States of Inversion: Book 1

IN THE SHADOW OF THE LUMINARIES

Kallen Samuels

Reproduction or transmission of this book in whole or in part by mechanical, electronic, audio recording or any other method is strictly prohibited, except with prior written approval from the author.

This is a work of fiction. Names, characters, events and incidents are the products of the author's imagination. Any resemblance to persons, living or dead, or actual events is purely coincidental.

2d9069d7f31da7f1eb4483a9a008d757c2eb70c573c07a4a754ad06f9ba9a fcf

ISBN: 978-1-7389011-3-5
Imprint: Innov@t Publishing - https://www.innovat.org

II

III

CONTENTS

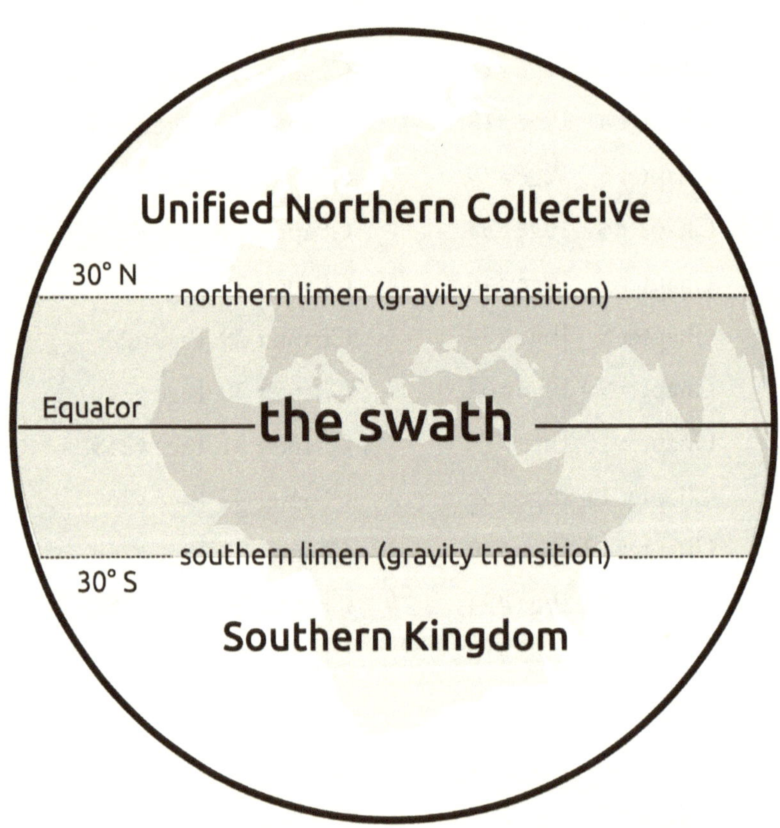

Unified Northern Collective
30° N
northern limen (gravity transition)
Equator
the swath
southern limen (gravity transition)
30° S
Southern Kingdom

Limen (threshold)

The swath is contained between two invisible, permeable energy fields that encircle the globe. They are called limens and extend from the surface to the upper atmosphere, separating regular gravity outside the swath from the reverse gravity within the swath.

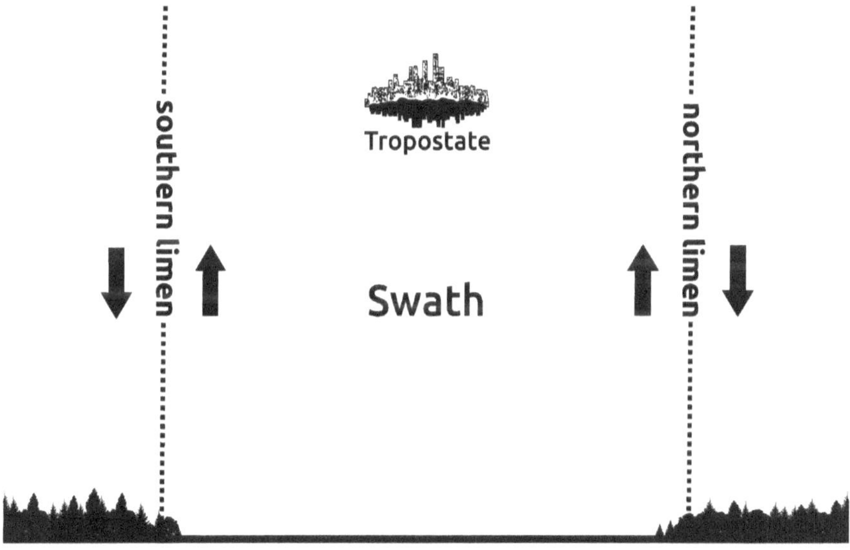

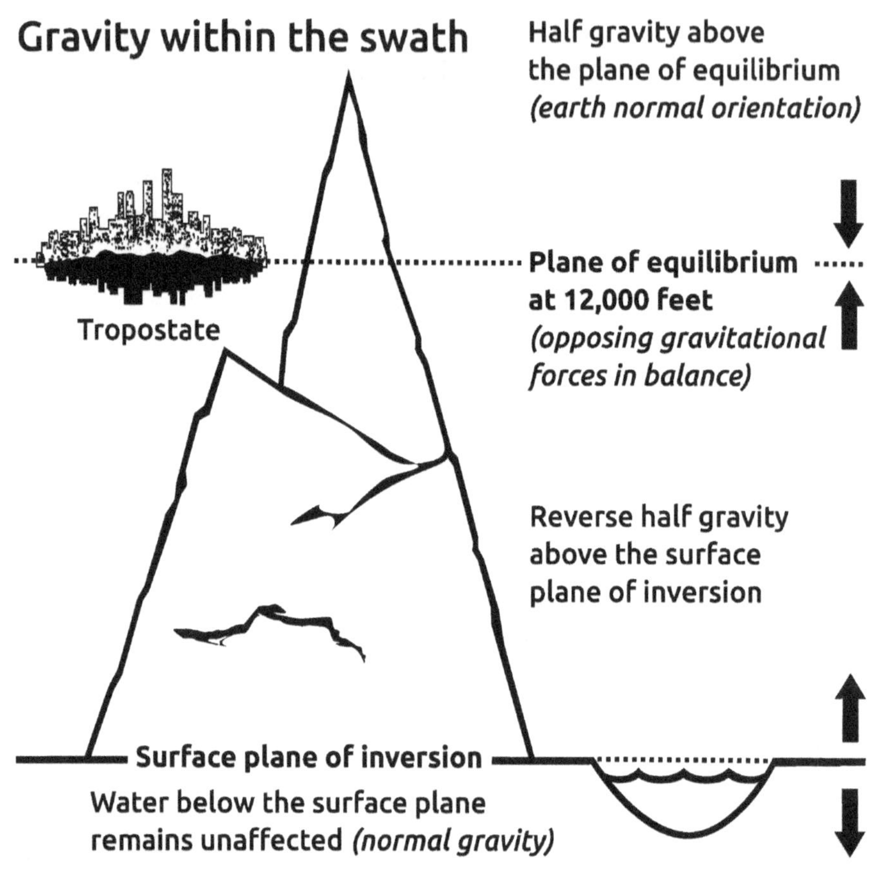

Gravity within the swath
Half gravity above
the plane of equilibrium
(earth normal orientation)
Tropostate
Plane of equilibrium
at 12,000 feet
(opposing gravitational
forces in balance)
Reverse half gravity
above the surface
plane of inversion
Surface plane of inversion
Water below the surface plane
remains unaffected (normal gravity)

2,700 nautical miles between tropostates

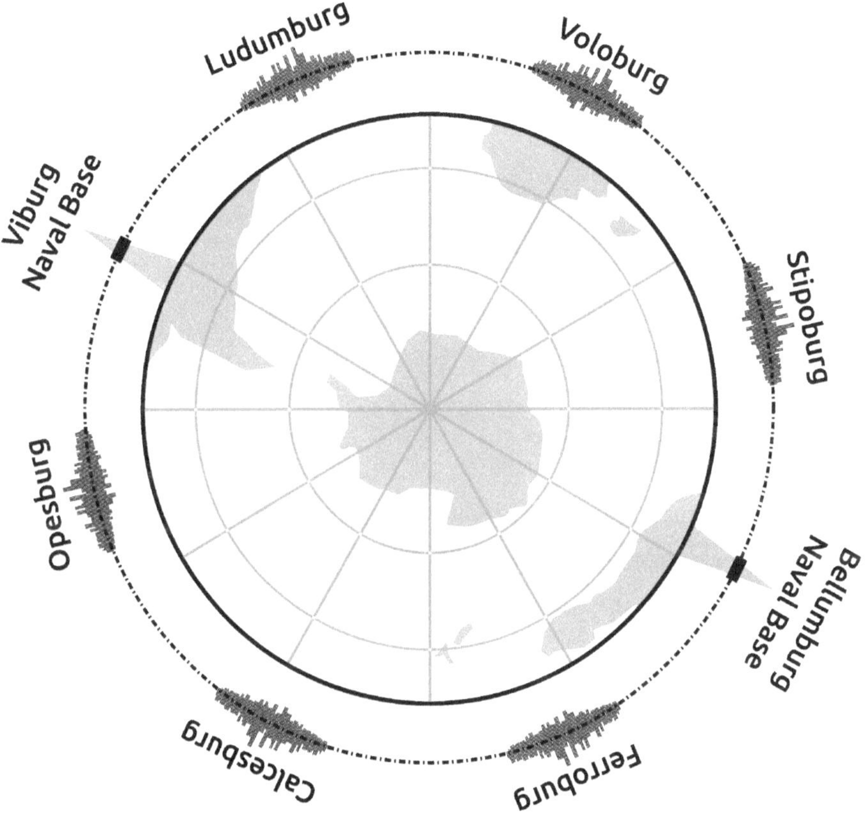

KALLEN SAMUELS

Chapter 1

Gravity is the foundation of our reality, or so we thought. That truth was torn from us and no one saw it coming. In the blink of an eye, gravity reversed in a massive swath that ringed the globe. Those outside of the swath were less affected, but not spared as seismic instability reshaped the face of our world.

Chaos spread across the planet, but nowhere so great as within the swath. We were thrust into the ether and set adrift. The electro-magnetic disturbances affected our minds, adding confusion to a place already lacking any familiar frame of reference. The icy upper atmosphere matched the cold terror in our hearts as we watched others perish, unable to prevent them from being crushed by floating rock or drowned by accumulating masses of water. Many more died of exposure or starvation.

Some of us had the presence of mind to come together, sharing warmth and using the flotsam to maneuver out of harm's way. We assessed our new circumstances and explored the unfamiliar environment, discovering our borders at great cost. No one knows how many were lost as a consequence of drifting across the northern or southern limens. We understand now that the swath is contained between those invisible thresholds where gravity transitions between normal and reversed. Armed with that knowledge, we avoid those places where rubble plunges back to earth.

We took action, gathering both people and debris, forming islands of refuge. A few men and women stood out as leaders, visionaries who saw a future and refused to give up. They are heroes who overcame impossible odds and brought order to upheaval. These same beacons of hope ultimately forged the world chain and built our civilization from the detritus of calamity. They are the founders, the Luminaries to whom we owe our survival. Because of them, we can proudly proclaim our status as the elevated of this world. — Memoirs of Hudson Ocon.

Nixon Ocon set aside the Chronicles of the Luminaries and grimaced, not from disapproval of the narrative, but because those tales of glory were no longer valued by many of his peers. The world was a very different place now. After five hundred years, a new normal was pushing aside the lessons of the past. The floating city-states of the Tropos Archipelago hung in the sky as testament to the ingenuity and perseverance of the Aerish, yet many were looking to the earthbound Tellusans for solutions to their problems. Why were Luminaries willing to lower themselves in that way? Nixon scowled in annoyance. The swath was bracketed by the Unified Northern Collective and the Southern Kingdom. He'd visited them both and quickly learned the differences between their worldviews and his own. The earthbound would never understand what it meant to be purified in the crucible of the inversion event, not to the degree that the Aerish had suffered.

As far as Nixon could ascertain, the Tellusan kingdoms were inferior. From a military standpoint, the Aerish had the advantage of high ground. From a technological perspective, the Aerish dominated. All trade between the northern and southern hemispheres had to pass through the swath and the Luminaries were the gatekeepers. They held all the cards and it galled him to imagine the Luminaries weakening their position with compromises.

Nixon would soon become the head of Sept Ocon and join the

Council of Luminaries. He wasn't about to let someone diminish his power before he claimed it. When that day came, he'd have the authority to force his agenda. By the time he was done, new heroes would arise and the Luminaries would become what they were always meant to be.

Chapter 2

"Welcome, Admiral Soren! What brings the head of the Luminary Navy to our humble friaerie?"

Quinto Soren rolled his eyes as his friend approached, then bowed his head slightly. "Friaer Kozen, I should think the reason would be obvious. I failed to visit that one time and I've never heard the end of it."

"Yes, that was a troubling occasion." Fisher grinned. "It's good to see you, Quinto. Walk with me."

Quinto fell into step as they headed toward the training hall. The friaers of Pax Montis were among the most feared fighters in the world. They weren't violent by nature, quite the opposite, but it had become a necessary part of their lifestyle as protectors of the sky lakes. He glanced out the window at one of the reservoirs hovering in the distance. It was an impressive honeycomb carrying several thousand gallons of water. The structure bristled with artillery reflecting off the calm waters, a visual dichotomy of peace and peril.

Fisher noticed the direction of his friend's gaze. "I never tire of looking at it." Fisher commented. "After the inversion event, it took decades to capture all of the water released into the atmosphere. Initially, we were just trying to prevent the drowning of countless survivors drifting helplessly in the swath."

Quinto shuddered. The thought of floating into the path of a suffocating bubble of water, with no way to escape, was the stuff of nightmares. He preferred to be in control of his fate.

"Today, it's less about preventing the immediate risk of death and more about sustaining life," Fisher continued. "The water and fish farm are provender to those in need." He lifted an eyebrow and stared pointedly into Quinto's eyes. "As an admiral, surely you could do more to educate the Luminaries about the suffering faced by the Lagan caste."

Quinto sighed. "You know it's more complicated than that; internal politics play a role. The Luminaries need a navy to protect the Tropos Archipelago from enemies beyond the swath, but the sky cities also need protection from their own competitive self-interests. The founders of those tropostates agree that the navy should remain autonomous. It can't be obligated to any one Luminary sept if it hopes to function as an unbiased police force."

Fisher waved a dismissive hand. "Yes, yes, you've told me this before, but if I'm not mistaken, that means you have a voice in the council chambers of the Luminaries. It also means that you've the backing of the entire navy, a force to be reckoned with. I would think that a wise Luminary would work hard to win your favour."

Quinto grunted. "You'd think so, wouldn't you? The Luminaries choose admirals from among the Lamina caste for a reason. Despite the latitude I'm given, the voice of a child from the Luminary caste holds more weight than my own."

Fisher snorted in disbelief. "I refuse to accept that a child could override your military command."

"That's not what I meant, and you know it. I'm free to make decisions where daily naval duties are concerned, and I have the authority to investigate actions taken by a specific sept if it affects other Luminaries. However, directly questioning the Luminary Council is a dangerous proposition. A majority vote of the Luminaries can undermine any decision I make. If I refuse their orders, or appear insubordinate, they can immediately vote to have me removed from my position. A misstep of that nature will result in a fatal retirement. My second in command is ready to assume control of the navy at a moment's notice. If I'm ever to speak out, it must be for the right cause at the right moment. It's not something I wish to squander, knowing I may only get one opportunity."

"Still, surely you can do something." Fisher stopped and rubbed his chin. Quinto left him to his thoughts while he took in the panoramic view beyond the glass. As gatekeepers to the sky lakes, the friaers benefited from a number of begrudgingly granted concessions, including property within the swath. The friaerie sprawled across the limen, part in full gravity, and part in reverse half gravity. The location permitted development of a coveted docking port. An aerotanker waited in a slip a short distance away from where they stood in the friaerie. It rested within the plane of equilibrium, pinned between the opposing half gravities of the swath, a curious and mysterious contradictory pull of gravity within the swath. From the surface of the planet to an elevation of twelve thousand feet, gravity was inverted and halved. At higher elevations, gravity returned to a natural orientation while remaining at half gravity. The physics were beyond comprehension. Some thought it was a punishment from God, some, a secret technology held by one of the world's nations. Still others considered it a precursor to an alien invasion. Regardless, after five hundred years, it was a continuing reality.

The plane of equilibrium was that neutral elevation where the opposing gravitational forces cancelled out each other, and nothing fell up or down. The phenomenon defied any known laws of physics. It was on this plane that loose rock and earth settled after the inversion event. The debris was gathered to form the floating masses that became the Tropos Archipelago, a staggering feat of engineering and determination. No one would call the Luminaries angels, but Quinto respected the achievement.

"I know what you're thinking, Quinto. You've expressed your admiration for the technological prowess of the Luminaries often enough, but look beyond the gleam of your shiny navy vessels and consider the cost." Fisher waved at the scene beyond the glass.

"The mountaintops are the only earthbound land masses accessible within the swath. Look at what the Luminaries have done with it! They've stripped away the beauty of God's creation. They razed these mountaintops to harvest rock for expansion, and ore for their forges. All that remains is this stone plateau as far as the eye can see."

Quinto wasn't sure he completely agreed with the assessment. Rows of glass covered channels penetrated the rock, creating thermal enclosures to grow what food they could at these altitudes. "They've made good use of the plateau. Look at the villages and greenhouses."

"That's my point exactly. By removing the peaks, they've reduced the usable square footage of land to this smaller cross-section. A substantial portion of their forestry industry has been eliminated along with a glacial water source to supply more greenhouses. The gardens have reached the limits of their expansion. They are watered from mountain streams outside of the swath, and we don't have the capacity to pump water any farther. Anything more remote would require water from the sky lakes, an unsustainable option.

"If that weren't enough, the Luminaries continue mining operations just below the surface of the plateau. They're riddling the mountain with tunnels that threaten to collapse. No one wants to build permanent villages over unstable land. Aside from the greenhouses, the rest of the plateau lies barren. What will happen, if the mountain crumbles and the loose mass floats away?"

Quinto furrowed his brows, but didn't reply. The answer was obvious enough. If the surface dropped below the plane of equilibrium, it would become much more difficult to farm, mine or harvest trees lower on the mountainside. He could attest to the barren expanse, having travelled it often by cable car to the naval base an hour away. That mode of transport would also be affected if the surface collapsed. Another thing to worry about as he travelled that track back to the naval base after the summit.

Fisher nodded. "You see? The Lagan caste is already deprived of much. What will happen, when the Luminaries further reduce their food rations? Do you have confidence that the Luminaries will give up their comforts to make up the shortfall? We both know the answer to that question." He turned abruptly from the view and continued walking toward the Hamo Sagitta training rooms. Quinto considered Fisher's words as he trailed behind. It was a legitimate concern, but he was at a loss as to what he could do about it.

"Friaer Fish!" The students hailed in unison. Quinto smiled. Many years ago he'd joined in that same chorus. Fisher Kozen was everyone's favourite instructor, and Quinto knew the friaer relished his nickname. Students loved him for his firm yet informal demeanour. One of the younger students ran to him excited about something he'd heard. "Friaer Fish! When are you going to teach us Invicta Manus?" Fisher knelt to bring his eyes to the boy's level. "I'm sorry, my eager young one. Those arts are reserved for friaers and tinkers. I suspect you would find their paths difficult to walk if you knew the cost."

Quinto chuckled at the confused expression on the boy's face. The Tinkers Guild consisted of itinerant eunuchs, men who chose to remove all temptations from their lives. They held no affiliation to nations or families. Proven reliable over centuries of service, the Guild garnered international respect. They were granted free passage anywhere in the world, and had become trusted mediators and record keepers for the governments of all nations. Sometimes, they also served as law keepers in remote areas.

It wasn't a surprise that the friaers taught Invicta Manus to the tinkers. The two organizations shared many common goals. Global peace and concern for the needy were the most obvious, but they also shared a desire to learn more about pre-inversion history. That knowledge might do much to reunite the world.

Both groups were appealing targets, the friaers for their water reservoirs and the tinkers for their privileged knowledge of international politics. Neither was a threat to each other and shared the distinction of being the only two truly non-partisan organizations in the world. They relied heavily on each other, having no one else they could turn to without jeopardizing their status.

Many nations sent military personnel to the friaers for combat training. Ironically, teaching martial arts was one of the ways friaers attempted to maintain peace. The friaers taught Hamo Sagitta to any who asked, intending that no faction gain an unfair advantage. Enemies who came to the school had to live, work and train together. It gave the friaers opportunity to open young minds to see their fellow students as people, and sometimes friends, rather than enemies.

The friaers held some knowledge back, of course. Their mastery assured a place in the order of things. They reserved the secret arts of Invicta Manus. It made them almost untouchable. Quinto knew that friaers made exceptions. They had trained him in the art of Invicta Manus, and he was neither tinker nor friaer.

While Fisher spent time with the students, Quinto watched the aerotanker prepare to leave port. Steam formed a cloud around the stern of the ship as the crew stoked the vapour engines. Ice crystals formed where moisture made contact with the cold steel surface. Some poor soul had been tasked with the chore of scraping ice from the exhaust ports. Soon the massive vessel would replenish its hold from the water reservoir and make its way across the swath, providing supplies to the Lagan caste or any Swathcombers they encountered.

Quinto understood Fisher's concern. The friaers' mission of mercy would become increasingly difficult if the Luminaries continued to expand beyond the ability to sustain their growth. Supply and demand were a precarious balancing act, as things were.

He sympathized with the friaer's quandary, but so many conflicting demands already rested on his shoulders. The burden pressed heavily, and he wasn't eager to increase its weight. The secrets he kept posed a constant threat, but he also believed it was the only way to move forward. Fisher returned and interrupted his thoughts. "You look exhausted."

"It's the full gravity in this section of the friaerie."

Fisher squeezed Quinto's arm to test the muscle density and snorted. "You've gone soft from all of your admiralish perks. You need to visit more often, and dedicate some time for training and conditioning."

"Admiralish? Is that even a word? If by perks you mean endless paperwork and lack of sleep, you can have them. You're right though, I should practise my forms more often. Speaking of which, Valtteri will be returning here soon for his final season of training. You'll keep an eye on him?"

"You know I will. How is the lad?"

"Headstrong as ever."

"It will serve him well in the future."

"I hope I live to see it." Quinto grew serious. "I have so many things to tell him, so much he needs to know. I suspect Sept Ocon will transfer him to active duty immediately after he completes his final training here. I'm not sure when I'll see him again. If something should happen to me...."

Fisher's expression shifted, mirroring Quinto's concern. "If this is his last session, I'll make sure to teach him myself. He'll have the special training he needs. As for other matters, I'll point him in the right direction. Don't worry, Quinto. I'll take care of things."

"I have to go, my friend. I'm late for the summit."

The two clasped forearms in farewell. "Quell the darkness, Admiral."

Quinto returned the expected response, "Bring truth to light."

Chapter 3

Quinto was running late. The trail to the friaerie was on the Tellusan side of the limen. He constantly forgot how long it took him to walk the narrow path in full gravity. His eyes judged the distance as short, but his body protested. He stopped to catch his breath and looked back to see how far he'd travelled.

The friaerie was a magnificent structure carved directly from the mountainside. It originated as a simple cave where the early friaers sheltered, each generation leaving its mark. As the facility expanded, the exterior carving kept pace with new tunnels and rooms excavated behind the facade.

A small glacier lake glistened nearby, glowing with a vibrant aquamarine hue. A village surrounded it, having sprung up to support the tourists. They came to admire the friaerie, to train with the friaers, or just to rest in the pastoral setting.

Quinto had many fond memories of this place and wished he had the time to visit his favourite tavern or paddle across the lake to a quiet place he knew, but it wasn't possible this time around. He inhaled deeply, invigorated by the scent of the spruce trees and the brisk mountain air as he quickened his pace. It wasn't a serious problem if he was tardy. He was only attending as an observer. Even so, his reputation as a punctual man was something he cultivated.

Arriving at his destination, he slowed to show his security credentials to the guards at the entrance. The tunnel was carved through a portion of the mountain in a place that straddled the limen. Ten paces took him to the ornate doors of the facility. He glanced around the foyer as he entered, and was relieved to discover that the transition gate was clear. He hated waiting in line, and disliked an audience even more. Crossing the limen could be jarring and people tended to take their time, hoping to avoid an embarrassing stumble.

Transition gates were stark reminders of all that humanity had endured. After so many centuries, it was easy for a person to forget. These unnatural thresholds separated the northern and southern lands from the massive expanse between the latitudes thirty degrees north and south of the equator — a desolate zone known as the swath. It was an appropriate name to describe the path of destruction that carved a ring around the planet. Every unattached item within that zone was flung into the heavens when gravity suddenly inverted. Life had settled into a new rhythm in the centuries since, but the world would never be truly normal again.

Quinto stepped into the half gravity of an antechamber surrounded by mirrors. He took a moment to straighten his dark blue uniform, and used his sleeve to polish the bars of his rank. Years of habit drew his fingers to a stubborn cowlick that he deftly pushed under his cap. His reflection passed inspection, and he quickly moved on.

It was a short walk from there to the assembly hall. International summits always took place at a declared neutral zone within the swath. The Aerish people of the Tropos Archipelago found it disagreeable to endure prolonged meetings under full gravity, while the earthbound Tellusans found the half gravity rather pleasant. The Tellusans, for their part, weren't used to the cooler temperatures found at higher elevations, which the Aerish found quite comfortable.

Quinto wrinkled his nose at the pungent scent of bodies crowded into a confined space. The Tellusans tended to overcompensate for the cold by wearing far too many layers of outerwear. He wasn't sure if the sweat scented assault proved to be a political weakness or an advantage in an atmosphere already filled with battles of the verbal kind.

As he searched for an empty seat, Quinto was dismayed to hear one of his fellow delegates antagonizing the other leaders.

"Do you think we haven't noticed your troops moving south beyond the range of our telescopes? What are you hiding?"

"This is getting tiresome, Luminary Ocon. You take every opportunity to remind us of your superior technology, yet you insist we're hiding some kind of gravity device responsible for the inversion. It's ludicrous!"

Zayd stabbed a finger in the southern queen's direction. "The Tellusans continue to benefit from the inversion at our expense. We're forced to beg for the necessities of life while you continue to raise prices, profiting from our suffering."

Across the room, a deep laugh erupted from Prime Palatine Duron Tagish, representative of the Unified Northern Collective. "If any of your people are suffering hardship, Zayd, it's only those from the Lagan caste of your so-called Luminocracy — the ones you so readily abuse."

Zayd's face flushed with anger. "You will address me by my proper title!"

Turning toward Zayd, Queen Melena Silvanus rose abruptly from her seat. "In your father's day, we addressed each other in the cordial manner of agreeable peers. It seems you've forgotten the progress we've made in that respect, along with the reforms your father was attempting to implement. The changes he proposed for your people would have gone far to improve international relations. If you feel set upon, then perhaps you should take your father's lead instead of antagonizing those with whom you trade, *Luminary Ocon.*"

Prime Palatine Tagish pressed the point. "You call yourselves Luminaries, or 'elevated ones'. Look me in the eye and tell me you don't think you're superior to Tellusans. You place more value on your status than the welfare of your people. You can't be both a victim and a conqueror, Luminary Ocon. The truth is that you have a tactical military advantage from the lofty position of your islands in the sky. You've accelerated the development of your war machines, much of it from ore we provided to your forges in good faith. Any reasonable man looking for a perpetrator of the inversion event would quickly find an obvious candidate. Your arrogant antagonism speaks volumes. Your father sought to remedy wrongs of the past, but you're a threat to all Tellusans — north and south of the swath."

Zayd bristled. "You're one to talk, Duron. The charade of a unified north does little to disguise your totalitarian regime. Even now, your war balloons patrol the northern limen, and you wonder why we have a navy?"

The Prime Palatine rolled his eyes. "Oh, we're on a first name basis now, are we?"

Queen Silvanus cleared her throat. "Speaking of Luminary Navy vessels, that brings us to the reason for this gathering — the recent bombing of lands within my borders."

Zayd clenched his fist. "I've already explained this to you. It was an unfortunate accident during a training exercise. A novice recruit loaded live ammunition by mistake."

Derisive hoots filled the air from both the northern and southern delegates. A number of them turned to look in Quinto's direction. He squirmed under their accusing eyes. As admiral of the Luminary Navy, he was culpable, but he couldn't admit that the incident occurred without his consent or knowledge. He had been furious when he found out, and the matter was still under review, but Zayd was hindering his investigation.

"That *mistake* destroyed over a hundred acres of prime woodland!" Melena shouted. "Your explanation is unsatisfactory!"

"Agreed!" Duron shouted, before growling a warning. "If any *accidents* occur along the northern limen, I promise you, my war balloons will provide a remedy for your faulty equipment and crew."

"I'm not the only one running military exercises near the limen," Zayd sneered. "Would the good Queen Silvanus like to explain why her men are operating in remote areas along Luminary borders?"

"We were investigating the damage caused by your bombs!"

"A convenient story, but rumours among the tether tribesmen suggest that Tellusans are crossing into the swath. Nobody risks crossing at the base of the swath unless they're hiding something. If you're trying to start a war, you've made a good start."

"Your accusations are baseless. I have nothing to hide."

"Then why do you have troops moving into the deep south? Surely nothing threatens your realm from within. What machines of destruction are hidden there, and for what purpose? Do you plan to point your gravitational device at the northern lands next?"

Duron Tagish growled at the mention of a potential inversion threat to the Unified Northern Collective, also known as the UNC. He turned questioning eyes towards the southern queen, but no answer was forthcoming.

Old Lord Calix was seated on a dais at the head of the chamber. As a high-ranking member of the Tinkers Guild, he was a regular fixture when world leaders gathered. Tinkers were often called on to mediate negotiations and treaties. He struck the table with a blade-less pommel that symbolized his neutral status.

"Order! Order! These accusatory speculations will get us nowhere. The Tinkers Guild has scrutinized the few available historical records about life immediately following the inversion. What we know for certain, is that aside from the destruction caused by the gravity shift within the swath, the event also caused massive volcanic activity and earthquakes outside of the swath. The cataclysm reduced cities around the globe to unrecognizable rubble. We have virtually no physical remnant of culture or technology from before the disaster. All of humanity was affected. The massive magnetic instabilities caused neurological damage that nearly annihilated life on this planet. For decades, that impairment afflicted the memories of those who survived. As a result, we've never been able to piece together a reliable record of what came before. For all practical purposes, our history began when the inversion took place."

Lord Calix scanned the room like a scholar estimating the impact of his words. "In five hundred years, we've failed to uncover any relics of that bygone era. If the technology to create such destruction ever existed, it's lost and forgotten. If the inversion was a naturally occurring phenomenon, then we can do nothing about that either. We're not here to lay blame for an ancient mystery. We're here to deal with present concerns."

"You're quite right," Zayd agreed, "my apologies, Lord Calix, fellow delegates."

Lord Calix scanned the report in front of him. "Fortunately, the incident at hand didn't harm any Tellusans. Trees will grow back, and wildlife will return in time. I suggest that the Luminary delegates offer a formal apology and an in-kind or monetary reparation of some sort. Is that agreeable to all parties?" Lord Calix directed his question to Queen Silvanus, who nodded in agreement.

"That would be acceptable."

Zayd rose from his seat. "On behalf of the Luminary delegation, we apologize for the incident and are willing to provide compensation."

Quinto furrowed his brows as he scrutinized Luminary Ocon's face. The quick acceptance was uncharacteristic.

"My staff has calculated the value of the lumber that was lost," Queen Silvanus began.

"If I may?" Zayd interrupted.

Lord Calix turned to Queen Silvanus, and waited for her nod of acceptance regarding the interruption. "Did you have something particular in mind, Luminary Ocon?"

"The southern realm has recently placed an order for two of our city-class power generators. We're willing to gift them to Queen Silvanus by way of compensation for the lost lumber, and as a show of our good will towards the Tellusans."

Quinto's eyes widened in shock. Everyone in the room knew that two power generators far exceeded the value of the lost timber. As the largest stakeholder in vapour engine production, Zayd's offer would place the greatest financial burden on his own Sept, and the Ocon family wasn't charitable by nature.

"Why that's — very generous — and unexpected." Queen Silvanus stammered.

Zayd smiled, something that looked disingenuous at the best of times. "I may not share my father's views, but we can still have a friendly and productive relationship."

"Will that be acceptable, Queen Silvanus?"

"Certainly, Lord Calix."

"Very well then, that completes our agenda for the morning. The paperwork will be ready in the early afternoon. I'll have a page summon you once they're prepared. Please make yourselves available to sign the documents at your earliest convenience, so we can conclude this business." Lord Calix struck the table signalling an end to the session.

Zayd remained seated as the other delegates rose to leave. He had a smug look on his face as though he'd obtained exactly what he wanted.

Quinto watched him carefully. The man was up to something. First he interfered with the investigation into the artillery incident, then he vehemently denied any wrongdoing. Now, he was ceding far more than anyone would have expected. Quinto didn't know what the Luminary was up to, but if he discovered that Zayd had overstepped, he was going to take great pleasure in bringing the man down.

Chapter 4

At first light on a weekend, four delinquents broke into the Viburg Academy's hangar to borrow a pair of aerosiren class scout ships for a few hours. Taking advantage of the launch catapults, they coasted far from the naval base before stoking the noisy vapour engines. If they were lucky, no one would notice the missing craft until they were well out of visual range.

Nixon and Jack were in one of the two passenger vessels. Sebastian had joined Valtteri in the other. It was an hour-long journey to the training buoys near the southern limen.

"You know we're strictly forbidden to be at the training area without an instructor."

Valtteri groaned. "How can I forget, Seb? You've reminded me three times in the past forty-five minutes. Why are you so worried? It's not like we're fresh recruits. In a few weeks, we'll graduate from the academy and we can come out here any time we like."

It seemed like a reasonable argument, but Valtteri knew some form of discipline would be waiting for them once they returned to the base. *Correction,* Valtteri thought. *Punishment will be waiting for me, Luminary Ocon's nephew won't get more than a gentle slap on his pampered wrist.*

Valtteri tried not to dwell on Nixon and switched his focus to the gauges arrayed before him. He loved piloting ships in the swath. It wasn't flying so much as perpetual falling, thanks to the plane of equilibrium. The navy referred to that zone as zero strata. Whether pointed at the heavens or the earth, you were always falling to z-strat.

Valtteri adjusted the elevators on the vessel's stubby wings to begin the return arc. He smiled, anticipating a stomach flutter just before the plunge. Some people couldn't handle that sensation over prolonged periods.

With a sadistic impulse, he tightened the arc. "How are you doing back there, Seb? You look a little green."

"Can we talk about something else, please?"

Valtteri laughed. "Honestly, Seb, why did you join the navy?"

"You know I didn't have a choice. My parents couldn't afford higher education for me, and the navy is free. It was this or a lifetime of scraping clinkers from a forge." Sebastian closed his eyes and choked back some bile as they wove their way along. Stitching the strata allowed gravity to do most of the work. Momentum carried an object to a z-positive peak before falling back across z-strat into a z-negative peak. Applying judicious bursts from the main thrust nozzles enabled an experienced pilot to maintain the serpentine motion until they ran out of fuel.

"Can we coast the plane of equilibrium for a bit?"

"If you want to pass the navigation course, you'll need to start using proper vernacular."

"I don't understand why the navy uses different terminology."

Valtteri rolled his eyes. "Have you tried operating the heliograph to flash a message using long words? It's much easier to spell out z-pos or z-neg."

"They could have shortened *plane of equilibrium* to *POE* and everyone would understand what it meant."

"You can make that argument to the instructor if you wish, but promise me you won't bring it up until after you pass the course. Let me know when you plan to make your case, I want to be there to watch."

"Ha, ha. Moving on to more important matters, I thought we were going to coast for a bit?"

Valtteri shrugged and levelled off at z-strat. Momentum could carry them a long way, at high speed, in that low resistance space where opposing gravitational forces cancelled each other out. It wasn't something pilots liked to do on a longer journey because it took more thrust to get moving again. The accumulated microbursts used for regular travel was more fuel efficient. Coasting was usually reserved for the last leg of a journey or for moments when a burst of straight line speed was necessary. As it was, they were close enough to their destination that he could afford to give Sebastian a break.

Sebastian was taking slow deep breaths as he worked to settle his stomach. The silence was a welcome break, but without the endless chatter, Valtteri's mind returned to the reason for this little outing.

"Ocon gets to me every single time." he whispered. It wouldn't be a problem if the taunt had come from anyone else. He'd been enduring insults his whole life, and ninety-nine percent of the time he could shed them like water off an oiled cloak. Unfortunately, Nixon Ocon fell into that one percent he found difficult to ignore no matter how hard he tried. Something about Nixon's smug attitude pushed him over the edge.

Valtteri had lost control at one point and beat Nixon senseless. He received twenty strokes of the cane plus a year on probation for his indiscretion. Since then, Nixon acted like he was invulnerable, and he took every opportunity to goad Valtteri into repeating his mistake.

"How do I get myself into these situations?" He muttered.

"Was that a rhetorical question?" Sebastian chuckled. "Because I'd be happy to explain it to you, if you'd like."

"Not if you know what's good for you."

The reason was simple enough. Nixon wanted to prove that he was a superior pilot before they graduated. Valtteri had brushed him off, but then Nixon spoke those hated words that overrode his better judgment.

"Why don't you run and hide behind the admiral's coattails, blight eye?" The insult cut deep. It wasn't just a dig at Valtteri, it was also disrespectful to the admiral who had taken him in after the navy found him floating in the swath. Valtteri was five years old at the time, an earthbound Tellusan child who unwittingly stepped through the southern limen. He was too young to understand the danger of crossing the invisible barrier that separates normal gravity from the reversed gravity within the swath. His transition into the heavens was rapid and terrifying, something he hoped to never experience again.

Valtteri had the heavier bones and musculature of those born in full gravity. It made him stand out. The fact that one of his eyes was gold-coloured and the other grey only drew more attention. He always assumed that Nixon called him blight eye in an attempt to associate his grey eye with death. It didn't seem like much of an insult. It was the way Nixon said it that got under Valtteri's skin.

It hardly mattered. Valtteri didn't care what others thought of his appearance. The true irritant was an insinuation that the admiral treated him favourably. It was a difficult accusation to stomach coming from the pampered nephew of Zayd Ocon. Nixon's uncle was one of the most powerful founders in the Tropos Archipelago.

Nixon was born into the Luminary caste. His education was little more than a formality. No matter what Valtteri achieved, he would never rise above Nixon in rank or privilege. It was a fact, and he could live with it. However, he refused to accept that Nixon was a better student, pilot, or man, for that matter.

Valtteri worked hard to become the best recruit of the academy. If anything, his status as a Tellusan put him at a disadvantage. Everyone treated him with derision except the admiral, and Sebastian, his one and only friend. Valtteri had no intention of letting Nixon discredit his hard-won accomplishments.

Sebastian seemed to sense the tension building in the cockpit. "You've nothing to prove, Val. Everyone knows you're at the top of our class."

"If that's true, why did you agree to tag along?"

"Are you kidding? I love watching you put that blowhard in his place. He has this bright purple vein that pulses at his temple when he's mad. A bunch of us have a running wager on when it will pop. I'm betting sooner rather than later. This little outing should help push the odds in my favour."

Valtteri eased to a stop as they reached their destination. "That's, a little dark. You're really that confident I'll win?"

Sebastian snorted. "No one would place a wager against you in a contest between you and Ocon. It's too one-sided. Why do you think we bet on his head exploding instead?"

Valtteri grinned. "Thanks buddy, you always know just how to lift my spirits. Now finish stoking the firebox, then get out and tether yourself to the buoy. I need you ready to declare my victory when I'm first to cross the finish line on the return leg. I don't trust Jack to make an honest call."

Sebastian arranged another load of coal for the hopper, and exited the cabin to join Jack at the buoy. Jack pulled out a flag and glanced at the two contestants, waiting for their thumbs-up to indicate readiness.

They'd already discussed the rules beforehand. Basically, there were none. An expert pilot should be able to deal with the unexpected. It was something Nixon insisted on. Valtteri rolled his eyes. He wouldn't let Nixon's dirty tricks affect the outcome.

They'd race to the warning buoy that marked the limen, round it, and return. The risk of inadvertently crossing the limen at this altitude was real. Improper timing could send the unwary plummeting to their death. As pilots, they'd practised the maneuver hundreds of times. Slow down, spin your craft with a combination of rudder plus vector bursts, and then initiate full vapour thrust from the rear nozzles. If done right, you'd be back across the limen and into the swath before full gravity pulled you to earth. It was both terrifying and exhilarating.

Following the one hundred and eighty degree turn at the limen, it was a hard run to the starting buoy for a win. The two craft were identical, so victory would be the result of skill alone. Without a passenger to feed the engine, power management was crucial.

Valtteri peered out the side window of his cockpit at the sneering face of Nixon Ocon floating twenty feet away. He checked his pressure gauges and gave Jack a thumbs-up. Nixon did the same, and then gave Valtteri a thumbs-down.

Valtteri growled and tightened his grip on the steering yoke just as Jack dropped the flag. Both craft rocketed toward the limen, leaving Jack and Sebastian struggling to hang on to the buoy as it bounced about in the wake of the departing craft.

Nixon made the first move, choosing to head z-pos. Valtteri immediately slipped into an opposing z-neg pattern. He planned to keep as much space between the two of them as possible. If Nixon planned to pull any stunts, it would be when they were both nearing z-strat from opposite directions.

Nixon was a decent pilot, but his limitations were immediately apparent in the greater distance he chose to travel from z-strat. It gave a pilot more room for error, but it also used more fuel. You couldn't win a race on speed alone.

Valtteri had always been hyper-aware of his surroundings. Sometimes, the information overload distracted him, but he'd learned to parse it at convenient moments and use the extra information to his advantage. That ability, coupled with quick reflexes, was a potent combination. He didn't require as much room for error. He could hold a shallow wave pattern, and save fuel to counter the inevitable shady tactics Nixon would attempt.

Nixon narrowed the gap between their two vessels as they neared the first point of intersection. He sounded the pressure whistle, prompting Valtteri to glance over just in time to receive a blinding reflection from Nixon's heliograph. Valtteri squeezed his eyes shut and yelped in pain. He instinctively veered off as Nixon's whistle sounded a second time in very close proximity.

Valtteri muttered in annoyance, blinking rapidly as he recovered. The course correction cost him precious fuel. He flashed displeasure with his own heliograph, but Nixon pulled ahead.

Valtteri knew his tighter pattern would allow him to catch up within a few passes, but he'd planned to be in the lead by this point in the race. He'd hoped to make his turn through the limen well ahead of Nixon and his schemes.

Nixon kept to himself through the next two arcs, but altered his course at the third. They were heading toward z-strat in what could easily become a collision course.

"What are you up to, Ocon?"

The answer came with a burst of steam from Nixon's forward braking vents. The unexpected cloud obscured Valtteri's vision while the screech of metal filled his ears. Nixon's wing caught his own and flipped him into an uncontrolled spin.

A moment of panic gripped Valtteri before his training kicked in. He applied full opposite rudder to pull out of the spin, and entered a dive into z-strat to coast. The opposing gravitational forces would help smooth out the erratic wobble introduced during his recovery. Valtteri pounded the armrest of his seat, and roared in frustration as he fell behind. Nixon couldn't win in a fair race and he knew it.

It took three more passes for Valtteri to catch up. They were approaching the limen. If he couldn't be well ahead for the turn, he'd rather trail behind so he could watch for other ploys. They reached the deceleration point before the turn, but instead of slowing down, Nixon increased aft thrust to climb z-pos. He was already past the point for a safe reversal.

"Nixon, no! It's too dangerous!" He recognized the risky maneuver immediately — Dok's Gambit — first hazarded by a famous pilot named Bennet Dokker. Few people attempted it. The intent was to cross the limen high above z-strat so you could build up speed in a dive beyond the swath and make your turn back into the swath vertically instead of laterally. Pulling out of the dive at speed with an assist from the reverse half gravity of the swath provided a slingshot effect. That momentum would propel you at high velocity toward your desired destination. The danger of the maneuver resided in the timing. If you didn't begin your turn back into the swath before picking up too much velocity, the sudden transition from full gravity to reverse half gravity would tear your ship apart. The point of no return was counted two seconds after crossing z-strat. Valtteri could already tell Nixon wasn't going to make it.

Valtteri's mind raced as he considered his options. What could he do? During training exercises, instructors attached tethers between the smaller training craft and a much larger aerovette. If something went wrong, the larger ship's engines could pull a small craft to safety, but this wasn't an exercise.

"Wait, the harpoon!" Harpoons were standard issue, used for boarding other ships during a police action. If he could line up with Nixon's dive and time it just right, he might be able to snag the other ship as it crossed z-strat. He'd still need to make his own turn while attempting to divert Nixon. It was a long shot, but it was all he had.

Valtteri used his port thrusters to line up with the second craft as Nixon began to turn into a dive. He quickly ran some calculations and determined that Nixon would be within two hundred feet as they crossed paths. He'd need to fire the harpoon a second before reaching that mark. He set an alarm and held his breath with his finger on the trigger.

Everything seemed to happen at once. The alarm sounded, the harpoon fired, Valtteri crossed the limen, and his ship began to plummet. He initiated full aft thrust while employing all manoeuvring surfaces and steering nozzles in an attempt to pull himself and Nixon back into the swath.

At first his efforts made no difference, but it was enough to turn Nixon's craft across the limen and back into the swath. Unfortunately, Nixon's velocity yanked Valtteri back into the swath with a ferocity that snapped the harpoon cable and sent him tumbling. Both were hurtling to the finish line at high speed, but Nixon was in control while Valtteri was still trying to sort out which way was up.

I can't believe this. Ocon's still trying to win this race! He's not even going to slow down to see if I'm okay. Well, he's not the only one with a few tricks up his sleeve.

Valtteri managed to pull himself into a controlled spiral. It was a technique he'd been practising on his own ever since he read about it in an old tactics manual. A pilot with sufficient control could employ an ever tightening corkscrew centred on z-strat. It provided the gravitational benefits of a traditional serpentine motion, but with far superior acceleration.

Valtteri's practice sessions hadn't progressed beyond a steady spiral. He was attempting to complete the maneuver for the first time. Slowly tightening the spiral into a spin, he guided the craft fully into the lower resistance of z-strat. Using his steering thrusters to arrest his spin, he struggled with the controls and waited for a wave of dizziness to pass. When his head cleared enough to read the gauges, he was shocked to discover that he'd added one hundred knots to the aerosiren's top rated speed of three hundred.

He spotted Nixon's ship just in time to smile and wave, leaving Nixon well behind as he crossed the finish line.

Valtteri's speed and momentum carried him far past the buoy. By the time he returned, Nixon was waiting with his canopy open and his arms crossed.

"That win doesn't count, Knox. You cheated!"

"Did you forget that you insisted on no rules? You have some nerve complaining after all the stunts you pulled during the race. For the record, I didn't cheat, I saved your life."

"I ran a clean race, blight eye!"

"First you blinded me with your heliograph, and later by venting steam so I couldn't see. You intentionally rammed my vessel and sent me into a spin. You call all of that a fair race?”

“Don’t blame me if a random reflection from the morning sun caught your eye. As for the rest, I was trying to *avoid* a collision. After you changed course, I had to make a sudden correction with the manoeuvring thrusters. That light tap could have been avoided if you’d kept to your lane.”

Valtteri stared incredulously. “Are you kidding me, Ocon? I never strayed from my lane until the moment I had to save your neck. You’re the reckless one. Only a lunatic would attempt Dok’s gambit.”

Jack and Sebastian had been watching the exchange with interest, but their focus was entirely on Nixon after that disclosure. Jack was first to speak. “You attempted Dok’s gambit?”

Sebastian added, “Are you crazy?”

“I had it under control,” Nixon hooked a thumb in Valtteri’s direction, “until blight eye harpooned me!”

“You harpooned him?” Jack exclaimed. Up to that point, he and Sebastian hadn’t noticed the tether trailing from a hole torn in the opposite side of Nixon’s aerosiren. Jack unclipped from the buoy and moved to inspect the damage.

Sebastian inspected the harpoon port on Valtteri’s aerosiren. The spool had been ripped from its base and was nowhere in sight. He slowly shook his head. “We’re in so much trouble.”

“When I explain to my uncle how Knox tried to kill me, no one will be worrying about a few repairs.”

“Are you really so stupid, Ocon? The instructors don’t teach that maneuver for a very good reason. The death rate is too high. When I fired the harpoon, you had already passed the point of no return. Don’t you get it? You were about to die! I barely managed to swing you back into the swath.”

“My timing would’ve been perfect if it weren’t for the distraction of a harpoon ripping through my starboard side. What were you thinking? That harpoon could have hit me! Maybe that was your intent.”

"Of course not!"

"I'd already caught the limen with my starboard wing. It was enough to pull me through before the harpoon tether tightened. The way I see it, Knox, I dragged your sorry butt back across the limen, not the other way around. You're lucky I didn't cut you loose and let you drop after that stunt. You knew that I was about to take a commanding lead, and you tried to stop me."

"Twist the truth all you want, Ocon. I won fair and square, and I saved your life in the process. If you think that the instructors are going to turn a blind eye to your reckless use of a navy vessel, you're dreaming."

"We'll see, blight eye. It's your word against mine. I don't know why my uncle puts up with you."

"Maybe because you're such a disappointment!" Valtteri shot back.

A vein began to throb at Nixon's temple. "You're nothing but a Tellusan infiltrator. The lowest of the Lagan caste is worth more than you. One day I'll be in charge, and your free ride will be over." Nixon gestured for Jack to climb in and spun the craft around before his copilot had a chance to buckle in. A blast of steam buffeted Valtteri and Sebastian as a parting insult.

Sebastian had a look of resignation on his face as he crawled into his seat. "We're in so much trouble," he repeated.

This time Valtteri didn't have an argument.

Chapter 5

Valtteri stood at attention. He could smell the leather of the unused chair tucked under the desk. Admiral Soren seldom sat, preferring to prop himself against the front of his desk. "What were you thinking, Val? Using navy vessels for an unsanctioned purpose, and without authorization? Worse, you took them to the training area without supervision! Damage to the craft can be repaired, but I can't guarantee the same for flesh and bone. Someone could have died!"

Valtteri kept his eyes forward, staring off into the distance. The office window overlooked the navy docks. A bit of frost had collected at the corner of the pane. Considering the atmosphere in the room, he wasn't certain if it was a byproduct of the inside or outside temperature. "No one was hurt."

Quinto tossed a warning glance at Valtteri. "Nixon is laying serious charges about your actions."

Valtteri lifted his eyes in the silence that followed. The admiral seemed to be waiting for a response, so he ventured a question. "Did you speak with Sebastian?"

Quito sighed. "I've met with everyone involved. Now, I wish to hear your side of the story."

"I'm sure Nixon spun a tall tale, but if Jack was honest, his story should corroborate Sebastian's version. Nixon attempted Dok's Gambit."

"Oh, everyone was very clear on that part of the story. Nixon was bragging about it, young fool that he is. His arrogance is going to cost him his life one day."

The comment surprised Valtteri. It was unlike the admiral to let his emotions rise so close to the surface. He'd never heard the man utter an opinion about a trainee, though he imagined senior staff heard more behind closed doors. The fact that he let it slip in front of Valtteri showed just how close the admiral was to losing his reputation for self-restraint.

Valtteri had no desire to be the first to see the admiral totally lose his cool, so he decided to recount events as though he were in an operational debriefing. "I witnessed trainee Ocon approaching the limen in a steep climb consistent with the maneuver known as Dok's Gambit. The speed of his dive indicated that he'd pass the point of no-return before he could change course toward the swath. If I'd failed to intervene, I have no doubt he would have perished. I did the only thing I could think of to save him."

"The need for a rescue should never have arisen. You weren't supposed to be there in the first place. I ask you again, what were you thinking? Never mind, I know you well enough to guess. Why do you let him get under your skin? People like Nixon Ocon will always be around. You can't allow them to influence your actions."

"He insulted you!"

"And you insult my intelligence! Your pride had more to do with this than a slight to my integrity. I'm sure you've heard many trainees impugn the character of superior officers. How was this any different?"

Valtteri lowered his eyes and took a deep breath to control his anger. "It's just... He's so arrogant!"

"He's a Luminary. Of course he's arrogant. Words like small-minded, short-sighted, selfish, and entitled also come to mind."

Valtteri's eyes widened a second time. The admiral of the Luminary Navy was speaking in derogatory terms about members of the founding septs. *This sounds nothing like the man who raised me.*

Noticing Valterri's surprise, Quinto removed his cap, ran his fingers through his hair, and sighed. "We owe much to the founders. They forged a path for our survival. However, the caste system is a consequence of everything that followed. Power once obtained is difficult to let go. Nixon was taught to believe in his superiority as a birthright. Practically speaking, his family has the wealth and influence to ensure that nothing threatens his station in life. He acts untouchable because in many ways he is."

Valtteri lifted his voice in protest. "It's not right! How can a man be superior by virtue of a name when the whole world can see his failings? You're an admiral, surely you hold the power to eliminate the caste system. You're part of the judicial structure within the swath, yet you do nothing. How can you allow the injustice to continue?" It was something Valtteri had often wondered.

"You're not the first to ask me that question. In time, I'll be able to give you the answers you deserve, but for now, I'll ask you a question in return. If I did what you're suggesting, how would I be any different from those I depose? On what would I base my claim of authority? On my title? Didn't you just say that a man shouldn't be considered superior by virtue of a name? Such an action would cost many innocent lives with no certain long-term outcome. I'm not willing to pay that price, not if I have another option."

Valtteri snorted in disgust. "So nothing will ever change. How do you stand it?"

"Not all Luminaries hold the same views, Val. Before Zayd Ocon came into power, his father was working on reforms. Some of the septs liked his ideas. Even now, they disagree on appropriate governance in the Tropos Archipelago."

Quinto raised a palm to forestall any further protest and turned the conversation back to the original topic. "We're not here to talk about the shortcomings of the caste system, but rather, your own. You took navy property without permission and damaged it. You disregarded regulations, and endangered the life of a fellow trainee."

Val couldn't believe what he was hearing. "I saved the life of that trainee!"

"I believe you endeavoured to do just that, but you and Nixon are the only witnesses, and your stories disagree on key points. You can't be one hundred percent certain that your calculations were accurate in those few seconds before you took action. You made a snap decision that likely saved a life, but the possibility remains that Nixon would've been fine without your intervention."

Valtteri shook his head in frustration. "I can't believe you're taking his side. If I hadn't stepped in, he would have died."

"Listen, Val, no one is denying that Nixon took a foolish risk. Considering how few have attempted Dok's Gambit and survived, most would agree that your actions saved his life. I likely would've done the same. That doesn't erase your own foolish choice to race him in the first place. I would expect this sort of behaviour from Nixon Ocon, but not from you."

Valtteri felt his anger rising. "Just one more disappointment from the Tellusan orphan they paid you to raise."

"That's not fair, Val. I never thought of you that way. When I offered to take you in, Ocon's money had nothing to do with it."

"You accepted it freely enough."

"We've been over this. Zayd Ocon finances your education. He saw an opportunity in you, and paid for your specialized training. You're a Tellusan born with heavier bones and musculature. You'll be able to mingle freely among the Tellusans in ways that the Aerish can't. You represent a potential for intelligence gathering that Zayd covets. I never personally received money from him for your care or training, nor would I have accepted if he offered."

"Instead, you just endorsed my shaping as a tool for his agenda. It's what a loving father figure would do." Valtteri knew his comments were unfair, but he couldn't help himself. The pain his words caused were etched in the lines of Quinto's face, and Valtteri immediately regretted saying them.

"Is that really what you think of me? That I'm using you? I know that I haven't always been available for you. Juggling my duties as the admiral with my desire to spend time with you hasn't been easy. I'm not trying to make excuses, only acknowledging that I was unprepared for the expectations you might have. I know I fell short, but you need to understand that I never thought of you as a burden. I regard you as my son."

Quinto paused to gather his thoughts. "Every Luminary sept maintains their own intelligence squad. Their recruits are trained by the navy, but once that training is complete, their primary allegiance is to the sept that supported them. I wasn't happy with Luminary Ocon's interest in you or how it would define your future. I tried to prevent it, but as a Tellusan, you held no legal rights. Accepting his demands to train you for eventual service to Sept Ocon was the price I paid to keep you in my care. Ocon was determined to get his way, and I didn't want to see you programmed like a machine without an alternative perspective."

The admiral struggled with his words. "I'm a military man who never married. I was ill-equipped to create a loving environment for a child, but I did what I could. By keeping you close, I was able to protect you from much more than you know. Strange as it may sound, you also benefited from Ocon's protection. I know it has been difficult for you, but no one would risk the ire of a Luminary like Ocon by interfering with one of his projects. I realize how harsh it sounds to hear yourself labelled as such, but know that I don't see you that way, and I hope that I was able to provide at least some joy in your life. I've been doing what I can to prepare you."

Valtteri was becoming increasingly uncomfortable with the admiral's confession. It was uncharacteristic, and he began to worry about the potentially extreme nature of his punishment. "So what's going to happen now?"

"I've discussed the matter with Luminary Ocon. He agrees that Nixon's risky behaviour warrants discipline. Nixon will spend the next week scraping ice from an aeronaught class warship that recently arrived in port for maintenance. I've agreed to pay for repairs to the aerosirens from my own funds."

Val spotted the aeronaught through the window. The corners of his mouth twitched upwards at the thought of Nixon's pampered hands covered in blisters and frostbite. No doubt he'd be cursing Valtteri's name the whole time. That thought stretched his mouth into a full grin.

Quinto lifted a brow. "Do you find something amusing about your current circumstances, trainee Knox?"

"No, Sir! Sorry, Sir!" Valtteri quickly schooled his face. "What about me, Sir?"

"You'll be heading to Pax Montis for your final training."

"And?"

"That's it. You'll complete your training. Luminary Ocon is eager to get you into the field. You'll leave two days from now. As far as anyone is concerned, we're sending you to the friaers for discipline in the form of additional training. Everyone will feel sorry for you. I suggest you play the part of someone metaphorically heading to the gallows if you don't want to see the implication become reality."

Valtteri couldn't believe what he was hearing. For once, Nixon was getting the short end of the stick, and Valtteri was the one escaping with nothing more than a slap on the wrist. Best of all, he'd be away from Nixon for a whole week before that pain in his neck was sent to complete training at the friaerie as well.

Valtteri's attention returned to the moment, at the sound of snapping fingers.

"Valtteri, this is no time for your daydreaming. I need you to focus."

Why do people always think I'm daydreaming?

"Tomorrow morning, you'll stand before Luminary Ocon to receive your deployment orders. He will be your commander. I'll no longer be able to protect you, and I don't know when I will see you again."

"We both knew this day would come."

"Yes, but I haven't had enough time to prepare."

"Prepare for what?"

"I don't trust Zayd Ocon. You shouldn't trust him either. You must obey his commands if you want to live, but rely on your instincts and be smart. Find ways to follow orders without compromising your integrity. There may come a day when he pits you against me."

"I don't understand. You're in charge of the navy. How can he come against you and why would he?"

"Recent military exercises have taken place without my knowledge or sanction. Zayd's been interfering with my investigation. The navy is one of Zayd's biggest customers, and he provides the engines we rely on. A potential for corruption exists within any large organization, and a bribe from Zayd can be very attractive to those with careers in the military. I know those whom I trust, but I can't know everyone under my command. As part of Zayd's intelligence squad, you may soon know more about his activities than I've been able to uncover. Zayd knows I'm investigating, and he won't trust you because of your relationship with me. He will demand your allegiance and he'll test it. You need to be very cautious. Don't blindly trust anyone.

"In answer to your second question, I was a supporter of Asher Ocon, Zayd's Father. You were perhaps eight years old at the time. The two had many arguments. Zayd wasn't in favour of the proposed changes. Asher died under mysterious circumstances just before an important treaty was about to be signed. Zayd was alone with his father when he died."

"You think Zayd Ocon killed his father?"

"I have no evidence one way or the other, but after that night, all of Asher's progress was systematically dismantled. The treaty was never signed, and Zayd has kept me at arm's length ever since. Shortly after that, he turned his attention to you."

"What if I refuse to swear allegiance?"

"That's not an option. You're a Tellusan by birth, born of no caste. You exist in the swath under the sponsorship of Ocon. As a Luminary, he can declare you a threat to the archipelago. If you betray him, you'll be hunted down and killed."

Valtteri's head was spinning with the revelations. He never asked for any of this. His entire life in the swath was that of a non-entity, one derided, mocked and dismissed no matter how hard he worked to please those around him. Nothing he did was ever good enough for the Aerish. Others decided every aspect of his existence. For many years he held onto the hope that as a future intelligence operative, he could see the world and perhaps find a place where he'd feel accepted. Now he was learning that after all his efforts towards that goal, he was bound even more tightly, a slave to a dangerous man.

"Valtteri, please pay attention. This is important!"

"Sorry, what did you just say?"

"I said, if something should happen to me, you need to find a tinker and tell him who you are. I've deposited documentation with the Tinkers Guild declaring you as my heir. It will automatically make you a citizen of the Lamina caste. You'll inherit everything I own. I'm sorry I couldn't gain your citizenship in some other way, but Zayd would have contested it because he's already laid a claim on you. Fortunately, no one can question a last will and testament filed with the Tinkers Guild. Your citizenship will afford you some protection from Sept Ocon. All of the founding septs must vote when serious accusations are levelled against a citizen of the Lamina caste. It's not a guarantee of a positive outcome, but it will prevent any single sept from making a unilateral decision against you. If you find yourself in that situation, seek an audience with Luminary Dewei of Ludumburg or Luminary Xandri of Opesburg. I have good relationships with them."

"Wait, back up. You've designated me as your heir?"

Quinto placed his hands on Valtteri's shoulders. "I'm so sorry, Val. I wish I could have told you sooner, but Zayd was watching me. If he suspected that I considered you anything more than an obligation, it's unlikely you would've made it this far. I love you, and everything I have is yours. I'm so proud of the man you've become, and I hope you'll find it in your heart someday to forgive me for waiting so long to tell you how I feel."

He loves me? He's proud of me? Val was having difficulty reconciling his feelings. The admiral had always defended him, and their life together was a reasonably good one, but the man was often absent. The navy placed many demands on an admiral's time. Valtteri knew Quinto Soren as a kind and considerate man, a side that few others saw, but the two of them never shared tender moments. *I could have used some emotional support on so many occasions.*

Valtteri suddenly realized that the admiral was speaking again. "I'm sorry, what was that you said?"

Quinto sighed and repeated himself. "Please pay attention, this is important. Remember, to expose the truth, you must quell the darkness. These words are trustworthy. Quell the darkness."

What an odd thing to say, and why the heavy emphasis on that last part?

"Repeat it back to me, Val."

"I think it was something like, be quiet at night."

"No! *Quell the darkness.* At least remember that part."

"Quell the darkness? What's that supposed to mean?"

"There may come a day when it means everything to you." Quinto glanced at the mantle clock. "I'm sorry, Val, I have a meeting scheduled. We can talk later. You have tomorrow off, but pack your bags and prepare to leave at 0600 hours the following morning. I'll take you to the docks where a transport will be waiting to escort you to the Ocon estate in Calcesburg."

The admiral rushed out the door, leaving Valtteri to sort through the unexpected information dump that was about to change his life forever.

Chapter 6

While not a very imaginative name, the tavern Valterri and Sebastian entered was appropriately called Shroud's Edge, located as it was at the edge of shroudside. A hint of cigar smoke drifted past. Cigars were a luxury item in the swath, suggesting someone of wealth was slumming or perhaps a crime boss was having a meeting of some sort. The latter thought put Valtteri on edge. *I'd better get used to it. My new job will probably require that I frequent such places to gather intelligence.*

"Relax, Val, we're here to have some fun before you deploy."

"That's easy for you to say. You don't stand out like I do. Everyone keeps looking this way."

"It's just your imagination." Sebastian glanced up at the waitress as she placed their food orders on the table. "Uh, miss? We didn't order these drinks."

"I know, the drinks are compliments of that table over there." The waitress tossed her long ebony hair over her shoulder, pointing with her chin.

Valtteri looked over to see two young ladies waving at him. He turned back to Sebastian and tilted his head. "You were saying?"

"So, now you're complaining about attractive women admiring us?"

Valtteri wasn't immune to the lure, but in his experience, Aerish women were just curious about his Tellusan physique. Most had no interest in a serious relationship, and he hated the objectification. It just reinforced how little he was valued in the swath. "You know how I feel about this. I have enough people laying claim to me. I'm not about to sell myself to yet another person for the price of a drink. When I'm ready, I want a relationship, and I'm not going to find it here."

"Suit yourself, but you don't mind if I show my appreciation, do you?"

Valtteri rolled his eyes as Sebastian made his way to their table. A burst of laughter initiated a hasty retreat by a red-faced Sebastian.

"Back so soon?"

Sebastian took his seat and rubbed the back of his neck. "The waitress must have made a mistake and sent the drinks to the wrong table."

"I guess you were right, I was just imagining things."

Sebastian quickly accepted the proffered escape. "What did I tell you? Anyway, the food smells great and I'm starving."

They both tucked into their meals. It had been a long eighteen-hour trip from Viburg Naval Base to Calcesburg, not to mention the four-hour layover at Opesburg. They travelled on an aerocruiser that didn't have anything appetizing to eat. To be honest, the typical fare at the naval base cafeteria wasn't much better. Silence reigned as they focused on the task of shovelling gravy drenched pheasant into their mouths.

As he chewed, Valtteri's mind wandered to his upcoming meeting. It seemed ridiculous that he should have to travel 2,700 nautical miles to meet with Luminary Ocon, and then immediately return to Viburg. He had decided to use his day off to get the long trip out of the way. Otherwise, he'd be worrying about the journey instead of enjoying his free time. Arriving early at his destination would give him time to explore the city, a brief moment of freedom before the demands of his new duties.

Quinto had reluctantly agreed with Valtteri's argument that leaving early would ensure he was well rested before his meeting with Zayd Ocon. Valtteri's promise to stop in Opesburg sweetened the deal. The admiral spent most of his time at the Viburg Naval Base, but his duties required him to spend time in Opesburg as well. It was the centre for judicial affairs, and on occasion, issues arose that only he could address. To accommodate extended stays in Opesburg, the admiral had purchased an estate there. Valtteri agreed to deliver some legal documents while checking on the admiral's property. It would save the admiral a trip.

Valtteri could tell that Quinto was disappointed with the early departure. Clearly, he had much more to share. The admiral's sudden openness was a bit overwhelming, and Valtteri didn't know how to respond. He needed some distance, and time alone, to ruminate before hearing more.

The admiral approved his travel plans, and even gave Sebastian leave to join him. Sebastian would have plenty of time to return to the base before the weekend came to a close. So, here they were, free to explore, and enjoy some downtime together before they had to say their goodbyes.

Sated for the moment, Valtteri leaned back in his chair. "I've been solarside of Opesburg many times. The architecture is very ornate, with cultivated gardens everywhere. I've never been shroudside. Here in Calcesburg, solarside seems more subdued. The buildings lend themselves to function over form. I've also noticed fewer green spaces in favour of paved plazas. This tavern is the closest I've been to the shroudside of a tropostate. It doesn't seem as bad as the stories suggest. Is it like this in Ferroburg where you come from, Seb?"

Sebastian seemed to laugh and grunt at the same time. "This isn't the *real* shroudside, Val. Some among the higher castes want to feel like they're flirting with danger. The fringes of shroudside cater to that sort of clientele. You need to move past the fringe to see how most people live."

"So, what's it like?"

"Living shroudside is the same in every tropostate. When we look up, we see the barren surface of the swath. The reflected light filters through in places, but shadows prevail. Light is too sparse to grow anything. When I first arrived at Viburg for training, I would spend hours looking up at the sky to feel the sun on my face. Consider yourself blessed that you were able to do so for your entire life. I know you've had it hard being a lone Tellusan in the archipelago, but even so, you've lived a better life than most of the Lagan caste. I can say that, having experienced more sunshine than most of my caste. I would find it very difficult to go back into the perpetual shadows. It's difficult to put into words how your soul is affected when all you can see in your future is endless grey monotony."

"I'm sorry, Seb, I didn't know."

"It isn't all bad. We find our joy where we can. A distinguishing trait of shroudside cities are the wide boulevards that run unobstructed from east to west. For a brief period of time, the streets come alive as the sun passes between the plane of equilibrium and the horizon. The sky darkens for the Luminaries and shines for us. What you would call sunrise and sunset is known as first and second bright watch by the residents of shroudside. All work ceases, and people flood into the streets to enjoy the light. No matter your station, in that moment we're all one, joined by the uplifting of our spirits."

Valtteri remained silent as he watched the memories play across his friend's face. Sebastian seldom spoke of his past, and this was a special insight.

"We bring out richly coloured objects to appreciate their full vibrancy. Music and laughter fill the air, along with the scent of extinguished candles, a small act of defiance against the darkness. We forgive and forget animosities born of hardship, as the desire for life is rekindled. Those are magical moments where hope exists in a hopeless place. All of our celebrations are scheduled during bright watch."

"It sounds amazing, Seb."

Sebastian nodded, his eyes glistening. "It's the only thing I miss. Shroudside is otherwise a depressing place. Sunny spaces filled with cultivated greenery don't exist here. The moon and stars aren't visible to inspire paintings or songs. Shroudside can't compare to the beauty of solarside, but I feel sorry for those who have never experienced bright watch. I'm convinced that nothing is more beautiful than that moment when hearts unite, forgiveness flows freely, and we remember what it means to love one another." Sebastian fell silent for a moment. "Did you know that the friaers prefer to locate their tropostate missions on shroudside? Most say it's because of their commitment to work with the poor, since the Luminaries would never allow the Lagan caste to remain solarside. That is a part of it to be sure, but I've noticed the friaer's faces when they join in bright watch. I believe they see something holy in those moments."

"Do you think I could see it for myself?"

"It's not something reserved for the Lagan caste if that's what you're wondering. Anyone can participate, but it won't happen for several hours. Are you sure you want to hang around that long?"

"I do! We have other things to see before then. You know how fascinated I am with machinery. All of the interesting equipment is housed shroudside. Apparently, it intrudes on the sensibilities of the upper crust. They don't know what they're missing."

"You're a strange one." Sebastian laughed. "What do you want to see first?"

"The world chains!"

As if on cue, a long horn sounded.

"Looks like you're in luck. Come on!"

Valtteri paid the waitress and ran after his friend. He caught up just as Sebastian swung himself onto a passing cable car. Valtteri followed suit and threw himself into an empty seat, coughing as he tried to catch his breath.

"Sorry, Val, I should have warned you. We're in an industrial area. There's a lot of coal dust and smoke. Try not to breathe too deeply."

"Why did the horn sound? What's going on?"

Sebastian pointed in the distance. "Look, they're raising the wicking masts. That means a cloud bank is nearby."

"I don't understand."

"You're about to see the world chains in action. We have to move Calcesburg into the cloud to harvest the moisture. The engineers need to unwind the chain reel to create slack. The vapour engines will provide the thrust we need to intercept."

The cable car lurched to a stop, and Sebastian hopped off. "We'll have to travel the rest of the way on foot. The system automatically anchors public transit while the chain reels are turning. The vibrations this close to the engines are pretty disruptive. It's not far, we're almost there."

Valtteri paced himself and followed Sebastian's lead. As they moved deeper into the industrial section, massive engines sprouted everywhere he looked. He'd seen the impressive drives of a warship, but those were dwarfed by the gargantuan dimensions of the machinery in front of him. Engineers designed this equipment to move an entire tropostate.

Sebastian led them to a rack of ear protectors beside a balustrade. Valtteri looked over the railing and was shocked to discover he'd only seen the tops of the engines rising from their bases three stories below them. It took three sharp elbows to his side before Sebastian interrupted his stupor.

"Pretty impressive, huh? Here, you're going to want these in a few minutes."

Valtteri accepted the ear protectors as he pointed to a crank assembly attached to the chain reel. "Look at the size of that piston! It's amazing!" He shook his head in awe. "How is it possible to forge something that large?"

Sebastian smiled at his friend's excitement. "Do you see that piston rod? Look at the words stamped into the side — Ferroburg Industries. Below that is a series of smaller circular stamps that denote the forges and families involved. They're used to track manufacturing defects to the source. You can just make out the second stamp from the end."

Valtteri squinted. "The one with the letter 'A'?"

"Yup, 'A' for Arguso." Sebastian straightened with pride. "My family forged that assembly. I helped with the mould."

Valtteri's chin dropped as he turned to his friend. "You made that thing?"

Sebastian laughed. "I played a small role. Forging something that large requires a lot of people. The Arguso family is recognized for the quality of their work, and the ability to forge any part no matter how large or complex. Now put these on, and get a good grip on the railing. It's about to get exciting."

Sebastian's warning was an understatement. The massive reel began to turn and the colossal world chain thundered as the links moved through their guides. A flagman was signalling from below to a booth not far from where they stood. The operator in the booth was rapidly tapping out messages. *He must be synchronizing with the second reel miles away on the opposite side of the tropostate.* The sheer magnitude of the equipment and coordination required for the effort was astonishing. *I had no idea.* "This is incredible!" Valtteri shouted into the cacophony, unheard by himself or anyone else.

Sebastian elbowed him once more, indicating that he should widen his stance and increase his grip on the railing. Then he felt it, a deep vibration gathering strength as the pressure valves were opened. The iron grates below his feet began to shake as the thrusters roared to a crescendo.

Just as Valtteri thought he could bear no more, the thrusters cut out, leaving a palpable absence of sound. At least, it seemed that way to his senses. In reality, he could see that equipment was still running. "I've gone deaf, Seb!" It felt like he was yelling, but Sebastian merely shook his head and pointed at his own ear as though it were perfectly normal. Sebastian hooked a thumb over his shoulder and lifted an eyebrow. Valtteri nodded and the two made their way back to the cable car.

With some distance from the engines, his ears began to provide a little feedback, but it was mostly in the form of a loud buzz. Valtteri glanced at Sebastian who was grinning from ear to ear. Valtteri laughed until Sebastian's face suddenly fell. His friend's eyes widened, and Val was about to ask what was wrong when his remaining senses failed him — the world went black.

Chapter 7

Zayd suppressed his irritation at being held to account, and put on a smile. The Council of Luminaries had been hastily convened following his own recently concluded summit with the northern and southern Tellusans. Keeping that meeting from his peers hadn't been easy. They were not happy when they learned about it later.

"Greetings, fellow Luminaries, and thank you for accommodating my busy schedule by coming to Calcesburg."

The meeting was originally scheduled to occur in Opesburg, the centre of justice and governance. Zayd considered the optics unacceptable. He wasn't about to come crawling to the Council as though he were a guilty child. Instead, he offered to host the gathering at his own expense. Zayd imagined they would view it as an act of contrition rather than manipulation. They were happy to take advantage of his generosity, and probably didn't realize how weak it made them look. They had come to him, as it should be.

"I hope your accommodations are acceptable, and that your comforts have been attended to."

"You've been a most generous host, Zayd."

It was no surprise that Luminary Kiraz spoke first. Voloburg was a pleasure tropostate, and its founder tended to overindulge in such things. Zayd mentally rolled his eyes. "I'm happy to hear it, Enzo." The man was inconsequential. He never took a hard stand on any issue, wary of scaring away potential customers.

Apart from the company, Zayd was pleased with the setting. He intentionally chose the grand library for this meeting. The scent of old paper from the shelves of books created an atmosphere of wisdom and history that would serve his purpose well. A large circular table had been installed in the middle of the room below a domed skylight. The surface displayed an exotic wood inlay depiction of the Tropos Archipelago. At the centre was an impressionist representation of chaos radiating outward. Beautiful interpretations of each tropostate encircled the table, strung together like gems on a gold chain that held them all together. They appeared as shining beacons of hope, stars sparkling in the heavens.

Zayd's staff ensured that each Luminary was seated at the appropriate depiction of their own tropostate. Every image was a monument designed to evoke passion and stroke egos.

The overall image duplicated the placement of each tropostate in the world chain, Stipoburg, Ferroburg, Calcesburg, Opesburg, Ludumburg, Voloburg, and back to Stipoburg. The favourable seating arrangement placed Zayd's two closest allies to his immediate left. It was a show of solidarity, but it seemed like an innocent acknowledgement of the illustration before them.

Zayd cleared his throat. "Well, this is a bit awkward. Typically the host would lead the agenda, but since I'm here to answer your questions, I yield the floor."

Silas Xandri stood to speak. "As I understand, you held a summit meeting with the Tellusans, yet many of us were not informed of your intent to do so. This is highly irregular."

Zayd rose and responded smoothly. "Straight to the point as always, Silas. It was a hasty affair at the insistence of the Tellusans. I made sure we had the minimum required number of delegates. Philo Stol of Stipoburg accompanied me, as did Tiago Damira of Ferroburg."

"For what purpose did the Tellusans request this meeting, and why didn't they go through regular channels? Opesburg is the centre of governance for the Tropos Archipelago. We should have been the first to hear of this."

"As you're aware, one of our recent naval exercises went awry, sending ordnance across the southern limen. The Tellusans had questions."

Jayla Dewei stood, suspicion clear in her voice. "That explains the Tellusans' request, but not the lack of transparency with your Luminary peers. Foreign affairs are clearly under the jurisdiction of Opesburg. At the very least, Silas should have been present."

"My dear, Jayla, I was merely sparing you all an unnecessary trip. As for issues of jurisdiction, Admiral Soren was also present. I'm sure he submitted a report. Hasn't he represented Opesburg on numerous occasions in the past? Since this involved a naval incident, he seemed the obvious choice. As I said, this was a rushed affair, but all of the governance requirements were met."

"Even so, we can't ignore the fact that you chose the delegates without input from the rest of us. This was a serious international incident that should have come before the entire Council."

Tiago Damira came to Zayd's defence. "During an investigation into the incident, a question arose as to whether the equipment was faulty. Ferroburg forges such parts and Calcesburg is responsible for assembly. Naturally, we were called in to discuss these matters early in the investigation. I think it's clear to everyone in this room that it was necessary for Zayd, myself and the admiral to attend. Regardless of who else you may have wished to be there, the issue had appropriate representation. I'm not sure why anyone would have a concern."

"And what is your explanation for requesting Philo's presence? Stipoburg is involved with mining and earth moving. They have no ties to the navy."

Philo responded in his own defence. "It was a matter of convenience. Stipoburg is close to Viburg. Zayd noted the urgency and asked if I would be willing."

"Yes, convenient." Silas muttered.

Philo took offence. "Are you insinuating something, Silas? Speak your mind!"

"You already know how I feel. Ever since Asher Zayd passed, we've been moving backwards. We were making great strides in international relations due to his proposed reforms. Now we walk a fine line with the Tellusans. It's important to tread carefully."

Zayd leapt to his feet, anger clear on his face. "This again? My father's proposed reforms were a mistake. It would've reduced us to nothing. How can you not see this? Why are you in such a hurry to cede authority to a foreign power?"

Silas shook his head. "This isn't about ceding authority, it's about improving the lives of our citizens."

"You insult our heritage, and all we've accomplished for the people."

Zayd caught the eyes of his peers in turn. He pointedly looked at the images on the table in front of them, dragging their gazes along as he did. "After the inversion, who gathered the rocks and soil? Who provided an oasis in the midst of the maelstrom? It was Sept Stol. They lost many good men in their efforts to gather those who were adrift. Later, they gathered food and cultivated crops. Without their selfless efforts, we wouldn't have survived. They're all heroes who continue their service to this day. What is it about their generosity and concern for the welfare of others that needs to be reformed?"

Zayd pointed to Tiago. "What of Sept Damira? It was they who found a way to build forges and fire them while adrift in the swath. To them we owe the heat and tools that enabled survival, and made all of our lives better. The world chain was fabricated through their ingenuity, linking us together as one people. These too are heroes who continue to perfect their craft, allowing us to build and grow."

Placing a hand against his chest, Zayd continued. "Sept Ocon builds the engines that keep us safely from the limen so we can sleep without fear of drifting across and plummeting to our deaths. My ancestors developed ships for the navy that protects us, and the generators that power our cities. We provide the means by which goods and services are transported so no tropostate is lacking. Is it this equity that needs to be reformed?"

"Last, but not least of the early founders..."

Enzo straightened with pride, knowing he was next.

Zayd smiled and offered a theatrical flourish. "How shall we thank Sept Kiraz? In a world seemingly without hope, they gathered musicians, singers, poets and storytellers. They provided a place to escape the drudgery of a difficult existence so we could remember who we are. Sept Kiraz continues to host our imagination, laughter, and hope. I ask you, Silas, are these things signs of failure?"

Silas protested. "I'm not diminishing accomplishments of the past. Merely looking to the future."

"The future?" Zayd thundered. "Are you suggesting that the rest of us do not? Have you so quickly forgotten that Opesburg and Ludumburg exist by the largess of the original three founders?" He looked pointedly at Jayla. "Sept Dewei provides the finest education in the world. The medical and research facilities of Ludumburg are unparalleled. The Tropos Archipelago continues to advance in all areas benefiting not only our people, but the Tellusans as well. This was always the intent of the Luminaries, and you have the audacity to suggest that we're not thinking of the people, or our future?"

Zayd shook his head vigorously as he built up steam. "And you, Silas, Luminary of Sept Xandri, founder of our banking, judicial and government infrastructure. You know very well that all who sit around this table have the freedom to speak, and vote on behalf of our citizens. Why do you look for direction from a totalitarian regime to the north, and a monarchy to the south? Two power-hungry individuals make decisions for all Tellusans and you say we're the ones moving backwards. Is it from people like these that we should seek a better future? Look at the bookshelves behind me. Our ingenuity spans five hundred years of history. The wisdom on these shelves continues to expand as testament that we have never stopped striving for a better future."

Jayla interrupted his tirade. "That is naive, Zayd. You're forgetting the plight of the Lagan caste who seldom benefit from the advances you've listed. You ignore the warnings Silas and I have presented to this body. We don't have the raw material to maintain the growth or prosperity you imagine. We rely on the Tellusans to supply the difference. We simply can't afford to make an enemy of them."

"I hear and understand, but you continue to dismiss more immediate warnings that speak directly to the very issue you raise. The Tellusans want what we have, and they know we're at a disadvantage. Mark my words. On the day we come begging for food, they won't be our saviours, but our conquerors. All that we have built will be lost. If you believe the Lagan caste will have more opportunities under Tellusan rule, you're sorely mistaken."

"Even if what you say is true, and I don't believe it is, the problem remains the same. We have no way to extend our resources. They're already stretched to the limit."

Zayd threw out his arms with impatience. "You're wrong! We can expand. You're just too blind to see it. We don't have to remain in the swath."

"Are you seriously suggesting we go to war?"

"What I'm telling you is that the Tellusans are coming for us. We can sit here passively and give up or we can go on the offensive. War is coming for us, whether we like it or not. If we move first, our resource problem goes away. We can provide better leadership and a better life for the Tellusans in the process. We can be liberators."

Jayla's eyes widened at the suggestion. "You're mad! We have no reason to believe that the Tellusans have aggressive intentions."

"Don't we? Have you taken the time to review our intelligence reports? They contain accounts from people who say they've seen Tellusans crossing the limen without invitation. That is a direct violation of the treaty, and a flagrant disregard for our sovereignty." Zayd looked pointedly at Silas. "I've noticed that our representative for international affairs has failed to challenge the Tellusans for their transgressions.

"I'd also like the Tellusans to explain how they reacted so swiftly to the recent mishap that occurred during our military exercises. That incident took place in a very remote location far from any inhabited areas. The Tellusans shouldn't have even noticed. Yet they did because they have troops operating along the southern limen where no soldiers should be. The motivations of the southern Tellusans are far from innocent, and the northern Tellusans are outright hostile."

Luminary Dewai cast questioning eyes at Philo and Tiago.

"The Prime Palatine did appear antagonistic," Philo confirmed. "He said that if such an incident ever occurred along the northern limen, his war balloons would shoot first and ask questions later."

Zayd picked up where Philo left off. "The Tellusans have been moving troops and equipment into the deep south beyond the range of our telescopes. When I asked why, Queen Silvanus held her tongue. I suggested she might have a gravity device hidden there, and that the next logical target would be the northern Tellusans. Prime Palatine Tagish became very agitated, and Queen Silvanus still refused to respond."

"This is exactly why I should have been present," Silas fumed. "You recklessly incite others with no real evidence to support your paranoia!"

"We have every right to demand answers from the Tellusans, considering they're demanding it of us."

"Is that how you dealt with the navy's mistake? By making demands?"

"Not at all, Luminary Xandri. My fellow delegates will confirm that I took full responsibility for the incident, even though it was the result of trainee error, not equipment. We discussed the value of the affected forest, and I offered reparations in the amount of two city-class generators at my own expense. I assure you, the value of those generators far exceed that of the lost lumber. I offered it as a show of good faith in our future relations. Queen Silvanus was very pleased."

Silas jerked in surprise, at a loss for words. "That's — that's —."

"A successful outcome?" Zayd looked around the room. "Those who wish they could have participated in the summit can still contribute. I'd be happy to accept donations to help offset the cost of my generous settlement, a gift given for the sake of international relations, if you recall."

The response was an uncomfortable silence interrupted by a guard who approached Zayd to whisper in his ear.

"My friends, an issue has arisen that requires my attention. We'll need to wrap this up or continue later. Are you satisfied with my answers and the outcome of the summit?"

Heads reluctantly nodded around the table.

"Excellent. Please stay as long as you wish. If I don't see you again before you leave, I bid you farewell and a safe journey."

Chapter 8

"Rouse him!"

One of the men threw a bucket of water in Valtteri's face where he lay on the stone floor. He gasped as the shock of the icy liquid woke him. The man with the bucket stepped back, rejoining ten others who surrounded him.

"Who are you?" Valtteri looked frantically around the room. "Why am I here?"

A voice from beyond his captors responded.

"That's a very good question."

Zayd motioned for his men to clear a path. Two of them stepped aside, granting him a clear view of the dripping truant. "Your appearance interrupted a conference of the Luminaries."

Valtteri struggled with confusion as he tried to focus beyond the ring of his captors. "Luminary Ocon?"

"Very astute, Mr. Knox. I certainly hope the money I've invested in your training amounts to more than an ability to state the obvious. That was a sorry display of deduction, but I'm more concerned by your lack of obedience."

"What happened to my friend?"

"Trainee Argus is on a transport headed back to Viburg, but that's really none of your concern."

"I don't understand. I wasn't scheduled to meet with you until tomorrow."

"Your instructions were to wait at the docks in Viburg for my men to pick you up. They arrived promptly at 0600 hours, you didn't. Some might wonder if you had decided to run from your responsibilities. My men don't appreciate having their time wasted. Imagine my surprise when I heard rumours of a young Tellusan, fitting your description, wandering shroudside in Calcesburg. You are fifty-four hundred miles from where you were supposed to be."

"I can explain."

"As I've said, I had to cut my meeting short because of you. Believe me, you have my undivided attention."

"I — I wanted to make sure I wasn't late. I had the day off so I thought I'd come early. Admiral Soren approved my travel plans."

"Did he, now?" Zayd nodded to one of his men. "Joseph, run to the communications room and check for messages. If you find one, I want to know why I didn't receive it."

Zayd sighed. "Stand up, Knox." He motioned to the men surrounding him. "Someone find the man a towel."

Two minutes passed in silence before Joseph returned with a piece of paper in his hand. Zayd read it and handed it back, eyebrow raised in query.

"Some confusion during a shift change, I'm told."

Zayd rolled his head back and stared at the ceiling, seeking calm. After a few deep breaths, he turned his attention back to Valtteri. "I regret the harsh welcome. My men can get a little rough when they're upset."

"My apologies, Luminary Ocon. I never intended for any of this to happen. I thought everything was in order."

Zayd held up a hand for silence. "You've spent most of your life answering to the navy. I understand that your first instinct was to approach the admiral. It's not your fault that his message failed to arrive in time. However, I'm disappointed that you made plans on your own and proceeded before receiving my approval. The authority of an admiral is not above that of a Luminary. Do you understand this?"

"Yes, Sir! I wasn't thinking. It won't happen again, Sir!"

"We were scheduled to meet tomorrow, but you're here now. I'm inclined to try and recover some of the time I've lost. You'll return to Viburg for your final classes, but as of this moment, you're officially in my employ. You'll continue to follow the navy chain of command for the duration of your training, so far as it doesn't conflict with my orders. Joseph will be accompanying you to supplement your training; you'll need to know our intelligence protocols. During your time together, you will obey Joseph's commands as if they were my own. Do you understand?

"Yes, Sir."

Zayd turned to his men. "The rest of you are dismissed. I wish some time alone with our latest recruit. Joseph, please make travel arrangements for yourself and Mr. Knox, and find him a room for the night. I want you to leave at first light."

Joseph nodded, and followed his team out of the room.

"I'm not going to ask you to declare allegiance to me or perform some ridiculous ceremony. It's not what you say, but what you do that matters. You will earn my trust over time if you obey my orders. However, let me be crystal clear, I won't condone betrayal. You'll be privy to secrets that put the lives of your fellow operatives at risk. You've met some of those operatives today. If you betray *me*, you betray *them*, and they will hunt you down. I know how threatening that sounds, but the threat is not without reason. These people have families whose safety relies on discretion. We don't put our families in harm's way. By accepting you into our ranks, you become one with Sept Ocon. We're placing our loved ones in your hands. Don't betray that trust."

Valtteri's face paled as the implications settled in. Zayd seemed not to have noticed. "I think you'll find it easy to maintain that trust. I'm not a monster. I don't command operatives to commit acts that go against their personal codes of morality. If a particular request is outside your comfort zone, you can approach me. Feel free to discuss this with Joseph. He'll put your mind at ease.

"I've observed your progress over the years and the results please me. I took a risk by sponsoring your placement within the Lamina caste. Some have questioned the wisdom of granting such privilege to a Tellusan, but I saw something in you, and felt confident enough to provide the financial support and training that led you here. I know it has been difficult for you, a Tellusan among the Aerish. I hope you can appreciate that you've otherwise had a good life, better than many. In fact, I suspect your life would've been worse had you remained among the Tellusans."

"Thank you for your aegis, Luminary. I will try to serve you well. If I may ask, why do the Aerish of the archipelago dislike me?"

"Another good question. Suspicion separates the Tellusans from the Aerish as effectively as the swath. People cling to painful memories of conflicts and loss. Grudges can live for a very long time. Do you remember much about your life before the accident that set you adrift in the swath?"

"Very little, Luminary. I was barely five at the time."

"As I thought. In many ways, you're more Aerish than Tellusan. Yet, I imagine you're reminded of your heritage daily by the way people look at you, among other things. In life, many people search for someone to blame for their circumstances. It's not fair, but you make an easy target. Surely you've found some friends among the Aerish?"

"A few, Luminary. Admiral Soren, of course, and Sebastian. Perhaps a small number of others who are at least peaceable."

"I'm disappointed that so few examples come to mind. I'm going to be sending you among your own kind. You'll be around people who look like you, and for a while you'll relish feeling ordinary. I expect that you'll begin to question your place among the Aerish. All the more since so many here have made you uncomfortable. However, I want you to consider something. Prejudice exists everywhere. An Aerish raised by the

Tellusans would face experiences similar to your own. You'll discover, soon enough, that darkness can lie within any heart.

"If you can set aside the injustices that you feel you've suffered, your efforts for me will help pave the way to a better future. When I send my operatives out, it's to break down barriers and uncover truth. I want you to be a bridge between our peoples. The history books will never record it, but you'll be a secret ambassador for change. You'll have a foot in both worlds, and I'm giving you an opportunity that will ultimately benefit Tellusans and Aerish alike."

Zayd paused before adding, "Do you have any questions?"

"Can I ask what I'll be doing to bring about this change?"

Zayd chuckled. "Nothing momentous, to start. I have a few tasks in mind. For now, I want you to finish your training at Pax Montis. After that, spend some time moving through the surrounding villages familiarizing yourself with Tellusan ways. Make friends in the local taverns where people speak freely. I've set up an expense account through the Tinkers Guild. You can make withdrawals as necessary. You'll have no financial restrictions placed upon you, but remember that you want to avoid unnecessary attention.

"If you hear rumours about political affairs, or strange events regarding the Aerish, or the Tellusans, those are things you should include in your reports. I will expect a bi-weekly summary of your activities. Joseph will explain how to use the drop sites and other means of communication. You may receive instructions in a similar manner. Aside from those regular expectations, I have one specific task that I need you to look into as soon as possible.

"I'm sending you to a remote village located near the southern limen. It's called Endelton. I need you to poke around, and determine the truth about rumours that Queen Silvanus has soldiers operating in the area. Sometimes, operatives disguise themselves as civilians. Suspect everyone. If you learn anything about people crossing the limen at the base of the swath, I need to know. That kind of activity would be a breach of international treaty, and could seriously jeopardize relations, if not addressed immediately."

"Why would anyone try to cross the limen at the base of the swath? I very nearly died as a child doing that very thing."

"Driven people do desperate things. That's why I train operatives. They uncover people's motivations before something disastrous happens. Do you think you can handle this mission?"

"Yes, Sir."

"Good. It's a simple task and relatively risk-free. It will give you time to settle into your new role. We'll start small, and then we'll see how you handle something a little more complex."

"I'll do my best, Sir. Will that be all?"

"I'll add one more thing. I know that you and my nephew dislike each other. I've chosen not to get involved because your rivalry has served to push you both to greater accomplishments, but now you're in service to Sept Ocon. Difficult as it may be for you to accept, Nixon will replace me as head of the sept one day. Sooner or later, you'll answer directly to him. You would do well to remember that."

"Understood."

"Excellent. You're dismissed. Find Joseph and he will see to your needs."

* * *

Zayd waited for his new operative to leave before calling out. "We're alone. You can come in now."

The door to an adjacent room opened and Nixon entered.

"That went fairly well, don't you agree, Nephew?"

"I wish you'd listen to me on this, Uncle. You can't trust Knox. He's too impulsive and easily goaded."

"From what I've heard, he only acts that way around you. Regardless, he has proven his abilities."

"You have *me*. I can accomplish anything Knox can, and I can do it better."

Zayd snorted. "You can do many things well, Nixon, but you'll never pass as a Tellusan. We need him."

"We can accomplish our goals in other ways without putting our trust in Knox. He's reckless, Uncle. He almost killed me!"

"Enough of that. You almost killed yourself!"

"I had everything under control."

"Nixon, you risked your life to make a stupid point. You're a Luminary, you have nothing to prove. When are you going to get that through your thick skull? You're my only heir. I can't have children of my own. You can't risk your life like that, or everything I've been working towards will fall apart."

Nixon glared at his uncle. "When are you going to tell me your plans?"

"Soon enough."

"Why won't you let me help you, Uncle? What was all this training for if I'm not going to use it?"

Zayd gave Nixon a sly grin. "Don't worry, Nephew, you'll get your chance to show me what you're made of. I plan to deploy you at the same time as Valtteri. I want you to follow him, and collect his reports from the drop sites.

"You'll need men and supplies to operate outside of the swath. I have a few contacts among the Tellusans who can connect you with the kinds of resources you'll need. Rely on these contacts to conduct business on your behalf. I need you to work from the shadows. No more risking your own safety! A Luminary gives orders for *others* to take. I expect you to learn how to accomplish your goals and manipulate people without getting your hands dirty. It will be an essential skill when you take my place one day.

"Another thing, stop competing with Valtteri Knox. He's not your equal, and soon enough, he'll be taking orders from you. Prove you're a leader of men, and not only will he do as you say, he will respect you as well."

Nixon nodded with an eager glint in his eyes. "I can do this, Uncle. Thank you for giving me this opportunity."

Chapter 9

Sunlight streamed through the floor to ceiling windows of the private training room. Valtteri had never been to this section of Pax Montis, it was reserved for the friaers. Navy trainees had been told that the area was off limits. Valtteri tried to protest when Friaer Kozen first brought him here, but he insisted it was the instructor's prerogative. Valtteri wasn't about to complain, the setting was much nicer than the space where he normally trained with the other recruits. The mats were clean, and potted plants sat in the corners. Best of all, there were no other students. Valtteri was constantly being approached by hotheads who wanted to test themselves against the Luminary Navy's token Tellusan. It made him a better fighter, but it was tiresome.

Fisher adjusted Valtteri's stance slightly. "You've always been a talented student, Valtteri, but don't let your success breed complacency. The forms we teach depend on a strong foundation. Always correct your stance before considering anything else. Ingrain that habit until it occurs without thinking. This is critical for the system we teach."

"Are you implying that a poor stance provides an exploitable weakness?"

Friaer Kozen nodded "That's a question too few of my students ask.

It's good that you pay attention to the posture of your opponents, but don't forget your own. What do you know about the history of Hamo Sagitta?"

Valtteri shrugged. "I know it surpassed all other styles and that it's pointless to study anything else."

"What has been drilled into you over the years?"'

Valtteri considered his answer. "We're taught to redirect attacks by hooking limbs, and to strike with the speed and accuracy of an arrow."

"Exactly so, but do you know why?"

Valtteri let out a nervous laugh. "To win the fight?"

Fisher lifted an eyebrow and said nothing until Valtteri's face took on a crimson hue. "Hamo Sagitta was developed over centuries. The friaers studied every style of martial art and analyzed the strengths and weaknesses of each. We discovered many similarities in the most effective fighting forms, but something else proved more difficult to quantify. Inevitably, practitioners would arise who seemed unbeatable, and they weren't students from the same school or style. We discovered that talent wasn't enough to explain these exceptions.

"A fighter knows many ways to strike a blow or block an attack, but the common denominator for success in these seemingly invincible fighters was the way they created and exploited weakness. They probably didn't even realize what they were doing. The developers of Hamo Sagitta catalogued the speed, balance, flow and resulting targets of opportunity that regularly appeared when these fighters sparred. A pattern began to emerge and we ultimately condensed it into the forms you practise.

"The stance you've been taught is unique to Hamo Sagitta. We didn't design it for stability in the way some might imagine. You can't use it to stand your ground. Rather, it's a state of balance that allows the practitioner to transition quickly into a hook or a strike. An effective fighter never stops moving. It's the best way to create openings and opportunities. Your stability comes through the speed and power of balanced motion. A poorly formed stance limits potential. You must be able to return quickly to a sound stance ready to explode into your next movement. This is critical if you find yourself fighting someone with superior skill."

Valtteri shook his head in wonder. "I've never heard any of this before. Did I miss a class or something? It seems like important information for a student to know."

Fisher gave Valtteri a penetrating gaze. "Many people come to Pax Montis to study Hamo Sagitta. We deny no one the opportunity to learn, but we reserve the right to limit what we teach. Those who seek to harm others obtain limited instruction."

"Like how you reserve the secrets of Invicta Manus for friaers and tinkers?"

"Actually, I was referring to simple things like I've just mentioned. Those who don't learn the importance of a strong foundational stance will fail to reach their full potential. Many similar infractions reduce effectiveness. We allow these failures among individuals who are too irresponsible to be granted such knowledge. It's safer for the world that such individuals remain at a disadvantage."

Valtteri cocked his head in confusion. "You just shared one of those secrets with me." His mind drifted as he considered previous sparring matches. He could picture his failures and realized many of them had indeed occurred when his stance felt unbalanced.

"You are granted that knowledge because you have the presence of mind to understand the consequences of unbridled power. Those who stumble in the darkness of their own ambition are not worthy. Only a fool engages an enemy at night without a light to quell the darkness."

Valtteri furrowed his brow at the cryptic response as he broke free of his contemplation. "So, you're saying I'm not your enemy? Wait, what did you just say?"

Fisher had a twinkle in his eye and his lips quirked to a sly smile. "No, young Mr. Knox. You're not my enemy, and I have much to teach you."

"I'm not sure I understand where this conversation is leading, but of course, I'm your student to mould for my remaining time here at Pax Montis."

Fisher began to pace the private training room. The scent of padded leather mats and an aroma of burning incense masked the tang of exertion. "Pay attention as I provide a little more context. The forms we teach focus on fulcrums and locks. Every hook or strike will take advantage of one or the other. It may be a balance point or a limitation in the human body's range of motion. While sparring, you can feel the difference between a well-executed throw and a poor one."

Valtteri nodded in affirmation. When the balance was just right, a throw felt effortless.

Fisher acknowledged the recognition and continued. "The forms of Hamo Sagitta, when well executed, will always place a practitioner in close proximity to a fulcrum or a lock juncture. Other fighting styles can't say the same. The exponential increase in targets of opportunity is what places Hamo Sagitta above all other styles. Talented practitioners will naturally begin to position themselves ever closer to fulcrum points. They may not understand what they're targeting, but they know that their movements become easier with better outcomes. When an instructor adjusts your stance, or the angle of a hook, we're pointing you in a direction that will help you discover these fulcrums."

Valtteri rubbed his temples. "Okay, let me try to summarize. Those who practise Hamo Sagitta have an advantage over other fighting styles by nature of the art itself. Further, those whom the friaers direct to finding these *fulcrums* will have an advantage over other Hamo Sagitta practitioners. Is that correct?"

Fisher nodded vigorously. "That's correct, but you haven't commented on an important detail."

"Wait, you said that the friaers developed their forms based on an analysis of all other martial arts. They catalogued the fulcrum locations. That means you know precisely where those points are!"

Fisher tilted his head in assent. "Every single one, including nerve cluster locations that we withhold from most students. We call them crux points."

"Why are you telling me this?"

"Because it's the first step in learning Invicta Manus."

Valtteri stiffened in shock. It took a full minute to shake off his torpor before he could respond. "Why me?"

"You don't wish to learn?"

"No! I mean yes, I want to learn! I just don't understand why you would entrust me with this knowledge."

"It's possible that you might abuse this honour, but we've become very good judges of character. Those who receive this gift are unlikely to share it. At least not broadly or they'd lose an advantage and put themselves at personal risk.

"When two practitioners of Invicta Manus fight, it's impossible to guess the outcome. They're too evenly matched. If the whole world knew the art of Invicta Manus, it would become irrelevant. To prevent that possibility, there remains a handful of very powerful crux points held in secrecy. These are handed down from one generation to the next. They're known only to a few keepers who have hidden the knowledge. If the secret of Invicta Manus became widely known, and the friaers found themselves in peril, the keeper would reveal himself. He would teach the brothers and regain an advantage."

"That explains your safeguards, but not why you've chosen to pass this knowledge on to me."

"The friaers have been around for a very long time, Valtteri. When we make plans, they have long-term implications. We're constantly cultivating friendships and allies. You never know who may find themselves in a position of influence one day. Invicta Manus is a gift we give to our potential friends and allies."

"But I'm a nobody to the Aerish, and have almost no history with the Tellusans. I'm not likely to be of any import or significance to anyone.

Besides, surely it takes years of study and I only have two weeks left before I have to leave Pax Montis."

"We have plenty of time. I won't be teaching you any new forms. Invicta Manus is nothing more than a layer of knowledge. It will add meaning to what you've already learned. The crux points are easy to memorize. I can teach them to you in a day. I'll have you spend the remainder of your time on what amounts to target practice so you can hit those points accurately and efficiently.

"You already know how effective Hamo Sagitta is, but when you interact with the crux points precisely and consistently, the cumulative benefits are astonishing. Your opponents will expend far more energy than you, and will suffer fatigue sooner. Your blows will become devastating as each assault connects with optimal force. In subsequent strikes, you'll be able to exploit a weakness you've created and introduce more. You'll take total control of an engagement. In short, you'll appear superhuman and practically untouchable."

Fisher walked to the edge of the sparring area where he'd left some bottles of water. He handed one to Valtteri. "It's important to stay hydrated."

Valtteri accepted the water and nodded. "In the navy, we're warned not to engage a practitioner of Invicta Manus without substantial backup."

"The friaers have spent generations inculcating fear and an air of mystery around Invicta Manus. When you openly engage, people will immediately recognize that you know it. That fear will go a long way in disarming your foes, but remember that you're not invincible."

Valtteri appeared doubtful. "Two weeks doesn't seem like enough time to master such a skill."

Fisher laughed. "Trust me, you'll have no trouble at all. Over the years, we friaers have trained a number of the Iridogen. Without exception they've cultivated uncanny reflexes and incredible eye-hand coordination. All of the Iridogen we've taught have mastered Invicta Manus within a week or two. You'll be no different."

Valtteri took several steps back, a look of confusion playing over his features.

"Valtteri? What's wrong?"

"You referred to me as Iridogen. Why did you call me that?"

"Oh dear. The admiral promised he'd explain things. I thought you knew. I'm surprised he kept this from you for so long. I suppose I understand why; it would only have served to make you feel like even more of an outsider. The admiral probably intended this omission as an act of kindness, but you can't continue in ignorance."

"So explain it to me. What makes you think I'm Iridogen, and why have I never heard that term before?"

Fisher sighed and gestured for Valtteri to sit with him on the mat. "The term *irido* is a combination of two words from the old language that mean *iridescent* and *rainbow*. The qualifier *gen* refers to a genetic trait, someone born with bicoloured eyes. When the genetic trait first started to appear, people labelled it *rainbow eyes*. Later it was discovered that people with bicoloured eyes didn't all fit into the same category. The range of possible colour combinations vary, but those with your particular genetic trait always have one gold eye and one grey eye. Not quite the spectrum of a rainbow, but the name stuck.

"Researchers have uncovered other common traits. During the inversion event, the massive magnetic flux did a great deal of harm to the neural pathways of the average human brain. It resulted in memory loss for a lot of people, but it affected the Iridogen in a positive way. Have you never wondered why you respond faster to situations than others do? We believe that something about the genetic make-up of the Iridogen caused neural pathways to open up rather than break down."

"Okay, so I have different coloured eyes and faster reflexes. Why would the admiral think he needed to keep that from me? Eye colour is hardly threatening, "

"To the contrary, Iridogen are hated and feared in the southern realm. It's different among the Aerish, though the reason is tragic. During the catastrophic events of inversion, the swath had a larger number of human casualties than the rest of the world. A devastating death toll wiped out the relatively small percentage of Iridogen. Generations of suspicion, isolation, and a caste system have prevented that rare genetic trait from crossing the limen to reemerge in Aerish society. You grew up in a culture generally unfamiliar with the Iridogen, so you were spared that particular bigotry, for the most part."

"That explains the admiral's motivations, but not why I should be concerned about the Tellusans. Why are the Iridogen hated in the southern realm?"

Fisher grimaced as he recalled some of the horrors recorded in their accumulated fragments of history. "That is a sad story. We don't know why, but the Iridogen first appeared in the southern hemisphere, and they seemed drawn to each other. The Iridogen began to multiply, and people started to take notice.

"A deadly plague afflicted the southern realm at about that same time, but the Iridogen were unaffected. Superstitious fools began to spread a rumour that the Iridogen were responsible for the plague. They claimed that the golden eye represented life and the grey eye represented death. They claimed that if an Iridogen looked at you with their grey eye open and golden eye closed, you would die. The idea is as preposterous as it sounds and perhaps it would have faded in time, but then the animals came."

Valtteri stiffened in anticipation.

"Judging by your expression, I'm guessing you know what I'm going to say next."

Valtteri swallowed past a lump in his throat. "On my thirteenth birthday, the admiral took me on a hunting trip to a remote plateau north of Viburg Naval Base. Trees still grew in the area at the time. We were hiding behind some rocks so we wouldn't scare the game. I haven't thought about this in a long time... I can hardly believe I almost forgot."

"What happened?"

"It was the strangest thing. Animals of all kinds came out of the forest from all directions and walked straight towards us. They stopped about twenty feet from us and just stood there. I was as mesmerized as the animals. I couldn't tear my gaze from their eyes ... my eyes. All of the animals had one gold eye and one grey eye. Apparently, I was the only one who noticed because the others in our hunting party couldn't believe their good fortune and opened fire. The animals didn't flee. They just stared at me as if they were waiting for something. It was — unnerving. The admiral doesn't talk about that trip much. I never told him about my connection with the animals. I figured it must have been my imagination, but after that, I refused to go hunting again."

"It wasn't your imagination. Quite a large number of iridomals thrive in the animal kingdom. They share some common traits with all other Iridogen. Those born with the trait are drawn by pheromones or some such thing. It's another unsolved mystery with tragic consequences."

"How so?"

"The rumours about the Iridogen being responsible for the plague was bad enough, but when strange eyed creatures of the forest began to follow their human counterparts... that was too much for most folk. It was a sign of witchcraft as far as they were concerned, and the rumours became truth in their minds. Many Iridogen were hunted and killed. That stigma remains to this day. You need to know these things, especially if you'll be travelling in remote areas. You may not be welcomed."

"Blight eye!"

"Pardon me?"

"Nixon Ocon calls me blight eye. I never realized what it meant."

Fisher ground his teeth. "Sadly, the small-minded tend to carry slurs across cultures. I suppose they think that if they denigrate others, they can somehow elevate themselves."

"I can't believe this! For most of my life, Aerish people have insulted and belittled me because I was a Tellusan. I learned to live with it because I knew that someday I would find myself back among my own kind. I hoped to finally find acceptance. Now I'm learning that Tellusans won't accept me either. It's not fair!"

"You're right it's not fair, but I assure you that you can find a place in this world. In the northern lands, for instance. Iridogen are seen as oddities there, but in that culture, as long as you're productive, no one really cares about peculiarities. Closer to home, you should know that the friaers and tinkers have a vested interest in supporting and protecting the Iridogen."

"And why would that be?"

"Tinkers and friaers share a common interest in understanding the inversion event. We feel that by solving the mystery, we can unite humanity. Together, we've spent centuries collecting whatever pre-inversion and post-inversion fragments we can find. We've discovered a few documents that suggest the Iridogen appeared shortly before the inversion event. That's incredibly significant, and we feel it's connected to the event itself. That fact alone makes you and all other Iridogen incredibly important. Earlier, you asked why I would offer you the gift of Invicta Manus. It's because you need protection, and for reasons we don't yet fully understand, you're important to the world."

"You said you trained other Iridogen. Are any of them in the southern realm?"

"Several, yes."

"How do they keep themselves safe?"

"Most of them opt for a disguise of some sort. Some wear sunglasses, but that can get awkward to explain while indoors. An eye patch or a tinted monocle is more popular. I suggest you consider one of those options for yourself."

Valtteri reclined on the mat and stared at the ceiling. "This is a lot to process. Things are changing so quickly. I have a lot of questions for the admiral, but I may not get to see him anytime soon."

"You can send letters to me, and I'll happily forward them to the admiral."

"Thank you, Friaer Kozen. I may take you up on that."

Fisher rose to his feet, and Valtteri followed suit. "I'd like to start your training, but we can wait until tomorrow if you need some time alone."

"No." Valtteri shook his head. "I'd rather distract myself. We may as well start now. In fact, it might do me some good to have this secret. I'll better tolerate Nixon's arrogance knowing I can make a fool of him in the sparring ring. He may be a Luminary, but he'll never have Invicta Manus." Valtteri threw a worried look at Fisher. "Um, he won't, right?"

Fisher laughed. "That spoiled child? Not a chance! Please don't tell anyone, but I may have taught him a few things that are detrimental to his progress."

Valtteri stared at him slack-jawed, and then burst into laughter. "Thanks for that, you just made my day."

Fisher smiled. "And your laughter made mine. Are you ready to begin?"

Valtteri fell into the foundation stance, then made a slight correction to the position of his left foot. His eyes shone with determination. "I'm ready."

Chapter 10

Almost a month had passed since Valtteri completed his navy training. The first week of his new assignment as an intelligence operative had been a trial. Joseph Admot, his fellow operative, had drilled him mercilessly. They shared a dingy room above the tavern in the village downhill of Pax Montis. The drinking establishment's patrons made merry well into the early morning hours. Joseph said it was the best way to ensure no one could hear their conversations, but it also meant Valtteri got very little sleep. Joseph took him through all of the protocols for sending and receiving messages. He had to memorize the cipher because they weren't allowed to write it down. Unfortunately, memorizing wasn't one of Valtteri's strengths.

Joseph grew increasingly frustrated as the days wore on, constantly grumbling about the waste of his time. When Valtteri finally proved himself capable of encoding and decoding a message, the man immediately began shoving clothes into his pack. All he said was 'don't forget'. No congratulatory speech or goodbye was offered, as he walked out the door.

Valtteri knew he could expect other training sessions with different agents. The navy endowed him with a high degree of proficiency in a variety of practical skill sets, but the true spy craft would only be taught as he proved himself worthy of trust. The founding septs protected their secrets. His education would consist of a series of increasingly difficult missions before they would grant him the keys to the kingdom, so to speak.

Valtteri wondered if his conscience would allow him to do some of the things he might be asked to do, but for now, this was his best chance to gain autonomy. It was freedom of a sort. He'd deal with the ethical implications when they arose. Until then, he had to gain what advantages he could.

Joseph's absence left Valtteri teetering between anxiety and elation. He was on his own for the first time in his life. The prospect was exhilarating. He could do whatever he wished. Unfortunately, it also meant he no longer had a safety net. Every decision he made from this point forward could have deadly consequences, and the admiral wasn't around to protect him. During his time in the navy, he hated it when others suggested the admiral gave him special treatment. Until this moment, he hadn't realized how much comfort he drew from that assurance.

Valtteri shook away his insecurities. The navy encouraged initiative and self-reliance. *Deal with each issue as it presents itself.* He frowned as he took in the room. His first task was to find somewhere else to sleep. It didn't take long to gather his few belongings, and he was quickly out the door to begin his search.

* * *

Locating an affordable room hadn't been easy with his limited supply of money. Joseph never offered to share the cost of their rent, at the tavern. They quickly burned through the funds allocated to him at the start of his mission.

Eventually, he found a widow willing to rent out a room in exchange for labour. He smiled, as he recalled the posting. The ad described it as a cozy suite with all of the comforts of home. The reality was a shed next to an outhouse, behind the primary dwelling. The tiny outbuilding had just enough space to house a single bed and a small table. A dented bowl sat on the tabletop to serve as a wash basin. A bucket of water rested on the floor, below the table. Still, it was a roof over his head, and Valtteri was grateful for the work. His newfound freedom was nice, but sitting around with nothing to do made him stir crazy.

He'd been waiting for a tinker to arrive so he could make a withdrawal and replenish his funds. While he waited, he spent time doing as instructed. He gathered nuggets of information and familiarized himself with Tellusan pastimes. It wasn't so different from life among the Aerish. The biggest difference he noticed was that no one stared at him and called him names. That could have turned out otherwise, but Friaer Kozen had purchased an eye patch for him before he left. The patch drew some attention of its own, but it produced looks of sympathy rather than the ire that one of the Iridogen might receive.

He later discovered a permanent tinker's station at the limen crossing. A high-ranking tinker was housed there to mediate international summits. Valtteri had been scrimping unnecessarily. Had he known about the station, he could have made a withdrawal shortly after entering the southern realm. It suddenly occurred to him that Joseph had been intentionally draining his funds to see what he'd do. It was a test, one that he had obviously failed. *No wonder the man was so surly. I must have seemed a hopeless student.* Somewhat chagrined, Valtteri made a mental note to take stock of his surroundings and resources in the future. Flush with currency once more, he used his first withdrawal to treat himself to a fine meal in an establishment situated in what looked to be one of the more affluent streets in the village.

By the end of the third week, Valtteri was ready to move on. He began watching the only road into town, willing another tinker to arrive. The exercise failed to hasten his arrival, but he had nothing better to do. Thankfully, the waiting was about to end. Today was the day that the travelling tinker was due. Valtteri heard from others that the tinker typically set up near the limen beside the trail to Pax Montis. It was a good intersection, equally accessible to friaers, villagers, and any international dignitaries who might happen by. Valtteri supposed it didn't hurt that the permanent tinker's station was also nearby. A man who spent weeks on the road probably looked forward to a shower, and the chance to sleep in something other than a wagon.

It was a fair spring morning, and the crocuses were waking to the sun. Valtteri had risen early, eager to get on with his mission. He was somewhat surprised to find that the tinker was waiting for customers. The fellow looked to be in his early forties, with the sun bronzed skin of someone who spent much of his time outdoors. His dark hair was pulled back in a tinker's braid with a red ribbon woven through it, to denote his rank within the Guild.

The tinker's wagon was already open, his wares on display. The wagon wasn't what Valtteri expected. He'd always imagined a rickety wooden cart drawn by an aging nag. This was a sturdy armoured vehicle with rubber wheels pulled by a team of six large and very healthy-looking steeds. He admired the majestic creatures as he neared the cart and was startled when one of them tried to give him a warning nip for getting too close.

The tinker gave a hearty laugh. "Best not to get too close to Mercury before she's had her morning oats. She's as temperamental as her name implies."

Valtteri eyed the beast warily as it pawed at the ground. "Has she ever bitten anyone?"

"It hasn't happened yet, but most folks know better than to come stomping toward an unfamiliar equid. I'm guessing you haven't spent much time around animals."

Valtteri shrugged. "You'd be correct in that assessment."

"I can tell you're not from around here." The sprightly man pulled off his cap and crumpled it in his left hand as he thrust his right out for a handshake. "My name's Adis Zekiah, travelling tinker at your service.

What can I do for you?"

Valtteri shook the proffered hand. "Two things, actually. I understand that the Tinkers Guild manages documents for various government organizations. Would that happen to include birth records?"

"Indeed. Are you looking for someone in particular?"

"My birth parents. I was separated from them at a very young age. I don't have a lot to go on, other than we lived along the southern limen."

Adis chuckled. "The limen encircles the globe, lad, you'll need to be a bit more specific."

Valtteri did some quick calculations. The admiral had always said that they found him floating in the swath somewhere between Viburg Naval Base and Ludumburg. "It would be somewhere within twenty-seven hundred nautical miles east of Pax Montis."

"Hmmm, well that's certainly more doable. Only a few villages lay in that direction. We'll get to that shortly. What was the second thing you needed my help with?"

"I'd like to retain your services as an escort."

"Escort services don't come cheap."

"Money is not a concern."

"Truly? I hope you don't mind me saying so, but you're very young to be making such a statement. You certainly don't dress like a person of affluence. I require payment in advance for escort services. I'll need some proof of currency before we take this discussion any further."

Valtteri nodded in understanding. "I have an account with the Tinkers Guild."

"Under what name?"

Valtteri hesitated, realizing for the first time that he might need an alias for this new life of his.

Adis gave him a knowing grin. "Out with it, lad, I'm a tinker. Any secrets you share are safe with me. We're honour bound not to divulge information about paying clients." The tinker waved his hands indicating an absence of customers. "I see no one here at the moment. It's just you and I. Besides, I can't search for your birth records without a name."

Valtteri felt his face heat. Some spy he was turning out to be. "Uh, right. My name is Valtteri Knox."

The tinker began to dig through some papers. "Knox you say? That's interesting."

"Why do you say that?"

"Now where is that ledger? Aha!" Adis grabbed a black binder and ran his finger down a list of names. "It's just that Knox is a common name among the Swathcombers. Let's see, Valtteri Knox — Valtteri Knox — ah, here we are."

The tinker's eyebrows climbed his forehead. "Well now, I see you have an account with no limit, courtesy of the Ocon estate. Interesting." He gave Valtteri a sideways glance. "You can obviously afford my services, but that doesn't mean I have to provide them."

The response startled Valtteri. He hadn't considered how he would accomplish his mission without an escort. He was wholly unprepared to travel alone over a great distance. The bigger problem was that he didn't really know how to get where he needed to go. He just assumed that tinkers granted passage to anyone who asked. "I'm sorry, what do you mean? Why would you refuse?"

"I need to consider my own safety, for one thing. Providing an escort service implies protection. No tinker will offer to protect someone against impossible odds. It would be foolish to accept a commission to travel through a war zone, for example. I wouldn't be much of an escort if I were unable to guarantee safe passage to my client's destination."

Valtteri breathed a sigh of relief. "Nothing dangerous, I assure you. I'll be trusting you to take any detours or precautions you deem necessary. In fact, I will be relying heavily on your knowledge as I know nothing about the area."

"You still haven't told me what your destination is."

"Oh! Well, I was hoping you would tell *me* after you complete a search of my birth records. I'd like to try and find my family, and if it's on the way, I'd like to stop in a little village called Endelton."

"Endelton. Interesting. Why would you be travelling to Endelton, of all places?"

Valtteri shrugged. "No particular reason. I've heard it's a nice village. I'd be interested in visiting any towns or landmarks you might recommend."

"No."

"No landmarks? Okay, whatever you think best."

"No." Adis shook his head. "What I meant was, I won't be offering my services to you."

"I don't understand."

"Young man, you've lied to me from the moment you approached my wagon. I won't take a job on blind faith. If you're not willing to tell me the truth, you can find someone else."

"I haven't lied to you! I told you my name. You saw it for yourself in your ledger, and you know it to be true."

"Aye that much is true, but you can't hide the small details from a tinker, I've seen too much. Do you think that we arrange treaties between nations without understanding politics and conflict? The nuances of such delicate transactions require a thorough understanding of the beasts involved. You may be a spy, but you'll never know half of what a tinker knows."

Valtteri sputtered in surprise. "Spy! What makes you think I'm a spy?"

Adis scoffed. "Please, an average citizen might not notice, but you exhibit so many suspicious proclivities that I had you half-figured before you approached my wagon."

"Like what? I mean, supposing it was even true."

Adis slowly moved his head from side to side. "You really are a green one. Very well, I'll fill you in on the issues your instructors failed to address." Adis began counting off on his fingers. "One, your bearing, haircut, and choice of clothes reek of military influence. That will fade with time, but you're obviously fresh off the base. Two, you walk with the shorter steps and cautious movements of someone recent to full gravity, and your accent has a hint of the Aerish. Three, you're still clearly trying to figure out Tellusan ways, and you're unfamiliar with something as commonplace as an equid. That begs the question... how did you get here without one? I can think of only one answer. You didn't travel far. You crossed the limen recently."

Valtteri tried to interrupt, but Adis pushed on. "The Luminary Navy sends its men to Pax Montis to study Hamo Sagitta. You recently completed your studies, but didn't return to Viburg Naval Base. That means you've earned a new appointment, but not within the Tropos Archipelago. Only a few roles fit that description. People who are specialists in maintaining Aerish equipment are a good example, or a student with a learning permit. Neither of those would require wandering about looking for transport to remote villages.

"On top of that, only a politician or an intelligence operative would have an unlimited expense account provided by Zayd Ocon. You're certainly not a politician. No Luminary would allow a Tellusan to function as a diplomat for the Aerish. On the other hand, a Luminary looking to infiltrate the southern realm would definitely leverage a Tellusan to go places that an Aerish spy could not.

"Luminaries require that their intelligence operatives complete their training in the navy. You're a military trained employee of Sept Ocon with no good reason to be here. You're definitely a spy, but you're not a very good one. Only two questions remain. What are you up to, and why is a Tellusan working with Luminary Ocon?"

Adis stared with a look of challenge in his eyes, and Valtteri withered under his steady gaze.

"If I'm so transparent, and you have me all figured out, why bother to tell me? You could just walk away and let me fail. Instead, you explained my mistakes so I could learn from them."

"Things are never as simple as they seem. You have a story to tell, and

I would like to hear it. Your choices from this point forward will have consequences. I don't yet know what those might be, but your survival could be as important as your failure."

"You have me at a disadvantage. I know nothing about you or your motivations. Why should I trust you?"

"I'm hoping your education contained at least a little socio political awareness. If so, you know that the tinkers have no ties to any one government or ideology. We provide the same confidentiality to everyone we serve. Our goal is a united humanity. If you need assurance, look to our history. The world relies on the integrity of the Tinkers Guild for good reason. If you can't trust *me*, who can you trust?"

Valtteri considered the tinker's words and remembered Luminary Ocon's warning about the cost of betrayal. Was it deemed treachery to consult with a tinker? Considering how little he knew, it was unlikely anything he shared would threaten the families of his fellow operatives. He didn't understand enough about his new role to leak something sensitive.

Adis responded as though he could hear the silent debate. "This isn't the last time you'll need to make a difficult decision. Your life is now a balancing act. You can't achieve your objectives without taking risks. Your job is to limit the exposure of your employer while achieving his goals. Most employers will overlook violations, as long as the damage can be repaired and the outcome meets their expectations.

"As you've noted, I have you at a disadvantage. You need me to complete your mission. Your employer knows this or he wouldn't have created an expense account with the Tinkers Guild. It's up to you to determine how much you'll share to protect your employer and satisfy me at the same time. You assume that I will ask more than you can offer, but that's not necessarily true. I have specific questions that need answers. Beyond that, your business is your own."

Valtteri knew the tinker was correct, but it felt like manipulation and he was getting tired of people controlling his life. He sighed. "What do you want to know?"

"Why don't we start with the most obvious question, the one least likely to compromise your mission. How did a Tellusan come to be working for a Luminary?"

"I was telling the truth when I spoke of the separation from my family at a young age. I was barely five years old when I crossed the limen. I was unaware of the danger and immediately fell into freerise. I don't remember much about the experience or how I survived. I remember being alone and shivering, as I floated helplessly on the plane of equilibrium. Eventually, a navy vessel rescued me. The ship's captain was a man named Quinto Soren. He took me in and raised me. If I reek of the military, as you say, it's because the navy has been a part of my life almost as far back as I can remember."

Adis whistled. "Admiral Soren of the Luminary Navy was your guardian?"

Valtteri rolled his eyes. "Why do people always respond that way? He's just a man like any other. Believe me when I tell you he's not as heroic as people make him out to be."

"And yet he saved your life and took you into his home. In your moment of despair, he was a light to quell the darkness."

Valtteri felt a sting of shame at the rebuttal. It was true he owed the admiral a great deal. His conscience warred with something else that tugged at the fringes of his mind. "What did you just say?"

The tinker ignored his question. "The information gathering potential of a Tellusan raised with Aerish values must have been very enticing for an ambitious Luminary. Still, it couldn't have been easy for you to grow up in that environment. How did the Aerish earn your allegiance in a caste society that mistrusts Tellusans in general?"

"Luminary Ocon granted me status within the Lamina caste. My care and physical comforts were met, but I never truly fit in. I had only two friends, the admiral and one classmate. I wouldn't say that I give my allegiance to the Aerish. It would be more accurate to say I know very little about any other way of life. Isolated as I am, the Tropos Archipelago is the only place I can call home at the moment.”

“That’s why you’re looking for your birth parents.”

“Yes.”

“I will complete the search for your birth records, regardless of my decision concerning your second request.”

“Thank you.”

Adis rubbed his hands together in anticipation. “Alright, then. Now comes the more delicate question. What did Zayd Ocon ask you to do?”

Valtteri considered what he might share without compromising his fellow operatives or his mission. He huffed with irritation when it finally dawned on him that it wasn’t a risk to verify rumours of a very public nature. Any information he gathered for Sept Ocon would be of no real value. This was just to see if he’d follow orders. He saw no reason to hold back and alienate the tinker. “I was told to travel to Endelton and search for suspicious Tellusan activity near the limen. I was also tasked with confirming rumours of Tellusans crossing the limen.”

Adis hugged his stomach as he roared with laughter. “Apologies for the outburst, lad, it’s just that you’ve been sent to chase your own tail. I can tell you right now that you’ll find Tellusan activity near the limen. The whole world knows about the incident at Endelton.”

“What incident?”

Adis choked on his laughter. “You’re a navy man, and you don’t know?”

The look of pity made Valtteri uncomfortable.

“I’m sorry, lad. I underestimated the extent of your isolation. Never mind, you’ll see the truth for yourself.”

“Does that mean you’ll escort me to Endelton?”

“Aye, lad. Your keepers have exploited you for far too long. Your innocence is a danger to yourself and others. It’s time you saw the world for what it truly is.”

Chapter 11

"So, how does this work?" Valtteri ran his hand along the side of the armoured wagon. "Where do I sit?"

Adis pushed his way between Valtteri and the wagon. "First of all, don't touch the wagon unless I give you permission. Second, you'll have to provide your own transportation, shelter and supplies. This wagon is my home, not some public transport. You're paying me to serve as guide, guard, and nothing more. You'll find me amicable company, but it's not my job to entertain you. The journey is long. If I need time alone, you'll know it. Just respect my personal boundaries and we'll get along fine. As for the transportation, I'll not have some steam driven contraption spooking my team. You'll need an equid. Do you know how to ride? Stupid question, of course you don't. You'll learn."

"Where do I find an equid?"

Adis pointed up the street. "The farrier should know if anyone in town has one for sale, I'd talk to him first. I recommend you ask for a draft equid that can also be ridden. If the farrier doesn't know of any, you can try Pax Montis. The friaers aren't in the equid business, but they have a stable of draft equids for their fields. They might be willing to part with one, given a big enough financial incentive. The village outfitter can sell you a saddle and a personal tent unless you want to sleep under the stars.”

Valtteri thought about wild animals and unintentionally shook his head. “Do *you* sleep under the stars?”

“Heavens, no. I sleep in the wagon, wouldn’t want a carniguar to drag me off in the middle of the night.”

Valtteri paled.

Adis laughed. “Relax, you’ll only need the tent for one night, and we won’t encounter large predators until we’re deep in the forest; they tend to stay away from populated areas. Our first stop is a larger city two days away. You won’t find a good covered wagon here, but Saxburrough will have what you need. We’ll be able to gather the majority of your supplies when we arrive. For now, you just need an equid and enough food to get you through a couple of days.”

Valtteri glanced at the six equid team attached to the tinker’s wagon. “Won’t I need more than one equid?”

“You won’t need a heavily armoured wagon like this one. All you need is something to protect you from the elements and curious critters. We’ll look for something small and light that a single equid can pull. If we can’t find anything that small, you can purchase another equid when we get to Saxburrough.”

Valtteri just nodded. He was completely out of his element.

“I’ll do my best to get you where you’re going, but you need to understand that the roads to the remote areas of the southern realm are more like hints of a path rarely travelled. You should be aware of the dangers. Carnivorous animals are a concern, of course, but brigands are the bigger threat. I need to know if you can handle yourself in a fight.”

Valtteri shuddered at the thought of some wild beast gnawing his flesh. He knew that wildlife could be a concern, but it hadn’t occurred to him to plan for human predators in remote areas. As for fighting skills, no problem there. He straightened with confidence. “I can fight.”

Adis rummaged through the contents of his wagon and pulled out a sword. “Can you use one of these? A blade will serve you better than a gun where we're going. Ammunition is scarce in the deep woods. Even bandits prefer to save their bullets for hunting. If we're attacked, and you start waving a gun around, you might as well paste a sign on your chest that says come and get me, I've got ammunition to steal."

Valtteri accepted the blade. "I've sparred with swords many times, but I've never drawn blood."

"Sparring is nothing like the real thing. The fear of injury can be overwhelming. If you hesitate, or lose your nerve for even a second, you're dead."

"I told you, I can fight."

"Perhaps, but I've never met a one-eyed man who could fight well."

"I have a light sensitivity, but I can remove the patch if I have to."

"I'd like something more than your word that it's not a serious injury. Come on, let's have a look."

Adis grabbed for the eye patch and Valtteri instinctively blocked his arm, only to find his block trapped in a firm grip.

Adis grinned. "We have confirmation that you've received training in hand-to-hand combat. Your reflexes are good, too bad about the blind spot."

Valtteri furrowed his brow in confusion before turning his head slightly to see the tinker's other hand an inch away from the eye patch.

"It can't be vanity that's getting in the way here. What are you hiding? I can still change my mind about taking you to Endelton."

"Don't you think you're getting a little too personal?" Valtteri fumed. "How could it possibly matter what's under the patch?"

"As I've said, it's important that I properly assess the risks. I need to know how much or how little assistance you can provide in a battle. It will determine where, when, and how we travel. You're hiding something from me, and it makes me wonder if I've misread you."

"Fine!" Valtteri made sure no one else was nearby and motioned the tinker under the awning of his wagon. Adis appeared amused by the theatrics, until Valtteri lifted the patch.

"Are you insane, lad? Cover it up! Cover it up! What are you thinking, exposing yourself like that?"

Valtteri crossed his arms over his chest and glared at the tinker.

"Right. Well, how was I to know? The Iridogen are very rare in the southern realm."

"Is this going to be a problem?"

"Not for me, but —." Adis scratched the stubble on his chin as he considered his inventory. He lifted a finger in recollection, and opened a panel to pull out the item he had in mind. "Here, try this on. It's a tinted monocle with an adjustable headband. It will allow people to look you in the eye without giving away the colour. Your light sensitivity excuse will make more sense, and you won't have a blind spot while fighting."

Valtteri accepted it gratefully. He knew the eye patch was necessary but the thought of covering a perfectly functional eye for however long he remained in the southern realm was incredibly unappealing. He'd already stubbed his toe numerous times.

Adis placed his hand on Valtteri's shoulder. "This changes things."

"You said it wasn't going to be a problem!"

"Let me finish. It changes things, but not in the way you might think. This goes far beyond the petty politics of Luminaries and queens. Thank you for trusting me with this."

Valtteri snorted. "It's not like you gave me much of a choice."

"Iridogen are important to the tinkers. Matters are more complicated now, but I want you to know that I will do everything I can to protect you."

"Friaer Kozen mentioned that the Tinker's Guild had an interest in Iridogen, but he didn't go into detail."

"Fisher Kozen was your instructor? Interesting."

"Why are the tinkers interested in the Iridogen?"

"I can't share more before consulting with the Tinkers Guild. I can hardly believe it, an Iridogen living openly in the swath for all of these years. The Aerish don't produce Iridogen offspring. It never occurred to us to search for those who might have travelled there. Outsiders aren't allowed to remain in the swath. Maybe the Swathcombers smuggled some in? We assumed we would have heard rumours, like we do everywhere else. I wonder how many more are living hidden lives shroudside of the tropostates?"

"I couldn't tell you, I've only seen the shroudside of Calcesburg, and then only briefly. I've certainly never heard of other Iridogen among the Lamina caste."

Adis pulled himself out of his musing and rummaged for some items in his wagon again. "It doesn't matter right now. We need to focus on our journey. Here... take these."

Valtteri looked at the strips of paper in bewilderment. "What am I supposed to do with this?"

"You're supposed to use it to buy an equid." Adis rolled his eyes. "You really are green. That's tinker scrip, recognized as the world's most stable form of currency. Have you really never seen it before?"

"Um, no? What do I do with it?"

"Listen. A young stranger like you can't go around making large purchases with local currency. People will assume it's stolen. Some unsavoury characters may accept it, but most will refuse to do business with you, and might call the authorities. You're trying to maintain a low profile, remember? Tinker scrip is notoriously difficult to duplicate, and no one has ever managed to steal notes from a tinker. If you have it in your possession, it was honestly gained. It gives your request credibility. Most people will think you're purchasing something on behalf of a tinker. I suggest you encourage that belief. Use one scrip per transaction. The shopkeeper will write the total on the scrip and ask for your signature plus a verification seal." Adis handed him a medallion attached to a leather thong. "Use this stamp to impress a seal onto the note."

"That's all I have to do? It's hard to believe I can just scribble my name on a piece of paper and someone will give me an equid."

"It really doesn't matter whether you believe it or not. Just go already. Focus first on getting the equid, saddle, food, and water. While you're doing that, I'll be at the tinker's station sending a request for your birth records. I should hear something before we leave. And, Valtteri, it's going to be a lot easier to find those records than I first thought. Very few Iridogen live in the southern realm. If your birth was officially reported, and it would be strange if it wasn't, it will be on a very short list. You're another piece of a puzzle, and the Tinker's Guild will have questions.

"I want you to hang onto that medallion I gave you, and wear it around your neck at all times. Keep it hidden beneath your clothes. After I finish sending my report, every tinker will know of your existence."

"Should I be worried?"

"Not at all. The Tinkers Guild can be a very powerful ally. If you ever find yourself in trouble, locate a tinker and show him that medallion. He'll help you with whatever you need."

Valtteri felt very exposed, and it showed on his face.

"Don't worry, Valtteri. This is a good thing, and the odds of finding your family just increased exponentially."

Chapter 12

Obitus waited patiently in the clearing he had chosen for this meeting. It was far enough from Pax Montis to guarantee that there would be no witnesses to the exchange. Finn and his men were out of sight, waiting for his signal. He heard his guests long before spotting them. They moved through the forest like a blind equid dragging the remains of a wagon. He shook his head. Somehow these inept thugs had managed to co-opt part of his intelligence gathering network. An organization he'd spent a long time nurturing.

Six men entered the clearing, a mountain of a man in the lead. He stopped an arms length away, wearing a sneer on his face. "So, this is the mighty Obitus. He doesn't look so tough to me." His men sniggered. They were an undisciplined bunch, and Obitus grimaced in disgust, although it was hidden by his mask.

The leader was a few inches taller than Obitus, an impressive stature for a Tellusan. As a rule, the Aerish were generally taller than the Tellusans, although slighter in build. It was the reason for the padded body suit Obitus wore. The disguise allowed him to move freely outside of the swath without his slight Aerish frame giving him away.

The extra bulk covered bladders of a red lubricant over a layer of thin metal scales designed to deflect blades. The combination had saved his life from lethal knife wounds on several occasions, leaving ugly, bloody-looking gashes. Those encounters lead some of his assailants to believe that he couldn't be killed. Every bit as impressive as his body armour was his instantly recognizable mask. The glistening black finish had a unique inlay that revealed a red hourglass when viewed from certain angles. He employed the illusion to great effect and his efforts had earned him the nickname Obitus, meaning death. It suited him and he adopted the moniker for all transactions conducted by his alter ego.

Obitus aggressively promoted rumours of his supposedly supernatural ability to cheat death. His preferred method was to incite a criminal organization and then send an unwitting victim to face their deadly retribution while wearing a cheap copy of his mask. Later, he'd reappear to exact vengeance. The fear instilled by his recovery from fatal wounds had gone a long way to establishing his power base. Apparently these men were unbelievers. That would change.

"What's your name?"

"What's it to you, masked man?"

"You've been dropping my name to serve your own agenda. I like to know the people who claim to work for me. I don't know you."

"Yeah? Well, we don't really know you either. You hide yourself behind a mask and expect us to kowtow and shiver in fear. Well, I'm not afraid of you."

"Then you have nothing to fear by giving me your name." Obitus looked past the brute at the men standing behind him. "Here's a little tip for you. If you expect to make a name for yourself and your little crew, people need to hear it."

He appeared to think about it for a moment, then responded in a smug tone. "People call me Cutter."

Obitus glanced at the ridiculously oversized knife at the man's waist and rolled his eyes, not that Cutter could see it.

"Well, Cutter, I've been told that you're smuggling narcotics across the limen."

"It's been very profitable, but I'm afraid you won't be getting a cut." A toothy grin followed the pun.

"You misunderstand. I'm here to tell you that your little enterprise stops now."

"And why would I do that?"

"I've spent several years securing a very large network of informants and mercenaries. Border towns, like Pax Montis, are particularly valuable funnels of information, but they are also susceptible to scrutiny by the military forces on either side of the limen. It takes finesse to keep them at bay, something you lack. Your actions are drawing unwanted attention from the authorities. Normally, I would just let them deal with someone like you. Unfortunately, like I said, you keep dropping my name."

Cutter snorted. "I don't know where you got your information. It can't be from the people who were working for you, I took care of them long ago. My operation is running smoothly. The authorities don't have a clue, and I'm not about to stop just because some freak in a mask doesn't like that I'm using his name."

"I'm guessing that means you don't realize someone from the Tellusan military has been tailing you for over a week. I can see by the expression on your face that you still don't get it, so I'm going to say this slowly and give your little brain the time it needs to comprehend. This... ends... now! I'm not asking you. I'm telling you. One way or the other, your presence in Pax Montis has come to an end. You will leave, immediately."

"I don't think so. You talk a big game, but there are six of us and one of you. I think, behind that mask, you're quivering in fear. Did you really believe we came here for our marching orders? We don't recognize you any more than we did your former employees, and soon you'll be joining them."

Obitus tamped down his rage. He would like nothing more than to remove his mask, and stare into the man's eyes as he put him in his place, but he'd wasted enough time. "Then you leave me no alternative."

Cutter uttered a low growl and gave Obitus a shove. In one swift motion, Obitus grabbed Cutter's arm, spun him around, drew the blade from Cutter's belt, and plunged it through his spine. Cutter's crew looked on in shock as Obitus dropped the body and casually walked ten paces to one side. Once out of the line of fire, he gave the prearranged signal, and his men released a volley of gunfire, taking out Cutter's men.

Finn came out of hiding and drew near. "What do you want us to do with the bodies?"

Take Cutter, and one other, back to Pax Montis. Place them somewhere the investigator can find them, along with some narcotics and money. Make it look like they had a disagreement. Hopefully, that will be the end of it."

"What about the rest of them?"

"Let them make a positive contribution to the world by fertilizing the ground where they lay."

Obitus felt no remorse for his actions. Tellusan criminals held less value than mud on the shoes of the lowest caste in the Aerish Luminocracy. They had no honour, thinking only of themselves. He carried no guilt for taking their lives or using their ill-gotten gains to further his own agenda. His mission was righteous, the preservation of the Aerish people. He would never tolerate such criminal activity in the Tropos Archipelago and a touch of pride bubbled up as Obitus reflected on his vigilante acts of justice.

This was an unfortunate setback, but he wouldn't let it interfere with his current plans. Every action was setting a stage for the right moment. That time was drawing near.

Chapter 13

Obitus sat at a workbench in the back room of an abandoned print shop he had rented. He toed a sheet of newsprint lying on the floor, raising a small cloud of dust. Apparently, the village once boasted a newspaper called the Pax Montis Bugle. "What printing press owner in their right mind would choose Bugle as the masthead for a newsletter in a place called Peace Mountain?"

The man in front of him ignored the rhetorical question. "The men are ready."

Obitus returned his attention to the mercenary who was clearly superior in physical strength and had the look of someone who'd won many battles. Even so, a touch of nervousness was apparent in the way the soldier comported himself around Obitus.

"Have you found a suitable location, Finn?"

"Yes, a valley, two days ride from Saxburrough. It's heavily treed and far enough from the city that it sees little travel, but close enough that someone will happen by, sooner or later. My men are in place waiting for my return."

"Excellent, make sure it appears to be a robbery."

"About that, the men would be more comfortable with this

operation if we could dispose of the bodies."

"That's not possible. The whole point is for the remains to be identifiable. It's less work for you, I don't see the problem."

Finn shifted to his other foot, looking decidedly uncomfortable. "It's just that we have a good thing going here and the men don't understand why we're taking such a risk. The military has a standing order to hunt down anyone who attempts to take the life of a tinker. I've participated in one of those hunting squads in the past and I've never heard of anyone escaping that brutal justice. If we're exposed, we'll have to spend the rest of our lives on the run. That's assuming we're the first to elude the military."

"You assured me that you would have enough men to guarantee success; now you seem to be second-guessing your ability to see this through. Are you concealing something I should know?"

"No, sir! We have twenty trained men ready for a coordinated attack. I have full confidence that we'll achieve our objective."

Obitus lifted a palm in question. "Then I don't understand your concern."

"We've heard rumours that tinkers have a way to signal the Guild from their wagons."

"Then, I suggest you lure the tinker from his wagon before you attack, and keep him from it."

"Yes, of course, that was indeed the plan, but something could go wrong. It's a small chance, but considering the consequences, my men are on edge."

"I see." Obitus stared at the man until he took an unconscious step back. "Will the men be more inclined to accept a greater risk if I pay double the standard rate of pay?"

Finn nodded vigorously. "That's very generous of you, sir. I'm sure that would make a difference."

"Very well, get it done. Ensure the bodies are easy to discover and submit a sighting of concern to the Saxburrough constabulary. When I'm satisfied that the authorities have identified the bodies, and made an official report, you'll get your money." Obitus held up a hand to forestall argument. "If I'm paying you double, I expect some added value. I'm sure you can find some clever way to approach the authorities without risking your identity."

Finn didn't look happy, but nodded his acceptance.

"I imagine a week will suffice for this business to conclude. I'll meet you in Saxburrough. You know where to find me."

Finn grunted and turned to leave.

"Oh, and Finn… I value your service, but don't abuse my generosity. I can find others who would happily take your place."

Finn paused with his hand on the doorknob. He tightened his grip to stifle a tremble before quickly exiting.

The mask came off as Nixon stared at his reflection in the mirror hanging from a hook in the brick wall. The Obitus personae was necessary, but the mask was uncomfortable. It was a relief to take it off. He reread the message in his hand. It was a message from Valtteri, left at the drop site a few hours ago. Nixon's lips twitched in amusement. He wondered how Knox would feel if he knew who he was reporting to. The message was brief. Valtteri had finalized his preparations for the trip to Endelton and was planning to leave in the morning.

"It's about time." Nixon grumbled. His own plans had been on hold for weeks now, as he sat in this tiny resort town. He was anxious to check on his assets.

Prior to his meeting with Finn, Nixon had made arrangements for an escort to Endelton. His escort managed to secure some of the few available equids for the three of them before Valtteri purchased one of his own. Nixon wasn't leaving anything to chance, he'd be following. If Valtteri and the tinker somehow managed to survive the ambush, he'd patiently wait for another opportunity.

Nixon couldn't understand why his uncle was placing trust in Valtteri. The risk was too great. Perhaps the head of Sept Ocon was losing his edge. It didn't matter, Nixon was determined to remove Valtteri from the equation. His uncle would be disappointed when he learned of Valtteri's demise, but it was common for bandits to attack people on country roads. Sometimes, fate had other plans.

He crumpled the report, imagining how it would feel to squeeze the life out of Valtteri with his own hands. The family crest embossed on his pinky ring caught his eye. He often stared at it when he needed to focus. Nixon would lead Sept Ocon one day and he needed to keep his mind on the end game.

He reflected on the circumstances that brought him to this point. Uncle Zayd had stepped in to help raise Nixon after his father died. It was years later that Nixon learned the reason. It wasn't because his uncle was a saintly man, it was because he couldn't have children of his own. If it weren't for the man's infertility, Nixon would have remained a lesser noble. He would still have a claim to the Ocon name, but little power. Now he was next in line for the throne, so to speak.

Thoughts of his uncle hadn't always been so critical. Nixon held fond memories of sitting near the hearth at Zayd Ocon's feet, enthralled as his uncle related tales of the great deeds accomplished by the magnificent Ocon family. As a child, he stood in awe of Zayd Ocon, but lately he'd begun to wonder if his uncle was becoming as impotent a leader as he was a suitor. Perhaps he'd always been less than Nixon imagined, but he was too young to see it.

Nixon shook his head and chuckled as he recalled his disappointment when he learned that most of those stories were embellishments penned by professional storytellers. It troubled him for a full week as he pondered whether his family held any true power. Eventually he realized that the ability to control a narrative was proof of power, and oh, how he coveted that power. He'd known it from the first moment he'd heard the stories.

Embellished history or otherwise, his family's dynasty existed because the leaders of each generation had proven themselves capable of making the hard choices necessary for survival. Sometimes, those difficult choices cost innocent lives, something he learned at a young age.

When he was in his early teens, Nixon had witnessed a murder. The assailant was unaware of his presence. He never told anyone about that day, but the memory remained fresh. He remembered the initial shock at what he was seeing, but he only felt it briefly. He was more surprised to realize it didn't trouble him as much as he thought it should. He understood in that moment that he was different, unaffected by the emotions that seemed to rule others.

When he recalled the memory, it was always with clinical detachment. That scrutiny led to a fascination regarding the necessary groundwork for such an endeavour. Over the years, he had tracked down the unwitting accomplices who supplied materials and cover stories. He'd compiled enough evidence to convict the guilty party, but never revealed it to the authorities. The exercise taught him how laxity could lead to self-incrimination. He embraced both the experience and the investigative exercise as a source of strength. It taught him that boundaries weren't necessarily a limiting factor for a fastidious individual, especially if that person could also control the narrative. As a result, he felt no fear of reprisal and knew he could make the hard decisions required of a leader.

Nixon accepted with absolute certainty that it was his destiny to lead Sept Ocon. He planned to lift the family name to greater heights than any who ruled before him. As such, he employed the family's resources as though they were already under his purview. The fact that he had been able to pilfer so much of the family fortune without his uncle noticing was part of the reason his respect for the man had declined. Details were important, and Nixon was very good at details.

Nixon slammed his fist on the rickety table. He was wasting time tailing Valtteri simply to appease his uncle. How many times had he told the man that they didn't need Knox to infiltrate the southern realm? He'd been doing it himself for years. Of course, his uncle didn't know about his activities. If he ever found out, it would compromise years of careful planning.

As a Luminary, Nixon had been sent to study abroad during his teen years. His uncle considered it important for a future leader to obtain a global perspective. Nixon had used his free time to establish contacts in both the southern realm and the Unified Northern Collective. None were aware of the youthful face behind his mask. People could form assumptions and nothing more. What he revealed was a keen intellect and a ruthless resolve with which he cemented his reputation.

That was in the past. Now he was an adult trained by the Luminary Navy and he was ready to take full advantage of the seeds he had planted.

Nixon knew his uncle had plans of his own and it galled him that he wasn't privy to those machinations. Somehow, Zayd Ocon had managed to keep a tight lid on those secrets. It was an endless source of frustration for Nixon that he'd not been able to learn what his uncle was up to. How could a man who didn't even realize his nephew robbed him on a regular basis, have enough awareness to employ such an effective subterfuge?

His uncle was supposed to be grooming him. Instead, Nixon felt like a child granted little tidbits of information, but never trusted with anything of importance. Nixon hoped his recent graduation would change things. Otherwise, he couldn't continue wasting time on the errands his uncle gave him. Still, if he could prove himself, if Valtteri were no longer a viable option, perhaps his uncle would finally bring Nixon into his confidence.

He didn't really believe his uncle capable of an inspired strategy, but Nixon needed to know what it was, so he could decide if it would enhance or interfere with his own plans. He couldn't wait forever. If his uncle didn't reveal his plans soon, he'd take matters into his own hands.

That inevitable confrontation would come soon enough, but first he had to take care of Valtteri.

Chapter 14

Pero Calix looked every bit his seventy years. Face framed by a long white beard, he carried his authority with a quiet dignity and a gravitas suggesting deep reserves of wisdom, at least while in the public eye. Adis knew better, having spent many a night at the tinker's station. Pero loved his wine and had a questionable sense of humour. His personal quarters were more a pigsty than a functional living space. Still, Adis held a deep fondness and respect for the man.

"Let me pour you another glass, Adis!"

"No, thank you, Pero. I have to leave early in the morning."

"Yes, yes, of course, but you won't mind if I indulge?"

Adis shook his head and grinned. "As long as you promise not to tell me any more of your feeble jokes. Seriously, Pero, they're getting worse."

"Come now, Adis, you're a travelling showman as well as a merchant. A tinker needs quality material to add to his repertoire."

"I never turn my back on quality."

"Pah! You wouldn't recognize a good joke if your entire audience were laughing at it."

Adis looked over at Pero as his smile faded. "I always miss our time together when I'm on the road. I hope my next visit isn't postponed indefinitely."

Pero sobered in appearance, despite his indulgence. "The lad has you so concerned?"

"I fear I've stepped into something much bigger than I can discern. It makes me uncomfortable."

Pero sighed. "Then I'm about to make things worse."

"Does that mean the Guild has completed a search for his birth records?"

Pero nodded as he reached for a piece of paper beside the telegraph key. A blackened silver bowl hinted at a recently incinerated message. Adis's pulse spiked at the sight.

"The young man who hired you remains a mystery. We have no record of his birth on file. You said he claimed the surname Knox?"

"Yes, his father's name was Bronto Knox."

"The Guild searched for references to that name in other records using the parameters you provided for the potential area of origin. They found a few references. It's a familiar Swathcomber name, but as you know, Swathcombers are relatively common among the Tellusans. Unfortunately, those who cross the limen seldom stay in one place for very long."

"So we've learned nothing?"

"I wouldn't say that. It turns out that a man named Bronto Knox has been living in the southern realm for quite some time. That's highly unusual for a Swathcomber, but not so surprising as what we learned about his wife."

"You're enjoying dragging this out, aren't you?"

Pero grinned, "If you're not going to accept my comedic advice, at least pay attention to the importance of a dramatic delivery."

Adis rolled his eyes and leaned back, resigned. If he showed impatience, Pero would turn the simple report into a four-act play.

Pero cleared his throat. "As I was saying, Clea Knox is a midwife of some renown."

"A midwife!"

Pero's eyes narrowed in rebuke at the interruption and Adis fell silent.

"We have no records to show that Bronto and Clea Knox ever had a child of their own. Despite the fact that Clea has submitted many birth records, she has never mentioned one of the Iridogen. That's not surprising in the southern realm where such births are extremely rare, but...."

Adis finished the sentence "...but it's too much of a coincidence that Valtteri Knox named Bronto as his father. It's more than that though, isn't it? If Bronto and Clea Knox are Swathcombers, then their progeny would have the fine bones of the Aerish. Valtteri has a Tellusan physique."

"Exactly. Bronto and Clea Knox are not Valtteri's biological parents. I suspect that Clea was present at his birth, but why she kept the child and failed to file a birth report remains a mystery. One we would like an answer to."

"Valtteri isn't going to be happy when I tell him."

"So don't."

"He paid for the record search. I have to tell him."

"The last known location of Bronto Knox is a small village called Swiftwater. It's on the way to Endelton and that's all Valtteri needs to know for now. He's going to want to meet the man. Help Valtteri find Bronto and he'll learn the truth for himself. Perhaps we can find some answers to our own questions in the process."

"That will work. I wanted to introduce the lad to some tether tribesmen who live in that village. It will help with the task Zayd Ocon gave him. Valtteri needs to know more about the kind of person he's working for."

Pero emitted a derisive snort. "Zayd Ocon. The man is determined to destroy the hard-won peace we've been working toward. That bombing incident has both Queen Silvanus and Prime Palantine Tagish in an uproar. At the recent international summit, Ocon directly accused Queen

Silvanus of hiding a gravitational device in the deep south."

"You can't be serious. We've never found any evidence of such a device. It's a divisive argument that the world needs to put to rest."

"I explained that very thing to the assembled delegates and I firmly believed it until early this morning. Now I'm not so sure."

Adis stared at Pero, incredulity written all over his face. "I know I asked you not to share any more jokes, but please tell me this is one of them."

"I'm afraid not. We've received a report about a strange artefact in the deep south."

Adis huffed a nervous laugh, not sure if his friend was being sincere. "Stories like that have been circulating for as long as the Tinkers Guild has been in existence. We deal in facts, Pero, not rumours!"

"We've known for some time that Queen Silvanus has been moving troops south. We've been unable to get close enough to discover why, but then again, we haven't put much into the effort. Every country has its secrets. You know we don't aggressively insert ourselves unless it affects international peace, but something has changed that warrants investigation."

"What could possibly provoke the Guild to investigate such outrageous gossip?"

"The information came from a highly placed official in the southern army. He was recently assigned to a secretive post in the deep south."

"And what gives his story more credibility than the many others we've investigated over the years? These things always end up being a hoax."

"Several things are different about this particular instance. This comes from one of our informants, someone who has always proven reliable. Placement into rotation for his current duty was pure chance; otherwise we may never have received a report about it at all. While his summary seems implausible, he's offered details that are compelling."

"Such as?"

"Do you remember the rash of missing person reports from a few years ago?"

"Yes, a military squad, as I recall. I don't believe an investigation even took place. I assumed that they all eventually returned with a reasonable explanation."

"That was the assumption of most people. At the time, one of our analysts noticed that among the missing were some of Queen Silvanus's top scientists. We noted it as suspicious, but when members of the squad began returning, it no longer seemed a viable lead. We now know that everyone returned except for the scientists."

"I don't understand what one has to do with the other, but you have my attention."

"Our informant named two of those scientists as part of the research team serving at his current post. He's unaware of the connection."

Adis shot to his feet. "That was six years ago! Why are we only hearing about this now?"

Pero answered by raising a brow.

"Don't leave me hanging in suspense, man! What's going on?"

"When Zayd Ocon asked Queen Silvanus what she was hiding in the deep south, the queen refused to answer."

"That's — that's suspicious to say the least."

"Our informant said the scientists are researching a strange device. He gave the impression that it was a preexisting piece of equipment, not something they built. However, that wasn't what most convinced us he was telling the truth."

Adis sat back down and stared at Pero. "I concede the point. You are indeed very good at dramatic delivery."

Pero chuckled. "Having graciously recognized my talent, I'll no longer keep you in suspense. Answer me this. What is the mystery we have been seeking to solve for so long, that most of the world has forgotten?"

"The link between the inversion event and the Iridogen."

"Only tinkers and friaers still seek the answer. I doubt most people are aware it was ever a question. I believe our informant is equally unaware, yet something spooked him, something he couldn't explain."

"Pero!"

Pero held up his hands in surrender. "Okay, okay, the report states that hundreds of animals have surrounded the research compound. Creatures with one golden eye and one grey eye."

Adis paled. "Iridomals."

"Now you understand. It can't be a coincidence and it's hard to believe our intelligence network is only hearing about this now. What is Queen Silvanus hiding? Why is Zayd Ocon suddenly going on the offensive? Why is the Prime Palantine increasing production of his war balloons? Global tensions are at an all-time high and we have no idea why."

"Does the Guild believe Valtteri is somehow tied to all of this?"

"That remains uncertain, but Adis, your instincts were correct. You've stepped into something big here and we don't know where it may lead. You've been ordered to protect Valtteri at all costs. Few Iridogen remain in the southern realm. Certainly none that would agree to place themselves in danger to satisfy our curiosity. These circumstances are unprecedented. If this device is what we think it is, we need one of the human Iridogen to interact with it.

"Valtteri is uniquely qualified. I think it's fair to surmise that Zayd Ocon trained the lad precisely for this sort of investigation. Who would suspect a Tellusan of working for the Aerish? Zayd has made clear his suspicion. If he hasn't done so already, I suspect that he'll be sending Valtteri to investigate what's happening in the south. You need to be with him when he does."

"I'm not sure he'll want to remain with me once his business in Endelton is complete."

"At the moment, he's a fish out of water. He needs someone to direct him, Adis. Someone who can open his eyes and show him the world as it truly is. You need to gain his trust."

"And if I fail?" "Then I fear we'll witness the global conflict we've been trying so desperately to avoid."

Chapter 15

An occasional pop from the campfire blended with the sizzling of sausage and eggs. The aroma made his stomach growl adding another note to the dawn symphony. Valtteri found it difficult to keep his eyes open as he stared at the hypnotic dance of the flames and the shifting patterns among the glowing coals. It was another experience to add to his growing list of differences between life among the Aerish compared to the Tellusans. Open fires weren't permitted in the limited green spaces solarside of the Aerish tropostates.

Having spent the majority of his life in urban or institutional settings, he hadn't expected to enjoy this rustic experience. His one hunting excursion with the admiral couldn't really compare. He was too caught up in the anticipation of the hunt to appreciate his surroundings at the time, and the chase was chaotic, lacking the pastoral serenity of this place.

Exotic scents from the forest evoked remnants of memories from his early childhood, triggering a pensive mood. The chirping of insects at night soothed him. It made him wonder if the stresses of his Aerish life were partially due to a lack of nature. *Or maybe it's that I felt trapped. Do I feel at peace due to my surroundings or is it because of distance from those who make demands on my life?* A little of both, he decided. *I need to find out who I truly am, before I can understand the motivations that drive me.*

Adis's voice interrupted his musing. "How did you sleep?"

Valtteri considered his response. The wagon he'd purchased in Saxburrough was intentionally small to limit the burden for his equid. That meant he had little room for his supplies and a tight squeeze when it came to sleeping. The thought of a cadaver in a coffin came to mind. Still, the mattress was luxurious compared to the hard ground of his first night on the road.

He was equally grateful for the addition of a suspension system below the padded driver's seat. That option had been an expensive add-on, but after a few days of equid riding, he'd have paid almost any amount to avoid reliving the experience. He still had difficulty walking. Adis assured him the tenderness would pass and eventually the saddle would begin to feel comfortable as his body adjusted. The price seemed too high for Valtteri.

He was exhausted and sore when he settled in for the night. A gentle breeze had lowered the temperature enough to make his wagon comfortable. He didn't remember falling asleep, the rustling of leaves generated white noise, and then it was morning. He felt better than he had in days, despite the cramped quarters.

"I slept well."

Adis gazed at him for a moment and then nodded in understanding. "Life on the road can be difficult, but the solitude has its benefits."

He lifted the pan from the fire and divided the contents into two bowls. Valtteri accepted his portion gratefully and savoured the aroma. They sat in companionable silence while shovelling food into their mouths. It was simple fare, but somehow it tasted better than anything Valtteri could remember.

His eye caught movement beyond the fire and his spoon stopped halfway to his mouth, appetite suddenly forgotten.

Adis noticed the direction of Valtteri's gaze and turned to see what had distracted him. "Huh, it looks like more arrived during the night."

Valtteri dropped his spoon into the bowl and set it down on a rock. He waved his arms and shouted. "Shoo! Get out of here!"

"You try that every morning," Adis chuckled, "It never works."

Iridomals encircled their wagons, always within twenty feet of Valtteri. That was unsettling enough, but not near so unnerving as the recent arrival of a carniguar. It didn't attack any of the other creatures, seemingly content to follow Valtteri along with the other animals.

"Why do you suppose they're drawn to you?"

Valtteri began pacing. "I have no idea. Friaer Kozen seemed to think it was pheromones or something."

"Perhaps, though pheromones are usually species specific and often elicit behaviours that require much closer proximity."

Valtteri stopped pacing and turned to face Adis, eyes wide with concern. "You don't think...."

Adis chuckled, "No, lad, we'd see some competition among the males if that were the case." The expression on Adis's face changed to one of confusion. "Valtteri could you start pacing again please?"

"Why?"

"Just do it and keep an eye on your followers."

Valtteri began walking. The animals kept their distance, but they moved with him. When he stopped, they stopped. "No way!" Valtteri broke into a run and suddenly changed direction. They mimicked his movements. He tried to confuse them by sprinting in a zigzag pattern and then running in a circle, but they moved in perfect synchronization, like a flock of birds, or a school of fish. Except they weren't a school or a flock, they were a hodgepodge of creatures who were acting in a very unnatural way.

Valtteri came to a panting stop, hands on his knees as he tried to catch his breath.

"Incredible. Definitely not pheromones. How are you doing that, Valtteri?"

"How should I know?"

"The limited records we have on the Iridogen make mention of animals following their human counterparts, but nothing about this type of coordination. It's almost as if they can anticipate your movements. What were you thinking about, while you were running around like a game bird with its head cut off?"

"I'm not broadcasting to them mentally if that's what you're wondering. Otherwise they'd have heard me screaming for them to leave me alone. This is really unnerving. How do I make them stop?"

Adis shook his head. "I don't think you can, but keep trying. At the very least, find a way to control them somehow."

Valtteri hoped that was possible because he'd noticed one thing that he chose not to share. For a brief moment, he felt an odd sensation. He couldn't quite describe it, but it almost felt like a sense of purpose and joy in running with the group. Valtteri shivered with the unwanted thought. *I hope I'm not losing my mind.*

"We should pack up and get moving."

Valtteri could feel hundreds of eyes on him. "Yeah, I think I'd like to focus on the road for a while."

"Why don't you hitch your wagon to mine and ride with me today? I think we could both use a little distraction."

Valtteri gave him a grateful nod and started packing.

* * *

The wagon swayed to a steady rhythm, dipping smoothly from rock to rut. The tinker's armoured carriage was outfitted with a suspension system for the wheels as well as the driver's bench. *I thought my wagon was luxurious compared to the back of an equid. I didn't know what I was missing.* Valtteri felt himself drifting off and decided to strike up a conversation to stay awake. *I may as well take the opportunity to gather some information, assuming I get a response.* Valtteri couldn't figure the man out. Sometimes, Adis was a fount of information, but on other occasions, he was as reticent as an eremite.

Valtteri decided his best approach would be to ask Adis to expand on something he'd already shared. "What can you tell me about Swiftwater? Why would my father and mother choose to live in such a remote place?"

"I didn't say they lived in Swiftwater, but I imagine the reason for their presence is a simple one. Clea Knox is a midwife. She and Bronto will travel wherever a need for such services exists. The last birth record she submitted was from Swiftwater, so the townsfolk may know where they went next. We'll pass through the village on our way to Endelton, so it's as good a place as any to begin our search."

Valtteri noted that Adis never referred to his parents as his father or mother, only by their names. *Perhaps it's the habit of tinkers when discussing genealogies.*

"What if no one knows where they went?"

"Midwives tend to work in a general area. A reputation is important, after all. I'd be surprised if she was difficult to find. Regardless, sooner or later she'll submit several birth records in one of the larger towns and we'll have somewhere new to search."

"That could take months!"

"I don't believe so. Are you in a hurry? I thought your mission in Endelton held priority."

"It does, I had just hoped...."

"Valtteri, you were separated from Bronto and Clea at a very young age. I know you have questions, but you need to understand that they haven't seen you in a very long time. They may think you're dead. As difficult as it may be to accept, they will have moved on with their lives. You can't expect to pick up where you left off. I know you've suffered a great deal, but it's not possible to reclaim your lost childhood. You're an adult now, and you grew up in a very different world. You'll be a stranger to them. You need to temper your expectations. They may be able to answer some questions, but they can't replace what you've lost."

Valtteri sighed. "I know you're right. I won't know how I feel until the moment arrives, so I should do my best to prepare for the worst. I guess I just want to know where I came from ... who I am."

"Young man, listen to me very carefully. Your identity isn't tied to a name or a title. It doesn't depend on status, appearance, culture or lifestyle. Identity isn't something that can be stolen, measured, put on or set aside. When your soul leaves flesh and world behind, that which escapes is who you truly are. Understanding that simple truth is key to being content within your mortal shell."

"How can you say that? Surely we're shaped by our circumstances."

"We experience things that can generate aversion or desire. We form habits and attitudes that may lead to certain outcomes, but none of these things are your identity."

Adis tugged on his earlobe, taking a moment to gather his thoughts. "You know that tinkers are eunuchs by choice. I became a tinker for all the wrong reasons. Suffice it to say, I was convinced that choosing a tinker's lifestyle would allow me to escape my mental torment. I thought that by adopting an entirely different way of life, I would finally be at peace with myself."

"Did it work?"

"The Tinker's Guild is a highly respected institution. A certain deference is shown to its representatives. That helped with self-esteem. I had a great deal to learn and, for a time, I was caught up in the excitement of it all. I felt I had successfully left my old life behind.

"Eventually, my new vocation became routine and discontentment returned. When faced with the distractions of life, I reacted with the same pleasure or annoyance as before and for the same reasons. My preferences and motivations persisted as always. Nothing about me had truly changed, apart from the wounding of my flesh.

"For a time, I was angry about what I had given up. That didn't bother me so much as what I'd failed to gain. I fell into a deep depression thinking I had no escape from the things I hated about myself."

"What did you do?"

"I contemplated taking my own life, thinking that in death I would find freedom. I remember a question insinuating itself into my deliberations. If death offered escape, what in particular was I fleeing from? Was it the world, or something in myself? I thought self-loathing was the obvious answer. On further reflection, I realized that I didn't find it all that hard to be alone with my thoughts. Rather, I found it difficult to live up to the expectations I placed on myself. The impossible to attain, constantly changing, cultural dictates of the world.

"It was then that I realized my identity was never lost, I had simply given it up. I had listened to others who convinced me I would find happiness down a particular path. I realize now that it was foolish to listen to the advice of others on such matters. It's not possible to exchange your soul, and nothing is wrong with my body or mind. I decided to embrace the simple truth. I threw myself into the work of a tinker, but this time, to grow instead of to escape.

"A tinker is privy to many secrets held by those in power. Lies, propaganda and more subtle methods of influence invade our lives to ensure compliance or for potential gain. Powerful people use social engineering for evil as well as for good. The troubles of my youth were nothing more than contrivances born out of cultural fads or manipulation. At the time, I didn't understand who my true abuser was. Had I known, I wouldn't have become a victim."

Valtteri shifted uncomfortably. It wasn't like Adis to share so much, and it was extremely personal. There had to be a reason for the sudden openness, but he wasn't sure what that might be or how best to respond. "I guess that makes sense, but if that's true, how will I know who my enemies are?"

"You're a Tellusan who lived among the Aerish, an outsider. As a conditional member of the Lamina caste, you've carried a stigma your entire life. A label given so you could be wielded as a tool. In reality, Sept Ocon considered you less than the lowest of the Lagan caste. You've recently learned that some view the Iridogen as a blight. Certain people will dismiss you wherever you go. You seek to find acceptance in a family, but what will you do if that doesn't work out as you'd hoped?"

"What else can I do?"

"You need to learn the truth, all of it. I will share what I know of this world if you wish to hear it. Other things you'll need to discover on your own. No matter what you uncover, remember that fleeing from yourself isn't an option. You've overcome enough to know that you can struggle on. All of us are born into this life to learn what we will do with what we're given. It's up to us to determine how we'll overcome our limitations and employ our strengths. The journey can feel oppressive at times. You must quell the darkness that threatens to consume you. Know this as well, you're not alone."

"What did you just say?"

"I said you're not alone."

"Not that, the other thing. Something about smothering the dark. I've heard that before...."

"Quiet!"

"You can't just unload like that and suddenly end the conversation!"

"Shhh! Something's wrong."

Valtteri was instantly alert. "I don't hear anything."

"I know this valley well. Wildlife are attracted to a stream that runs through it. It's a busy place, but you wouldn't guess that at the moment. The forest has gone silent. Look, even the iridomals are wary."

"Could it be a predator?"

"That, or highwaymen. Listen to me carefully. I know you've probably been told to hide the fact that you practise Invicta Manus, but now isn't one of those times. If we're attacked, your life is at stake. Thieves in these woods don't leave their victims alive."

"Why would you think I know Invicta Manus?"

Adis rolled his eyes. "Do you still believe you have secrets, lad? You're Iridogen, and you've studied under Fisher Kozen. That means you were taught Invicta Manus. I can teach you how to use it in ways that mask your ability, but we don't have time for that right now."

Valtteri nodded as Adis slowed the equids to a stop at the bottom of the valley.

"I'll check it out, stay with the wagon."

A mossy expanse separated the road from the treeline sixty yards away. Adis crossed it quickly and drew his sword as he slipped through the underbrush. After ten minutes, Valtteri began to worry. *Should I go after him? What if something happened? How long should I wait?* He swung to the ground just as Adis reappeared. "It seems to be clear," he yelled from the treeline. "We may as well fill the water jugs while we're here. Would you mind grabbing them? The stream is close."

Valtteri sighed in relief as he unstrapped the water jugs and followed Adis deeper into the forest.

Sunlight filtered through the humid valley. Fallen logs covered in vibrant green moss created a surreal backdrop for the crystal clear creek that meandered through the valley. Adis waited at a pool where the creek seemed to end.

Valtteri looked back from the way he came. "Why doesn't the water continue to the road?"

Adis grinned. "It makes the whole valley seem kind of magical, doesn't it?"

Valtteri could see how Adis would think so, but the iridomals had followed them into the glade, giving it an otherworldly feel. It made him shiver.

Adis bent down to fill one of the jugs. "It's not much of a mystery. A short walk on the other side of the road reveals a ten-foot drop. The water travels below ground and emerges from a crack in the rock there. I've used it as a shower on occasion."

Valtteri glanced in the direction he imagined an underwater stream would flow, thinking it might come to the surface in spots. Instead of water, he saw shadows moving over the mossy logs disrupting the dappled light. He rose quickly to his feet, alerting Adis. A group of men confidently walked towards them from the direction of the road. His glance in the opposite direction revealed more men. They were surrounded.

Chapter 16

Valtteri's heart was pounding. Cut off from the road, they were trapped between two groups of ten men who were slowly advancing. Only one of them had a gun, which confirmed Adis's assertion that ammunition was too valuable to waste in the remote areas of the southern realm. It was small comfort when facing nineteen swordsmen. Adis fell into position back-to-back with Valtteri, the two of them slowly turning in unison as they sized up their adversaries.

"These aren't thieves, lad, they're mercenaries."

Valtteri didn't have enough experience outside of the swath to know one from the other. "What difference does it make? They all have weapons and it looks like they know how to use them."

"Correct, and that's a very important distinction. Thieves in these parts are usually desperate and weak from hunger. These men look well fed and well trained. They're not likely to make mistakes that play in our favour."

"Tell me what to do."

"We need to get back to the wagon. I have defensive measures there that can give us an advantage."

Valtteri glanced nervously at the mercenaries blocking their path to whatever tricks Adis had in mind. "How in the world are we supposed to do that?"

"Just stay alive and wait for an opportunity."

Valtteri felt a nervous laugh building at the suggestion, as if it were that simple. "Shouldn't we have some kind of plan?" He felt some small comfort as he remembered who was watching his back. Adis settled into the iconic fighting pose of a tinker. A variation of the Invicta Manus stance, it accentuated the tinkers' unique enhanced physical characteristics. The position gave them an advantage in stability and speed. Most men wouldn't risk the exposure of an obvious male weakness in that fashion, but tinkers no longer had that vulnerability.

Valtteri knew that Adis had suffered a lot more than the loss of a part of his anatomy when he became a tinker. As confidence keepers, the Guild went out of their way to provide ways to protect their secrets. That included some barbaric sounding physical enhancements. Recruits suffered long and painful surgeries to lengthen their forearms and shins. Bones were reinforced with titanium bars supporting subcutaneous plates. It gave them a reach advantage in hand-to-hand combat. Similar plates were attached to the rib cage to protect vital organs.

Valtteri stared at the hand gripping Adis' sword. The larger than normal knuckles hinted at the metal implanted there as well. *I wouldn't want to be on the receiving end of that fist, even in a friendly sparring match.* Very few men were foolish enough to pick a fight with a tinker. Still, at some point, even those advantages could be overcome, and they were facing twenty opponents.

The mercenaries who were blocking the road stopped and waited for their cohorts to attack first. Apparently, they understood the importance of keeping a tinker from his wagon.

Adis gave Valtteri an encouraging nod. "You wield Invicta Manus, the invincible hand, don't hold back."

Valtteri knew that his training gave him a deadly advantage, but he wasn't battle seasoned. His instructors had warned him about the danger of giving in to fear. The shaking of his arms declared how they might betray him. The unfamiliar weakness exacerbated his fear. *I have to push those thoughts from my mind. I know my opponent's weaknesses, that makes me strong. I just need to focus on the crux points and forget everything else.*

The first attackers surrounded them and took turns testing their defences. Adis dispatched two of them immediately. Valtteri was more tentative. He managed to parry and land blows on the two opponents who consecutively challenged him. Unfortunately, he hadn't targeted any crux points with a potential to cripple and his efforts only seemed to make them angry.

A third assailant felt the tinker's wrath as Valtteri watched. Adis disabled his attacker's sword arm by targeting a lock crux point below the elbow. It looked like nothing more than a blocking maneuver, but Valtteri saw the bone break. Adis used his crippled opponent as a shield from a fourth man while he finished off the third.

When Adis moved, it looked choreographed, a deadly well-practised dance. Valtteri began to understand why Invicta Manus was so potent. The devastating results were obvious, but more importantly, he saw Adis's distilled responses to targets of opportunity common in a fight of this type. Adis was repeatedly attacking the same few crux points presented to him like an offering by every opponent. *I've been overthinking, trying to find the optimal key points.* Valtteri watched Adis for a moment longer, and everything fell into place. *I don't need to think about it, I just need to watch for those opportunities as they are presented.*

As if answering a summons, a sword whistled towards Valtteri. This time the blade didn't register as a priority. Instead, his mind locked on two crux points that were completely exposed. It was as though his opponent was willingly sacrificing himself. Valtteri's heel broke a kneecap. It caused the man to fall, throwing his swing off balance and striking the thigh of another mercenary. In the momentary confusion, both opponents offered easy targets for Valtteri to exploit. In two swift strikes, both were lying unconscious on the ground, as Valtterri searched for new combatants.

The remaining mercenaries pulled back realizing they'd need reinforcements. One of them whistled and motioned to the group blocking the wagon.

"Well done, lad, but these remaining men won't commit to one-on-one contests. I suspect that these first attackers were less experienced and felt they had something to prove. The others won't make the same mistake. If they attack as one, we won't be able to defend ourselves."

"What do you suggest?" Valtteri panted out.

"Our only hope is to somehow scatter them and make a break for the wagon."

The mercenaries took their time, discussing strategies as they approached. Valtteri scanned the glade for possible escape routes, but the mercenaries had chosen well. Their attackers could easily cut them off no matter which direction they ran.

Adis began to laugh.

"Would you mind telling me what you find so amusing about our imminent deaths?"

"The iridomals — they're here."

Valtteri hadn't noticed in the heat of battle, but there they were. They stood like sentries twenty feet away. He glanced at the mercenaries. They hadn't noticed either. The creatures stared at him in that unnerving way, like they expected something from him. He couldn't help feeling that this time they came to witness his demise.

He shook off the morbid thoughts as an urgent whisper claimed his attention.

"Valtteri! Are you listening to me?"

"Huh? What did you say?"

"I want you to run directly towards the wagon as fast as you can. I'll stay here and deal with these five."

"Are you crazy? Ten men are blocking my path. You said that we can't take them all on at once and now you want me to fight the majority on my own?"

"We don't have time to debate. Run straight towards them and when you get within twenty feet, make a ninety-degree turn and run for another forty feet. They should move to intercept. Then stop, turn one hundred and eighty degrees and run back the way you came. The way should be clear for you to pass them and run for the wagon."

"They'll just turn around and follow me back!"

"I don't think so."

"You said these fighters have training. They aren't going to fall for that!"

"Just trust me, you'll be fine. I'll be right behind you."

Valtteri felt like shouting with exasperation, but he didn't have a better idea, so he ran. The fear he'd been trying to suppress replaced the confidence he'd felt moments ago. *What am I doing? I'm going to die!* As he neared the waiting assassins, he saw them crouch in anticipation of a clash and then pause in consternation as he suddenly veered left and sprinted away, running parallel to their defensive line.

He heard their surprised outrage and imagined them angling to intersect his path in an attempt to overtake. Another frantic yell sounded a moment later, but he didn't turn to look. *Thirty feet … just a little further and then a one hundred and eighty degree turn.* He readied his sword expecting to fight as he spun to run back towards his point of origin. What he saw caught him completely off guard, and he stumbled for a few steps before running with a new purpose.

As before, the iridomals were syncing with his movements approximately twenty feet from him. Their path of travel collided with the mercenaries who had turned their backs to pursue him. The stampede caught them completely off guard. Now that Valtteri was running in the opposite direction, iridomals trampled the screaming mercenaries a second time.

Adis was running for the wagon with two remaining mercenaries in pursuit. He was shouting and waving for Valtteri to do the same. One of the two remaining attackers had a gun pointed at Adis' back. Valtteri's whole body shouted a silent warning in support of the words from his mouth. His body reacted as if to attack, but he was too far away to do any good. A second later the gunman fell and screamed in terror as a carniguar pounced.

Valtteri looked on in shock. *Did I do that?* He angled towards Adis who was still running for the wagon, no longer checking to see who might be chasing them. They arrived at the same time, with Adis pinning Valtteri against the wagon as he pushed on a hidden panel.

The wagon rumbled, as powerful clockwork springs came to life. Valtteri froze in wonder as the wagon unfolded to create a perimeter of steel shielding. The noise ceased a moment later with the two of them standing in a narrow space between wagon and shielding.

Adis opened another panel and pulled out two crossbows. He handed one to Valtteri and pointed at the swivels mounted behind the crenels in the shielding. Valtteri followed Adis's example to mount his own bow and loaded the bolts that were handed to him.

"Six men survived." Adis counted as he peered through the gun hole. "The situation just became a lot more complicated for them."

Adis pulled out some curious looking devices and handed one to Valtteri. It was spherical with a bore through the centre where a propeller resided.

"What are these?"

"These are aerial dispersal canisters. They're loaded with powdered fire spice. Wind them up and turn this dial to set the timer."

"What am I supposed to do with these?"

"Climb up to that platform above you, so you can rise above the shielding. I'm going to fire a bolt. When our attackers take cover, pay attention to their positions. I'll continue firing to keep them pinned down. I need you to set each canister to a five second delay. Push and hold the red button until you're ready. When you release the button, a propeller will engage to keep the canister aloft for a short period of time. Try to aim just above your target. The goal is for the canister to hover above your objective when it releases its payload. If we manage to hit them all, they'll be in no condition to put up a fight."

"And if that doesn't work?"

"Don't worry, this wagon has many deterrents. Let's try this one first, it's the most cost-effective."

Valtteri shrugged and climbed into position. It was surprisingly calming to hear Adis shift from concern about their odds to worry about his budget. Valtteri wound six canisters, set the timers and placed them within easy reach, giving Adis a thumbs up when he was done.

Adis didn't waste any time. His first target went down with a bolt in his chest and the remaining mercenaries fell to their bellies to scramble for cover. Caught as they were in the clearing between the treeline and the road, they didn't have many options. Fallen logs and small moss covered boulders were the only choices.

Valtteri noted the positions of his intended targets. He tossed the first canister which fell short of his objective. The payload released too soon, but he got lucky when a gust of wind carried the fire spice to his target. The assassin started coughing and stood without thinking, rubbing his eyes as he staggered about. Adis put him out of his misery.

The others looked at their comrade with confusion. Adis fired another bolt and they quickly put their heads back down. Valtteri took the cue and tossed three more canisters in quick succession. Three of the mercenaries were scattered behind a row of shrubs. This time his aim was true. The targets heard the whirring and looked up in time to watch the payload release. Coughing fits cut off their shouted warnings. They tried to crawl away, exposing themselves when they left their meagre cover.

"That's almost all of them," Adis commented. "I count one more. Stay here."

Valtteri descended from his perch and manned the crossbow to cover Adis, who had donned a mask before heading out into the cloud of fire spice. Adis disabled the man quickly and appeared to be questioning him. When the man no longer moved, Adis proceeded to check each body in the clearing. He continued to the stream, presumably to ensure no threats remained there either. Valtteri felt unsettled by the ruthless efficiency of the tinker, even while he was grateful to be alive.

When Adis finally returned, he was carrying the water jugs they'd dropped earlier. He looked weary but not in the physical sense alone.

"Are they all dead?"

Adis nodded. "They were dead from the moment they chose to attack, either by my hand or that of the military. Attacking a tinker is a death sentence in all jurisdictions. I'm legally bound to carry out such sentences when possible. It's one of the things I hate most about being a tinker."

"The role of executioner?"

"That and the target that I carry on my back. Some fool is always willing to spend his life by testing his metal against the Guild." Adis shook his head sadly. "Such a waste."

"You didn't ask for this, it's not your fault."

"I'm the one who must carry the weight of their deaths."

Adis cleaned his sword on the grass and returned it to the scabbard on his belt. "We can't stay here. Someone planned this attack. Sooner or later, they'll wonder why they haven't received a report and they will come looking."

Adis turned to the task of restoring the wagon to its original configuration. His words had Valtteri nervously scanning the area. A large spruce tree overlooking the valley rustled from some disturbance. He stared at it for a full minute, but detected no further motion. *Probably just some rodent.* Even so, he couldn't shake the feeling that someone was watching.

Chapter 17

Silence greeted them as they entered the valley. It was as if the wildlife knew something terrible happened in this place. The equids had proven skittish when they descended. Probably from the scent of blood.

Nixon received no response when he kicked the body. He wasn't really surprised, it had been the same with all of the others.

"So, you thought you deserved twice the normal rate of pay, for all the good that incentive did. I guess your fear of being caught was the least of your worries."

Nixon knew tinkers were formidable fighters, but he could hardly believe his eyes when he arrived on the scene. Bodies were scattered everywhere, showing no evidence of a coordinated assault like one would anticipate from a military operation.

Sunlight filtered through the trees, illuminating the verdant growth. Most would consider the setting tranquil under normal circumstances. As it was, bodies rested alongside fallen logs, marring the ambience, or did it? Wasn't peace found in death? Nixon wondered how long it would take for the moss to cover the mercenaries as it claimed everything else that had fallen.

The victims exhibited lethal blade-inflicted wounds. Other injuries seemed more like mutilation than swordplay. Nixon couldn't imagine wasting time to inflict such damage in the heat of battle. It almost appeared as though animals attacked his men. If this was a tinker's battle signature, no wonder people feared the Guild. It looked like someone set a berserker loose.

Nixon cast a glance at his escorts. One of them had lost his lunch and the other clearly wished he was anywhere else. No doubt they'd be expanding the tinker mystique at the next tavern they visited.

He crouched to continue his analysis with clinical detachment. The abdomen had a gaping hole. An unnecessary waste of effort, the number of bodies was more than sufficient. The wounds looked like claw marks and he wondered what sort of tool was used.

Nixon sighed as he rose. At least he wouldn't have to pay them for their failure. It was an unfortunate turn of events. Replacing so many mercenaries would be difficult, harder still to replace Finn. He'd invested a great deal of time cultivating the fear that made Finn pliable.

Nixon had glimpsed just a small view of the engagement from his vantage in a tree overlooking the valley. Information gleaned was disappointingly limited. He wished he could have witnessed the tinker's post-battle activities. Even so, what he *did* see proved enlightening. The tinker didn't appear to be concerned about the safety of his ward. At one point during the conflict, he completely abandoned Valtteri. That had surprised Nixon until he saw Valtteri dispatching opponents with the same ease as the tinker. Everyone knew that tinkers were practitioners of Invicta Manus. Valtteri was undeniably a student of the art as well and the tinker was aware of the fact.

How could Knox have learned Invicta Manus? Nixon knew for a fact that Valtteri spent very little time away from the naval base, certainly not enough to explain his level of prowess. Surely it took years to gain that kind of competence. They were classmates with the same schedules and training so how could this have come about? Did the admiral manage to sneak an instructor onto the base? How would he have convinced the friaers or tinkers to divulge their secret arts unless he was working with them? The admiral had been a supporter of the reforms proposed by Nixon's grandfather and didn't try to hide his disdain for Zayd Ocon. Was he approached by others dismayed by Zayd's rise to power?

Invicta Manus! Nixon felt a stab of jealousy followed by irritation at the thought of Valtteri possessing something he didn't. Envy turned to wrath as Nixon was further tormented by Valtteri's survival. The threat was greater than he'd imagined. Knox was keeping secrets. Worse, he had a benefactor apart from Sept Ocon. Valtteri's loyalties were divided as he'd always known they must be.

Friaers and tinkers were the keepers of Invicta Manus which meant one or the other had an interest in Valtteri, possibly both. The two organizations had international reach. An association with the tinkers in particular would be troublesome. They had powerful political connections. When was the relationship established? Were they using Valtteri to gather intelligence about Sept Ocon's activities? How was the admiral involved?

Nixon scowled as he recalled the frustrating arguments he'd had with his uncle in the past. How could the man possibly believe he could turn a Tellusan into a trusted asset? It made no difference that Knox grew up among the Aerish, they treated him as an outsider. Valtteri had less reason to vow allegiance than the Lagan caste who toiled shroudside. He wore resentment on his face for all to see. The only exception was when he was with the admiral. Why would that be?

Nixon wondered how many of his uncle's plans were under scrutiny, or his own, for that matter. Perhaps the loss of these mercenaries was a sign that he needed to purge and rebuild. He nodded to himself. It would require a lot of work, but this time he didn't have any other commitments holding him back. Besides, he'd already established the reputation of Obitus, so he wouldn't need to start from scratch.

Sept Ocon was another matter. He couldn't rebuild the sept while Zayd remained in charge. His uncle could face censure from the other

Luminaries if an intelligence breach led to an embarrassing international incident. If that happened, Nixon would have to deal with the fallout. He would prefer to rebuild on his own terms. To do that he needed to find out what his uncle was up to. He had to prepare to distance himself from his uncle's activities if necessary. It would mean accelerating his own plans, but that was unavoidable. If things went badly for his uncle as a result, well, he'd made his bed. In the meantime, he still had to deal with Valtteri.

"We're leaving."

Both of Nixon's escorts looked up, but only one answered. "Shouldn't we bury them or something?"

"Do I pay you for your opinion?"

"No, Obitus."

Nixon nodded in the direction of some scavengers creeping towards one of the bodies. "The cleanup crew has already arrived."

Nixon considered whether the fellow might serve as a replacement for Finn. He seemed suitably shaken. "What did you say your name was?"

"My friends call me Leo."

"I'm not looking for a friend, Leo, but it seems I have an opening in my organization for a... facilitator. Is that something you think you could handle?"

Avarice replaced the fear in Leo's eyes. "I think I can help you with that, Obitus."

Nixon smiled behind his mask as he mounted his equid. Fear and greed, he could work with that.

Chapter 18

The plodding of hooves mingled with creaks and thumps from the wagon as it jostled along the rutted path that Adis called a road. Valtteri was riding alongside the tinker once more. He'd taken a seat without an invitation. After the attack, they both felt a need to discuss the situation.

Adis was first to break the silence. "You fought well."

"I struggled at first, but then I saw what you were doing, limiting your blows to targets of opportunity. That made things easier."

"Don't make it a habit. If you do that in public too often, someone will notice that you're striking repeatedly at the same spots. I'm sure you're aware that Invicta Manus only offers an advantage if the crux points remain a secret. Overwhelmed as we were, it would've been difficult to conceal our movements."

Valtteri grimaced. "Not that anyone lived to tell the tale."

"It's a very difficult thing to end a life, and not something I take lightly." Adis paused and then added, "I don't know if it will change your opinion of me, but those men chose to engage in an illegal action punishable by death. They'd be hunted down regardless of the outcome. They were dead from the moment they engaged us, whether they lost their lives to me or someone else."

"I get that and I wouldn't expect either of us to lay down and die. I understand we needed to defend ourselves. It's just going to take me some time to process."

Adis nodded his acceptance.

Valtteri changed the subject. "So, what do you do to conceal your skill when you aren't fighting for your life against impossible odds?"

"As I've mentioned before, there are always those who want to test their skill against a tinker. It's not necessary for every encounter to end in death. If someone isn't trying to kill me, there's no point in reporting it to the military. It's better to teach them a lesson they won't forget. I do that by dragging the conflict out. It's possible to strike near a nerve crux point and only cause limited damage. I like to strike near the shoulder crux points early on in a fight. If you graze a nerve bundle, it will weaken your opponent's blows without putting his arms out of commission. With subtle redirection, I let him connect with a glancing blow and react as if it was more severe. It gives him confidence that he has a chance while I continue to weaken him. To a casual observer the fight appears to be a closer match than it is. I can often win a fight by only coming close to a few crux points. People don't pay as much attention to what you're doing if they're lulled into thinking you have less skill than they thought."

"I think I can see how that could work."

"It takes practice, something a tinker gets in abundance. I can show you when time permits."

"I'd appreciate that, thank you."

Dipping his chin in acknowledgement, Adis turned his attention to the road and fell silent in that abrupt way of his.

Valtteri furrowed his brows in thought. "I'm curious, what made you think to involve the iridomals in our escape?"

"I noticed the creatures lurking at the edge of the clearing near our attackers."

"How did you know it would work?"

Adis shrugged. "I didn't. It was a hunch."

Valtteri tore his gaze from the road to stare wide-eyed at his travelling companion. "You told me to run towards armed men on a hunch? I can't believe this. You're supposed to be protecting me, not wagering with my life to save your own skin!"

Adis snorted. "We both know you're not that helpless."

Valtteri's mouth hung open in disbelief. "That's besides the point. I paid for your services!"

"They outnumbered us. If we had waited for them to surround us, we would've died. An opportunity presented itself. It was a strategic gamble."

"Isn't that convenient? Since it all worked out, it was merely a calculated risk and if we had died, no one would be around to question your math."

Adis quirked an eyebrow. "Let's suppose the animals didn't respond the way I'd hoped. You still succeeded in startling our attackers. It took a moment for them to react when you suddenly headed in a different direction. When they finally took chase, it spread them out, forcing them to approach you one at a time. It gave you control of the battlefield dramatically increasing the odds in your favour. It also kept them from surrounding us and gave me an opportunity to take out a few more assailants. I had plenty of time to come to your aid if necessary.

"Besides that, I wanted to see what they'd do if we split up. Would they abandon me and go after you, or the other way around? Their actions would've been helpful in determining their motivations. As it turned out, the animals prevented us from discovering that answer. Considering the odds, I believe that I performed my services adequately."

"Maybe you gave it more thought than I credited. I apologize."

Valtteri expected Adis to rub it in a little, but instead he looked a little sheepish. "I have to admit that the iridomals didn't react quite the way I expected. You were running in the other direction by that point, so you didn't see what happened."

"What do you mean?"

"I thought they'd stampede through the group in their attempt to keep up with you. Distraction was my goal, but I got more than I bargained for. They stopped and attacked."

"What do you mean, attacked?"

"I mean they stomped, gored, clawed and chewed their way through the interlopers in their path."

Valtteri's jaw dropped. "Why would they do that?"

"You tell me. What were you thinking about while you were running?"

"This, again? I wasn't contemplating anything in particular. I didn't give orders. I can't communicate with animals. All I know is that every fibre of my being was convinced I was going to die."

"Hmmm, like a cornered animal?"

"Do you think they somehow sensed my fear and it became their own?"

"I like that explanation better than thinking the animals were intentionally trying to protect you."

Valtteri froze.

"What's wrong?"

"I may have missed the attack of the animals that first time, but I saw something you didn't. While you were running to join me, the mercenary with a gun had it pointed it at your back. I instinctively moved to intercept even though I was too far away to help. Before I could warn you, a carniguar attacked the gun man."

Adis looked shaken. "That would explain a great deal about what I saw when I went to check for survivors. It seems you saved my life, lad. You have my gratitude."

"Thank the carniguar. Do you really think I might have influenced the actions of those animals?"

"That's a mystery for another time. We have bigger concerns at the moment."

"Right. You said the men who attacked us weren't thieves but mercenaries. Why would mercenaries attack us?"

"That's what I've been trying to figure out. These were professionals. They wouldn't be wandering around in the wilderness hoping for a lucky score. They chose the location well and were waiting for us. Men like these would know better than to attack the Tinkers Guild. They wouldn't attempt it unless it was a very lucrative contract. They were paid very well. Hiring that many men is expensive. The contents of a tinker's wagon wouldn't hold enough value to offer a return on investment."

"Then what else could they have wanted?"

"Someone might seek access to sensitive documents which once again suggests someone with resources was behind this attack. However, most know that a tinker's wagon contains measures to destroy the contents if anyone attempts to enter by force. People looking for information usually attempt a bribe or some other means to get what they want."

"They didn't seem to be interested in the wagon so much as keeping us from it."

Adis lifted a brow. "You might have the makings of a spy, after all. I suspect you're right. They weren't after valuables, they were after us. More specifically, you."

Valtteri laughed nervously. "I only recently entered the southern realm. I hardly know anyone apart from you. What makes you think they were after me?"

"I've been travelling this route for years. This is the first time professionals have targeted me. This wagon carries little of value, mostly birth, death, and marriage certificates. I carry a few land titles, but that would only interest other locals, not the type of people with the resources to hire twenty trained fighters. Any valuable or politically sensitive documents would travel the highways between major cities. Only a simpleton would look for that type of information out here in the middle of nowhere. You're the only detail that's different about this particular trip."

"I haven't even been here long enough to make an enemy."

"I suppose that means that you have enemies elsewhere. Perhaps dangerous, wealthy enemies?"

"Nixon Ocon is the only person I know of who openly hates me, but Sept Ocon supported and trained me for years. I think it unlikely they'd invest all of that time and money only to hunt me in the southern realm. They're not known for their generosity."

"That's not what I was suggesting." Adis fell silent, gathering his thoughts.

Valtteri let his eyes wander, not wanting to dwell on the possibility that someone might be trying to kill him. He spotted some of the iridomals keeping pace and shook his head. *I'm some kind of freak.* All he wanted was to feel normal, but his life seemed inevitably drawn to the bizarre. Why were so many forces set against him? He was a nobody with modest aspirations who tried to keep to himself. He wasn't a threat to anyone, yet life kept setting him apart, making him stand out. *Why won't people leave me alone to make my own choices?*

"Are you listening to me?"

"Huh?"

"I said I agree, it doesn't make sense that Zayd Ocon would try to get rid of you. He did set you up with an unlimited expense account through the Tinkers Guild, after all. Even so, something else is happening here and I think it's time you knew a little bit more about the man you're working for."

"So, you've finally decided you can trust me with the information you've withheld?"

"I've decided we're both in more danger if you're totally in the dark."

Valtteri rolled his eyes. "One more thing I have no control over."

"Pardon me?"

"Never mind. Go ahead, I'm all ears."

"It's not a coincidence you were sent to Endelton. The village and surrounding area are the subject of an investigation regarding an international incident."

"You mentioned something to that effect when we first met, but didn't elaborate."

"A Luminary Navy vessel bombarded a section of woodland in the southern realm."

Valtteri was shocked. "They fired across the limen? That's against international treaty!"

"Now you understand why I was surprised that someone who attended the academy at Viburg base was unaware. At a recent summit meeting, Zayd Ocon claimed a fresh recruit had accidentally loaded live ordnance during a routine military exercise. That seems like something everyone on the base would be talking about."

Valtteri shook his head in denial. "That's not possible. All live ammunition is under lock and key during training exercises and we never aim ordnance towards the limen during weapons training. Besides that, one person loads ordnance while another plots targeting coordinates. A third person dials in those coordinates. A mistake like you're describing could only happen if several people aligned to make a mistake all at the same time."

Adis smiled. "The other delegates at the summit didn't buy it either. Even so, they seemed willing to overlook the incident since it happened in a remote area. Luminary Ocon was extremely generous with his offer of compensation."

Valtteri snorted. "That's as unlikely as a gunship making a targeting error."

"And you never heard even a rumour about this incident at the naval base?"

"No, and we definitely would have. The admiral tends to make an example of failure as an incentive to improve. He has this broken compass that he straps to the forehead of error-prone ind7viduals. The needle on that thing spins wildly, it's impossible to look at someone wearing it without laughing."

Adis smiled at the mental picture. "Do you think the admiral was involved?"

"When the admiral is in charge of a military operation, he doesn't leave room for error. He wouldn't have allowed poorly trained personnel on board. Neither would he have fired across the limen to risk an international incident and incite a war. I don't believe he was involved or that it was an accident. It shouldn't be possible for something like that to occur without the admiral's knowledge or authorization. The implications are disturbing."

Adis scowled. "Now you begin to understand my caution."

Valtteri shook his head in confusion. "Who could accomplish such a thing and for what reason?"

"That's what you need to find out."

"What? Why me?"

"Because you're already in the thick of things."

Valtteri laughed as he gestured at the road before them. "Out here, in the middle of nowhere?"

"It wasn't operator error. Someone intentionally sent bombs across the limen, but missed the target. The intent was to level the village of Endelton."

"Endelton! What makes you think that?"

"Because I played a part in confusing their targeting coordinates. I also witnessed the attack and saw the devastating aftermath. If you'd like, I can show you the images I recorded. I'm responsible for exposing the incident."

Valtteri felt a stab of fear. Adis was actively investigating the attempted bombing of Endelton. He knew Valtteri was an agent for the Luminaries, an agent sent to Endelton. *Am I in danger?*

Adis seemed to be reading his mind. "You've nothing to fear from me, lad."

Valtteri shifted a little further down the bench. "Words to invoke complacency."

Adis laughed. "The moment we met, you proved yourself a very bad liar. You're obviously not directly involved. However, I can't say the same for your employer, though evidence is circumstantial at the moment."

Valtteri eyed Adis skeptically. "You declare me a spy knowing full well that I work for Zayd Ocon and you expect me to believe that you suddenly consider me above suspicion?"

"I *am* trying to put you at ease, but not for nefarious reasons. Perhaps it would help if I explain my reasoning. First, I know Fisher Kozen very well. He's a vocal critic of the Luminary caste system and a thorn in their collective sides. He would never teach Invicta Manus to someone working for a return to the traditional caste structure. It's telling that he was willing to overlook the fact that you're an intelligence operative for Zayd Ocon."

"All he knows is that I was one of many students sent to Pax Montis for training."

Adis snorted. "Trust me, lad, he knows a lot more than that, but let me continue. You're an Iridogen Tellusan raised among the Aerish. I would imagine that anyone in your shoes would want to know more about where they came from. You made that clear from the moment we met. That means you have divided loyalties."

"I do hold affection for the admiral, the man raised me. Other than that, I don't feel particularly loyal to the Aerish. It's not a life I would've chosen, but it's all that I know. I serve Zayd Ocon as a required obligation, no more."

Adis nodded. "I believe you. Zayd Ocon sent you to Endelton without providing any real information. I can only guess why he sent you on such a vague mission, but the fact that you're first learning this from me means you're not part of his trusted inner circle. Additionally, someone made an attempt on your life, presumably to prevent you from learning anything at Endelton. It doesn't add up that Zayd would send you there without warning you of that danger. I still have many questions, but I'm confident that you're not a critical part of Zayd's plans."

"You haven't explained why you think Sept Ocon is responsible for the bombing."

"As I said, I don't have anything definitive, only suspicious circumstances. For starters, an international incident involving a treaty violation should have brought all of the Luminaries to the summit. Only a few Luminary delegates appeared and only supporters of Sept Ocon. I don't believe the other Luminaries were aware of the proceedings. That limits the number of suspects among the founders. Further, it was Zayd who offered to compensate Queen Silvanus for the destruction of Tellusan timber and he paid out of his own pocket. I would have expected a coordinated effort of the Luminary Council which would entail a great deal of haggling over the details. Instead, it was a one-man show with a goal of ending the proceedings quickly. If Zayd isn't the primary suspect, he's certainly one of them."

Valtteri knit his brows. "I can't believe the admiral would be part of this."

"Admiral Soren was present at the summit, but probably not willingly. Apparently, the admiral wore a scowl the entire time. Considering what you've said about his professionalism, I suspect he was unaware of the training exercise. Very few Luminaries could arrange such a thing right under the admiral's nose. As a ship builder, with access to the fleet, Zayd Ocon is one of them."

Valtteri gasped. "A non-commissioned vessel?"

"Speculation at this point. It's more important to know why than it is to know how."

Valtteri picked up the thought. "You want to know why Ocon is concerned about the activities of Tellusans."

"I think he's less worried about their proximity and more worried about the possibility of Tellusans crossing the limen. Something is happening within the swath and Zayd Ocon is desperate to keep it secret."

"And that's not speculation?"

Instead of responding to the verbal jab, Adis redirected. "What do you know about the tether tribes?"

"Tether tribes? I've never heard of them."

Adis snorted. "An uncomfortable institution of the past conveniently excluded from your history classes. Early on in the formation of the Tropos Archipelago, criminals were sent to the base of the swath to work in chain gangs. The Vigils literally tethered them to trees to keep them from flying to their deaths. It was a harsh punishment that resulted in a dramatic decrease in criminal activity.

"Eventually, the Luminaries grew dependent on this free labour and needed to find a way to replenish their workforce. In an attempt to keep up with demand, they treated minor misdemeanours as capital offences. It was unsustainable and the public was in an uproar over the unjust sentencing. The international community began to put pressure on the Luminaries to discontinue the practice."

"When it ended, did they free those who had been working in the chain gangs?"

"Who said it ended?"

Valtteri straightened in surprise and then quickly regretted it as a bump in the road sent a jolt up his spine. "They're still sending criminals to the surface?"

"Orphans, actually."

"What!?"

"Since both men and women were sent to the surface, it was inevitable that a child would be born there. The Luminaries quickly realized that they had a solution. After they officially discontinued the sentencing of criminals to the base of the swath, they initiated a darker practice. To this day, they gather abandoned babies and raise them as part of a fictional society. Nobody noticed or cared when the infants began to disappear. It's a dirty secret that the Tinkers Guild has been trying to expose for many years.

"Boys are told they are children of the tether tribes, reuniting with their fathers and brothers when they're old enough. Girls become state sanctioned ladies of the night. Tether tribesmen work for credit applied towards the hope of a wife granted by the Luminaries. They struggle with the wait for a bride while avoiding the taboo of an incestuous relationship. Tribesmen have no idea who among them might be a biological son or brother and the Luminaries deny them that information. To deal with the forced abstinence, many chew on tarma leaves which cause temporary impotence. They rely on the Luminaries and their records to provide an appropriate bride. When that day comes, one of the working girls is sent to the surface for a single night. To the girls it is routine, but the tribesmen believe that they're consummating a marriage."

"That's obscene!"

"Indeed, but it gets worse. After the consummation of their marriage, the tribesman never see their wives again. They're under the impression that their brides are immediately delivered to a safe place to bear and raise children. They're told it's a necessary evil since the base of the swath is a dangerous place. These aren't their biological children, of course, they come from the orphanages. It's how these all-male tribes remain viable from generation to generation.

"The tether tribes willingly work for the Luminaries thinking they're earning credits for the care of their wives, children and a future together. Tribesmen look forward to three special days in their lifetime, the day a new brother joins the tribe, marriage day, and the day of their retirement. On their day of retirement, what they call *the hoisting*, tribesmen believe they will be reunited with their wives and daughters in the sky lands."

"How can this be a secret? Surely the retired tribesmen learn the truth once they take up residence in a tropostate."

Adis shook his head and grimaced. "The promise of retirement is a lie. The hoisting isn't what the tribes believe it to be. After a brief ceremony, the tribe bids goodbye to their retiring brother and they return to work, leaving him behind. Once the tribe has vacated the campsite, their retiring brother learns the terrible truth. The Vigil, a proxy of the Luminaries, cuts the poor soul's tether as he makes his way to the sky elevator. Instead of a happy reunion, the tribesman is sent hurtling upwards to his death. The tether tribes remain in the dark, isolated as they are from the rest of the world. They're surprisingly happy in their ignorance. Similar to something you said earlier, it's all that they know."

Valtteri couldn't believe what he was hearing and suddenly thought maybe he shouldn't. A nervous chuckle escaped his lips. "You almost had me going, but this can't be true."

"Just because something is hidden and forgotten doesn't negate the truth. I can show you the historical documents housed in the archives of the Tinkers Guild. You can't trust the edited history of the Luminaries. The first three founding septs are complicit. Sept Ocon, Sept Stol and Sept Damira. The remaining three septs may be unaware, I'm not certain."

"You're saying Sept Ocon has been doing this for centuries?"

Adis tilted his head and held Valtteri's eyes. "You need to understand who you're working for."

"I get it, Sept Ocon has skeletons in its closet. It's not like I thought they were angels."

"That's not the only reason I bring it up. The bombing is tied to the tether tribes."

Valtteri closed his eyes and pinched the bridge of his nose. "Okay, you've lost me."

"Luminaries monitor the tether tribes through the Vigils. The interaction between a Vigil and his designated tether tribe has remained consistent for hundreds of years, but something has changed. Out of necessity, the Luminaries have kept the tether tribes secluded, but recently the Vigils have been giving the tether tribes orders."

"What kind of orders?"

"They've been told to patrol the limen and report suspicious Tellusan activity."

"That can't be a coincidence."

"It's not, lad. It's an act of desperation and Zayd made a mistake by involving the tether tribes. That order led to a chance meeting between a tether tribe scout and a female Tellusan who happens to be a descendant of a tribesman who witnessed the truth about a hoisting, a man who avoided a similar fate by crossing the limen to escape. I've spoken with that scout and provided him with evidence about the tether tribe deception. The proverbial cat is out of the bag and tether tribes are beginning to rebel."

"I still don't understand what that has to do with me."

"Remember when I told you I was involved in preventing the bombing of Endelton?"

"Yes."

"The man I'm talking about is a scout named Tallow from the Blackspike Tether Tribe. The Vigil for his area ordered him to release a buoy marking the location of Endelton. That order came shortly after Tallow mentioned his encounter with the Tellusan woman I spoke of. Tallow followed my suggestion to release the buoy at a different location. The Vigil told Tallow's tribe that Tellusans were about to invade and then promised protection for the tribe. He told them that the Luminaries would rain fire on their common enemy."

Valtteri gasped. "The bombing!"

"I was able to set up equipment before Tallow released the buoy. It allowed me to record the attack. That, plus testimony from Tallow, has enabled the Tinkers Guild to open an official investigation into the tether tribe atrocities. The sudden spotlight on Luminary activities seems to have triggered a response at the base of the swath. Tallow tells me that the Vigil has ordered some dramatic changes for the tether tribes.

"The Luminaries wanted Endelton destroyed for a reason. The village is too near to something sensitive and it can't be the tether tribes since they tend to keep to themselves. No, the tribes were an information gathering tool of last resort. Someone was concerned that something else might be exposed. I believe Zayd Ocon sent you to Endleton to determine if his reparation for the bombing has convinced Queen Silvanus to reduce her scrutiny of the area."

Valtteri suddenly understood. "You want me to discover what the Luminaries are hiding at the base of the swath."

"You're already comfortable in a half-gravity environment. It makes you a perfect candidate. It will be easier for Tallow to teach you how to travel the treeline within the swath. A Tellusan would have more difficulty."

"I *am* a Tellusan!"

Adis waved off the objection "You know what I mean."

"I haven't agreed to help and maybe we should talk to this Tallow fellow before you get too carried away with your plans."

"Oh, I'm sure he'll agree. We can discuss it with him when we get to Swiftwater."

Valtteri eyed Adis with suspicion. "Tallow just happens to be in the village where we're hoping to find my parents?"

"Tallow and his wife live in Swiftwater. Did I forget to mention that?"

"Yes," Valtteri responded dryly, "It seems to have slipped your mind. What else have you conveniently forgotten to tell me about your master plan?"

"While you're searching for Bronto and Clea Knox, I'll arrange a meeting between you and Tallow. You can also meet other tribesmen who have chosen to make a home there. After that, we'll continue on to Endelton. You'll have plenty of opportunity to question the people there as well and confirm what I've been telling you. I've been completely honest in the things I've chosen to share with you, Valtteri, but you can't blame me for being cautious. Listen to what Tallow has to say and then you can decide what to believe."

Chapter 19

Admiral Quinto Soren brushed his hands down the front of his uniform to smooth out some imagined wrinkles. He stood at attention waiting to be ushered into the presence of the Luminaries. Well, some of the Luminaries. He'd been expecting a summons, but not quite so soon. It was concerning.

He didn't have long to wait before an attendant opened the chamber doors and beckoned to him. "The Luminaries will see you now."

Quinto nodded once and entered the brightly lit room as the attendant closed the door behind him. Sunshine streamed through large glass doors leading to a solarium. Well-manicured plants spoke of Luminary wealth. Beyond lay the architectural wonders of Opesburg where topiary ringed the central park.

A haze of smoke drifted past, disturbing his view. From the aroma, it was a Duron brand cigar if he wasn't mistaken. It was surprising Silas managed to get his hands on one of those. Duron cigars were custom-made for the Prime Palantine of the UNC and carried his name. Very few found their way onto the black market, and those that did were prohibitively expensive, a concern not likely to cross a Luminary's mind.

Luminary Silas Xandri sat one side of a semicircular table admiring his cigar. Luminary Jayla Dewei sat across from him and gestured Quinto towards a chair positioned between them, and in front of the table. She frowned as she fanned away the noxious cloud. "Must you smoke that thing now, Silas?"

"My house, my rules."

Jayla scowled. "I offered to hold this meeting at Ludumburg, but you insisted we convene here. I had to rearrange my schedule to make the journey. You could at least try to be an accommodating host."

Silas sighed dramatically and put out the cigar as he nodded to Quinto. "Please take a seat, Admiral."

Quinto grabbed the proffered chair and pulled it back a few feet. The new position allowed him to see both Luminaries without rotating his head from side to side when addressed by one or the other. That elicited a wry smile from Jayla and a raised brow from Silas, but Quinto wasn't in the mood for their power games. "I arrived as quickly as I could upon receiving your summons. How may I serve?"

Quinto tried to ignore the way Jayla undressed him with her eyes. She'd made it clear on several occasions how she'd like him to serve. She was an attractive woman, but a fleet admiral was expected to remain impartial when dealing with the founding septs. Jayla knew this, of course, and took perverse pleasure in making him uncomfortable at every opportunity. He wasn't in the mood for that either.

"We would like a report on your investigation into the incident. What have you learned regarding the navy vessel that fired live ordnance across the limen?"

"Perhaps if you were to share what your own intelligence operatives have uncovered, I could add relevant details without unnecessarily wasting your valuable time."

Silas grunted dismissively. "You report to us, Admiral, not the other way around. It's your job to make certain that the activity of a sept does not interfere with the autonomy of any other sept. However, it's also your job to make sure Luminaries don't exceed their authority where it concerns our entire nation. In the event of such activity, you have authority to respond in the manner you deem necessary to preserve the Tropos Archipelago.

"An overreach of this nature has clearly taken place. The Luminary Navy isn't allowed to take action that may provoke a foreign power without the consent of the entire Council. I know I didn't vote to attack Queen Silvanus's trees. How about you, Luminary Dewei?"

"Had anyone asked my opinion, I'm sure I would've voted against such a poorly conceived plan. Pitting the firepower of our navy against the pointy sticks of a forest seems an unnecessary waste of valuable resources."

"There you have it, Admiral, no unanimous vote was ever carried out to permit such an operation to take place. Seeing as how Zayd Ocon decided to inform only Sept Stol and Sept Damira about the resulting international uproar, you can imagine our concern. We should have been consulted, not kept in the dark. We're very interested to know how the navy's participation came about, lacking the required authorization."

Quinto surged to his feet. "I received no orders, nor would I have acted on them!"

"Calm yourself, Quinto. You're one of my constituents and we've known each other a long time. I don't believe you're capable of such duplicity, or recklessness. On the other hand, I have no difficulty imagining such questionable behaviour from some of my peers. Assuming you've come to the conclusion that this was an intentional transgression, and not an accident, we would like to know what you've learned. How could this have occurred?"

Quinto settled back into his chair. "The incident happened without my knowledge or endorsement."

"Something I'm sure you find intolerable."

Quinto nodded curtly in response. "All of my people were accounted for, as were all of the fleet's ships. Someone used a non-commissioned vessel manned by unknown operatives. I'm still investigating, but someone is hindering my efforts."

"Our intelligence has come to a similar understanding regarding the ship, but how did you come to your conclusions?"

"A vessel of that size can't leave the Viburg, or Bellumburg naval bases without notice. That means it came from the shipyard. An aerosloop is under construction there, but I was told three weeks ago that it wouldn't be ready for six more months. When I investigated the staff at the shipyards, all they'd tell me was that they were handed orders carrying an umbrella-class Luminary seal."

"It shouldn't be possible for a warship to leave the shipyards with anything less than a director-class seal. This is an outrageous breach of security!"

Quinto nodded in agreement. "As you know, the shipyards are not under naval command. Those manufacturing facilities belong to Septs Ocon and Damira. The Lamina and Lagan caste workers in those facilities aren't likely to question a Luminary order, no matter how generic. No one was willing to risk the ire of their superiors by discussing the matter with me.

"I had to come at it from a different angle. A few men under my command have relatives from the Lagan caste who work at the shipyards. I gave them a few days of shore leave to visit their families and glean some gossip. It turns out that the men who requisitioned the ship weren't part of the crew who normally make test runs. In fact, none of the shipyard workers had seen them before. Even so, the newcomers spoke with authority and had a Luminary seal of authorization. It happened very quickly during a shift change, and the yard master wasn't on the site at the time. The ship returned within a few hours and appeared undamaged, so the workers assumed everything was legitimate."

Luminary Silas Xandri was tapping his foot vigorously, as he often did when agitated. "Zayd has been spewing his aggressive rhetoric with increasing frequency at Luminary Council meetings. He's been intentionally unravelling all of his father's reforms, and threatening hard won peace in the process. We need to stop him, or he'll start a war that none of us wants."

"I must caution you about your choice of words, Luminary. Unless you can prove that he's directly menacing Opesburg, I have no authority to intervene. However, if you openly harass a member of Sept Ocon, I will be obliged to stop any attempt to interfere with his right to rule Calcesburg."

"Bah! Do you agree with Zayd Ocon's beliefs, or his recent actions?"

"I don't personally agree with the views of Zayd Ocon, as you well know. I supported Asher Ocon and his reforms. Regardless, I'm in no position to question how he rules Calcesburg, any more than I question your right to rule Opesburg. My job is to maintain peace within the Tropos Archipelago."

"Silas wasn't threatening anyone," Luminary Dewei interrupted. "He's merely pointing out a potential danger. Something that definitely falls within your purview. Zayd's reckless bombing threatened the safety of the entire archipelago."

"We have no proof it was him, or that it was intentional."

"Please, you don't believe that for a minute." Jayla snorted. "He all but admitted guilt when he paid off Queen Silvanus. Even if we lack physical evidence, he declared his involvement and lied about the circumstances. The three original Luminary septs conspired to act without the blessing of the entire Council. That is unacceptable. If unilateral decisions like these go unchallenged, then where does authority lie within the Tropos Archipelago? How will you decide when to act, Admiral, without a united Council to give you orders? Will you declare yourself as the only authority? Do you think the Luminaries wouldn't challenge you? Mark my words, Admiral, this is going to escalate."

"Jayla is correct, Quinto. The Council must identify the guilty parties and hold them accountable. Due process must take place, but everyone in this room knows that outcome is unlikely. The original three septs will vote together against Jayla and myself. Enzo Kiraz is more concerned about the draw to his gambling establishments than Luminary politics. He's the wild card, if you'll excuse my pun. Assuming he could be convinced to get off the fence and side with us, his endorsement would only split the vote. This problem has been building for years and now, Zayd is emboldened. He won't be content to play the charade much longer, not with the misguided zeal he's been displaying of late. He'll either plunge the tropostates into civil war, or start a world war that forces us to side with his misguided ideals."

The two Luminaries stared silently at Quinto until he began to squirm. "At the moment, we have no proof that Zayd orchestrated the incident for a nefarious purpose. He claims it was accidental. I agree that those claims seem suspicious, but until we discover otherwise, I have no authority to do anything more, and neither do either of you. If I don't hold you all to the same standard of Luminary law, we *will* have that picture of chaos you've painted."

"Always the cautious one, Quinto. I suppose that's why you were universally endorsed for your current role. You have my word that we won't make threatening advances against other Luminaries. However, as you've pointed out, we're well within our rights to ensure the safety of those within our own tropostates. We have plans that I will share with you in the spirit of transparency, but first I need to know something."

Quinto furrowed his brows in suspicion. "And what is that?"

"If it comes to pass that the Luminaries are divided, and the Council disbands, or we're plunged into a world war that none of us agreed to... with whom will you stand?"

"I — I'll do all I can to protect the archipelago."

Jayla interrupted. "Admiral, you haven't been listening. If someone outside of the swath instigated a war, the entire Council would likely agree to respond in the interest of self-preservation. However, a unanimous Luminary decision in favour of *provoking* a war beyond the swath will never come to pass. If international war unfolds as a result of Luminary action, it will be the result of a unilateral decision. In that scenario, the council will disband. Without the council, you're no longer beholden to anyone. The navy will be yours to command, unless a Luminary manages to wrest control from you. I hope you're prepared for that possibility. You'll have as much or more power than any of the Luminaries. If someone wants control, you'll be the first target."

Quinto hadn't given much thought to such a scenario. The existence of the Council spanned generations, a tranquilizing tradition. Despite the obvious inequities of a Luminocracy, there remained a perverse comfort in the consistency of routine. An unspoken fear of disruption maintained the status quo, even if change promised something better.

Quinto made a career out of promoting positive change, yet here he was, falling into the same trap, the discomfort of something he'd never considered. It caught him off guard. Could everything really fall apart so quickly? He spent years working to effect change through the rubric of his station. It never occurred to him that the chance to make real change might be handed to him. Maybe that scenario wouldn't be a falling apart so much as a coming together. He couldn't afford to think that way, the cost was too high. The brief temptation was frightening in its allure. His mind took a taste of the possibility even as his mouth tried to reject it. "That's wildly speculative conjecture."

"Please indulge us, Admiral. Since this is all speculation, speaking your mind will do no harm. Who can hold you accountable for actions you never took in a hypothetical situation? We're merely asking you where you would stand if such a thing actually did occur. For instance, would you support instigating a war between the Tropos Archipelago and the Unified Northern Collective?"

"Of course not! I don't believe we should start a war with anyone."

"Not even if we run out of resources and our people are starving?"

"That was the intent of Asher Ocon's reforms. He worked to create good trading relationships, to prevent a shortage of resources. I believe that could still be achieved without bloodshed."

"I see. So you agree that Zayd Ocon should not be allowed to provoke a war."

Quinto refused to be baited.

"Very well, let me return to the hypothetical. If Zayd Ocon started a war or forced the collapse of the Luminary Council, would you cede control of the navy to him? Would you work with him to achieve his goals based on what you know of his character?"

"Hypothetically speaking," Quinto responded, "If *any* Luminary started a war without the consent of the entire Council, or caused the council to disband, I would conclude that their reasons were self-serving. In that case, I would command the navy to stand against the instigators and protect those who are innocent of wrongdoing, particularly the Lamina and Lagan castes who have no way to shield themselves. I have sworn to protect that which is in the best interest of the Tropos as determined by Luminary law."

"Well spoken, Admiral. If parties outside of the swath offered to help you achieve a return to peace, would you accept their help?"

"If I were able to discern that their offer of help was genuine, and without ulterior motive, then yes, I would consider outside help for a return to peace."

"Thank you, Admiral." Silas craned his neck to speak over his shoulder and raised his voice. "Have you heard enough?"

A door in the back of the room opened and a tall man in military attire strode in like he owned the room.

Chapter 20

Quinto recognized the face immediately. He rose from his seat, backing away while subconsciously reached for a weapon that he didn't have. Neither of the two Luminaries reacted with alarm. Instead, they sat calmly, waiting for him to speak. "Would either of you care to explain to me, why the Prime Palatine of the Unified Northern Collective is standing before me grinning like a madman?"

The deep voice of Duron Tagish filled the room before either Luminary could answer. "Greetings, Admiral. It's good to see you again. You look just as uncomfortable as you did the last time I saw you. On that occasion, you were staring daggers at Zayd Ocon who was insinuating that the officers under your command were incompetent. I didn't believe that fabricated story for even a moment. I've made my distaste and mistrust of that man abundantly clear. He's up to something, and anyone with an eye to see could tell you weren't in the loop. You just confirmed as much."

Quinto glared at Silas and Jayla. "You deliberately directed our conversation. Explain yourselves!"

Jayla stood and moved to Quinto's side, resting a reassuring hand on his arm. The calming effect was more alarming than it was reassuring. He scowled at her and shook her hand away.

"Consider where you stand!" Silas barked. "Opesburg is the judicial centre of governance for the archipelago. We regularly receive foreign dignitaries here. You will show proper respect to the leader of the UNC. His presence here is no more questionable than his attendance at the recent summit."

"It's not his presence in Opesburg I question, it's your reason for bringing him here. You allowed him to eavesdrop on a conversation involving sensitive details about an ongoing investigation."

"The recent summit was convened in response to a provocative action. The Prime Palatine wanted some assurances. He didn't feel that Zayd Ocon responded appropriately to legitimate concerns raised during that assembly. Opesburg is the proper forum for such inquiries. Your investigation is a matter of public record. Our discussion here has revealed nothing that would be deemed classified information. To the contrary, it assures our guest that Zayd doesn't represent the entire council."

Duron pointed at the chair Quinto had vacated. "Are you planning on using that?"

Quinto shook his head and Duron pulled the chair around the table, setting it next to Silas. He sat heavily and groaned. "I'm getting too old to be standing for long periods with my ear to the door. That was most undignified, Silas."

"I offered you a chair."

"How is that more dignified? I still felt like a busybody fetching about for some gossip to share. I could have talked with the admiral instead of skulking about."

"Would that have been enough to convince you that he's genuine?"

"Probably not." Duron conceded.

Quinto waved his hands in exasperation, catching everyone's attention. "Hello? I'm waiting for an explanation."

Jayla was still standing next to him, perhaps her proximity prompting her to speak first. "As Silas mentioned, we have plans to prepare for our own security. Unfortunately, that would require the help of Calcesburg and Stipoburg. They provide the forges and engines of our society. Considering recent developments, we're not confident that they'd provide us with the means to defend ourselves. We need to find an alternate source for materials and production facilities."

"Resources the UNC can provide." Quinto's eyes widened as the pieces came together.

Silas gave Quinto a stern look. "This transparency is a courtesy for your ears only, Admiral. As per our laws, you can't repeat what you've heard unless it poses a threat to another sept. This meeting is a disclosure of our plans in order to satisfy any questions you may have about our intentions."

Duron chuckled. "It's refreshing to know that the politics of the Luminaries are as convoluted as those of the UNC. We're not so different in that regard, despite the constant reminders of your imagined superiority."

Quinto hid a smirk as the Luminaries flinched from the slight. It wasn't often someone from the Lamina caste witnessed a superior taken down a peg. "If I'm to assess risk, I'll need more detail about the kinds of materials you plan to exchange. I can't allow you to source munitions from a foreign power."

"Only raw material and manufactured structural components will be imported. All technology will be homegrown. Ocon and Stol may have a stranglehold on refining, manufacturing and propulsion systems, but Ludumburg is home to the universities and research centres of the archipelago. We're not without resources of our own."

Pride entered Jayla's voice as she discussed their progress. "We've completed blueprints for a massive hydro-garden structure. Sept Stol already approved a contract to forge the skeletal components, and Sept Ocon has agreed to sell generators and basic vapour engines for the project. We've opted for hundreds of small engines instead of the few city class engines typically used on large installations. Zayd can provide the smaller models quickly, an important consideration for us. We've also ordered an equal number of backups for redundancy. The recent events, previously discussed, prompted us to make that decision. We feel a need to move quickly in light of building tensions.

"As we told Zayd, a food supply is too important to trust to a large engine which could take weeks to repair if it breaks down. What we didn't tell him is that our researchers have designed tanks, pumps and thrust nozzles that can function at higher pressures and with far more efficiency than anything he can provide. We already know that we can retrofit these components onto a standard Ocon vapour engine. The redundancy will make us far less reliant on others if supply issues arise in the future.

"We've decided that we're not willing to share our improvements with Zayd Ocon. However, we can't keep it a secret from him if we're required to have Sept Stol forge our new designs. That's where the UNC comes in. They're keen to take advantage of the increased manoeuvrability our engine modifications will provide their war balloons."

Quinto turned his head to direct a question at the Prime Palatine. "Why is it you're so eager to advance the capabilities of your war balloons if you're not interested in war?"

"You were at the summit," Duron responded, "How can you ask that question?"

"Aside from Luminary Ocon's theatrics, what in particular are you referring to?"

Duron considered Quinto for a moment. "I suppose it's possible you couldn't read the room. Sometimes, I forget that politicians are made, not born."

The UNC leader idly played with one of the medals adorning his uniform as he considered the best way to explain. "When you've been in the political sparring ring as long as I have, you learn to observe the habits and moods of your adversaries. Over time, you collect an arsenal of tools that can help you achieve desired outcomes. An example might be a touchy personal subject that you know will put your opponent off his game. It might be a temperament that's easy to inflame at a convenient moment, something to create a distraction. If you're lucky, you may discover a nervous habit. Such mannerisms can be very revealing. Queen Silvanus has a tell that she's completely unaware of. When she's about to lie, or someone comes close to a truth she's trying to hide, she tugs on her left ear. It's subtle but consistent.

"Zayd Ocon's theatrics, as you call them, were disturbing enough. It's not just for show. That man is a noxious ideologue. He plays the part of a politician, but he does it poorly. His language is always threatening. As a man familiar with war, I can tell you that he's already committed to a course of action, placing his words in a dangerous context. It comforts me to learn that not all Luminaries are like Zayd Ocon. I am reassured that the man in charge of the Luminary Navy is not itching to participate in a war.

"Even so, that may not be enough. I don't trust Zayd Ocon to abide by the wishes of his peers. He already sent ordnance across the limen into the southern realm. I won't allow him to do the same to my lands. As an admiral, you of all people, know the importance of preparing in advance."

"It won't come to that."

"That's not something you can promise. Besides, Zayd's rhetoric isn't the only concern. Do you recall what happened when Zayd accused Silvanus of hiding a gravity device in the deep south?"

Quinto rolled his eyes. "Fables that have existed for as long as I can remember. The queen didn't respond, if I recall. Why would she? The accusation is baseless."

"I have a different perspective. Silvanus held her tongue, but she tugged on her left ear not once, but three times."

Quinto shrugged. "Even if she's hiding something, it doesn't mean she has a gravity device."

"You may be right, but her silence suggests something significant. She's definitely preparing, just as I am. My people fought battles in the northern lands for many years before coming together. I can sense when war is coming and I'm telling you that it's inevitable. Tensions are high around the globe. You may not have noticed it, but it's there and growing.

Look for the signs and prepare. The two Luminaries in this room know it's approaching as well. As for Zayd, and those with him, I can see an eagerness in their eyes that's all too familiar."

Quinto wrung his hands with concern. "I don't like this at all. Why is everyone preparing for war instead of looking for peaceful solutions?"

"Do you really think I'm only here to strengthen my arsenal? Oh, I know I have a certain notoriety. I've even benefited from that reputation at times, but that's not the whole story. The truth is, more victories are won at the table than on the battlefield. The northern lands are vast and the people are hardy. Maintaining unity through brutality is cost prohibitive, especially if you expect it to last for more than a generation. My people don't hate me as much as you think. We maintain many mutually beneficial agreements. I prefer allies to enemies, and I'm here with a show of goodwill."

"What might that be?"

Duron turned to Silas and Jayla. "I haven't discussed this with you yet, but I've cordoned off a body of water in the UNC. The lake is close to the limen, and not too far from Ludumburg. If you're amenable, I'd like to offer to fill the tanks we produce with water before delivery. We've already arranged to launch the tanks into the swath for you to recover, but not their exact location. I propose that you build a collection and launching platform near the lake coordinates."

"Collections *and* launching?" Silas asked in confusion.

"As you consume water, the empty tanks can be launched across the limen into that same lake. We will collect and refill them. Your people will have a steady supply of water. Over time, the water gardens will have a large reserve. It's an extra show of gratitude for the financial infusion our manufacturing industry is about to receive."

"That's very generous of you, Prime Palatine."

"Not at all, the lake is remote and unused. With an infusion of water and the new food production facility you're planning to build, perhaps the pressure to go to war will diminish. It's a small cost to build better relationships. In all honesty, I'm also hoping you'll be willing to return the favour by sharing more technology in the future."

Quinto looked from one smiling face to another, finding it difficult to believe what he was witnessing. "I applaud the efforts to develop friendships and resources for the archipelago, but you mentioned defensive measures...."

"Right!" Silas clapped his hands together. It's quite elegant, really. Each new pressure tank can double as a fuselage. The tanks will have mounting points for the modified engines. They'll be integrated into the superstructure to serve as water storage. The combined engines will allow us to maneuver the entire structure as necessary. If we come under attack, each tank will vent its contents, creating a steam cloud for cover. The tanks can then detach, providing hundreds of rudimentary ships that the population can use for escape. At least we won't be sitting ducks."

"That's very creative."

"Are you satisfied then, Admiral?"

"I don't see anything in your plans that contravene Luminary law. I will hold your confidence, but I still believe your fears are unfounded."

Silas inclined his head. "Perhaps your investigation will show that Zayd is as innocent as he claims."

Quinto frowned. He didn't believe that either.

"Well, this has all been very enlightening." Duron took Quinto's hand in a firm grip. "I'm sure you don't trust me, but I'm now fairly confident I can trust you. Make allies while you can, Admiral. You've already heard how the Luminary Council could fall. When the day arrives that you find yourself cut off and left to your own devices, you'll want friends to help you in the righteous battle to come."

With that said, the two Luminaries escorted the Prime Palatine from the room and left Quinto to his thoughts. He knew much more about a looming disaster than he'd let on, but it was better to maintain a facade and now was not the time to fan flames. He needed to get a message to his contacts about these new developments. None of them had anticipated potential help from the UNC. It was certainly worth investigating.

Chapter 21

The remainder of the journey to Swiftwater was blessedly uneventful. The iridomals had stopped following as they neared the village. They didn't seem comfortable around large gatherings of humans. At least that much about them was normal. Valtteri had observed that the number of animals following him tended to increase over time. Once they left, for whatever reason, they seldom returned unless he crossed their paths again. It was evidence that the creatures didn't possess advanced reasoning. Their response to his presence was instinctual.

He knew that his bizarre retinue would begin to form anew once he left civilization, but he was thankful for the respite. He worried about having such conspicuous companions while questioning people. He had an official mission to complete, after all. Valtteri tried to imagine anyone taking him seriously with a tree creature on his shoulder and a ground rodent on his shoe. He shook the image from his mind. It was a ridiculous state of affairs for someone in the intelligence gathering business.

Villagers poured from their homes as word spread of the tinker's arrival. Children ran alongside the wagon, leaping and waving their arms. The small community was a hive of excitement by the time they finally came to a stop. Adis barely had time to park and open the side of his cart before the crowd swarmed him. Everyone clamoured for news of the outside world.

Adis had warned him to expect enthusiasm, but the turnout was overwhelming. Valtteri found himself smiling with the villagers, caught up in the impromptu celebration. Soon enough, they seemed to realize that he was merely a passenger and directed their attention to Adis.

Valtteri did manage to distract a few people to ask if they knew of any Swathcombers living in the area. Apparently, a group of them lived in the woods. They were doing business with the tether tribesmen who had also settled nearby. Eventually, he spotted one of the tribesmen sitting on a rock near the edge of the crowd. His thin Aerish frame stood out among the hardy townsfolk.

Valtteri grinned when he noticed the bemused expression on the tribesman's face as he watched the buzz of activity. "Hello, friend. You don't seem to be as excited as the rest of the crowd."

"Curious is a better word. I've witnessed this display on several other occasions and I still don't understand."

Valtteri sat on the grass beside the tribesman to share his view. "You don't understand the excitement?"

"No, it's not that, the tether tribes live in isolation, much like these folk. We also celebrate on those rare occasions when we can gather together. The sharing of news is a welcome thing."

"Then, what is it that you find confusing?"

The tribesman turned to look at Valtteri. "These people work hard to make a life for themselves. They have very little in the way of disposable income. Yet, every time the tinker arrives, they hurry to spend their money on completely impractical trinkets. I've seen the tinker's wares, he carries some fine knives and other useful tools. Why don't the people wait until they can afford something of true value?"

Valtteri burst out laughing. "Value is a very subjective thing, my friend."

The tribesmen shrugged and then joined in the mirth. "I suppose that's true. I have a friend from my tribe who spent much of his earnings on paper and pencils. He enjoyed sketching. I never understood that either." He hesitated, struck by a thought, and then began to chuckle again. "Come to think of it, many of us traded items for his drawings, myself included. I guess that makes me the spendthrift, and my friend the practical one."

He held out a hand and introduced himself. "My name is Bull. What brings you to Swiftwater?"

Valtteri shook the proffered hand. "My name's Valtteri. I came here to find my family. I'm told that your people deal with some Swathcombers in the area. Would you happen to know if a man named Bronto Knox is among them?"

"You mean the midwife's husband?"

Valtteri looked skyward and silently chastised himself. *I should have started by asking about the local midwife.* "Yes, I'm looking for Clea Knox and her husband, Bronto. They're my parents."

"Truly? They've never mentioned family. I imagine they'll be happy to see you."

"Can you take me to them?"

Bull pointed towards the tinker's wagon. "That's my wife over there, standing in line to view the tinker's wares. She'll be buying something completely impractical and taking her time about it. She won't be happy with me if I leave without her. My apologies, but you don't really need a guide anyway. Just take the main street to the edge of town. It becomes a path that parallels the river. Follow the path until you reach a small stream branching from the river. Continue along that stream and you will soon spot the tents of the Swathcombers. You can't miss the campsite."

Valtteri thanked the man and wandered back to the wagon. Adis had the side open and his display tables spread out on either side. It didn't seem possible to get through the crowd that surrounded him, so he moved to the other side and climbed onto the driver's bench, leaning over until he could catch Adis's attention from above.

Adis saw Valtteri waving, and the crowd made a path for the tinker to join him.

"I think I may have found my parents. I'm told some Swathcombers have a campsite not far from here. It's just down the river path. I'm going to pay them a visit."

Adis nodded. "Do you want me to join you?"

"That's not necessary. It looks like you have your hands full. Besides, the villagers would probably lynch me if I took you away from them."

Adis was in flamboyant peddler mode and grinned as he spread his arms expansively. "A tinker is always in demand."

Valtteri rolled his eyes, knowing the man's preferences were closer to those of a hermit. How he could switch so easily from one personality to the other was a mystery. Adis turned back to his customers and Valtteri left the crowd behind as he made his way through the town.

The noisy milieu near Adis's wagon dwindled as he continued down the main street. Simple log homes were the norm, with a few mud and straw buildings sprinkled in. The packed dirt thoroughfare was probably a muddy nightmare after a heavy rain. Wooden plank sidewalks fronted the buildings, no doubt to address that very issue.

As he progressed along the recently deserted streets, the quiet had him looking nervously over his shoulder. On two occasions, he was convinced that someone was following him, but whenever he backtracked to investigate, he found nothing. *I must still be skittish from the attack.* The sensation of being watched faded as the street converged with the river and narrowed to a path.

Twenty minutes later, he arrived at a crude bridge spanning a creek that forked from the river. The path continued along the river on the other side while a narrower trail turned to follow the creek. Valtteri followed the trail as the creek meandered deeper into the forest.

The trees and mossy ground, so near to the river, brought to mind a recent ambush in a similar setting. The feeling of being watched returned. Valtteri heard the rustle of grass behind him and glanced over his shoulder.

A branch snapped in front of him and his head spun back in time to see two men stepping out from behind some trees.

Judging by their dress, if he could trust Adis's description, these were Swathcombers. *Don't overreact, you're the stranger here. They're just being cautious.* "Hello, there. I've just come from the village. I was told I might find —."

The tallest among them held up a hand. "Stop where you are, Luminary lapdog."

How could they know he worked for the Luminaries? "I'm no one's lapdog."

"Then you won't mind answering some questions. We'll learn the truth, soon enough." The dark smile hinted at more than a polite inquiry. Two more men stepped into view on either side of him. He should have taken Adis up on his offer to come along. *Don't panic. I'm better prepared this time, and I only count four of them.* Two more men appeared behind him. *Okay, six. Still doable.* The circle closed in and Valtteri fell into a fighting stance. He calculated targets of opportunity, prepared to burst into action as they advanced. A net fell from above and they rushed him.

Valtteri cursed as he tried to fend them off, but the net hampered his movements. They deftly wound the net around him, pinning his arms and legs. He yelled and struggled, but his captors merely laughed as they hoisted and carried him the rest of the way to the Swathcomber campsite. They threw him unceremoniously inside a tent where they bound his ankles and wrists. One of them tied him to a short length of rope and attached it to a peg firmly embedded in the ground.

"This is completely unnecessary! I came freely with no ill intent."

"We have no doubt you came here of your own volition. Do you think this is the first time that Luminaries sent an agent to flush out some Swathcombers?"

"Do I look Aerish to you?"

"Of course not! Why would they send one of their own? The Luminaries have no imagination. It's always the same. Hire some Tellusan thug to locate a Swathcomber encampment, then send in more thugs to toss them across the limen. Ships wait to collect anyone who survives freerise. I lost a brother to one of those raids!"

A finger poked Valtteri hard in the ribs, followed by hot breath from an angry face inches from his own. "All we want is to live free! We're no threat to the Luminaries. You should be ashamed of yourself for helping them enslave others. Why can't they just leave us alone?"

"I'm not here on behalf of the Luminaries! I'm here for personal reasons."

"You're a stranger, and this is Swiftwater. People don't come here, they're born here. Strangers don't travel to Swiftwater for personal reasons."

"You came here, and so did a tether tribe. I doubt either was born in Swiftwater."

"That's not the same thing. Remote villagers, tribesmen, and Swathcombers alike, have chosen to live in isolation. We share that in common. As for the tether tribes, they're victims of the Luminaries just as we are. We do business in remote places like this precisely because the people here are like-minded. It also helps us avoid uninvited guests. You're not a villager, neither are you a tribesman or Swathcomber. That makes you an unwelcome surprise."

"Maybe not such a stranger. I think you may know my parents, Bronto and Clea Knox."

The interrogator jerked in surprise. "You lie! Bronto and Clea are Swathcombers. You're clearly Tellusan. How do you know their names?"

"I'm telling you the truth. My name is Valtteri Knox."

The group stepped away and whispered among themselves. The tall one nodded and two of the men left the tent. "We'll know soon enough. As it happens, Bronto is here. The others have gone to fetch him. I'm only giving you this chance to prove yourself because of a memory from my childhood. My name is Sato Knox. Remember it, because if I learn you're working for the Luminaries, I will avenge the death of my brother by throwing you across the limen."

Valtteri huffed. "It won't be the first time I suffer that fate."

Sato frowned and furrowed his brows. He nodded at Valtteri's headgear. "Why do you cover your eye like that?"

Valtteri stiffened. "My eye is sensitive to the light."

"Only one eye?"

"Yes, does it matter?"

"It might."

The conversation ended and they waited in silence for Bronto to arrive. Sato continued to stare at Valtteri as though he were puzzling out a problem.

Twenty minutes passed. Valtteri tried to get comfortable, but no matter what position he chose, the ropes chafed his wrists or his ankles. His ears perked up at the sound of footsteps outside the tent. The flap lifted and a figure paused at the entrance, his features cast in shadow by the sunlight at his back. Sato placed a stool near Valtteri and the figure fully entered to take a seat. As the tent flap dropped, Valtteri saw his face clearly for the first time. He looked familiar. He was certainly about the right age. "Papa?"

"Who are you?"

"It's Valtteri. Don't you recognize me?"

"Valtteri died a long time ago. I'll ask you again, who are you? How do you know that name?"

"I didn't die. A Luminary navy vessel found me floating near the limen. They rescued me."

"That's not possible. Who are you, really?"

Valtteri shook his head in frustration. "Ask me something only Valtteri would know."

Bronto lowered his head and closed his eyes in thought. "I once carved a toy figurine. What was it?"

"It was a pelican. You told me it was a symbol of the swath divers. You said they always return with their pouches full of food."

Bronto opened his eyes, but kept his head lowered as if he didn't want to face the possibility. "It's a common Swathcomber icon. You could have guessed."

"I named it Dipper."

Bronto's head jerked up, eyes searching Valtteri's face. They settled on the striking gold colour of his exposed eye. "Why do you cover your other eye?"

Sato spoke up. "He said it was sensitive to light."

"Why don't you see for yourself? I'd show you, but —." Valtteri tilted his head to indicate his bindings.

Bronto's hand moved to Valtteri's face. He hesitated for a moment. Valtteri tilted his face to the ground to make it easier to reach the strap from the back of his head. Bronto slowly pulled the headgear away. Valtteri lifted his head to lock eyes. Bronto gasped, "Iridogen! It can't be," he whispered.

"But it is." Valtteri whispered.

"It really is you." A tear rolled down Bronto's cheek. "How is it that you're here now, after all of these years?"

"I've spent my life among the Aerish. It hasn't been easy. Circumstances limited my options, as you can imagine. I have very few memories of my life with you. Certainly not enough to claim a Swathcomber heritage. However, I know what I am not. In my heart, I was never Aerish, despite my upbringing. I'm left with many questions. I don't know who I am or where I came from. Now that I've found you, I'm hoping you can provide some answers."

Valtteri saw hope in Bronto's eyes, but he seemed to be struggling with something. "What's the last thing you remember?"

"We were in an unfamiliar area. I think it was behind our home, beyond the cultivated portion of our yard. You warned me never to play there, but I felt safe because you were with me."

"Is that all you remember?"

"Things are a bit fuzzy. I remember that the sun was setting. I should have been in bed, but you seemed excited or on edge about something, and I was elated to stay up later than usual. You pointed to a boulder. It was a short distance away and you said that a surprise waited for me on the other side. You told me I had to hurry if I wanted to claim it. I tried to obey, but I found it difficult to move and I was overly warm for some reason."

Bronto was nodding in quick bobs. He avoided Valtteri's gaze as though he were ashamed. "We dressed you in many layers of clothing. Do you remember anything else?"

Valtteri squeezed his eyes shut, trying to focus on his memories. "I think I was carrying something. A heavy blanket, or — ."

"Yes, that's right." Bronto confirmed. "It was a drogue chute, attached to a harness you were wearing."

"When I reached the boulder, it felt like a giant hand grabbed me and threw me across the sky. I was tumbling and spinning. I didn't know which way was up. I yelled for you, but the wind carried my voice away. Then, I felt something jerk my body and I stopped spinning. The deafening wind slowed to a steady howl. Eventually I stopped. The light was fading fast and I couldn't tell where I was. It felt like I had been alone in that place forever. I still have nightmares about it. I was so cold, and I couldn't keep my eyes open any longer. That's the last thing I remember before waking up in the boiler room of a ship, wrapped in blankets with worried faces looking down at me."

Bronto was rubbing the back of his neck with a look of wonder on his face. "So... a navy vessel found you? That explains a great deal."

Valtteri's mind snagged on something Bronto had mentioned. "Did you say I was harnessed to a drogue chute?" His eyes hardened in accusation. "You intentionally sent me across the limen. It wasn't an accident!"

Bronto turned his head to the side. "We didn't have a choice."

"I was five years old! How could you do that?"

"I had to believe you'd be safe. I dressed you warmly, and we use drogue chutes to send up packages all the time."

"I was a child, not a bundle of produce! I could have been killed!"

Bronto lifted his voice in defence. "If I hadn't sent you across the limen, you definitely would've been killed! True, it was a risk, but they came for you, and we were out of time."

Bronto was struggling with his emotions. "Cut him free."

"Are you certain, Bronto?"

"Cut him free, Sato! He's family."

Sato drew a knife and cut through the ropes. "No hard feelings, I hope. We didn't know who you were."

Valtteri sighed as he rubbed his wrists to get the blood flowing again. "I understand. You were protecting your people."

Sato reddened. "Not quite. We were warned of your arrival, and we were paid to toss you across the limen."

"What? Why would someone pay you to do that?"

"A man arrived a few days earlier. He was a peculiar fellow wearing a ridiculous mask. There's not much call for bounty hunters or mercenaries in these parts. I suppose he came to us, because he had no other options. We wouldn't normally accept that kind of work, but he claimed that you were an Aerish spy and that you had a bounty on your head. He said he represented a consortium of Tellusan interests who wanted to send a message, and offered to split the bounty with us." Sato shrugged. "It was a very large sum, and I wasn't lying when I told you that I lost my brother to an Aerish raid. Receiving money to see justice done is a once in a lifetime opportunity for a Swathcomber."

"I don't suppose he gave you a name?"

"He called himself Obitus ... I know, the moniker is as ridiculous as the mask he was wearing, but his money was good."

Valtteri rubbed his temples. He felt like laughing at the absurdity of it all. Previously unknown factions were already tailing him before he managed to complete his first task. It made no sense. He hadn't threatened anyone or ruffled any feathers.

Sept Ocon trained Valtteri to function as a secret operative, but apparently, he was completely incompetent. How did he so quickly become a target? First mercenaries, and now some lunatic calling himself Obitus. Not that long ago, Valtteri would have suspected Nixon, but he was a world away. Besides, Valtteri's orders came directly from Zayd Ocon, and not even Nixon would have risked the ire of his uncle.

"I don't know who this man is or why he led you to believe that I was targeting your family. You already know I'm not who he said I was. I came here looking for relatives. I'm beginning to wonder if that was a mistake. What kind of family tosses children to their death and threatens to do the same with long-lost relatives?"

Valtteri glared first at Bronto and then turned to Sato. "You people have to stop treating me like baggage. The navy saved me that first time you threw me into the swath, but I'd rather not push my luck."

"Don't be too hard on Bronto. He immediately sent out search parties. I was ten years old at the time, old enough to help. We spent days looking for you. It devastated Bronto when we came back empty-handed."

Bronto's eyes were pleading. "You have to believe me, we were only trying to protect you. It should have worked. Now we know why it didn't, it was the Luminaries. Somehow they keep managing to ruin our lives."

The tent flap flew open and Clea Knox rushed in, almost knocking Bronto from his seat before her eyes adjusted to the darker interior. "Is it true? They said Valtteri is alive." She spotted him sitting on the ground and her eyes grew wide in recognition. She fell to her knees and wrapped her arms around him, weeping into his neck and begging for forgiveness. Valtteri stiffened for a moment, but his emotions took over and he hugged her fiercely in return.

After a few minutes, Valtteri pulled back to get a better look at Clea's face. It was older than he remembered, but her eyes were familiar. She smiled tentatively and brushed a strand of hair behind his ear. He looked from Clea to Bronto and back again. His countenance fell. "You're both Aerish."

Bronto and Clea exchanged confused expressions.

"It's just that, well, I assumed one of you would be Tellusan." Valtteri shook his head. "I'm not your biological child, am I?"

Clea's eyes widened in understanding. "Oh, you poor dear. You don't know. What am I saying? Of course you don't know. How would you? You were so young when we lost you." Clea looked accusingly at Bronto. He held up his hands in surrender. The men of the camp deferred to Bronto, but apparently someone else was in charge.

"Valtteri was asking about our decision to risk his life in freerise. I was about to explain, just before you entered. The subject of his birth didn't come up."

"Foolish old man! Why would you start with a story of how we sent him away? Didn't it occur to you to welcome our long-lost son home? To tell him how much we loved and missed him? You could have given him some context so he understood how difficult the situation was. The poor boy probably thinks we didn't want him!"

"Well, I —."

"Shush. Let me do the talking, before you make matters worse."

Clea faced Valtteri with the no-nonsense demeanour of someone practised at giving uncomfortable news. "If you asked after us in the village, I'm guessing you learned that I'm a midwife."

"I'm aware of that fact, yes."

"Judging by that headgear you're clutching, I'm guessing you're also aware that the southern realm isn't particularly friendly to the Iridogen."

"I was warned."

Clea nodded. "Sometimes, we travel to very isolated locations where only small nomadic groups of people live." She circled her index finger to indicate their immediate surroundings. "Our campsites always seem like a village to the nomads. They typically start to make an appearance after a day or two, drawn to the cook pots and singing. It was that kind of setting where you were born.

"When the group discovered I was a midwife, their leader bade me to come see a young woman in their midst. The girl was heavy with child. I asked her who the father was, but she insisted that she didn't know. It might be true, monogamy is often eschewed in such groups. The only name she gave for herself was Beth.

"I checked on Beth every few days and stayed when it was her time to give birth. It was an easy delivery, and you came into the world under a canopy of trees. She was holding you when you opened your eyes for the first time. I remember the look of horror on her face. It was such a contradiction to the smile from a moment before. She dropped you, and backed away. I chastised her soundly. I couldn't imagine what had gotten into her. You squeezed your eyes shut as you howled from the shock of the fall. I held you until you fell asleep and placed you in a bassinet.

"I had business to attend to, so I gave her some instructions and promised I would be back in the morning to check on her. When I returned, she was gone, along with the rest of the group. You were still in the bassinet where I'd left you, wide awake and looking around. When I saw your eyes, I understood." Clea's face clouded. "Superstitious fools!"

"I wasn't about to abandon you like your mother had, so I took you back to the campsite. We remained in the area for several months, but Beth never returned. I had no way to find her. Bronto and I are unable to have children of our own, so we happily took you in. We're not your biological parents, but we *are* your family in every way that matters.

"Bronto and I settled in the small village of Mulpika. It's very near the limen, which is convenient for a Swathcomber outpost. We wanted some stability for you until you were old enough to travel with the Swathcombers. The first few years were a happy time. You made us laugh and filled our hearts with joy. We kept to ourselves, and it was relatively easy to hide you.

"As you grew older, things became more difficult. We couldn't keep you indoors forever. People were becoming suspicious. We did what we could to hide your eyes, using wide brim hats and sunglasses. That worked for a while, but then the animals came. They followed you around the yard and we had to keep you indoors again.

"One day, you decided to explore on your own. We still don't know how you managed to unlock the door. You walked straight down the main street, oblivious to the parade of iridomals in your wake. You created quite a stir. Bronto heard the shouts, and went to check on the commotion. He saw you surrounded by angry men and pushed his way through. Bronto picked you up and ran home.

"I tried to reason with the crowd over the next few days. They knew me well, and I hoped to make them understand. Instead of listening, they accused me of bringing a curse on the village. Suddenly, they had someone to blame for every little inconvenience of the previous four years.

"The crowd turned ugly, and several men went to get their guns. They vowed to remove the curse. I ran home to warn Bronto, who was already preparing for the worst. The Swathcomber campsite was too far away to get help in time, the villagers were approaching. We came up with a desperate plan. I ran to the front yard to do what I could to delay the crowd while Bronto completed the preparations and rushed you out the back door.

"I couldn't hold them for long and they broke into the house to search for you. Someone noticed the back door was open and they rushed through it in pursuit. They reached Bronto just as you crossed the limen."

Valtteri was rapt through the retelling. "I assume they were satisfied when they saw me spin into the ether."

"They were, but Bronto lost his temper, and almost his life, when he attacked the armed villagers. He did a fair bit of damage before they were able to stop him. They allowed us to grab a few items from the house before they drove us out of town. We had no intention of staying and headed straight for the Swathcomber encampment where we could gather limen divers to form a search party.

"We travelled by moonlight through the worst night of our lives and arrived at the campsite by daybreak. Limen divers were dispatched immediately, and relatives in the upper swath quickly joined the search. You had completely disappeared."

Valtteri rose to his feet, dumbfounded. "I need some air." He left the tent and walked a few paces. Bronto and Clea followed.

"Valtteri, are you okay?"

He turned to face them. "I've never fit in with the Aerish, and my biological parents are lost to me. All I really know is that I am Iridogen, hated for the sin of opening my eyes for the first time."

Bronto shook his head. "That's not true. We're your family. We loved you from the moment we held you in our arms."

"I was only in your life briefly as a child. You don't know me at all."

"It doesn't matter. You're a member of the Knox family, and you'll always have a place with us."

"That's very generous of you, but it's unnecessary. I'm no longer your responsibility."

Clea stepped up to Valtteri and placed her hands on his cheeks. "Love doesn't work that way. It's not something you lose. This is a miracle. I haven't felt such joy since the day we first claimed you as our son. I understand that many years have passed, and perhaps we have no right to ask, but can you give us a chance? We've missed out on so much of your life. Please don't walk away forever. We can still get to know each other. "

Family. Valtterri looked into those familiar eyes and his heart softened. "I — I think I'd like that."

A tear rolled down Clea's cheek and she pulled Valtteri into a hug. Bronto joined the embrace. "We may have failed you in many ways, Valtteri, but know this, Swathcombers take care of their own. Word will get out of this reunion. Everyone will know of your status among us. If you ever find yourself in trouble, the Swathcombers will be ready to render aid. You can count on it."

The sun shone down on the bittersweet reunion, no one noticing the glint reflecting off the lens of a telescope watching them from a distance.

Chapter 22

Valtteri shifted his position on the bench. He was sitting by the river near the edge of town, staring pensively into the turbulent stream.

Game birds erupted from the tall grasses alongside the path, warning him of someone's approach. He turned to see Adis waving as he drew near. Valtteri returned to his contemplation of a water scavenger. It was making short work of some grisly remains. He wondered how long it would be before he met a similar fate, victim of an agenda that was never his own.

"Valtteri! How was your search? What did you learn?" Adis drew up short when he noticed the morose expression on the face of his ward. The Tinkers Guild tasked him with guarding the young man, but some wounds were unavoidable.

Valtteri spared a momentary glance at the tinker. "I'm guessing that you knew Bronto and Clea Knox were not my biological parents."

"It wasn't my place to say."

"You could have told me, it would've saved us both a lot of time."

"I promised I would help you find them. You wanted to know more about your past. Those early memories hold a place in your heart and this is your journey of self-discovery. Would you have ignored this opportunity had you known?"

"It might have been better if I did. They were planning to kill me."

Adis did a double take. "Why in the world would they do that?" He scanned their surroundings nervously, searching for potential assailants.

"It's okay, Adis, they're no longer a threat."

Adis took a deep, slow breath and settled back into a more casual stance. "I'll note in the official record that you acted in self-defence."

"What? No, I didn't kill them! Valtteri rolled his eyes. "We just talked."

"You talked them out of killing you? Either I'm missing something important here or I've seriously underestimated your negotiating skills."

Valtteri's lips twitched upward despite his mood. "Bronto was at the camp. Once I convinced him that I was his lost child, they abandoned any plans to kill me."

"That explains why you're alive, but not why they wanted you dead in the first place."

"They accepted a contract. Someone approached them with an opportunity to eliminate an Aerish scout who was supposedly planning to expose their camp. Apparently, the Swathcombers are not on friendly terms with the Luminaries."

Adis snorted. "That's an understatement. They go out of their way to irritate the founders. Swathcombers regularly cross the limen, making deals with local Tellusans and sharing information. The Luminaries have outlawed those activities, calling it a breach of border security. Swathcomber independence has been a bone of contention for as long as the swath has existed."

"I'd always assumed the Luminaries considered them lower than the Lagan caste and generally ignored them. I've never encountered Swathcombers in my time with the fleet. I thought they were outcasts hiding on the fringes."

"The Swathcombers are very good at avoiding the fleet, but don't take that to mean they stay away. They're very active in support of anti-

Luminary activity. The Luminaries don't want anyone to know how successful Swathcomber raiding tactics are. Instead of acknowledging it, they use some innocent soul from the Lagan caste as a scapegoat. That injustice further infuriates the Swathcombers. They seek an end to the caste system and Luminary control, but they don't want innocent people to suffer because of their actions. It forces the Swathcombers to dial back their incursions, but the Luminaries are just making matters worse. It's one of several flash points that are building within the swath."

Yet another thing I didn't know. "How could I be so blind to all of these things happening around me?"

"It's easy to miss the obvious when you're lulled by routine and reassured by those in charge." Adis paced behind the bench where Valtteri sat. "Did they happen to mention who hired them?"

"The man wore a mask, so they didn't know what he looked like. They said he called himself Obitus. Does that ring any bells?"

"The Guild is aware of a man operating under that moniker, but he's as much a ghost as his name implies. He's feared in criminal circles, yet doesn't seem to be involved in any illegal money-making ventures. Rumours suggest he has hired mercenary groups on occasion, but no one seems to know for what purpose."

"Like those mercenaries who attacked us on the road?"

"That's where my thoughts were heading as well. The first attempt was probably supposed to look like the work of uncoordinated bandits rather than the professionals who were waiting for our arrival. This second attempt was less direct, and the Swathcombers were offered a story to suggest a different motivation. Someone is working hard to obfuscate possible connections. If your death were investigated without proper context, I doubt anyone would look beyond the narrative provided. This all points to someone with guile and connections. Now we have a name, but the implications are worrisome. It appears that this Obitus fellow provides services to politically motivated clients. It's troubling when someone with his apparent resources and global reach is successful at remaining hidden. This is a dangerous opponent. We'll need to stay vigilant."

Valtteri nodded and silently turned back to his study of the river.

Adis placed a hand on his shoulder. "Was it so bad?"

"Actually, no. At least not once they recognized me. I met them both, Bronto and Clea. They want to get to know me better. I promised I'd come back one day and spend some time here. They were only trying to protect me from a lynch mob when they sent me through the limen. I was foggy on the details, but they filled in the gaps."

Valtteri snorted. "Can you believe they thought I'd be safe because they harnessed me to a drogue chute? They arranged for Swathcomber relatives to pick me up, but the navy found me first. I guess they saved my life despite the ill-conceived plan. We really were a family for a time, and they truly loved me. Even so...."

"It wasn't what you were expecting."

"I still don't know who I am. My biological parents wander the forest. They could be anywhere, or perhaps they're no longer alive. My birth mother didn't know which of several men got her pregnant. That eliminates any chance of learning who my father was. Clea can't remember what my mother looked like, so even if I went searching, I have no way to identify her. They're lost to me. They obviously wanted nothing to do with one of the Iridogen anyway."

"I'm sorry, lad."

"You warned me not to get my hopes up. I don't know what I was expecting. It's not like I could so easily replace those lost years, although that relationship may develop over time. Maybe I was just hoping to find someone who thinks the way I do. Someone with familiar features or characteristics, some common family trait that ties me to a person or place. I've been adrift for so long ... I guess I was hoping for an anchor."

"A family is comprised of those who stick with you through good times and bad. Perhaps you haven't been paying close enough attention to the people around you. The admiral has always been by your side, and others have gone out of their way to help you. Fisher Kozen is one, and I've already told you that the Tinkers Guild has your back."

"Bronto said something similar about the Swathcombers."

Adis perked up. "What, precisely, did he say?"

"Just that the Swathcombers would be there if ever I needed help. Come to think of it, he did something peculiar after he said it." Valtteri reached into his pocket. "He took off one of his earrings and handed it to me. I'm not sure what I'm supposed to do with it."

Adis broke into a wide grin. "He gave you a family bijou in front of witnesses, and declared you as his heir. You now have a bigger family than you've ever imagined. The Knox clan is large, and a little notorious. They're also fiercely protective of their kin. Bronto wasn't making shallow promises. That bijou will gather a small army to your side if need calls for it. I suggest you let me pierce your ear at the earliest opportunity. You don't want to lose that."

Valtteri examined the small hoop and pendant in his hand. Unfamiliar symbols delicately engraved the surface. "Huh. Can you pierce my ear tonight?"

"I'd be happy to. I have equipment for that in the wagon, alongside the jewellery cases". Adis shook his head in wonder. "I've never met someone who could so quickly make both powerful allies and potent enemies simply by stumbling about."

"Instead of making light of my predicament, why don't you help me figure out why I have a target on my back?"

"I haven't forgotten. I'll need to think more on the Obitus connection, but for now, I've arranged a meeting with Tallow. He may be able to shed some light on what Zayd Ocon is hiding. Sicily said he was due back at the tether tribe campsite this afternoon. She'll meet us there. It's a five-mile walk. If we start now, we should get there shortly after he arrives."

* * *

The tether tribe camp was like nothing Valtteri had seen before. It was a miniature village spanning both sides of the limen. The dwellings on the swath side were a hodgepodge of baskets and platforms connected by ladder-like bridges. Tribesmen walked upside-down on the bridges carrying their burdens. They moved in a well practised, if somewhat awkward, gait. Their odd-looking foot wear alternately clipped to and then disengaged from the rungs as they made their way. It was a rather ingenious solution and provided a measure of safety in the reverse half gravity.

Spherical domiciles clung to the trees, barely large enough to sleep in. They looked like nests made of woven river reeds, tethered together with intricately braided cords.

Tube-like structures crossed the limen, anchored between pairs of trees on either side of the crossing. Woven in a similar fashion to the dwellings, these tunnels were reinforced with a framework of sturdy branches. Tribesmen were crossing from one side of the limen to the other, as though the shift from reverse half gravity to regular gravity was a trivial matter. From his own experience, at Pax Montis, the transition was disorienting and it took time to adjust. The people here seemed to take it for granted. Indeed, though the tribesmen were fine-boned like all Aerish, these men were both lithe and heavily muscled. Valtteri wondered at the blend of strength and grace until he noticed some of the tribesmen leaping from tree to tree instead of using the bridges. The dexterity required was mesmerizing. He was envious as he recalled his own long and clumsy transition to full gravity.

On the Tellusan side of the limen, the tribesmen took advantage of full gravity to construct domes instead of spheres. They had cleared an area to create a rudimentary market, complete with covered booths to display their wares. It served as a place to trade with the locals and to hold larger gatherings than would be practical while clinging to trees within the swath.

The atmosphere was festive as music from one of the booths filled the air. A trio of talented tribesmen were piping a lively tune from finely carved flutes. The instruments seemed to be a coveted commodity among the locals and a crowd gathered around the display table. Dancing had broken out in an open area as tribesmen twirled with local ladies, or anyone close at hand for that matter. They seemed to relish the gravity-bound activity and used their instinctive balance and poise to great effect, adding dramatic flair to traditional dance steps.

Adis had explained some of the history. The Blackspike Tether Tribe abandoned their previous life to escape Luminary oppression. They had settled here and seemed to be integrating well with the villagers of Swiftwater. Their hybrid village gave them the best of both worlds. It also provided a level of security. If a Luminary corrupted tether tribe attacked, the Blackspike tribe could quickly cross the limen, something traditional tether tribes would fear. At the same time, if any Tellusans were to take umbrage at their presence, they could flee to the swath, something very few gravity bound individuals would risk since one slip would send them flying into the ether. Opposition was unlikely in this remote location and the residents of Swiftwater had clearly adopted the tribe who offered a much-needed infusion of helpful hands. Combined, the two groups were thriving instead of merely surviving. It was a win-win for everyone.

Adis was smiling contentedly. He had arranged for the two groups to come together and was immensely gratified with the result. "Over there," he said, pointing to a couple hovering over a cook pot across the clearing. "That's Tallow and Sicily."

Sicily waved in greeting as they approached. Tallow offered a quick glance and a nod before returning his focus to the stew he was stirring. He dipped a mug into the pot and tested it. "Needs more salt." He declared.

Sicily gave him a swat. "And before that, it needed more sour leaf, then more heat root. Stop taste testing, you've already consumed three mugs worth of dinner."

Tallow closed his eyes and smiled as he inhaled the aroma. "I've been living off dried meat and berries for the last two weeks, can we please just eat already?"

Sicily rolled her eyes. "I suppose it's close enough to the evening meal." Tallow grabbed a bowl and quickly filled it. Before he could find a spoon, Sicily grabbed his arm and removed the bowl from his hand. She handed it to Valtteri. Tallow had a stricken look on his face and Sicily lifted a brow in response. "Guests first." Tallow's face reddened as he reached for a second bowl, which he filled and handed to Adis. He offered a bowl to his wife before filling his own.

Sicily pointed to a series of logs arranged near the edge of the clearing. "We can sit there, and talk over our meal." She moved towards the designated spot, Adis in tow. Valtteri followed and glanced over his shoulder to see Tallow quickly consume half the contents of his bowl and top it off before joining them. Tallow, caught in the act, shrugged with a grin and trotted to catch up.

Adis spent some time sharing news from abroad as they ate their meal. When his update touched on the current political climate, discussion shifted to the reason for their meeting.

Tallow broached the subject first. "Adis tells me you're looking into Tellusan activity near Endelton."

"That was the task given to me." Valtteri acknowledged. "From what Adis tells me, it has less to do with the Tellusans than it does the Luminaries."

"Then you know how the Luminaries have been using and destroying my people."

"I feel like I should apologize for my ignorance. I'm sorry for what you've gone through, but I never heard of the tether tribes before I came here."

"It's not your fault. Our people live in anonymity and isolation. If Sicily and Adis hadn't opened my eyes to the truth," Tallow swept his arm to indicate the other tribesmen, "these people would still be suffering. Unfortunately, many others continue to toil in ignorance. It's difficult to ask someone to give up the only culture they've ever known. Some tribes have accepted the truth and rebelled only to be slaughtered for their defiance. We lack the means to stand against the Luminaries. Our only option is to flee. I've managed to convince a few tribes to join us here, but much work remains."

Sicily placed an arm around Tallow and gave him a squeeze of encouragement. "My husband does what he can, but Adis believes that our best chance to end the atrocities is to expose the Luminaries. Unprecedented changes are taking place among the tribes, and Tallow has been moving deeper into the swath, searching for answers. Some of what he's discovered is disturbing."

Tallow placed a hand on Sicily's knee, silencing her. "Tell me, tinker. Why should we confide in this man? You said he's an agent of the Luminaries."

"You trust *me*, don't you? I can vouch for him."

"You've earned my trust, Adis, but I don't know this man. Forgive me for saying so, but I've given people the benefit of doubt before, with deadly consequences."

"Look at him, Tallow. He wasn't born in the swath. The Luminaries are using him just as they used you. They've tried to kill him twice since he crossed into the southern realm."

"I know you have no reason to believe me." Valtteri interjected. "I hold no love for the Luminaries. They've made my life miserable since the day I was dragged into their service as a five-year-old child. They consider me property. If I can gain my freedom by uncovering the truth, then I think we're after the same thing."

"We shall see. I've been tracking some strange activity near Endelton. I'll meet you there in three days. Tell me what you learn while you're there and we'll compare notes. After that, we can discuss next steps."

"Thank you."

The sun was beginning to set, and Tallow rose to his feet. "If you'll excuse me, I need to get some sleep. Travelling the base of the swath is tiring." Tallow reached for Sicily's hand.

"You go on, I'll be there shortly," she smiled.

Tallow nodded and moved towards the sleeping domes.

"Would you be willing to deliver a care package to my father while you're in Endelton, Adis?"

"Of course, Sicily. It will be good to see Ryo again."

Sicily turned to Valtteri. "Adis is being kind. My father can be a cantankerous mule. Even so, he can introduce you to the townsfolk, making it easier for you to conduct your investigation. I'll send along a letter explaining things, and he'll offer you a place to stay. He can show you the stone of witness while you're there and give you some historical context."

"That's very kind of you."

"Not at all. Adis is a good judge of character, and I'm inclined to accept his assessment. Even so, it will comfort me knowing my father is observing your activities as well. Tallow and I have become understandably suspicious, but our enemy is powerful and we need allies." Sicily's eyes took on a dangerous glint. "If any harm comes to my husband because of your actions, I promise you that this entire village will hunt you down and send you back to the Luminaries..." Sicily looked upwards. "...by the most expedient route."

Valtteri watched in stunned silence, as Sicily walked away.

"That went well." Adis commented.

"It went well? Why does everyone keep threatening to throw me across the limen?"

"I guess you have one of those faces? Never mind, we need to get an early start tomorrow. We may as well call it a night. The guest domes are this way."

Valtteri shook his head. He felt a wave of dread as he followed Adis. Endelton... would he find answers or a masked man waiting to end his questions? He'd find out, soon enough.

Chapter 23

Valtteri followed in silence as Adis led them through a thicket of underbrush. They'd left the wagons secured on the main road and tethered the equids in a small meadow near the treeline so they could feed. They only planned to stay a short time and the wagons couldn't get where they were going anyway. The tinker paused every now and then to look for marks he'd carved into trees on his previous visits. "We're nearly there."

The underbrush thinned as soil gave way to rock. Trees still managed to stake their claim in fissures, providing shade. The walk became far more pleasant, but ended minutes later as they arrived at a clearing with evidence of a former campsite. "Here we are." Adis set down his pack and rummaged through the contents looking for his recording instruments. He wanted to capture a few more images and take some measurements.

The campsite sat on a ridge overlooking a valley, and Valtteri felt drawn towards the edge to take in the view. What he saw made him gasp.

Adis joined him at the edge. "Shocking, isn't it?"

The valley was a desolation of craters running along the limen for miles in every direction.

"Endelton was the intended target."

Valtteri had been part of live ordnance exercises within the desert areas of the swath. He'd seen the impact craters through telescopes and had a rough idea of a single bomb's explosive radius, but this? "This wasn't the result of an accident during a routine military exercise with an inexperienced crew. The breadth and intensity of the barrage that caused this..." Valtteri did some quick calculations. "This bombing would've taken hours of sustained and coordinated effort."

Adis nodded. "Whoever ordered this attack wanted to make sure no one from Endelton survived. Thankfully, they miscalculated. Unfortunately for them, what they intended to keep quiet became a political bombshell instead. Pardon the word choice."

"You're a hero, Adis."

"I don't feel like one. It was my evidence of Luminary oppression that incited the Fleetwood Tether Tribe to rebel. They died from a similar bombing within the swath.

"As I understand, it was Tallow who showed them that evidence. You had no way to know how they would respond, or the consequences."

"Plenty of blame to go around. It's guilt that drives Tallow. Very few people are aware that an entire tribe was wiped from existence. The Luminaries managed to keep that secret from the general public. It's unacceptable."

Adis set up his tripod and took some optical measurements.

"Two bombings." Valtteri shook his head. "It's not possible for something like that to remain quiet without high-level collusion."

Adis looked up from his work. "Now you understand why I wanted you to see this place with your own eyes. Images don't do it justice. You were on the naval base when this happened, and no one knew. Even the admiral was in the dark. Something of this magnitude and precision can't have taken place without Luminary involvement. No one else has the resources or the political clout to minimize the repercussions like we've seen. Zayd Ocon was the one who responded, and it was his money that silenced Queen Silvanus, that and the threat of exposing the queen's own secrets."

Valtteri sighed. "I'm working for a dangerous man, I don't doubt it for a moment. I just never thought he was capable of wholesale slaughter. He was targeting innocent people."

"Dangerous games are playing out across the planet, lad. You don't yet understand the breadth of the problem and have little time to learn."

"I'm standing right here, and I'm willing to listen."

"It's better if you learn for yourself."

"Oh, so we're back to this again, are we?"

"We should get back to the wagons. We still have several hours of daylight for travel. We'll arrive in Endelton before nightfall."

* * *

Valtteri woke to the smell of eggs and freshly baked bread wafting from the kitchen. Adis had dropped him off at Ryo Basurto's home, along with Sicily's letter and care package. The tinker preferred to set up in the heart of the village where he had a spot reserved for his wagon. He planned to spend his time there, catering to his customers. Valtteri had been uncertain of his welcome in the Basurto residence, but Ryo seemed delighted to have a guest. He behaved as a perfect host, contrary to Sicily's warnings about her father's curmudgeonly ways. It made him wonder what she'd written in that letter to her father.

Valtteri rubbed the sleep from his eyes and stumbled outside to use the outhouse. He found a trough nearby and splashed water on his face before entering the kitchen.

Ryo stood at the cook stove with a towel slung over his shoulder. "Good morning, young Mr. Knox. I hope you like eggs. It's been hard to keep up with the hens now that I'm here all alone. It will be good to eat these before they go bad. I hope you have a hearty appetite."

"Eggs are fine, Thank you."

"You'll find hot cocoa in the pot, courtesy of Sicily. Thank you, again, for delivering her package. I don't hear from my daughter much these days. It's good to know she hasn't forgotten me. I imagine she and

Tallow are still hunting for evidence to make their case against the Luminaries?"

Valtteri helped himself to a mug. "Yes, that's actually why I'm here. We have similar goals and I was hoping to learn more about what happened. Sicily suggested you might be willing to take me to see the rock of witness?"

"Ah, you'd like to start at the very beginning of all this?" Ryo placed a plate of food in front of Valtteri and grabbed a second plateful for himself, before joining him at the table. The aroma was heavenly. Valtteri tucked into his food as Ryo fell into that storytelling mode so common among older men. "It all started when a tether tribesman showed up on the edge of town. I was very young at the time, but I remember it created quite a stir. No one knew what to do with him. He showed up every morning, and left every night.

"He just sat, waiting for... well, no one knew what he was waiting for. He turned gaunt as time passed and Sicily's grandmother took pity on him. She was always taking in strays, and caring for the wounds of people in the village. She couldn't bear to watch him wither away, so she took him in and fed him. He helped around the house and eventually the townsfolk decided he wasn't a threat. Life went back to normal.

"His name was Trapper, and in the course of time, Sicily's grandmother fell in love with him. They married and had children, one of whom became my wife. Over time, we learned about his life in the tether tribe. Eventually, he shared the story about how he witnessed the death of a tribesman at the hands of a Vigil working for the Luminaries. Trapper fled for his life, and with nowhere safe to go, he risked crossing the limen.

"Trapper wanted to warn other tribesmen about the duplicity of the Vigils, but he was afraid to return to the swath. He decided to leave a message in the hope that others would find it. He located a boulder close to the limen, polished the side facing the swath, and carved his testimony into the surface. The stone encourages other tribesmen to escape across the limen. Trapper wanted to form a bridge. He hoped to make the transition less threatening by planting a tree beside the stone. It grew to span both sides of the limen, creating a convenient transition point.

"That old scout made many trips to the stone, hoping to spot a fellow tribesman passing by. Sadly, he died before he could see the fruit of his labour. Sicily and her grandfather were very close. She continued to visit the stone after he died. That's how she met Tallow."

"So, Sicily met a tribesman and followed in her grandmother's footsteps? That's quite a story."

"Yes, except it didn't have the same happy ending. Tallow had a rival for Sicily's affection who turned the townsfolk against him. The villagers formed a lynch mob based on false accusations that the tether tribes were preparing for an attack. They were convinced that Tallow was an advance scout for an invasion. I'm ashamed to admit that I believed the lies. I'm not sure Sicily has forgiven me for that failing."

"Wait," Valtteri interrupted, "I remember Tallow saying that a Vigil named Strom told the Blackspike Tribe that Tellusans were crossing the limen to attack *them*. Doesn't it strike you as odd that someone was stoking fear on both sides of the limen?"

"I hadn't really thought that far, but now that you mention it — it does seem suspicious."

"What can you tell me about Tallow's detractor?"

"His name was Lomar Romero, the wealthiest man in our village. He'd been paying off my gambling debts. I've come to understand that he was leveraging that debt in an attempt to obtain Sicily's hand in marriage. At the time, I considered him a generous benefactor. I should have trusted Sicily's instincts about the man. She's still angry at me for encouraging his courtship."

"Would I be able to talk to him?"

"No, I'm afraid he died."

"Do you think he might have spoken to an outsider at the time this took place?"

"In the past, I would've said no. Our isolation tends to deter visitors.

On rare occasions a stranger passes through, but the tinker is our only regular visitor. Having said that, we've seen an increase in visitors since the bombing incident. Most of those are soldiers working for Queen Silvanus. Others are men like yourself, looking for answers. Considering everything that took place, I suppose it's conceivable that provocateurs were speaking from the shadows. I couldn't say if Lomar spoke to someone like that. I *will* say that he seemed to be acting out of character. I never saw a stranger other than Tallow during that time, but it might be a question to ask others."

"Do you have any suggestions about where I might start?"

"You'll probably want to speak with Mayor Hawton. Everyone comes to him with their problems, so he has a good grasp of community dynamics. He may have insight that others wouldn't."

Valtteri scraped the last of his meal from the plate. Ryo reached for it, to clear the table, then paused with a frown.

"Is something wrong?"

"It's just that Sicily would've admonished me for not asking if you wanted a second helping, and here I am attempting to take your plate from you. I miss that girl, she reminded me how important small acts of kindness can be."

"It's fine, Mr. Basurto." Valtteri pushed his plate across the table. "I've had my fill. Thank you for the meal, it was delicious."

Ryo nodded and placed the dishes into the wash basin. "I can clean these later. I imagine you'd like to get started. Do you wish to see Trapper's stone of witness?"

"Perhaps later. I'd like to speak with some of the townsfolk first, if that's alright?"

"Certainly. If we hurry, we might catch some people before they begin work." Ryo grabbed a wide-brimmed hat from a peg near the door, and stepped into the sunshine without waiting for a response. Valtteri chuckled, imagining what Sicily might have to say about her father's brusque behaviour, then hurried after his host.

IN THE SHADOW OF THE LUMINARIES

* * *

The interviews weren't going as well as he'd hoped. Everyone seemed either suspicious of him, or filled with guilt for their part in chasing Tallow and Sicily away. He supposed they didn't want to be fooled a second time. Valtteri didn't blame them, a lot of strangers wandered the town. As the day progressed, he'd spotted several of the queen's soldiers. The villagers resented their presence, despite assurances that the military was there for the protection of the people. Many of Endelton's citizens had moved to the remote location to get away from big-city problems. The sudden interest in their town left everyone uncertain whether their happy seclusion would ever return. Mayor Hawton was particularly vocal in his objections. His volume increased for the third time as a soldier passed within earshot. "I don't know what to tell you. These interlopers refuse to give me any idea how long they will remain, and they are rapidly depleting our food stock."

The nearby soldier shrugged, clearly familiar with the mayor's tirades. Hawton yelled at the departing soldier's back. "Tell Queen Silvanus I'm keeping a record of how you are abusing our town's resources, and that I expect to be fully reimbursed!"

The mayor shook his head in disgust. "None of this makes any sense. The bombing took place miles from here, but the tinker tells us that Endelton was the intended target. We're far from any important trade routes. We keep to ourselves, and have no enemies. Destroying Endelton benefits no one. What possible strategic advantage could anyone hope to gain? We're in the middle of nowhere. We've seen no sign of Aerish in these parts, yet the queen's men gather as though there's an imminent threat of an enemy crossing the limen."

"Adis assures me that the Aerish are up to something in the swath." Valtteri offered.

"Yes, we've heard much the same from these unwelcome scoundrels who make themselves at home in our town!"

Valtteri winced as the mayor lifted his voice in the direction of

191

another convenient target. Villagers were fuelling the mayor's invective with angry glares of their own. Soldiers in the area wisely found alternative routes. One remained immune to the icy stares. He leaned against a building across the street, unaffected by the townfolk's attempts to make him feel unwelcome. The peculiar stranger wore a hooded cloak over his uniform. Valtteri had no idea if the cloak was an acceptable part of military attire in the southern realm, but it was an odd thing to wear on a hot sunny day. The soldier pulled his hood low to obscure his face and Valtteri had the distinct impression that the man was watching him rather than the Mayor.

Valtteri interrupted the mayor's harangue and pointed at the soldier. "Have you seen that man around here before?"

Hawton glanced in the indicated direction. "I can't say that I have, but who can tell? They come and go in a steady flow. Just when I think I'm starting to make headway with someone in charge, that person is replaced. It's unacceptable."

The mysterious figure pushed off the wall and moved out of sight between two buildings.

"Mayor Hawton, I want to thank you for answering my questions. I'll make sure to include your concerns in my report." Valtteri didn't say who he was reporting to, but the mayor made his assumptions and seemed to be happy that someone was listening to his complaints.

"You're very welcome. If you have any more questions, Ryo will know where to find me." The mayor turned his considerable bulk decisively towards the market. His approach caused the baker to roll her eyes as vigorously as the dough she was rolling on the table.

Ryo laughed at the display. "Poor Clair, the mayor will be hovering until her next batch of sweet rolls comes out of the oven. Where would you like to go next? I could take you to the camp to talk with the soldiers."

"Actually, Ryo, why don't we take a break for a few hours? I'd like to walk alone, and process what we've heard so far."

Ryo seemed uncertain, so Valtteri dropped a few coins in his hand.

"Why don't you wait for me in the tavern, and I'll join you in a bit?"

Ryo grinned as he accepted the coins. "I'll have a mug waiting for your return."

Valtteri lingered until Ryo entered the tavern. He looked up and down the street searching for a hooded figure, and rushed to the spot where he'd seen the man disappear. Slipping between the houses, he passed into a narrow green space behind the dwellings. It separated the buildings from the forest beyond. Looking left and right revealed nothing of his quarry.

Vaguely recalling his father's tracking instructions on their one joint hunting trip, he knelt to the ground to look for spoor. The mown grass had perked up, but it was still slightly askew, indicating someone had recently passed that way. He followed until the trail turned onto a narrow path winding through the forest. He hesitated. No one knew where he was going. He should have spoken with Adis, but if he turned back now he'd lose the trail completely. Anger and determination made the decision for him. Someone had tried to ambush him, twice. This time he was the hunter, and he wasn't about to waste the opportunity to be on the offensive for a change.

Valtteri followed the narrow trail for an hour. He moved swiftly on the well-packed soil, hoping to catch up while he could still move in relative silence. He spotted footprints near the edge of the track in a few places. Signs of someone's passage made an occasional appearance, branches missing leaves, a snapped twig, a flower turned away from the sun. He felt confident that his quarry hadn't left the trail.

Somewhere along the way, he picked up some tree-dwelling shadows as iridomals formed a wake behind him. He slowed, realizing that he hadn't seen any disturbances on the trail for a while. Valtteri was suddenly concerned about the noise the creatures were making in the trees. Had his quarry heard him and turned off the path to hide? He stood motionless, hoping the iridomals would do the same. The forest grew silent for a moment and Valtteri heard a commotion in the trees south of the trail. A moment later, the creatures above him began to chitter in response, reminding him of a telegraph machine. It couldn't be.... He didn't have time to consider the implications and lacking any leads, he retraced his steps. *There!* A lesser travelled path was visible beyond a bush at the edge of the trail he'd been following. No wonder he missed it. The path led downhill into a large grove of old growth trees. The moss-covered ground silenced his footsteps as he moved quietly from one trunk to another.

Valtteri heard voices and froze. He discovered the source a moment later in a small clearing to his right. Two soldiers, one of them wearing a cloak. This time his hood was down revealing a mask. *Obitus!*

The conversation was brief, and the soldier grinned as he accepted money from his masked benefactor. *What are you up to?* Valtteri wondered. He needed to warn Adis about this new threat, but Obitus continued on alone, and Valtteri wasn't about to turn back now.

Eventually, Obitus came to a stop. He inspected several hidden trip lines as he approached a gap in a patch of thicket. Once he was satisfied they were undisturbed, he disappeared into the thicket. Valtteri couldn't see any other entrance. He'd taken a careful note of the trip lines, but he had no way to know what other deterrents lay in or beyond the brushwood.

Iridomals were making noise above him, and Valtteri ground his teeth with the fear of discovery. He cast his eyes to the tree tops and glared until he noticed them racing back and forth across the stout branches of the immense trees. It was like a highway through the canopy, and it passed right over Obitus's hiding place. *If I can get up there....*

Keeping out of sight, Valtteri searched for a tree with branches low enough to reach. Eventually he found a partially fallen tree snagged in the branches of its neighbours. It provided a convenient ramp, and soon he was picking his way above the thicket. It took longer than he imagined it should, but his slow progress rewarded him with a view of a clearing within the thicket. It was the perfect hiding spot, a protected haven. Valtteri couldn't imagine how Obitus discovered it in the first place.

IN THE SHADOW OF THE LUMINARIES

A tent sat on one side of the clearing. A nearby ring of stones surrounded the remains of a fire. The campsite had seen several days of use. Valtteri watched as his objective circled the fire pit several times before stopping in front of the tent to pull off his cloak and toss it inside. The man was heavily muscled, a common trait among Tellusan warriors, but he moved as though burdened. Valtteri almost fell from his perch as the fellow suddenly shrugged off his muscles like a snake shedding its skin.

Aerish! As the suit was discarded, Valtteri could see metal plates lining the inside. *Some kind of armour. It must be incredibly heavy.* His suspicions were confirmed as the fellow rotated his neck and stretched his limbs. The audacity was astonishing. This man, known as Obitus, and feared by Tellusan criminal organizations around the world, was Aerish!

Valtteri's thoughts were scattered as he tried to imagine possible reasons for one of the Aerish to take such a risk. One inference rose to the surface, the stranger's presence in Endleton screamed of Luminary involvement. *If that's true, and the Luminaries already have assets in the field, why was I sent here?* His musings were interrupted as he watched the fellow sit down on a rock and remove his mask. Obitus set his mask on the ground at his side. Unfortunately, his back was turned to Valtteri. *I need to see his face.*

Valtteri plotted a path through the branches. As he began to move, the iridomals moved with him, creating a disturbance. Obitus jumped to his feet and spun to face the noise, drawing a pistol and firing in one smooth motion. Valtteri froze. One of the iridomals lay dead on the ground and the rest chittered their indignation as they scattered in a noisy withdrawal.

Toeing the carcass at his feet, the gunman chuckled and returned his weapon to its holster. He looked up with a wry smile on his face, shook his head, and returned to his seat.

Valtteri trembled with a mixture of relief and rage. Relief that he wasn't spotted, and rage at what he saw. Nixon Ocon! Nixon was Obitus. Nixon was the one plotting to kill him! It took every ounce of self-control he possessed to keep himself from leaping into the clearing to vent his anger. Deep calming breaths brought him back to rational thought. A knowledge of Invicta Manus wouldn't protect him from a bullet. He'd come unprepared. Adis would be furious with him for the risk he'd just taken. He recognized his own foolishness. Together they could have subdued and questioned Nixon.

As anger and frustration waned, Valtteri remembered the transaction between Nixon and the Tellusan soldier. That meeting had taken place several hours ago. *Adis could be in danger, I have to warn him.*

Valtteri quietly moved away from Nixon's campsite. He had to get to Endelton. It took a while to move far enough away from the thicket before it was safe to descend. When he reached the packed trail, he broke into a run. Every footfall was accompanied by a prayer that he wasn't too late.

Chapter 24

Valtteri was nearly in a panic when he found the tinker's wagon locked up with Adis nowhere in sight. Not knowing what else to do, he ran for the Basurto residence at the edge of town hoping Sicily's father might have seen Adis. He burst through the door, startling Ryo, who let out a yelp.

"Have you seen Adis?"

Eyes wide, Ryo pointed to the guest room where Valtteri was staying. The door was open and voices drifted from the room. "His belongings appear undisturbed. When did you say you'd seen him last?"

Valtteri walked briskly to the door, filled with relief at the sight of Adis sitting on the bed. His pulse spiked as he spotted a soldier standing to one side.

"Valtteri? You're okay! Where have you been?"

"We have to leave, Adis. It's not safe here." Valtteri moved in front of Adis and fell into a fighting stance.

Adis furrowed his brows in confusion. "Have you lost your mind, lad? Stand down, this is Sergeant Rimes of the queen's army."

"I saw Obitus giving money to a soldier, so you'll forgive me if I don't have a lot of faith in the queen's men at the moment."

"You spotted Obitus, and went after him without me? What were you thinking? We talked about this."

"I'm sorry, I didn't have time to find you. If I hadn't followed when I did, I would've lost him."

Adis shook his head in disbelief. "You take too many risks. I can't protect you if you keep running off on your own."

"It's *because* I followed him that I know we're in danger from the military. Look, you can lecture me later. Right now we need to get away from here."

Sergeant Rimes listened with interest. "Obitus. Is this the person you were telling me about? The one you believe orchestrated the attacks?"

Adis nodded.

The sergeant turned to Valtteri. "Can you describe the soldier you saw?"

"Short bald guy, missing part of his left ear."

Rimes snorted. "That would be Krebs. He's been nothing but trouble from day one. The queen has spread the army out along the limen. We don't have enough regular recruits, so we've been hiring mercenaries to pad the ranks. Krebs and his crew are a bunch of undisciplined misfits who take orders reluctantly, if at all. I've been looking for an excuse to have them removed from my unit, so if you have any evidence, I'd very much like to hear it."

"I'm sure you would. I'm less sure about what you'd do with the information."

"It's okay, Valtteri. I trust the sergeant. We've worked together before. Do you remember when I told you that governments around the world are contractually obligated to provide a military police force to hunt down those who attack a tinker? Sergeant Rimes has helped me in that regard on several occasions. When I heard he was running the operation here in Endelton, I tracked him down to bring him up to speed on recent attacks. He can help if someone makes another attempt on our lives."

Valtteri eyed the sergeant warily. "I don't have any physical proof to offer you, but you might want to search Krebs for a large sum of money."

"Oh, believe me, I'll take great pleasure in tearing his tent apart, and I don't need an excuse to do it. Unfortunately, a bundle of money won't be enough to charge him with anything. Attempting to assassinate a tinker, however, that's a very serious charge with deadly consequences. I'd have to catch him making the attempt."

"It's nice to know you'd hunt down our killers after we're gone, but that's small consolation to the dead."

"Give the man a chance, lad. What are you suggesting, Rimes?"

The sergeant's face split into a grin. "I'm thinking, we set a little trap of our own."

* * *

The small fishing pond was Ryo's idea. He claimed few people knew the place. It was off the beaten track, a perfect spot for an ambush. After scouting the location, Sergeant Rimes agreed that it would serve their purposes.

Valtteri, Adis and Ryo spent the afternoon in the tavern waiting for one of Krebs's men to arrive. Rimes had pointed them out earlier in the day, confident they'd show up at the tavern sooner or later. He wasn't wrong. It was Krebs himself who first made an appearance. Surprising no one, he sat nearby to listen in on their conversation. Ryo made sure he could be overheard as he explained how to find his secret fishing hole. Valtteri and Adis displayed appropriate enthusiasm and discussed their plans to try their hand at catching something on the following morning. They arranged a time to set out, and knew their intended catch had taken the bait when Krebs quickly got up to leave.

That was yesterday. Today they sat on a log in front of the pond, pretending they knew what they were doing. The temperature was climbing quickly, and Valtteri regarded the wide-brimmed hat on Adis's head with envy. They'd been hard-pressed to cobble together some convincing fishing gear on short notice. Among the selection was Ryo's one and only hat, and Adis quickly claimed it. *For someone who's supposed to be protecting me, he doesn't seem to care too much for my comfort.*

"I'll probably die of heatstroke before Krebs and his crew even get here."

Adis raised an eyebrow and chose to ignore the comment.

Bulrushes surrounded the natural basin, fed by a tributary. Occasionally, a fish would break the surface, feeding on the insects hovering over the surface. Valtteri would find it idyllic if he could keep his fight or flight response from ruining the moment. He watched a spreading ring as it raced away from the pebble he'd tossed into the water.

Adis frowned. "Stop it. You'll scare the fish."

"Um, we're not really fishing, Adis."

"We need to make this look convincing. Real fishermen wouldn't scare the fish."

"This is a bad idea." Valtteri muttered.

"I assure you that I've noted your objections... with each repetition over the past half hour."

"So you say, yet here we sit, pretending to fish. Ironically, the bait isn't on the hook, it's holding the poles. We may as well paint targets on our back."

"Everything will be fine. Rimes and his men planned to arrive long before we got here. I'm sure they're in position, watching us as we speak."

"A fat lot of good that'll do if someone shoots us in the back."

Adis gave him a sideways glance. "Not that long ago, you thought it was a good idea to run off on your own without backup. Now we have backup, and you're complaining?"

"That was different, no one knew I was there. These men are coming to kill us. They're not going to be like those ammunition stingy mercenaries we met when we first set out. These men are armed to the teeth, courtesy of the queen's coffers. You can bet they've been told what we're capable of. I'm guessing they'll shoot as soon as they see us."

"That *is* what we're hoping for. If they show intent to harm a tinker, it's over for them."

"It's a terrible plan, Adis."

"As long as we appear oblivious, they'll take their time. Rimes is watching. When he sees our attackers line up a shot, he'll give the signal and we can dive into the bulrushes. If anyone points a gun at us, Rimes will have proof of intent."

"This is insane! We can't move faster than a bullet."

Adis shrugged. "I don't think it will come to that."

A harsh chuckle sounded behind them. "I'm afraid Rimes won't be coming to your aid. He's dead, and as far as his men are concerned, they believe the operation was called off."

Valtteri turned his head far enough to see Krebs and two of his cronies pointing rifles at their backs. "Tut, tut. Eyes forward."

Valtteri returned his gaze to the water.

"You didn't really think I was stupid enough to fall for your obvious set-up back at the tavern, did you?"

Valtteri shrugged. "Honestly, I wasn't sure if you were smart enough to follow the directions to get here. I thought you'd get lost along the way."

The comment earned him a jab to the back of the head with a rifle barrel. Adis cast a warning look, and subtly shook his head.

"If this is about money, I can give you more than you were paid." Adis suggested.

"I sincerely doubt that. Our employer was very generous."

"The Tinkers Guild has more wealth than you can imagine."

"And will the Tinkers Guild offer me future jobs like this one?"

Adis held his tongue.

"That's what I thought. I don't know what you did to get on that masked psycho's bad side, but it hardly matters to me. This will be easy money."

The cocking of rifles sounded loud to Valtteri's ears, drowning out everything else. *I'm going to die.* He held his breath, waiting for the inevitable.

A staccato of gunfire overwhelmed his senses and Valtteri fell to the ground in shock.

A moment of confusion followed before the ringing in his ears resolved into a voice. "Valtteri?"

Valtteri didn't know what to expect in the afterlife, but he'd hoped for something sweeter than Adis's voice followed by the toe of a boot in his side. Valtteri took a deep breath and felt for injuries. "I'm not dead?"

"I believe I told you to dive into the bulrushes, not fall off the log, but yes, you're fine."

Valtteri sat up and looked around. Krebs and his men were lying motionless on the ground.

"What happened?"

Adis jerked his head toward the tall grass ten feet away where Rimes was standing with a cadre of men.

"I don't understand. Krebs said he killed you."

Rimes let his hand drop to the bandage around his midsection. "He certainly tried. Thankfully, he missed any vital organs, and he didn't stick around to make sure the wound was fatal. The coward stabbed me while I was still in my bed. I'm sorry we didn't get here sooner, but the medic insisted we stop the bleeding first."

Valtteri couldn't stifle his laugh. It was probably nervous tension, but the release felt good. He was still alive after three attempts on his life, and now he knew without a doubt who was responsible. He didn't understand what sort of game Nixon was playing, but Adis was right, they couldn't trust Sept Ocon. Having that assurance allowed him to shed any vestiges of obligation. If that meant he was a traitor, well, they were trying to kill him either way. It made no difference. More importantly, he had real allies now, friends who could help him survive what was coming. Adis had been right about that, too. True family revealed itself through its actions, and Valtteri was slowly gathering a group he could call his own.

Chapter 25

It was a humid morning. Valtteri couldn't tell if his clothes were soaked from the weather or exertion. It was a curious sensation, crossing from the arid swath side of the limen into the light drizzle outside of the swath, only to return. The abrupt transition was almost like entering and leaving the shelter of a house, except they were outside. They had been crossing back and forth across the limen for hours. Tallow insisted that Valtteri become familiar with the transition from the reverse half gravity of the swath to normal gravity and vice versa.

Valtteri had crossed the limen many times during his naval training, but that was always accommodated through special transit points with accompanying hand rails and other stabilizing comforts. Jumping into the swath with nothing but open space between you and a target tree was exhilarating, to say the least. It had taken the better part of the morning to master the acrobatic roll that would put him in the correct orientation as he flung himself towards a tree.

The reverse half gravity left very little room for error. Missing your target could mean a terrifying freerise past the treetops and into the sky with no way to stop yourself. Tallow had shown him how to use an anchoring tether between trees when travelling, but the initial leap without a tether across the limen into the swath was both disorienting and terrifying. Tallow ignored the safer methods for crossing, insisting that Valtteri learn to leap through quickly. The maneuver had saved Tallow's life, on several occasions, from threats on both sides of the limen.

Valtteri looked down at himself. He was wearing a harness equipped with a tether, pitons, and a grappling hook. Numerous rings and clips provided options for attaching water bladders or other necessities. His legs sprouted climbing spurs, ungainly on the ground but an undeniable asset in the trees.

Most impressive were the gauntlets. Valtteri admired the craftsmanship as he sheathed and unsheathed the multiple blades several times, enjoying the smooth mechanism and the sound they made when engaging. Traditionally, tether tribesmen used a simple blade in each hand while traversing the trees, but Tallow had designed these gauntlets to provide a more efficient means of gaining purchase when approaching a tree. Valtteri was grateful to have them. Learning to travel like a tribesman was daunting enough. He had no doubt it would be far more difficult to use knives. They certainly didn't have time for him to learn such advanced techniques.

Valtteri thought he was making good progress. As a navy pilot, calculating trajectories was second nature and those instincts were helping him now. He had always loved the feel of cresting an arc and diving to a target. It was one of the things that made him a skilled pilot while others found it disorienting. When he sat in the cockpit of a navy vessel, he thought that he knew what it felt like to fly, but this.... Pouncing from tree to tree under his own power without a shell of protection was on another level. It felt like freedom and he revelled in it.

Valtteri had spent most of his life in half gravity, but even so, diving towards the surface instead of the sky felt counter-intuitive. He regularly did the same in a scout ship, but the surface was so far away from the plane of equilibrium that it never registered in his mind. Here, the close proximity of the surface introduced a real risk of impact, even as reverse gravity pulled him towards the ether. On a few leaps, he came near enough to the surface that he could feel the taller grasses brushing his scalp. The experience was surreal, and his senses struggled with the contradictory input. It should have been nausea inducing, but he felt only pleasure. Every leap was dangerous, yet exhilarating. Valtteri couldn't keep the grin off his face.

"Pay attention!" Tallow barked. "This isn't a game. If you lose focus, you die."

They stopped for a short break on the Tellusan side of the limen. Valtteri let the rain wash his upturned face as he cooled down. He paced, trying to keep his muscles from tightening as he adjusted to full gravity.

His wandering brought him to the rock of witness again. He'd heard Adis speak of it, and he listened as Ryo, Tallow, and Sicily verified the tinker's account. Even so, the narrative held a fairy tale quality that planted a seed of doubt. It wasn't until their meetup with Tallow that the truth finally sank in. Here it was, staring him in the face. A real person had etched words into the polished surface of the stone. It was a testament to atrocities of the past, crimes that continued into the present. It served both as a cry for help and a warning, yet it sat in the middle of nowhere. It was far away from the authorities who might be able to do something about it. It felt both impotent and powerful at the same time.

The testimony stirred something inside of him, a fierce desire to protect innocence. *Definitely powerful.* Valtteri suddenly understood the passion Adis displayed when he discussed the tether tribes. These people were victims of manipulation. They trusted their wardens, never realizing they were prisoners. They accepted exploitation because they knew nothing else. Somehow, that made it more disturbing.

"This is so wrong." Valtteri muttered.

"It is," Tallow agreed, "but it has become something far worse."

"How could it get any more appalling?"

"Before the truth came out, we didn't realize we were living a lie. We were unwittingly serving the Luminaries, but we believed we were receiving something in exchange. As far as we knew, our choices were our own, and we were happy. Since I crossed the limen, I've experienced many new things. I've seen wonders to be sure, but also much evil. Some days, I long for the simplicity that I once knew. I miss the brothers I could rely on without question. On this side of the limen, I'm never certain whom I can trust."

"I think, perhaps, we have that in common."

Tallow nodded. "Adis shared a little of your story. We both need to find answers."

"And you think we'll find them in the swath?"

"I told you things were worse now. Much of what is happening to the tribes is my fault. When I discovered the truth, I told others. One of those tribes rebelled, so the Luminaries destroyed them. Since that time, the Vigil has been making unprecedented changes to the tether tribe culture. They separate longtime brothers, and gather impressionable youth into new tribes. They're taken away from those who know our history, so they'll adopt new ways. They are tempted with gifts and the immediate granting of brides, but they're too young to recognize a bribe. As a result of this largess, the members of these newly formed tribes believe whatever the Vigil tells them. The Luminaries are rewriting history to raise doubt about the challenges put forth by the Tinkers Guild. I fear that the tribe elders are dead, or soon will be. No one will hear about the atrocities of the past."

"Adis will find a way."

"I fervently hope so, because I believe this goes far beyond the tether tribes."

"Adis has a similar fear, but I'd like to hear your perspective."

Tallow laid a hand on the stone of witness, a wistful expression on his face. "I've been trying to understand why things progressed the way they have. This all began when the Vigil ordered tribesmen to monitor the limen for possible Tellusan incursions. That's never happened before. Tether tribes avoid the world and its politics. It has always been a

Luminary policy that we remain apart from international affairs. That protection was one of the things we thought they did for us. Vigil Strom went so far as to suggest that the Tellusans were our enemies, even though we've never had a conflict with them, or contact, for that matter."

"Perhaps when they learned you were communicating with a Tellusan, they were worried that the truth about their crimes would get out." Valtteri suggested. "Maybe they hoped to instill fear to make sure no others would follow you."

"That's what I thought at first as well. You could apply that same reasoning for the destruction of the Fleetwood Tribe, as well as the attempted destruction of Endelton. It was risky, but if it had worked, they would have silenced everyone who knew the truth. However, that doesn't explain why they wanted us to patrol the limen long before any of those events took place. They were already worried about something. Worried enough to risk an international incident. It doesn't make sense that they'd take such a risk for the tether tribes. Most of the world doesn't even know we exist. No, they were worried that Tellusans might discover something other than the tribes."

Valtteri furrowed his brows in confusion. "But you spent your life at the base of the swath. Surely one of the tribes would've known if something strange were happening."

"Along the limen, sure, but not the interior."

"I don't follow."

"The majority of tether tribes live near the limen. An extensive root system allows the forest to encroach partway into the swath. This greenbelt is fed by rains that still fall outside of the swath. We rely on the forest to anchor us. It provides food, shelter, and a means to travel without fear of being flung into the ether. However, we have another reason to remain near the limen. The Luminaries have chosen to place their sky lifts there. It's how we trade with them. They are our primary contact with the outside world. We don't have much incentive to travel into the interior, but sometimes we're forced to search further abroad when resources are limited."

"I thought the swath was a desert wasteland."

"Most of it is, but some rivers remain. Those streams crisscross the swath, and where water exists, trees flourish along the banks."

"I've never heard of this. How can any water remain on the surface within the swath?"

"The swath has two transition planes. The first is at the surface where reverse half gravity begins, and the second is the plane of equilibrium at twelve thousand feet, where the gravity reverts to its proper orientation, albeit still at half gravity. The Aerish don't know this?"

"Yes, of course, but why weren't the rivers taken up during the inversion event?"

"The largest portion of water within the swath, along with the loose soil above the surface transition plane, disappeared into the heavens. However, the removal of that soil exposed underground streams, and of course, some rivers exist in valleys below the surface plane. Those were never affected. I can't say if any of those rivers cross the entire swath. I'm sure the Luminary Navy has mapped them. Adis tells me you trained with the navy. I'm surprised you haven't seen the rivers from one of your vessels."

"Recruits seldom travel far from the base. I suppose I might have seen the rivers for myself eventually, if the Luminaries decided I should serve in a traditional navy role."

"Luminaries control lives beyond the tether tribes, I see. Nevertheless, we have an interesting intersection of coincidences. Endelton happens to be near a river that flows to the interior. As far as I've been able to ascertain, over the past several months, only two tribes were asked to patrol the limen. The Fleetwood Tribe, which resides on one side of that river, and my own Blackspike Tribe, which heralds from the other side of the river."

"Interesting."

"Yes, and that's not all. The Vigil has been gathering malcontents and bullies from the tribes into a special group dedicated to his service. They show up at the campsites of other tribes and make trouble, flaunting their special status. Witnesses say they're under the influence of a narcotic. They're not sure what it is. They do know it's not vision berries. These men are exceedingly aggressive and armed with high-quality knives and other weapons we've never seen before. No one has risked following them, but all have seen them head into the interior via that same river route."

"So, you believe the Luminaries have created a private little army to protect something deeper within the swath."

"I do, and it's a venture that I think is separate from their attempts to rewrite tether tribe history."

Valtteri nodded. "It would explain the request for tribesmen to patrol the limen, and the risks they've been taking to silence anyone in the area. It would also explain why Zayd Ocon wanted me to investigate Tellusan activity in and around Endelton."

"Do you agree with my assessment?"

"You've highlighted too many coincidences for me to think otherwise. We need to find out what's happening along that river."

"I'm prepared to leave immediately."

"Do you think I'm ready?"

"You're as competent as a seven-year-old tribesman."

"That bad, huh?"

"You misunderstand. That's the age when we trust our children to explore without supervision. You've adapted surprisingly well for an adult travelling in this manner for the first time. I'm comfortable enough with your progress that I believe you can follow without assistance. You'll learn far more by taking a journey than continuing with the rudimentary exercises we've been practising."

Valtteri released a nervous laugh, "So, we just leave? Shouldn't we gather provisions or something?"

"The swath will provide everything we require."

"There he is!"

Tallow and Valtteri both turned, searching for the source of the unexpected voice. A group of armed men burst into the clearing, led by a man in a dark mask.

"I think you're right, Tallow, now would be a very good time to leave."

The two men extended their claws and turned to face the limen. Valtteri chose a tree to aim for, and vaulted across the limen, spinning as he'd been taught. The reverse half gravity drew him skyward as he approached his target. He felt a moment of panic, then his spurs and claws sunk into the wood as his arms and legs cushioned the impact. It was his first jump without a tether connecting him to Tallow.

"Valtteri! Take cover!"

He barely had time to move behind the tree trunk before a volley of gunfire peppered the spot where he'd landed. He glanced over at Tallow who pointed skyward. He knew it was better to start a second jump near the base of a tree. It allowed more time to reach a second tree before passing the canopy, but he understood that they couldn't make a leap without exposing themselves. Their only hope was to remain hidden from sight and change location vertically. That way they could leap from an unexpected position. It would take a moment for the gunmen to spot them and adjust their aim. If they were lucky, that was all the advantage they'd need. The next jump would take them out of range.

Tallow climbed swiftly and waited as Valtteri struggled to match him. Tallow turned sideways, allowing the left side of his body to hold his weight with spur and claw, while preparing to push off with the right side of his body. Valtteri mimicked his movements and selected a new target. When he was ready, he nodded to Tallow. They had to time this perfectly. Tallow signalled to make the jump at the count of three.

Three, two, one, jump! They were halfway to their new destination before a second volley of shots rang out, but they were no longer in the spot where their attackers had aimed. Valtteri scrambled behind the cover of his new location. He peered around the tree trunk and saw the mercenaries lowering their rifles.

Nixon shook his fist and shouted. Valtteri couldn't help himself, he stuck his head out, smiled, and saluted. Nixon ran towards the limen. For a moment, Valtteri wondered if he'd actually try to cross. It was the kind of reckless behaviour he'd expect from Nixon. Instead, he drew up short, whipped out his pistol, and fired. The shot flew wide, but it was surprisingly close, clipping some nearby leaves. Nixon had always been a good shot, but that shouldn't have been possible with a pistol at this range. He made a mental note, *don't underestimate that man in the future.*

A sigh escaped his lips. Here he was, clinging to a tree dangerously close to the canopy, and he felt safer than he'd felt in weeks. The primary threat to his life was on the other side of the limen with no way to follow. He smiled at the irony of returning to the swath to escape Sept Ocon. It couldn't last, but he'd enjoy the reprieve while he could.

Chapter 26

Quinto crossed the gangplank between his aeronaught and the equally massive water tanker. He nodded to his men, who fanned out for the routine inspection. The Luminaries had a long-standing point of contention with the friaers over their water monopoly. Quinto snorted at the absurdity of the accusation. The friaers had done exactly as the founding septs, they built something in the aftermath of the inversion event. While the septs were busy gathering soil to make their floating islands, the friaers were gathering water.

The difference was that the friaers were trying to help those in need. This tanker would be docking shroudside of a tropostate to provide free water to the struggling Lagan caste, or perhaps the occasional Swathcomber they came across. As far as Quinto could tell, the Luminaries were disgruntled because it hadn't occurred to them to make water a first priority. They simply didn't like that it was out of their control. It probably didn't help that the wealthy were the only ones who had to pay for their water. The friaers gave it to the needy for free. Quinto thought it only fair, since the Luminaries didn't give anything to the friaers for free either. The friaers typically used those earnings to help the downtrodden in other ways. They were often filling in the gaps left by the

Luminary failure to take care of their own people.

Regardless, as admiral of the Luminary Navy, he was tasked with filling a quota of random spot checks on the tankers. The friaers knew about the requirement, and that the admiral considered it a pointless exercise. He always made certain it was a painless affair for everyone. His officers vied for the opportunity since it was a ridiculously easy duty. Was the vessel carrying water? If so, the only thing left to inspect was the latest batch of Pax Montis beer. Everyone was a winner. The friaers made a pretty penny selling pints, and some of his officers earned a brief shore leave.

On this occasion, Quinto was using the opportunity for a clandestine meeting with Fisher Kozen. It was safer for them to discuss private matters on one of the friaer's water tankers, far from any of the tropostates.

Fisher was waiting in his stateroom with the door ajar. A plate of cheese from Pax Montis, and two frothy mugs of the friaer's finest sat on a small table. Quinto considered it an invitation to enter, if ever he saw one.

"Are you a mind reader now, my friend?"

Fisher grinned. "The desires of an uncomplicated mind are easy to guess, no supernatural powers required."

Quinto chuckled at the backhanded compliment, and the friendly banter continued while they drained their mugs.

"Refill?"

"Probably not a good idea. I can't stay long, best we get down to business. Do you have any news?"

Fisher grew serious. "We're hearing more rumours from the deep south. Some claim the discovery of a lighthouse located miles away from any water."

"A lighthouse?"

"Or something similar. It's apparently casting a beam of light into the sky."

Quinto leaned back in his chair. "Another fairy tale."

"I don't think so. This time it's different."

"Care to elaborate?"

"I can't say much without revealing my source, but we have a highly placed contact in the southern military. He was stationed at a facility set up to study the structure. It had him spooked."

"Okay, you have my attention. What had him on edge?"

"I don't think he understood what he was seeing, but from what he described... Quinto, iridomals have surrounded the facility."

"I'll admit, the presence of iridomals is an intriguing addition to the typical stories."

"This could be the break we've been waiting for. When the inversion event happened, we lost our collective memories to the effects that the magnetic disruption had on our nervous systems. The global seismic destruction destroyed our cities. Crumbling pieces of technology hint at what we once were. All we have are scraps of memories and fragments of documentation. We've been collecting those clues for centuries, with very little to show for our efforts. Even so, we've learned enough to know that the answers we seek are the panacea our world needs. We need to explore every possibility if we hope to see unity."

"You're placing a lot of faith in questionable evidence."

"Isn't the truth important to you?"

Quinto rounded on Fisher. "How can you ask me that, after all I've sacrificed for Enigma? Of course, I want to know the truth!"

"Somewhere in the deep south, an edifice from our past is still standing. It may be the missing piece of the puzzle. This could be key to understanding the incomplete picture we've been examining all of these years. We can't leave it in the hands of Queen Silvanus. She'll try to use it to her advantage, but without knowing its true purpose, she'll end up starting a war."

Quinto leveled a hard stare at his friend. "The fact that Queen Silvanus is hiding something is reason enough to investigate. We don't need some fantastic tale of light beaming into the heavens." Quinto waved his hands in the air and let them drop. "It doesn't matter what I think. This is what we do. It's just that we've followed far too many dead-end leads, based on unreliable testimony, for me to believe that this will be any different."

"When did you become such a pessimist?"

"I'm just being realistic. You're every bit as pragmatic as I am, and as far as intel goes, this is one of the more outrageous things we've heard. Why are you suddenly convinced that this will be any different?"

"It's there, Quinto. It's real, and it calls to the iridomals. If it calls to them, then it's reasonable to believe that the Iridogen are somehow tied to this. You know what this means."

Quinto's jaw dropped. "You're the one who taught me to tread lightly where myth is concerned, and now you invoke it? We have never encountered anything other than oral tradition regarding a special purpose for the Iridogen. We've no documented evidence to verify the claims."

"Yet those claims exist with unwavering consistency. We've heard them from diverse sources in distinct cultures all around the world. When you consider that most other memories are lost to us, how can we ignore the significance? Those stories survived for a reason, and we can't deny that the Iridogen possess unique qualities that set them apart. You've seen it in Valtteri. I'm not saying that we should accept the stories at face value. We need context. Even so, we can't ignore the fact that an ancient structure is responsible for the massing of iridomals. That can't be a coincidence."

"It's more realistic to believe that we'll find partial ruins with a few random iridomal sightings than indisputable evidence to support mythology. This isn't like you, Fisher, why are you so convinced? Who gave you this information?"

"You know I can't tell you that. We're each allowed three contacts. One mentor, one peer, and one initiate. It's a necessary precaution to keep anyone from learning how widespread the organization is. We can only solve the riddle by keeping secrets. It's the paradox of the Enigma Mandate."

"You know how I feel about that, Fisher. The process is too slow. If the navy functioned that way, I'd get nothing done."

"We live in a fractured world, Quinto, with each faction holding on to their secrets. It's only through patient infiltration that we've come this far. We've successfully gathered people of influence who can access those pieces of the puzzle we seek. Every bit of information has the potential to unlock the mysteries of our past. If the world knew of our existence, it would compromise everything we've worked for. Suspicion would drive nations to lock down precious data for generations to come."

"If you can't tell me more, then why are you telling me at all?"

Fisher rose and walked to the portal looking out over the swath.

"Fisher? What aren't you telling me?"

"Orders have come down from the top. They want to bring Valtteri into the fold."

"What? No! Absolutely not. I didn't spend my life protecting that boy so we could put him in danger."

"He's Iridogen, Quinto."

"Here we go with the fables again! Even if the legends were true, it just reinforces my aversion to having Valtteri involved."

"Perhaps they're true, perhaps they're false, or merely allegory. We'll never know for sure until we test the hypothesis. Either way, it will inform how we move forward. The question needs to be answered and we may finally have a means for validation."

"That doesn't explain why we're considering Valtteri. We could recruit others."

"The very few surviving Iridogen of the southern realm live in fear of the prejudices found there. They'd never risk exposing themselves to help us. Valtteri was sheltered from all of that. He doesn't harbour that crippling fear. The Iridogen cultures of the north are insular and would be difficult to petition for help. They're one of the few people groups we've been unable to infiltrate, for obvious reasons. We have no way to find out how many memories they carry. Valtteri stands apart, yet they might accept him as one of their own. For that reason alone, his involvement is worth consideration. Apart from that, Valtteri is the only Iridogen on record having grown up in the swath. He has a worldview that no other Iridogen possesses. He's uniquely qualified, and you know it. Would you choose him for this role if he weren't your son?"

"That's not fair!"

"But it's true. You've had to keep things hidden from him for too long. He's out there now, searching for answers that you could give him."

"What do you expect me to say?"

"You still haven't taken on an initiate. I've proposed to the Chapter Primaries that you should be the one to mentor Valtteri."

"They'd allow this?"

"Not normally, but these are uncommon circumstances. In this case, everyone agrees with you, the regular process is too slow. I know it's risky, but the potential reward is too great to ignore."

Quinto ran his hands through his hair and groaned. "If you expect me to explain this to him properly, I'll need more time."

"Valtteri is an adult, he can accept the truth. At the very least, you should have told him about his Iridogen heritage. I encouraged you to tell him years ago."

"I didn't want him to feel different."

Fisher grunted in disagreement. "You didn't want a foreigner to feel ostracized in a caste system? How did that work out? This was never about Valtteri fitting in. This is about your guilt for failing to protect him from Zayd Ocon."

Quinto hung his head. "I hoped that Zayd would forget about him...."

Fisher placed a comforting hand on his friend's shoulder. "You've been a good father, Quinto. You know that Zayd would've taken Valtteri long ago if it weren't for your efforts. As a result of your care and influence, Valtteri found the strength to weather every storm. Despite his circumstances, he has grown into an incredibly well adjusted, and resilient, young man. You should be proud, not filled with regret. Valtteri is ready to hear the truth... he's discovering it on his own."

"What do you mean?"

"He already knows that he's Iridogen, and some of what that means. He also located the people he lived with before he came into your care."

"He's met his biological parents? I didn't think we knew who they were."

"We don't. These were the people who took Valtteri under their wing as an abandoned infant, and claimed him as their own. They're Swathcombers, and we both know how Swathcombers feel about the Luminaries. Between his discussions with them and revelations provided by his recent travelling companion, who happens to be a tinker, Valtteri has been receiving a very enlightening perspective of his present employer. I doubt you could tell him much that would come as a surprise."

"How is he taking it all?"

"You'd have to ask him yourself, but my sources tell me that his desire to do the right thing is strong. I believe we have you to thank for instilling those values. He's questioning his purpose, but he knows it doesn't align with the Luminaries. He's looking for direction, but doesn't know who he can trust. You can provide what he needs, and we both know that only one source can provide suitable answers for someone as driven as Valtteri. Dangerous though it may be, we need to introduce him to..."

Quinto interrupted, resignation in his voice. "...Enigma."

Fisher nodded. "His path was never going to be an easy or safe one. With Enigma, he'll have the help and resources he needs to survive. He'll have a just cause to fight for, and I think we both know he won't stop looking for a purpose until he finds one. You can give that to him."

Quinto offered a sigh of surrender. "I guess I have little choice. Tell the Chapter Primaries that I'll accept Valtteri as my initiate. When do we begin?"

"Valtteri will be out of touch for a while. When he surfaces again, we'll do everything we can to help him return to you. I don't know how that will look, you might have to improvise."

"Because our methods of communication are too slow?"

Fisher smiled, and shrugged. "I suspect that some of our practices will begin to change in the very near future."

Chapter 27

Valtteri stopped to catch his breath, clinging to the tree as though his life depended on it, which it did. He'd quickly learned the importance of placing a piton and securing his tether. Twice, he had miscalculated a jump and found himself hurtling skyward in a state of panic. Each time, the tether attached to his harness brought him to a sudden stop.

Tallow was always there to reel him in, something Valtteri was still learning to do on his own. Tallow shrugged it off and insisted it was nothing to be ashamed of. Even the most seasoned scouts fell victim to freerise on occasion.

"On occasion." Valtteri muttered, not at all comforted by Tallow's encouraging words. He took a moment to observe Tallow's progress, searching for tips to improve his own efforts. He needed to learn quickly. The tether tribe scout was moving slower than normal to accommodate his inexperienced travelling companion. Valtteri was determined to prove he could keep pace.

Watching Tallow move through the forest was like watching a river run. He revealed no hesitation as he moved from tree to tree, simply flowing around obstacles like water over a rock. When he landed at his target, the tree barely trembled upon his arrival. Tallow embedded pitons with a single stroke, never interrupting his preparation for the next jump. By comparison, Valtteri's tree shaking impacts sent birds screeching from their perch. He needed to do better if they hoped to stealthily creek up on their quarry. He checked his own recently placed piton for the third time, a piton that took three strokes to secure. Valtteri shook his head in dismay as he noticed Tallow looking back and waiting.

Two jumps later, he was placing a piton in a tree within arm's reach of Tallow.

"You're getting better at choosing your targets," Tallow observed. "We'll rest here for a while."

"I'm fine," Valtteri insisted, "we can keep moving."

"Our lives depend on our limbs when travelling in this manner. Endurance means little if muscles are too weak to do what they must in an emergency. An exhausted tribesman doesn't just fall to the ground in the swath. It's best to rest frequently." Tallow shortened his tether and shifted weight to his spurs so he could free his arms. Rummaging through his pack, he found some jerky and handed it to Valtteri. "Eat this; we need to keep up our strength."

Valtteri sniffed the offering. "What is this?"

Tallow nodded at the creatures running along branches in the canopy.

Valtteri frowned and took a tentative bite, chewing the tough meat for longer than he'd have expected before swallowing. "Not bad."

Tallow laughed. "You're a terrible liar. I know it's not very appetizing, but it keeps well, and expands in your stomach. It will provide energy for hours. Don't worry, you'll get used to it."

Tallow took a bite of his own, and chewed thoughtfully. "You know, I've been considering my future outside of the swath. Maybe I could open a restaurant featuring authentic tether tribe food."

Caught mid-swallow, Valtteri almost choked in response before noticing the big grin on Tallow's face. He shook his head and smothered a chuckle before deadpanning. "I think that's a great idea. I can picture the sign above the door. The Tallow Grill. Don't worry, you'll get used to it."

Tallow burst into laughter. "Sicily would like that one."

They chewed in companionable silence while Tallow gazed at the treetops. He had a look of confusion on his face.

"Is something troubling you?"

Tallow pointed at the commotion above them. "I've never seen so many in one place before. It's like they're following us. They don't normally act this way."

"I'm afraid that's my fault."

"Is that more Tellusan humour? I don't always understand the nuances."

"No, I'm serious. The iridomals follow me. I have some kind of connection with them that I don't understand."

"Iridomals?"

"Yeah, Iridogen of the animal kingdom, you know?"

"I'm not familiar with that term.

"You've never heard of the Iridogen?"

"Should I have?"

"Huh, I guess the tether tribes are more isolated than I thought. I can't tell you how relieved I am to learn that places still exist where a stranger can accept me for who I am as a person. Most people judge me by my genetic heritage."

"I'm still not following."

"Have you noticed anything peculiar about the creatures following us?"

"Well, they don't seem as afraid of us as they should be. Something else seems off, but I can't quite put my finger on what that might be."

"Hold very still for a moment, and let's see if they come closer. If one of them draws near, take a look at its eyes."

The two of them remained immobile until a few brave creatures came closer. Tallow gasped, and the iridomals scurried away. "Their eyes! I've never seen anything like that. At least, I don't think I have...." Tallow looked to Valtteri for an explanation, and gasped for a second time as the Tellusan removed his tinted monocle in answer.

"You're the same."

"I'd like to believe I'm more intelligent than our little friends up there," Valtteri laughed, "but yes, we share some of the same genetic makeup."

"That's..."

"Really weird, I know.

"So you don't really need the eye covering?"

"No, it's a disguise. I don't really want to get into the details right now. Let's just say the Iridogen aren't very popular in many parts of the world."

"The tether tribes have never heard of Iridogen. You won't need your disguise here, leave it off. You'll find it much easier to pace me with a full range of vision."

"I'm sorry, I should have mentioned all of this sooner. The eyepiece has become part of who I am, and sometimes I forget it's there. As for the iridomals... I generally don't share that information. Who'd believe me?"

Valtteri followed Tallow's gaze as it returned to the treetops. "I'm still having trouble accepting it. I don't know why they follow me. We seem to share some kind of synchronization. I don't have a clue how that works. Watch."

Valtteri moved away in a zigzag pattern. The iridomals matched his movements and followed him back as he returned. Tallow shook his head in amazement, and then in dismay. "This is going to make it very easy to supplement our food supply, and very difficult to conduct any kind of reconnaissance."

"They've served as a distraction in the past, and even as an early warning system."

"That display certainly is distracting, but tree-dwelling creatures don't naturally congregate like that in the swath. Resources are limited to the narrow green spaces and life tends to spread out. Seeing so many animals in one place is suspicious. Can you make them go away?"

Valtteri shook his head. "I don't think I can directly control them. I have noticed that they will leave if I enter places that make them uncomfortable, or remain stationary for too long. Eventually I gather new followers once I start moving again."

Tallow said nothing as he considered their surroundings. "We're seeking tribesmen. No offence intended, but they'll see you coming from a mile away, with or without your iridomal escort. I've been contemplating possible solutions, and I keep returning to one in particular. Can you swim?"

Valtteri glanced at the river. Travelling upside-down as they were, it was above his head from their current perspective in the reverse gravity. "You want us to swim? Can we do that in the swath?"

"Gravity is normal below the surface. So yes, you can swim if you're careful to keep the majority of your body submerged. You'd need to swim underwater, and employ a great deal of caution when coming up for air. It's not something we risk very often. However, it's possible to navigate along the shoreline. Just cling to roots that break through the riverbank. You can return to the trees by those same roots."

"Won't that be too slow?"

"It's something to consider. For the moment, I'd just like to see what happens to our iridomal friends if you travel underwater for a distance."

Valtteri nodded in understanding. "I'd be willing to give it a try. How do I do this?"

"Find an exposed root and use your claws and spurs to pull yourself into the water. Tie your tether to a root, and use the roots to pull yourself along the riverbank while remaining underwater. When you need some air, bring your head up between the roots so you remain hidden from sight. I'd like to see how far you have to travel before your furry friends lose interest. When that happens, I'll give your tether a tug and untie it so you can gather it up. You can keep your head out of the water at that point, but wait for me before you try to leave the river. Slap the water every few minutes so I can find you and I'll join you at your new location."

Valtteri followed instructions and slipped into the cool water. It was a welcome reprieve from the heat of the day. It didn't take long to establish a rhythm. The roots were plentiful, and he had no difficulty finding purchase to pull himself along underwater. Numerous gaps appeared where he could lift his head clear of the surface. The exposed roots and boles of trees that crowded the river banks kept him hidden. He came up for air five times before he felt a tug at his tether. Valtteri surfaced, and anchored himself by wrapping his legs around some roots. By the time he finished gathering his tether, Tallow had arrived and was appraising him with a lifted brow.

"Oh! Sorry... I forgot to slap the water."

Tallow rolled his eyes. "When I suggested slapping the water every once in a while, I was imagining something natural sounding, like water lapping the shoreline. What I heard was more like an animal in its death throes, thrashing among the roots. Next time, wind the rope under the surface quietly. "

Valtteri felt his face heating, but chose to ignore the jab. "Did it work?"

"Yes, it did. When you disappeared, the iridomals began scurrying about as if they were trying to find you. They seemed confused. I suspect they could sense you somehow, but without any visual cues, they didn't know how to respond. Shortly after that, they went about their business. Very peculiar."

"So does this give you any ideas?"

"I'm thinking that when we set up camp at the end of each day, I should scout ahead. That way, if I come across anything, we have time to slip away from the iridomals before carrying on."

Valtteri winced. They both knew his lack of stealth put them at risk. Tallow was just making the best of an imperfect situation. Valtteri needed to witness what was happening firsthand, and he couldn't hope to do so without Tallow's help. Valtteri's connection to the iridomals was a serious handicap for Tallow as they entered a potentially hostile situation. Neither of them had a choice, they both needed evidence to effect change. Valtteri felt guilty for not having prepared Tallow for the possibility. Adis once told him that Iridogen didn't live in the Tropos Archipelago, so Valtteri hadn't really expected to find iridomals in the swath. That was a foolish assumption, and now they had to deal with an unexpected complication. Tallow could have refused to continue, but he handled it gracefully, and Valtteri was grateful.

* * *

They were into the third week of their new routine. Tallow had left to scout ahead while Valtteri set up camp. He had just tethered the cook stove when Tallow suddenly reappeared, breathing heavily.

"Good, I'm glad I caught you before you made a fire. Pack up, we'll be laying low tonight."

"You found something?"

"I spotted a sky lift approximately a day's travel from here."

"I thought you said sky lifts are located near tether tribe communities."

"They usually are. I've never heard of one this far inland. It could be legitimate. Tribes are widely dispersed, and I've only met a few. This may be good news. Part of my mission is to find new tribes and warn them about the Luminaries. If we're lucky, that's what we'll find, and they may have helpful information to share."

"You don't look convinced."

Tallow sighed. "We know the renegades came from this direction. This could just as easily be their campsite."

"Then we've found them. That's good!"

"If this is the renegade campsite, and they have direct access to a sky lift, then things are worse than we thought. The Luminaries only place lifts at high priority locations. If this is what we're looking for, they'll be well supplied, likely with Luminary weapons.”

"What, exactly, is a sky lift anyway?" Valtteri asked. "I mean, I get that it's some kind of elevator, but I've never heard of the navy using one."

"I can't tell you much about the history. Adis told me that it's a mining technology produced by Sept Stol, strictly Luminary tech. I don't think it's widely used, and I doubt they'd lease it to the navy. I'm not sure what the navy would even need it for."

Interesting, Valtteri thought. *Sept Stol is a close ally of Sept Ocon. I wonder how much they know about Zayd Ocon's plans?* "I know that Sept Stol is still involved in mining and gathering, but I assumed that was mostly on the mountain ranges. I never imagined they'd try to harvest from the surface. That's a long haul."

"I'm sure it's not the preferred method, but some things you can only find at lower elevations. The Vigil who dealt with our tribe always told us that moving and operating a sky lift was labour-intensive and an expensive endeavour. I could best describe it as a heavy-duty tether anchored to the surface and suspended from a buoy. As for why you've never seen one, apparently they're really difficult to spot from on high. Locating one would require coordinates, and the buoys are placed well below the plane of equilibrium. The chance of stumbling across one by chance is slim. Sky lifts aren't of much use without ships anchored to them. The mass of the vessel pulls the tether taut allowing it to support an equal mass of material lifted from the surface. Over the years, I've loaded a lot of peat onto lift platforms." Tallow shook his head. "That's one thing about my old life that I don't miss at all. I'd hoped I would never see a sky lift again."

"Unfortunately, we need to check it out."

"Agreed. We'll know more tomorrow. The approach will be slow, it's going to be a long day. We should get some sleep."

The two men shared a simple meal of cheese and dry bread, choosing to eat in silence. Caught up in thoughts of what the morning would bring, they settled in for the night with a subdued nod of agreement.

Valtteri tied himself to a sturdy limb and listened to the wind blowing through the treetops. His search for truth had led him here. He knew, deep down, that whatever they discovered would change his life forever. Eventually, he fell into a fitful sleep filled with equal parts anticipation and dread.

Chapter 28

Nixon mumbled with irritation as he waited for an audience with his uncle. It galled him that he had to show deference like some Lagan worker. He would be in charge one day, but his uncle treated him with no more respect than a coal porter. Nixon had returned three days ago, and only now was he finally ushered into his uncle's presence. He sat on his hands, waiting as the wise Luminary Ocon completed some mundane function of municipal insignificance.

He was so caught up in his indignation that the voice of Zayd's assistant startled him.

"Luminary Ocon will see you now."

"It's about time!"

The lackey lifted a judgmental eyebrow and Nixon shouldered him as he passed by. Things would be different when he was in charge. He flung open the office doors and strode inside, umbrage colouring his countenance.

"Why have you kept me waiting?"

"That's a little dramatic, don't you think?" Zayd peered past Nixon's shoulder and nodded to his frowning assistant who promptly closed the office doors.

"I don't have time for this!"

"And yet, your time is mine to command. Sit down."

"I'd rather stand."

"I said, sit down!"

Nixon glowered, but took a seat.

"I know you chafe at my authority, but until you prove yourself capable of self-control, you're not ready to fill my shoes."

Considering Zayd had created their current predicament, Nixon wanted to throttle the man. That wouldn't serve his purpose at the moment, so he held his temper.

"That's better. Now tell me what was so important that you've been harassing my assistant for the past few days."

Nixon stared in disbelief. "Have you forgotten the task you gave me?"

"Of course not. How is our latest operative doing?"

"Uncle, I've repeatedly warned you that we can't trust Valtteri Knox."

"Don't be ridiculous. He knows his life is forfeit if he ever double-crosses me. He'll be a valuable asset one day, and I have plans to deploy him among the Tellusans."

"How can you be so blind? He has no loyalty to Sept Ocon!"

"Nonsense, he owes me his life. I've supported and provided for him. He was a foreign foundling, yet I've granted him a standing among the Lamina caste. I have no reason to doubt the sincerity of his service. He has been a model citizen, excelling at the tasks I give him, which is more than I can say for you."

"You don't know him like I do!"

"When are you going to set aside your petty rivalry? You're destined to lead, and he's destined to follow. Grow up and stop wasting my time with your obsessive jealousy."

"Wasting your... do you want to hear my report on the activities of your innocent operative?"

"Oh do tell, what grievous error has the lad made in the remote borderlands where I sent him? Let me guess. He spent some time in the tavern and slept late into the day instead of submitting a report?"

Nixon bit back his response. Arguing with his uncle was pointless. He had to make him see the truth. "According to your orders, Knox was supposed to complete his final naval training with the friaers before continuing on to Endelton, correct?"

"That is correct. His first mission was a simple one, interview the locals at Endelton and report back."

"Did you request any special training from the friaers?"

"No, just the standard instruction given to all navy recruits. You know that my operatives handle all other training."

"Then perhaps you could explain why the friaers singled out Valtteri for one-on-one training?"

"What do you mean?"

"His training took place apart from the other recruits. No one saw him the entire time we were at Pax Montis."

"That's peculiar, but if no one saw him, then how do you know he was receiving special training?"

"I'll get back to that in a moment. After leaving the friaerie, operative Admot took over Valtteri's training and explained our security protocols. I suggest you change those protocols, by the way. The training didn't take long and Admont departed. Left to his own devices, Knox spent an increasing amount of time with a tinker."

"That's to be expected," Zayd interrupted, "all of our operatives have accounts with the Tinkers Guild. Besides, a tinker escort is the only practical option for travel to Endelton."

Nixon snorted, "*I* managed to find an alternative escort, but that's not the point. I overheard Knox making arrangements to travel to a different destination before moving on to Endelton. I decided to discourage his extracurricular activities. I hired twenty mercenaries to pose as bandits along the way, just to frighten him, you understand."

"I forbade you from putting yourself at risk! You were told not to engage directly with anyone in the southern realm."

"I was in disguise, and working through intermediaries." Nixon lied.

Zayd settled back into his chair and motioned for Nixon to continue.

"As I was saying, I sent a company of mercenaries large enough to overcome a tinker, leaving no recourse but to flee. I thought if Knox were to learn how dangerous travel could be, he'd avoid unnecessary detours and stick to his mission."

"And the result of your ploy?"

"The entire company of mercenaries perished."

Zayd leaned forward in his seat, fully engaged. "I knew that tinkers were formidable fighters, but twenty men?"

"I witnessed part of the battle. The tinker didn't fight alone. Knox fought at his side. They moved together, like men who had done so many times before. Uncle... Valtteri knows Invicta Manus."

"That's not possible. Like you, he's only been to Pax Montis on three occasions as part of his naval training. It would take years to master Invicta Manus."

"I thought the same, and yet, it's true. Knox dispatched trained mercenaries with the same ease as the tinker. They moved alike. I'm not misinterpreting what I saw. On how many other occasions, over the course of his life, did Knox receive private instruction from the friaers? Invicta Manus is taught only to friaers and tinkers. Explain it to me, Uncle. How is it that Valtteri Knox was granted such training, unless he's in league with one or the other?"

"I have no explanation, unless... could Admiral Soren have arranged such a thing? He has become an irritant of late. I'll do some digging. Continue with your report."

"I followed Knox for some time. When he switched paths, my escorts identified his destination. The trail led to a remote village called Swiftwater. We took a route less travelled to beat him there. I thought I'd try to deter him once more. This time, I hired some local thugs,

Swathcombers who had set up shop there. I told them that Knox was a Luminary operative, knowing how Swathcombers despise the founding families. They were told to question him about his contacts. I hoped Knox would reveal something that could explain his activities. The Swathcombers were warned that he was dangerous, but they didn't seem concerned. I have to say, I was surprised when they employed a net to capture him instead of confronting him directly."

"Swathcombers have no honour."

"Indeed. They happily accepted payment in advance, but ended up helping him instead of doing what I paid them to do. When confronted later, they claimed that the contract was negotiated under false pretenses. They said that the Knox family doesn't harm their own."

Zayd bolted from his chair. "The Swathcombers claimed their family name was Knox? They knew Valtteri?"

"It appears that way. I don't believe it was a coincidence that Valtteri travelled to Swiftwater. Apparently, you don't know Knox as well as you think you do," Nixon smirked. "It looks like he has connections with tinkers, friaers, and also Swathcombers."

"How can this be? Why didn't you tell me sooner?"

"I've been trying to tell you, for the last three days, but you had better things to do."

"Watch your tone, boy!"

"Enough!" Nixon barked back. "I'm not a child. I've been warning you about Knox for years, but you refuse to listen."

Zayd lifted his hands in surrender. "It appears that I've underestimated Valtteri Knox, and you as well. Your report has been very thorough, and you've given me a lot to think about."

"I'm not finished."

Zayd's temper flared at the presumption of his nephew. He took a deep breath before he ground out the words. "You're trying my patience, but I'm listening."

"Would it surprise you to learn that a community of tether

tribesmen live near Swiftwater?"

"Outside of the swath? Impossible! I had them destr —." Zayd caught himself before he finished his sentence.

Nixon chuckled. "I saw the aftermath of one of your bombings, Uncle. Very impressive. Unfortunately, you missed the target by a ridiculously large margin. Don't worry, your poorly kept secret is safe with me."

Zayd muttered something about incompetent help before speaking again. "I don't suppose you collected proper coordinates for this encampment?"

Nixon handed a slip of paper to his uncle. "It's here, but I'm not sure it would be politically wise to make a second bombing attempt. Besides, you have bigger problems."

Zayd sighed and slumped in his chair. "You have more to report?"

"When Knox arrived in Endelton, he met up with a tether tribesman who took him into the swath. Whatever secret you're trying to hide is about to be exposed. If we don't stop him, I imagine friaers, Swathcombers, tinkers, and maybe others, will soon know your plans."

The blood ran from Zayd's face. "No," he whispered, "I'm so close."

"I can help you, Uncle! Tell me what this plan is. I'm on your side. Together, we can fix this."

"I can't risk that. If my plans fall through, the heir apparent must be above suspicion. I need to ensure that you can step into my role without opposition. Sept Ocon must retain power at all costs."

"I'll be at greater risk if I don't know what I'm dealing with. You need to tell me what I'm getting into."

"I'm nearing the final phase of my plan. You'll know soon enough. Right now, we need to deal with Valtteri. I can accelerate my schedule, but I need a little more time. I want you to hunt him down."

"You can count on me. My sources are already searching."

Zayd raised a questioning brow. "You have informants?"

"It's what you taught me to do, Uncle."

Zayd gave his nephew a look of suspicion. "I really *have* underestimated you."

"Trust me, Uncle. I only serve the interests of our Sept."

Zayd called out to his assistant who responded immediately. Nixon eyed the man suspiciously, wondering if he had been listening at the door.

"Write this down." Zayd ordered. "I want you to send an archipelago-wide notice with the following message. Valtteri Knox, an operative for Sept Ocon, has been found guilty of treason. By Luminary agreement, an operative who discloses sept secrets will be refused amnesty or support from any tropostate of the archipelago. A bounty is in effect for the capture of Valtteri Knox, wanted alive. Anyone with information as to his whereabouts should immediately contact the Luminary Navy outpost in their district."

Zayd's assistant scribbled furiously.

"Did you get all of that?"

"Yes, Luminary Ocon."

"I want that distributed within the hour."

"I'll attend to it immediately, Sir."

The assistant rushed out, closing the door behind him.

"Do you trust that man?" Nixon wondered aloud.

"Not really," his uncle replied, "but that can be useful."

Zayd rubbed his temples and paused to look up at his nephew. "I'm going to be very busy for the next little while and I don't have anyone else I can trust. I need you to take care of this personally. I'll have all operatives report directly to you. You wanted to prove yourself. Here's your chance. Don't mess it up."

Chapter 29

Progress had been slow. Tallow would move well ahead and wave when he deemed it was safe for Valtteri to make his noisier approach. Eventually, they came to a stop, when Tallow spotted two sentries on either side of the river. The sentries were chatting and laughing, making no attempt to conceal their presence. Tallow expressed his disapproval at their lack of diligence, but it confirmed they had found the renegades. All reports suggested they were a tribe of bullies who considered themselves untouchable.

"What do you think?"

"I think they're intoxicated. The rumours of the vigil controlling them with an addictive substance must be true."

"That could work to our advantage."

Tallow glanced at his claws and then back at the sentries. "They carry Luminary long-range weapons. If we're spotted, they'll cut us down before we get close."

"If they're intoxicated, they may have difficulty aiming those things."

"Do you want to test that theory?"

"Not really. What do you propose?"

Tallow looked to the canopy and smiled at the iridomals who had gathered once more. "Perhaps a slight modification to our strategy. We'll both enter the water, one on either side of the river. We can tether to each other, rather than the roots. It's not as safe, but we'll have to make do, and we'll need to keep moving."

"I don't know…. We'll be in very close proximity to the sentries when we pass."

"It's a risk, but I can't see any other way. They chose the location well. The tree stand is sparse on either side of the river at this point. We can't pass overland without the sentries noticing. By taking the river, we have the option of submerging if we're spotted. It will be more difficult for them to target us in the water."

"It will also be harder for us to move quickly if we're discovered."

"I'm hoping your entourage can provide a distraction. You said they've done it before?"

"I also said I don't control them."

"I don't think you'll have to. Originally, I was worried the iridomals would give away our approach, but what would happen if we entered the river here and made our way towards the sentries *without* hiding from the iridomals?"

Valtteri grinned, "The commotion in the canopy would have the sentries looking to the treetops instead of the river! I'll just need to surface often enough that the iridomals can keep track of me. That could work."

"When we reach the sentries, you'll need to disappear so the iridomals stay put until we're far from the area. How long can you hold your breath?"

"Long enough to find a place to slip between the roots before I need to surface. I'll make sure the iridomals don't see me."

Tallow nodded, and tied a tether between their harnesses. He slipped into the river, crossing to the other side.

"I guess we're leaving immediately." Valtteri muttered, as he followed Tallow into the water.

It took a few tries to determine how long it would take the iridomals to relocate Valtteri whenever he surfaced. He found a rhythm long before they were within earshot of the sentries. Now came the difficult part. He needed to remain hidden from the sentries without losing their furry procession.

As they drew near, he became acutely aware of the sentries' weapons. He had trained with something similar and was familiar with their power and accuracy. If the sentries targeted them, the water wouldn't offer any protection. He hadn't had the heart to share that detail with Tallow. This was their best tactic, and it had a good chance of succeeding.

Tallow slipped below the surface across the stream. Valtteri took a deep breath, preparing to submerge as well. They were about to move directly past the sentries. This was the point where they were most vulnerable. He could feel his heart pounding with tension. Something in the water brushed against his hand, startling him. His hand jerked in reaction, losing its grip on the root he was holding. Valtteri lost his balance, splashing as he tried to regain purchase. His fear spiked as the heads of the sentries began to swivel in his direction. *They're going to see me*. Time seemed to slow in that moment of panic. The iridomals went crazy.

The canopy filled with a cacophony of piercing screeches, grabbing the attention of the sentries. They suddenly found themselves surrounded by an army of angry tree dwellers who lunged at the renegade tribesmen, baring their teeth and dropping cones. The sentries swatted at their attackers and fired blindly into the treetops, further enraging the creatures. Valtteri watched in awe until he felt a tug on his tether and came to his senses. He quickly submerged and moved away from the excitement, careful to keep himself from view.

They followed the river for much longer than Valtteri would've thought necessary, before Tallow finally signalled that they could return to the trees. Valtteri pulled his adrenaline fatigued body up the nearest tree, secured himself, and let his body go limp. Tallow tethered himself to a nearby tree of his own.

"I thought you said that you couldn't control them."

"As far as I know, I can't."

"Then what happened back there? They clearly came to your aid. Are iridomals more intelligent than other animals?"

"I don't believe so. Something similar happened on another occasion when I thought I was about to die. The nearby creatures reacted as if they were threatened. I don't know how to trigger that response. I've been in danger at other times, and the iridomals didn't react at all."

"Huh. Well, they certainly saved our skins this time around. That was both inspiring and disturbing, at the same time. It's going to be more difficult for me to eat jerky in the future."

"Will we encounter more sentries?"

"I doubt it. What we saw was a typical tether tribe protocol. Everyone else will be at work or at the campsite. Those two will have a story to tell, but they have no reason to leave their post. We can expect a shift change by nightfall which means we need to move quickly. Are you rested enough?"

"I'd like to be far from here. Let's go."

* * *

Valtteri did his best to compensate for the swaying of the tree as he studied the scene through his telescope. They were at the treeline, and as close to the treetops as they dared.

"That sky lift is at least an hour from here." Tallow noted. "Usually they're closer to the treeline."

A surface tether ran between the treeline and the base of the sky lift, with anchors spaced evenly between. Nobody travelled it at the moment, but Valtteri noticed a few tribesmen stationed at the sky lift and more activity beyond. "The surface tether continues for an equal distance on the other side of the lift. There seems to be a lot of movement at the far end. Do you think that could be the renegade campsite?"

"A tribesman wouldn't choose to camp in the arid part of the swath.

It would be far too difficult to access water.

"I see something that looks like a water tank."

"Still, why go to all that effort? Maybe they're protecting something valuable?"

"Or something they want to keep hidden. This has all the earmarks of Luminary activity."

Tallow huffed in agreement. "From what we've seen so far, these renegades are a lazy bunch. If they're out that far, it's not because of their industrious nature."

"This must be what Zayd has been covering up. I wonder what's out there. It's too far away for my scope. We need to get closer."

"And how do you propose we do that? If we're seen anywhere along that surface tether, we'll be trapped."

"Wouldn't they just assume we were the sentries?"

"Perhaps, but then they'd wonder what kind of emergency would cause them to leave their post. At some point, they'd get suspicious."

"We only need to get to the lift. We should be close enough to use the scope at that range. I only see two men guarding it."

"Two men with long-range weapons!" Tallow protested.

Valtteri lifted the scope to his eye for a second look. "They don't appear to have scopes of their own." Valterri wiped clay from the riverbank off his hand and had a thought. "This clay is a similar colour to the sand. If we coat ourselves with it, we might blend in. I don't think they'd even notice us until we were almost upon them. They seem to be sticking to the shady side of the lift. In a few hours, that patch of shade will be on the opposite side of the lift from our approach. If we time things right, they won't even be looking in this direction."

"That's a lot of ifs...."

"Do you want to turn back?"

"I'm not saying that, but it will be at least a three-hour return trip. Anything could happen during that time. Someone could travel the line from either direction, and we'd be stuck in the middle with nowhere to flee. We need an escape strategy if we're going to attempt this."

Valtteri thought in silence for a moment. "Do you see the spacing of the surface tether anchors? The range of their weapons is approximately the distance between two of those anchors. If we can keep two anchors distance between any pursuers, we should be safe. That gives us a bit of breathing room to turn around and head back if we're spotted. If we get within two anchors of the lift, I'm sure we can cover the remaining distance quickly. It's a small risk."

"And if we make it to the lift?"

"We incapacitate the two renegades and cut the tether leading beyond the lift. That will ensure that the bulk of them can't get to us."

"You make it sound like incapacitating two tether tribesmen will be an easy task."

"Trust me, once we're on the underside of that platform where I have a solid footing, I can take care of two men. We only have to worry about the sentries by the river. If they block our return, we'll have a problem. We'll need to deal with them sooner or later, but I hope to have some confiscated weapons before we face them again. Besides, you said yourself that they won't leave their post until nightfall."

Tallow made some quick calculations. "That gives us about six hours. If we're going to do this, it has to be now."

"You don't sound convinced."

"I'm not, but you're right. We came all this way to find evidence, and they're not expecting us. We may not get a better chance."

* * *

After a quick trip to the river to fill their water skins and apply some clay, they were on their way. During the first half of their journey, the heat from the sun forced them to take regular water breaks. At the halfway point, a bit of cloud cover moved in, providing some relief. They moved more quickly in the cooler temperature and successfully traversed the distance to the second anchor from the lift. They paused to catch their breath while Valtteri pulled out his scope.

"They haven't moved. I think they're taking a nap!"

"Let me see."

Valtteri handed the scope to Tallow. "What do you think?"

"I think you're right, and I'm tired of feeling like a target pigeon on a tether, keep going."

Nervous energy had Valtteri feeling like a coiled spring by the time they reached the sky lift. He fully expected one of the tribesmen to wake up and confront them before they arrived. Thankfully, that moment never came.

The surface tether was attached to an anchor stone at the base of the sky lift. The two tribesmen guarding the lift were hidden from view on the other side. Valtteri and Tallow quietly set their feet on the mesh underside of the lift platform and disengaged from the surface tether.

Valtteri's confidence increased dramatically with the solid footing. He circled to the right of the anchor stone, envisioning hand-to-hand attack strategies. Tallow pulled a bamboo baton from his harness and moved to the left. They needn't have bothered. The two renegades weren't just taking a nap, they had passed out, even more intoxicated than their counterparts at the river.

"That was a little anticlimactic."

Tallow snorted in disgust. "You take care of cutting the tether, I'll tie these two up."

Valtteri moved towards the tether and stopped short. "I think we have a problem. I can't cut the tether."

"Don't tell me you forgot your knife." Tallow finished his last knot and moved to Valtteri's side. "Here, you can use mine."

"Thanks, but I don't think that's going to work."

Tallow looked at the ground tether in dismay. "What kind of loads are they toting that would require a steel cable? Never mind, we'll soon know. What do you see?"

Valtteri steadied his scope on the platform railing and focussed on the activity at the far end of the cable. He gasped at what he saw. Row upon row of explosive mines were anchored to the ground and interconnected with a complicated system of release wires. They were painted in a sand-coloured camouflage pattern, rendering them almost invisible from a distance. "For what possible reason would they place so many explosives in this remote location?" He whispered.

"Valtteri? Why is that site sitting in shadow?"

"It's just the cloud cover."

"The cloud cover cleared ten minutes ago."

Valtteri turned his scope to the sky and felt his blood run cold. "They're going to bomb a tropostate!"

"What are you talking about?"

"That minefield is directly below a tropostate!" Valtteri pointed skyward. "If they release those mines, they'll strike shroudside and thousands of innocent people will die!"

"Why would the Luminaries strike one of their own tropostates?"

"I don't know, but we have to get back. We have to warn them."

Tallow's face paled. "That's going to be more difficult than we'd hoped."

Valtteri turned to look where Tallow was gesturing. Someone had fired a flare from the treeline. In response, tribesmen were flowing from the minefield like angry bees. Several were already moving along the ground tether towards the sky lift.

Valtteri quickly considered their options. They could cut the tether to the treeline and prevent the two sentries coming to the lift, but that was their exit and they'd have to confront the larger force coming from the other direction. They were trapped, and the weapons they'd expropriated seemed woefully insufficient. He cast about the platform for anything useful and spotted an emergency symbol on one of the equipment lockers. Valtteri rummaged through the contents. It was typical emergency gear — a drogue chute, thrust canister, signalling mirror, thermal tarp, and a tote pack with food and water rations.

Valtteri found several leather loading slings clipped to the platform. He grabbed two and waved Tallow to his side. He attached the drogue chute to the tribesman's harness and clipped the food pack to his belt. The signal mirror was shoved into one of Valtteri's pockets. He clipped the thrust canister and tarp to his harness.

"What do you want me to do with this stuff?"

"Ditch the weapon, Tallow, we're leaving."

"How? We have nowhere to go."

"That's not true. We can go up the cable."

"Are you insane?"

"It's okay, every navy officer practices emergency freerise evacuation."

"The navy practises this from the surface?"

"Well, no … not from the surface. Ships seldom travel beyond 2,000 feet of zero-strat, but the procedure is the same."

"Do you know anyone who survived freerise from the surface?"

"As a matter of fact, I do. I made the journey when I was five. I don't recommend it."

"That's a story you'll have to tell me someday." Tallow shook his head. "I don't think I can do this."

"Look, I'm not going to lie. This may be a fatal move, but if we stay here, we *will* die. I trusted you in your element. Will you trust me in mine?"

Tallow's eyes were wide with apprehension as he nodded.

Valtteri unfurled the chute connected to Tallow's harness. "Okay, we only have one drogue chute. It's going to add drag to slow our ascent, but it can only slow us a bit, and they didn't design these chutes for two people. We'll remain tethered together, but I'll be moving faster and ahead of you. We need to slow ourselves to compensate for the lack of a second chute. I hope the sky lift tether can help us with that. We'll let the cable slide between our spurs and claws. Keep your foot spurs on the cable and use the claws of one gauntlet to hold yourself away from the cable."

"How do we keep from flying free of the cable?"

Valtteri looped a leather sling around the sky lift cable and grabbed the rings with his free hand. "We're going to try and use the leather strap like a brake. It won't stop us, but if we can slow our ascent even a little bit more, it will lessen the impact."

Tallow's eyebrows rose higher. "Impact?"

"We'll reach the end of the tether and hit the buoy at high speed. If you see it coming, try to let go just before we hit. You'll see me disappear first, so that will be your cue. Realistically, I don't know if we'll have time to register all of that before it happens. Either way, we'll be torn free. While we're rising, you need to maintain your grip on the cable. Try to ignore what's happening around you. Hang on for dear life, and don't let go." Valtteri moved further up the cable until the tether joining them was taut.

Tallow looped the second strap around the cable and mimicked Valtteri's pose. "What happens after we reach the top?"

"Our momentum will carry us past zero-strat. We'll bounce above and below it, several times, until we come to rest at zero-strat."

"Zero-strat?"

"Sorry, that's what the navy calls the plane of equilibrium. Are you ready?"

"No, I'm terrified. The elders trained us to avoid this exact scenario, and freerise is the method of execution used against my people. You're asking me to ignore every instinct screaming within me."

"The renegades are nearing weapons range...."

Tallow let out a visceral roar and loosened tension on the sling, just enough to begin freerise. Valtteri quickly relaxed his sling as well, and the rapid ascent began. He watched as the jerk of the drogue chute almost pulled Tallow free when it expanded, but Tallow clung to the brake strap with the tenacity that kept him alive as a scout travelling among the trees. Valtteri turned his attention back to his own battle. Fear and fatigue consumed him. *It's happening again.* He wondered if the swath would claim him this time.

The wind of motion howled and buffeted, threatening to rip Valtteri free. Memories of his childhood experience came roaring back, but this time he saw daylight rather than darkness, and Valtteri wasn't a child any longer. This time, he knew what was happening, and he could see where he was going. The cable rushed past in a blur. They were quickly approaching the buoy. Valtteri tightened his leather strap, hoping to brake a little more. He yelled for Tallow to do the same. The words were ripped from his mouth, and he didn't know if Tallow heard them. A second later, the strap was torn from his numb fingers, and he had nothing left to do but pray.

The tether connecting Valtteri to Tallow gave a sharp tug each time they were dragged back towards zero-strat. After five passes, they levelled off and Valtteri pulled Tallow to his side.

Tallow was shivering uncontrollably. He'd never experienced the frigid temperatures of high altitude. "Let's n-never d-do th-that again."

"The first time was enough, twice was pushing my luck." Valtteri took out the thermal tarp and wrapped it around their shoulders. "Here, eat these rations. You need food to generate heat. That jerky you love so much may fill your belly, but it doesn't have the calories you need to survive up here."

Tallow took a bite and made a face.

Valtteri laughed. "You get used to it."

"Now what?"

"The sky lift was near a tropostate. We can see it in the distance." Valtteri pulled out the thrust canister and aimed the nozzle. They began to drift slowly towards the tropostate as the contents vented, and then it fizzled out.

"That's it? We hardly moved at all!"

Valtteri shrugged. "Zero-strat offers very little resistance. You may not feel it, but we're still slowly drifting towards our destination. As long as we don't encounter any headwinds, we'll eventually reach the tropostate.”

“And if we *do* run into a headwind?”

“Then we trust that someone finds us before we’re blown across the limen and plummet to our death.”

“Seriously? You give me a little nugget of hope to cling to, and then you throw headwinds into the mix?”

“You asked.”

“I asked for a contingency plan from your navy playbook.”

“Oh, that.” Valtteri handed his telescope to Tallow. “The workers on the shroudside of a tropostate have a system for situations like this. The perimeter of a tropostate has monitoring stations scanning the horizon for distress signals. Occasionally, a worker drifts free. Keep your eye on the tropostate and let me know if you see a flashing light.” Valtteri pulled the signal mirror from his pocket and directed it towards the tropostate, reflecting the sunlight as he formed a message.

“I see a flashing light!”

“Is there a pattern?”

“It looks like one long flash, one short, another long, followed by three short flashes, and then long, short, long, long.”

“Good, they know we’re here.”

“They’re sending help?”

“It’s going to be okay, Tallow. We made it.”

Chapter 30

Admiral Soren had officially cancelled the inquiry into the so-called accidental bombing of the southern realm. Clearly, someone was intentionally hindering the investigation. That wasn't to say that he'd let it drop.

As admiral of the Luminary Navy, he was directly responsible for the operation of the fleet. The idea that a mistake of this magnitude could have occurred under his command was unacceptable. It was also implausible. Quinto was a stickler for protocol, and numerous safeguards were in place. This sort of thing simply didn't happen.

The bombing incident had tarnished Quinto's impeccable record. He could live with that, people make mistakes. Far more troubling was the realization that someone had managed to manipulate the system for unknown reasons.

The archipelago formed a navy to meet two objectives. The most obvious was for protection of the archipelago from outside forces. The second was to police the archipelago itself. The second objective was arguably more important, or at least it was the primary focus of naval activity. Simply put, the power-hungry septs didn't really trust each other. The tropostates were kingdoms unto themselves, answerable to no one.

Formation of the Luminary Navy provided a non-partisan force to ensure that every tropostate could exist without fear of open hostility from within the archipelago. No sept could move against another founding family, without fear of reprisal from the overwhelming power of the navy. The balance was carefully maintained. A combined offensive of septs, put forth by a majority of the Luminary Council, could stand against the navy if it went rogue, but anything less could not.

For that very reason, strict regulations were in place to monitor warship construction. Despite those restrictions, a non-commissioned warship managed to run an unsanctioned exercise in secret. That should have created an uproar in the Luminary Council. He knew Sept Xandri and Sept Dewei were nervous, but none of the other septs had come forward to express concern. Someone had orchestrated a masterful act of misdirection, and the underlying threat remained hidden.

Quinto was from the Lamina caste and while he had some friends among the Luminaries, his concerns carried little weight without irrefutable proof. So far, he'd been denied the necessary evidence to support his suspicions. The admiral publicly declared the inquiry closed, but he wasn't willing to let it go. The investigation became a personal effort, continuing without staff or resources that might indicate his continued interest.

Quinto didn't have much free time, but that was remedied through efficiency. An admiral had unfettered access and the loyalty of many officers. Subtle queries, through seemingly unrelated interactions, opened many avenues of investigation that were previously closed. It was a circuitous route to actionable intel, but it paid off over the course of time.

His best leads surfaced when he visited the Lagan caste factories that supplied parts for the Viburg shipyards. Luminary agents had little respect or influence shroudside of a tropostate, so sept operatives didn't always know who to lean on. Quinto, on the other hand, had cultivated friendships among the factory workers over the course of decades. A military force created enemies by its very existence, so it made sense to gain as many friends as possible. Over the years, he had learned how to join in the friendly banter, gaining access to gossip filled with valuable insight.

His conversations uncovered a questionable individual who regularly disappeared for weeks at a time to places unknown. Looking into the shipbuilding contracts, Quinto discovered that this individual had his fingers in many pies. Determined to follow this suspect, he monitored the man's comings and goings until a pattern formed. He set a date in his calendar and made flight plans for a trip to the Bellumburg Naval Base, thirty-six hours away. That would give him plenty of time to drop off the grid without raising suspicion.

It was the perfect opportunity to test a pet project of his. Several years ago, he had ordered his staff to experiment with stealth add-ons for aerosiren class ships. Part of that research was applied to diffusion and cooling units, to hide the vapour trail from thrust nozzles. The team had also developed panels with non-reflective surfaces, painted to blend with a range of atmospheric conditions. It wasn't perfect, and they were of limited use during rapidly transitioning weather patterns. However, on a day when the sky was uniform, the appropriate colour-matched panels were surprisingly effective. It was a simple matter to clip them to the supports on the scout craft sitting in his personal hanger.

His preparations led to this moment, following his suspect at a safe distance. The sky was overcast, as far as the eye could see. Conditions were perfect for the panel colour he'd chosen. He wasn't worried about being seen. He'd tried to follow a stealth panelled craft under similar conditions early on in the testing phase. He knew how difficult it was to spot the craft if you didn't know what you were looking for.

Quinto's quarry gave no indication that he was aware of a tail. The pilot reversed course a few times shortly after leaving Viburg, then abandoned any further attempt to obscure his direction of travel.

He glanced at his chronometer. They'd been travelling for almost twenty-two hours, having stopped once at Calcesburg to top off their fuel supply. His quarry was slowing as they approached the Casini Mountain

Range, not quite halfway between Calcesburg and Ferroburg.

Mountain peaks that intersected zero-strat were few and far between. The Casini Range, in particular, held little of interest, stripped of resources centuries ago. It was as far from the main inter-tropos travel route as you could get. The craft he was following altered course for a cluster of those peaks.

Quinto reduced his forward momentum as he watched the craft dart into a valley and drop out of sight. He marked the coordinates on his map and cautiously coasted toward the mouth of the valley, chastising himself for a lack of foresight. He didn't dare leave zero-strat. If he climbed above the mountain range, the noise from his thrusters would draw attention, and it was impossible to hide venting steam from close-proximity observation. He could continue at his current altitude, but his choice of stealth panel colour would stick out like a sore thumb against the mountain backdrop. Trouble could literally be around the corner, as he wound his way through the valley.

He was taking a dangerous risk, but he decided to make the attempt. It was the only lead he had. If the location turned out to be a temporary meeting point, there would be nothing to see if he left now to return with backup.

After some consideration, Quinto decided to remove the stealth panels and stow them. The standard dark grey of a scout ship was less noticeable against the mountainside.

Quinto opened the canopy and quietly used a grappling pole to pull himself along the cliff face. Every scout ship had one for boarding maneuvers. It was slow going and it taxed his arms, but shadows cast by rocky outcroppings provided cover and respite between frantic sprints. It was during one of these rest stops that he heard the telltale noise of industry. Quinto anchored his aerosiren in the shadows and attached a long tether to his belt. He travelled the remaining distance with nothing more than the grappling pole. What he saw as he rounded the corner, astonished him in both scope and audacity. There, under a large overhang, sat a fleet of ships to rival that of the Luminary Navy.

Quinto scrambled backwards, terrified that he might have been spotted. He'd imagined a clandestine meeting, not an entire shipyard. Something of this magnitude would have regular patrols. This solo mission was a mistake. Quinto made a hasty return to his ship, praying the entire way. For the first time in his career, a genuine threat of war loomed, the kind of war that could destabilize the entire archipelago.

Thoughts of stealth fled his mind as he stoked the engines for a quick escape. He needed to get back. He needed to prepare. Quinto realized he was panicking. He forced himself to slow his breathing and think like an admiral. He couldn't leave under full thrust and draw attention to himself. hardening his resolve, Quinto used gentle bursts of thrust to navigate the valley, picking up speed as he backtracked.

He had one more corner to negotiate, when a munitions round penetrated his hull, filling him with dread. The shadow of a patrol craft crossed his bow and any hope of a clean escape evaporated. Quinto increased thrust and rolled into an evasive maneuver. The patrol craft continued to fire, but the shots went wide.

Quinto forced himself to remember his training. He couldn't afford to react blindly. He needed to assess and take control of the arena.

The hull of his ship had a puncture where a round had nearly pierced his leg. It didn't hit anything critical on the craft, but he decided to pretend otherwise and stuck a smoke flare partway through the hole.

Darting erratically, he flew toward the limen and then skirted it as he increased distance from the illegal shipyard. The last thing he needed was for more ships to take notice. With a little luck, the other pilot would prove less skilled and make a fatal mistake by getting too close to the limen.

It was wishful thinking. The enemy pilot never came close enough to endanger his vessel. Fortunately, the patrol craft hadn't been able to line up another shot, but it was still in pursuit and better shielded than Quinto's scout ship. A dogfight was out of the question. He needed options.

Out of the corner of his eye, he caught movement in the distance. It was a Swathcomber platform, near the limen, about ten minutes away. His mind filtered probabilities at a furious pace. Everything at this point was high risk, but one crazy plan had a small possibility of success. If he could keep the patrol craft off his back until they got closer to that platform....

Quinto reached behind his seat and pulled out two of the stealth panels. He used stowage straps to attach them to the front and back of his torso. That done, he disengaged the canopy and began throwing out anything that was loose in the cabin, scattering it into the path of his pursuers. Hopefully, they'd think his ship was breaking up.

The next part was critical, and he had to time it just right. He needed to create enough of a distraction so they wouldn't see him eject from his ship. Navy vessels had pressure tanks designed to handle brief spikes for emergency thrust. A pilot could disable the pressure relief valves for that purpose, but the navy frowned on the practice. Overburdening the tanks put the vessel out of commission, until it could be recertified as mechanically sound. Quinto decided this qualified as an emergency. He disabled the relief valve and watched as the needle on the pressure gauge moved into the red. The scout ship began to shake as the main tank groaned in protest. He pushed his luck and waited two more seconds. A rivet popped, and he decided he'd waited long enough.

Quinto released his harness, banked hard, and pushed himself out of the scout ship, as it veered towards the limen. The craft exploded in a cloud of steam, forcing his pursuers to alter course to avoid the shrapnel.

Quinto tucked into a ball, hoping the stealth panels would hide him as the explosion created a distraction from his fall toward the Swathcomber platform. He bobbed across zero-strat twice, before levelling off.

The patrol craft circled the area of the explosion, watching as scattered wreckage from the aerosiren rolled across the limen and plunged earthward. Quinto held his breath, waiting to see if his pursuers would begin a search pattern. A tense minute followed before they turned away and moved off. He could hardly believe that his ploy had worked.

Quinto shouted and waved until the Swathcombers noticed him. They began moving in his direction. Relief accompanied a sudden weariness as exhaustion caught up with him. He should have died. The security detail responsible for that shipyard was hopefully convinced he *did* die. They would think their secret was still safe and Quinto would have another chance to do something about it.

Quinto calculated that it would be days before the Swathcombers found a water tanker to take him aboard. It would take another day before the friaers could drop him off at a port where he could commandeer a ship to go home. The naval base would be frantic, but he could do nothing about that.

As the Swathcombers pulled him onto their platform, Quinto recalled the words of Duron Tagish at their recent meeting. 'When the day arrives that you find yourself cut off and left to your own devices, you'll want friends to help you in the righteous battle to come.'

That day might be coming, sooner than he'd thought.

Chapter 31

They had been luckier than he knew. The sky lift was beyond the limits of monitoring equipment typical for a tropostate. Fortunately, Ludumburg was home to the finest scientific community in the archipelago. A new long-range telescope was undergoing some fine-tuning when he flashed his distress signal. The scientists had the instrument pointed in a random direction. If Valtteri and Tallow had arrived at any other time or place, they might still be drifting. He didn't bother telling Tallow, who was still recovering from the whole experience.

Lucky? Valtteri reconsidered his choice of words as he gazed at the surface of the planet from his vantage point on the shroudside of Ludumburg. He was standing at ground zero of a catastrophic detonation waiting to happen.

He crossed his arms to stifle an involuntary shiver, thinking of the arsenal anchored to the surface. *What if the minefield is released before I can warn anyone?* It was a question he'd asked himself numerous times in the past few days. He considered approaching the Luminary of Ludumburg, but Valterri had seen the posters declaring him a traitor. No one in authority would listen to him. They'd deliver him to Zayd Ocon, and no one would ever learn the truth.

Valtteri shook his head in disgust. The Luminaries were so ensconced in their ways that they protected their social structure, even while stabbing each other in the back. He corrected himself. *They protect their status within the caste system. They don't care about those who are below them in stature.* It wasn't lost on him that the Lagan caste were the only true victims. Those who lived solarside would merely suffer an inconvenient lack of comforts, they wouldn't suffer loss of life. Put into that perspective, it seemed Zayd adhered to some twisted form of ethics. He did value life, at least those of his fellow Luminaries. Valtteri's blood boiled thinking Zayd considered the loss of the Lagan caste as nothing more than an inconvenience.

He knew that Zayd Ocon viewed the Luminaries as loftier than others. They called themselves the elevated ones, after all. What Valtteri couldn't understand was the insane plan to attack a tropostate of one of his peers. Even if he considered the Lagan caste as nothing more than a commodity, he'd be crippling Ludumburg, which weakened the archipelago. *Unless that's his plan.*

Valtteri shook his head in dismissal of the thought. Zayd must realize that blame would fall on the Tellusans for any attack from the surface. The Luminary Council would want to retaliate, and Tellusans wouldn't forgive a second bombing across the limen. It would mean war. If that happened, weakening the archipelago would have disastrous consequences. What was Zayd thinking? It was madness.

It was a waste of time to guess at a Luminary's mindset or motivations. Valtteri didn't have enough information to make an informed assessment. What he did have was knowledge of an imminent threat. He needed to get that knowledge into the right hands before it was too late. That was his biggest problem, and not one easily solved. He didn't know who he could trust in the Tropos Archipelago, and the bounty on his head would make travel difficult.

Valtteri took in his surroundings. He was sitting on a cold stone bench in the tiny courtyard of a mission managed by the friaers. The architecture was simple and functional, like most places shroudside. Sculptures and bolts of cloth sat near the entrance, ready to decorate the street at sunrise for that brief period when shroudside filled with light. He knew the display would be full of vibrant colours, but at the moment everything looked grey. It should have been depressing, but the smiling faces of the friaers, and those they helped, filled the place with an infectious hope, something he desperately needed.

The friaer mission was the only destination he could think of after they were ferried to Ludumburg and left to their own devices. He'd hoped that he could gain the friaers' help, by invoking the name of Fisher Kozen. Thankfully, they knew Fisher well and were more than happy to provide what assistance they could. It wasn't much, taxed as they were by the many needs of shroudside. However, they had no respect for the Luminaries and happily provided a safe haven for Valtteri and Tallow. It met their greatest need while they decided what to do, and Valtteri was immensely grateful.

Tallow entered the courtyard and joined Valtteri on the bench. "Have you decided where you'll go?"

Valtteri spread his arms. "More places like this, if I want to continue living. I can never return to my previous life."

"You know, Sicily and I would welcome you into our home."

Valtteri offered a sad smile and placed a grateful hand on Tallow's shoulder. "I'll miss your company, tribesman, but I know you need to return to the southern realm as soon as possible."

"Yes, Sicily will be worried, and I need to tell Adis what we've discovered. It may be that the Tinkers Guild can help stop it."

The two men sat in companionable silence, enjoying the restful moment. It felt odd to sit after weeks of clinging to trees.

"I want to thank you for saving my life."

Valtteri chuckled. "And for putting it at risk in the first place?"

Tallow shook his head. "I was planning to search for that place, with or without you. I don't think I would've survived if I'd gone alone. I never would've attempted that stunt with the sky lift cable on my own."

"And I could never have entered the swath to find what I needed to see, without you," Valtteri responded. "I was struggling to understand who I was and where I belonged. I don't have all of the answers yet, but now I know for certain that the Luminaries are my enemy. I have you to thank for that."

"I walked a similar path of discovery, not long ago. You'll find your place if you surround yourself with good people."

"Are all tribesmen so humble? You do know that your selfless efforts could save millions of innocent Aerish families, don't you?"

"Only because I surround myself with good people."

Valtteri rolled his eyes and smiled. "*You're* good people, Tallow."

"If we don't get a warning into the right hands, history may have a different opinion."

"The friaers tell me a water tanker is due within the next two days. They assure me that the brothers will take us aboard. The tanker visits each tropostate and returns to the sky lake near Viburg to refill. It won't be a fast journey, but you'll be able to disembark at Pax Montis, and Adis can get you back to Swiftwater from there."

"I plan to leave the tinker a message to deliver to Sicily. She needs to know I'm okay, but I might take the opportunity to travel via the swath for the return trip. It will give me the chance to search for other tribes between Pax Montis and home."

"Be careful out there."

Tallow laughed. "After that freerise scare, I need to get comfortable travelling through the forest again. I'm worried that I might never go back if I wait too long. Still, I plan to purchase a drogue chute in Pax Montis... just in case. What about you?"

"I need to find a way to get in touch with the admiral. He's the only person in a senior level position who I know will take the threat seriously. He's also the only one who wouldn't immediately take me into custody and deliver me to Zayd Ocon. The admiral spends most of his time at Viburg Naval Base, but I can't go anywhere near it. We're actually very close to Viburg, right now. Unfortunately, the tanker we're waiting for is travelling in the other direction. Ludumburg is the first stop on the tanker's journey. It will be another seven days before it returns to Viburg.

"I've weighed the pros and cons of finding someone here who could send a message to the admiral, but I don't feel safe leaving shroudside, as things stand. I haven't dared leave this building. I can't afford to take unnecessary risks. If I'm caught, you're the only other person who knows what's going on. Even if you get a message to Adis, the Tinkers Guild may not have enough influence to stop something taking place in the swath. I think I need to play it safe and take the chance that Zayd isn't ready to make a move. The renegades were still working on the minefield, so I have to believe we have a little time.

"That leaves the second to last tanker stop as the next best option. The admiral maintains a personal residence solarside of Opesburg. It makes sense to try and reach him there. It's close to Viburg and the admiral visits it often. Unfortunately, I've spent a lot of time there, and

people will recognize me. Zayd's operatives will be watching the estate to see if I turn up. On the plus side, I'm very familiar with the streets. I know how to avoid public areas. Even so, I'll likely remain shroudside unless I have no other way to get a message to the admiral."

"I think you're right, Valtteri. It would be foolish to take unnecessary risks. Even if the minefield is close to completion, it seems unlikely that Zayd Ocon would release it immediately. I can only imagine that he has a particular moment in mind, one that will be politically beneficial. Regardless, even if I'm wrong and the unthinkable happens, it's not your fault."

"I'm not sure I can agree."

"Is it my fault if more tether tribesmen die before I can find a way to expose the Luminaries?"

"Of course not!"

"You and I are a small part of a very big world. We're slugs sent to battle leviathan. Our intent is honourable and I know we'll make a difference, but never forget who the monster is."

Valtteri took a deep breath and slowly exhaled. He stood with a determined look in his eyes. "Then we'll rest, and in two days' time we'll begin our journey to the battleground. There we'll face leviathan and show him what a couple of slugs can do."

Chapter 32

It was a restful week other than a few tense hours one morning when the tanker was stopped for a random inspection. Valtteri had expressed his wish to remain hidden. He didn't explain why and the friaers didn't pry. They were quick to distract the inspectors with their latest batch of ale. A few hours and pints later, the officers waved a cheery goodbye and wobbled their way back to their own vessel.

Valtteri was happy to be on a ship again, even if it wasn't a navy vessel. The serpentine motion of travel in the swath was like the company of an old friend. The familiarity of ship life put him at ease and he felt doubly blessed by the appearance of a familiar face. Fisher Kozen was aboard. He had slipped away from his duties at Pax Montis to visit the tropostate missions. It was something he did on a regular basis. That was a surprise to Valtteri who had only ever known him as an instructor in a friaerie context. Their current setting didn't prevent the friaer from dragging Valtteri to the ship's sparring area for more practice.

In truth, it was nothing more than an open space between crates in the dry goods section of the cargo hold. Even so, it had training mats on the deck and since this was a friaer ship, Valtteri didn't need to hide the fact that he was practising Invicta Manus. Fisher introduced Valtteri to a different sparring partner each day. Valtteri found it fascinating how individuals manipulated crux points in various ways. He consumed the new knowledge like a child discovering sweets for the first time.

As they neared the end of their trip, Valtteri found himself spending more and more time with Fisher. The man was a wealth of information. On several occasions he'd been tempted to tell him about the minefield and ask for advice, but he chose to remain cautious. He felt he could trust Fisher, but he didn't really know the rest of the crew and someone was always within earshot. Adis had made it clear that Valtteri's spy craft was lacking and he didn't want make a mistake that might cost thousands of lives.

"I'm surprised you spend so much time out here. Surely it's more comfortable at the friaerie?"

"I'm of more help out here than at Pax Montis. So many people are suffering in the darkness on tropostates throughout the archipelago."

"I don't think the Luminaries appreciate your help."

"Yet they tolerate it because we save them the trouble of serving their people as they should."

"I've often wondered why the friaers bother. The Lagan caste isn't their responsibility."

"If we don't provide hope, who will? The Luminaries cast everything in shadow instead of the light they claim to represent. Some of us work to illuminate the truth so all can reach their destination safely. Only a fool runs at night without a light to quell the darkness."

"Wait, what was that last part? I've heard that before."

"Have a seat." Fisher gestured.

They sat at a familiar bench placed before a large viewing port in the gallery section of the ship. Valtteri often found Fisher here gazing out at the empty sky.

"How much do you know about the religions of our past?"

Valtteri shrugged. "How much do any of us know? I'm familiar with the friaers, of course."

"Do you know why you don't run across other religious groups?"

Valtteri made an uneducated guess. "Some say that the inversion event was a punishment for our sins. Maybe the false prophets were weeded out?"

Fisher laughed. "Adherents lived all over the world before the disaster. The majority of those who died were in the swath. I don't think God punishes based on geography. Would it surprise you to learn that most of the world's religions were still present shortly after the inversion event?"

"That's an unexpected detail. So, what happened?"

"Actions spoke louder than words. Controlling or hierarchical belief systems had expectations that became impossible to sustain in a broken world. Victims of the disaster had both spiritual *and* physical needs. People were drawn to spiritual leaders who met the needs of God's children with displays of practical love. Institutions faded away. What remains isn't an official organization so much as a collection of individuals with a common belief and a heart for God."

Fisher turned to face Valtteri and held his gaze. "We can all learn a valuable lesson from this about people in authority. It doesn't matter if the organization is a business, a religion, or a government. If their activities are more about helping themselves than helping others, they are not serving the will of God."

"You're referring to the Luminaries."

"Not only the Luminaries, but they are most germane to this conversation."

"How do you know so much about our past? I thought our history was lost."

"Much of it is, but, between the friaers and the tinkers, we've been able to piece some of it together. We've had five-hundred years to gather artefacts and fragments of documents. For some of us, the search is a passion. Perhaps I can show you the archives at Pax Montis one day."

"The admiral has spoken highly of them. I never understood what he found so fascinating. I'm beginning to comprehend."

Fisher smiled. "The admiral is a good man. He sees the value in knowing our past."

Valtteri snapped his fingers. "That's where I heard the phrase. 'A light to quell the darkness'. The admiral said something similar before I left for my first mission. What does it mean?"

"Ask him when you see him. I believe the two of you have much to discuss."

Valtteri furrowed his brows in confusion and waited for more. Fisher held his tongue. *The man can be as taciturn as a certain tinker I know.* "What do your archives have to say about the Iridogen?"

Fisher brightened at the opportunity to discuss his favourite topic. "That depends. I can tell you a great deal about the Iridogen of today. We understand less about their presence before the inversion. What would you like to know?"

"Let's begin with the better-known details. What can you tell me about Iridogen in the Unified Northern Collective?"

"The UNC began as a collection of fiefdoms with no single authority. They didn't have a coordinated response to plagues or other disasters. The rumour that Iridogen caused plagues didn't reach the northern lands. People judged others solely by their ability to contribute to the community. The Iridogen are very effective hunters and highly valued for their skill. They had no difficulty finding their place. Even so, they tend to stick with their own kind. I'm not sure why that is. They seem to have some kind of connection to each other that we can't fathom. They're like-minded in a way that differs from the general population. I've only had limited contact with the northern Iridogen, but my experience was that they had difficulty trusting others."

Fisher rubbed his chin. "You don't seem to have those same trust issues. I wonder if it's a culturally learned phenomenon or a consequence of being reared apart from other Iridogen?"

"Would you mind not talking as though I were the subject of an experiment?"

Fisher reddened in embarrassment. "Apologies, lad. I find the Iridogen fascinating, but believe me when I tell you that I see you for the man you are."

"No apology is necessary. The truth is, I still don't know who or what I am."

"You can find many Iridogen in the northern lands. It might help your journey of discovery if you spent some time in the UNC. I'm sure they could answer your questions. If you ever need a safe place to go, I know some people there who could help you."

"Someday, I might take you up on that offer. For now, maybe you can tell me why the friaers and tinkers believe that Iridogen have some special purpose."

Fisher seemed to struggle with an appropriate response. "I'm not sure how much I can tell you about that before you've spoken with the admiral."

"What does my foster father have to do with any of this? He's not Iridogen."

"He can give you context that will help you understand the specifics about friaer and tinker interests."

"I'm getting really tired of half answers." Valtteri's eyes bored into Fisher's until the friaer began to squirm. "You're right. You deserve to know, but you have to understand that what I'm about to tell you is more myth than fact."

Valtteri laughed. "I doubt you could surprise me after all I've experienced in the last few months."

"Very well, I'll tell you what I can. As you know, the magnetic flux that occurred during the inversion profoundly affected the memories of survivors. Some people remained more lucid than others. Much of what we know is a compilation of repetition in coherent narratives. For whatever reason, several poetic verses in particular survived more or less intact. These lyrics always involve the Iridogen."

Fisher waited for a response and, after receiving none, he continued. "I'll give you an example:

No access to the gate, the world must face its fate.
Pressing to the goal, favoured not the bold.
Discovered far too late, the envoys missed their date.
Window to the soul, eyes of grey and gold."

Valtteri was astonished. "Okay, I was wrong. I can still be surprised. You say that poem existed before the inversion event? That's... curious."

Fisher grinned. "A blander description than I would have used, but apt."

"What does it mean?"

Fisher turned his palms up in a questioning gesture. "The full meaning will become clear when we've collected all of the puzzle pieces. We suspect that the inversion may have been preventable. Our ancestors realized too late that the Iridogen were part of the solution."

"That's a pretty big assumption."

"Perhaps, but for a people that tends to avoid the public, they seem to be front and centre in our history. Extant documents and oral tradition mention the Iridogen far more often than their small numbers should merit. They have a function that is often alluded to but never fully revealed."

"You said many Iridogen live in the north. If they have a purpose, surely someone would've stumbled upon it by now."

"Not if it requires a catalyst. The archive contains an artefact. Well, it might be better described as a fragment of an artefact. The substance it's made from is harder than anything we've ever encountered. Under certain conditions, this fragment glows from within."

Valtteri hesitated. "I'm afraid to ask... what kind of conditions?"

"It glows when it comes in contact with one of the Iridogen."

Valtteri stood and began pacing. "I don't know what I'm supposed to do with this information. I'm trying to figure out how I fit into the world, but the more I learn, the less it seems possible."

"You're thinking of this in the wrong way. You are one of a unique minority, but you're also integral to this world. That makes you more a part of it, not less."

"Others don't seem to feel that way."

"A lack of understanding can cultivate fear, but people didn't always dread the Iridogen. One day when the truth comes out, they will accept you again. That should be your goal. Not just for yourself, but for the sake of everyone. If we learn the truth about the cause of the inversion, perhaps we can stop the fighting and finger-pointing. Perhaps we can move forward and rebuild this fractured world."

Valtteri placed a palm on the frigid glass of the view port, and shivered at the cold reality of a life he never expected or asked for. "It's a worthy dream, but first we need to prevent an imminent disaster that could set those goals back another hundred years."

Chapter 33

Nixon found Zayd Ocon in his chambers. The man had slept in and was still eating breakfast. Nixon shook his head as he took in the scene.

"Don't look at me like that, nephew. I was working late and I sleep when I can. The endless paperwork of running a tropostate is taxing beyond belief. When you take on the mantle one day, remember this moment."

Zayd motioned to a seat at the table. "Sit, have something to eat. I can't possibly finish it all."

Nixon sat at the small table. Sunlight poured through the window, illuminating a banquet of sliced fruit, cheeses and pastries. Zayd took a bite from his pastry and a sip of tea. Nixon decided to let the senior Ocon have his moment. He'd be removing the contented look from his uncle's face soon enough.

Nixon had already eaten, but took a slice of cheese to nibble as he looked around the room. The chambers once belonged to his grandfather, and not much had changed since his uncle moved in. The floor had a different carpet and the desk had been replaced with one too ornate for the rest of the room. Other than that, everything looked the same. Even the smell was familiar. Nixon had many memories of his time in this room as a child. He didn't understand what people meant when they claimed to have a *fond* or *bad* memory of a particular place or time. His memories were just a collection of occurrences that he could recall when necessary. Some events, however, held more significance than others.

Zayd leaned back in his chair, finally satisfied. "It's not like you to come to my chambers. I assume you have something important to discuss. Have you located the elusive Mr. Knox?"

"My informants tell me that he was spotted boarding a water tanker."

Mention of the tanker distracted Zayd from the point. "Those accursed friaers with their hoarded water! They're given far too much leeway."

"We need their water reserves. Our wicking masts can barely collect enough to run the vapour engines."

"One day the sky lakes will be ours."

Nixon lifted an eyebrow at that proclamation, but he held his tongue.

Zayd leveled an accusation at his nephew. "I thought you had men posted at all of the limen crossings. How did he manage to find his way to a water tanker?"

"I suspect he had help from the Swathcombers. I've heard they have methods to transit from the base of the swath to the plane of equilibrium."

"A drogue chute? Swathcombers are madmen. Only a fool would risk such a transit. With a fifty percent failure rate, even the navy will only consider it as a last resort. It's not in Valtteri's character to be that reckless."

"I suppose that depends on what he discovered at the base of the swath." Nixon tilted his head and looked his uncle in the eye. "Is the thing you're hiding important enough that Knox would risk his life to expose it?"

"Send the fleet to search every tanker. I want him contained."

"I've already searched the tankers, Uncle. Knox has disappeared and no one seems to know where he went. I'm afraid your secret will soon be exposed."

Zayd glowered. "I'm not ready."

"It won't be easy for Knox to approach someone in authority. The bounty is high and we have eyes everywhere. Our intelligence network has been vigilant and our operatives tell me that he hasn't popped up anywhere. Knox is laying low. I suspect you have a little time. If you need help accelerating your plans —"

Zayd cut him off. "We've already discussed this."

Nixon rose from his seat and walked to a nearby bookcase. "Did you know that Grandfather used to sing when he was alone?"

Zayd snorted. "Another one of his weaknesses."

"He was quite good, actually. I listened to him sing whenever I could. I found his voice soothing."

"He sang for you? He never sang for me."

"I liked to imagine he was singing for me, but the truth is that he didn't know I was listening." Nixon dropped to a knee and ran his hand along the spines of the books. "Ah, here it is." He looked over his shoulder at his uncle and pointed to a hole just below one of the shelves. "I drilled this hole with my pen knife. I'm surprised it has gone unnoticed all of these years." Nixon shrugged. "I suppose these books are mostly for show."

Zayd furrowed his brows. "Why would you do such a thing?"

"So I could look through it, of course."

Nixon smiled at the confusion on his uncle's face. "I'm sure you're aware that this building has undergone many renovations in the five hundred years since this tropostate was founded. Some of those changes left voids behind the walls. I spent my early teen years exploring the ventilation tunnels and uncovering those hidden spaces. I once discovered a fully furnished room hidden away, entirely forgotten. It was my secret world, a place where I could escape to be alone with my thoughts."

Nixon rapped the back of the bookcase with a knuckle making a hollow sounding thunk. "An empty space exists behind this bookcase. I used to sit there in the dark and listen to Grandfather sing. For a time that was enough, but my curiosity got the better of me and I wanted to see what he was doing. In a way, I wish I hadn't. My imagination provided far more inventive possibilities than the mundane reality. Apart from his singing, Grandfather was actually quite boring."

Zayd's eyes widened as he realized that his own activities may have been observed as well.

Nixon laughed. "Relax, Uncle. If you recall, I was sent off to school in various places shortly after Grandfather died. When my formal education was complete, you sent me to the naval academy. I believe it was several months subsequent to the time of mourning before you claimed these quarters for yourself. It's been many years since I spent time in this building. Whatever hobbies you pursue in these rooms remains a mystery to me."

Zayd blew out a sigh of relief, but it was short-lived.

"That's not to say that everything I saw through this peephole was mundane. One event in particular changed the entire trajectory of my life, and I have you to thank for it."

Zayd froze in dread anticipation.

"On the day I'm thinking of, you had joined Grandfather for tea. You offered to pour and I watched as you added a sedative to his cup while he was distracted. Eventually, he fell asleep. I saw you remove a hidden panel from the back of the wardrobe and pull out a strange device. I later learned that it was a small high-pressure steam thermos. You had commissioned someone to build it for the occasion. I watched you slip a tube down his throat and open the valve, releasing the piping hot contents. The steam that curled from his nose and throat left a lasting impression on my mind as I watched you scald his organs.

"You returned the thermos to its hiding place and left the room. I imagine you made yourself very visible far from the scene of the crime. It's always a good idea to establish an alibi. Grandfather suffered for several days before succumbing to his mortal wounds. Unable to speak, he couldn't express his symptoms. No one suspected foul play since he'd been on his deathbed for some time. When he died in your arms, you appeared the doting son, having cared for him until the end. It was a perfect crime. Well — almost perfect."

Nixon stood from his place in front of the bookcase and walked across the room to a particular wall panel. He felt for a hidden catch and engaged it with a click. "Here's a hidden space that I'm certain is familiar to you. It's an escape tunnel that leads to the garden." Nixon held up a hand to forestall his uncle's protest. "Shortly after your cowardly attack, a small wiry fellow used this tunnel to enter the room and remove the thermos along with any evidence of your treachery."

"I followed the man and confronted him. When I told him who I was and what I had seen, he was terrified. He insisted that he knew nothing about an assassination attempt and that he had only been hired to build the device, secure it in the room, and then remove it again at a specific time.

"Since that day, he has been quite a source of revenue. The fellow was eager to pay some sort of recompense to ease his guilt. I suppose he also felt that he'd prolong his life if he had something to offer. I certainly didn't need the money, but who was I to stand in the way of his self-imposed penance? It was the least I could do after you put him in such an uncomfortable position.

"I've accumulated a surprising amount of evidence. It's amazing what an enterprising teen can do, given enough money. I procured the steam thermos with your fingerprints on it. I have the requisition for its construction along with a ledger entry for a payment you made in an equivalent amount on the same day. I have tracked down the apothecary where the sedative was purchased and the shopkeeper confirmed that you purchased it yourself. You told her you were having trouble sleeping and she remembered thinking it was odd that a Luminary would make such a purchase shroudside.

"I even hired a doctor to perform a post-mortem autopsy on the body. I led him blindfolded into the family tomb. He had no idea who the victim was, but confirmed the severe burning of Grandfather's internal organs. I have the report of his findings and a way to tie that report to the victim. The combined facts and testimony are overwhelming."

Zayd stared at his nephew in horror. "Nixon... Let me explain..."

"I don't need an explanation. I understand completely. It's like the stories you used to tell me about our family history and our role as Luminaries. Sometimes we need to make difficult decisions for the greater good. Grandfather was giving away our authority... our strength. If he'd been allowed to continue, we all would've become as weak as he was. The Tropos Archipelago is in a fragile state. Now is not the time for weakness. Now is the time for hard decisions. You made a hard decision. I approve."

Zayd shook his head. "A child should never witness the murder of his grandfather. I can't imagine what you must have gone through."

"I learned what it means to consider the bigger picture. I had to grow up a little sooner than I might have otherwise, but you had already prepared me for it. I knew that one day I would need to make hard decisions of my own. The shock was fleeting and without remorse. I knew it was the right decision for my future."

"That's a disturbingly cold perspective."

"Is it more twisted than a son cooking his father from the inside out? All things considered, I think between us, I may have the healthier mentality. I suspect our family tree contains a number of dark individuals. Let's just agree that neither of us are normal. I consider it a strength in times that call for atypical solutions."

The two watched each other in silence. With everything out in the open, neither felt certain how to proceed.

Having the most to lose, Zayd broke the silence first. "You never said anything."

"That's the point. I could have had you removed from power at any time, but I didn't. How much more proof of loyalty do you need? I stand for Sept Ocon, I want to see our power expand, not diminish. Grandfather thought we could secure our future through treaties. I disagree."

Zayd's eyes narrowed as he leaned forward. "And how would you secure our future?"

"I would take what we need by force. Your actions suggest similar thoughts. You antagonize the Tellusans while provoking the Luminary Council with tales of past glory. You test the waters while keeping secrets, but you're running out of time. We have the same goals and you need an ally. It's time to let me in."

Nixon waited patiently. It was now or never. If Zayd didn't disclose his plans, Nixon would move forward with his own.

Zayd stood and began to pace. He seemed to have made a decision. "Our resources are dwindling. The friaers control the water in the archipelago and we're dependent on the Tellusans for much of our food. We're technologically more advanced than the Tellusans, yet we're at their mercy. The situation is growing worse every day. My father influenced the Luminary Council into believing that some tenuous peace treaty would bring us a future filled with prosperity. They would trade away the very technology that gives us an advantage. Already the war balloons of the UNC threaten our borders. Are we to give them our strength so they can defeat us?

"If we could push our borders beyond the swath, it would give us some breathing room. We would be better able to defend ourselves and we would possess arable land to sustain our people. Much of the land along the limen is unoccupied, yet when we've discussed these things with the international community, they refuse to consider selling it to us. Why? The answer is simple. They don't want us to thrive. They want to pen us in and control us. They've already succeeded in the former and it's only a matter of time before they succeed in the latter."

Nixon was nodding in agreement. "I take it the Council remains unconvinced of this threat to our sovereignty?"

"A few of the founding septs have similar concerns, but the rest are blind fools. If the Tellusans were to start a war, the Council would finally see the truth. Unless that happens, they will never be convinced of what must be done. Our only hope is to create a situation they can't ignore."

"I agree with you, Uncle, but short of an actual war, I don't see what kind of situation would serve the same purpose. The Luminary Navy won't go to war without the consent of the entire Council. If you try to start a war on your own, the navy will see it as a threat to the other tropostates and move to stop you."

"Indeed, but what if they didn't know it was me?"

Nixon chuckled. "Are you a magician now, Uncle? How will you perform this sleight-of-hand?"

"The bombing near Endelton was a mistake, I admit. That error continues to threaten my plans, but if we move quickly enough, it has also provided an opportunity. My reparations at the international summit allowed me a podium to plant seeds of doubt. I accused Queen Silvanus of sending her military across the limen. My operatives have long suspected that Silvanus is hiding something, so I also accused her of concealing a gravity engine within her realm. Silvanus made the mistake of refusing to answer my accusation, leaving the impression that both statements may be true. Now the delegates of that summit think that Silvanus is provoking the archipelago by entering the swath against treaty agreement. I may not be a magician, but my indignation was a noteworthy performance."

"I would've liked to have been there."

"You may have missed the drama, but you've made a valuable contribution to the narrative with your reports. I've submitted your observations of increased military presence in the Endelton area and requested confirmation from the international community. UNC operatives have noted the same. The Tinkers Guild has confirmed it and filed an affidavit."

Zayd stopped his pacing and turned to look directly at his nephew.

"By failing to deny that they crossed the limen, the Tellusans have already committed an act of war in the minds of the international community. The Luminaries have shown a remarkable constraint in light of this flagrant violation. If it were to appear that Silvanus was making a more aggressive move... something in the same neighbourhood as the increased military presence you've reported...."

Nixon's eyes widened at the implications. "The world would believe that the Tellusans were the instigators regardless of Silvanus's protestations. This is tied to whatever it is you've been concealing in the swath. What might that be, Uncle?"

Zayd looked around the room, worried that eyes were watching them. He beckoned Nixon closer before dropping his voice to a whisper. "I've anchored a minefield beneath Ludumburg. I can trigger its release on a moment's notice."

Nixon jerked in surprise. "That would kill tens of thousands!"

"Keep your voice down!"

Nixon took a deep breath and nodded for his uncle to continue.

"Further installations are in progress below Opesburg and Voloburg. It's important that the attacks occur simultaneously so those tropostates don't have time for defensive maneuvers."

Zayd stared hard at Nixon, willing him to understand. "It's a hard decision."

"Explain the rationale."

"Luminaries Dewai and Xandri are strong advocates of your grandfather's policies. They vigorously oppose me at every Council meeting. My words fail to sway them, but the facade of a Tellusan attack might change their minds. Even if they're not convinced, they can no longer directly oppose me if I weaken them."

"Perhaps they wouldn't be in a position to oppose you with force, but they could still withhold their vote to engage the navy. You won't be able to escalate the situation without a direct assault on the southern realm."

"I don't need the Luminary Navy."

"If you make an aggressive move that threatens the safety of the archipelago, the navy will intervene."

"They won't be able to stop me."

Nixon burst into laughter. "Our small personal fleet has some of the fastest engines and the heaviest armour, but we're no match for the Luminary Navy."

"Yes, we are. I've been secretly building a war fleet, one that is already a match for the Luminary Navy. If we add the resources of even one other tropostate, we will possess an overwhelming force."

Nixon's mouth hung open in disbelief. "How is that possible? The logistics alone..."

Zayd waved the protest aside. "It doesn't matter how. Just know that the fleet already exists."

"No sept is allowed to possess a stronger force than the navy. If the rest of the Council finds out, they'll join forces with the navy to destroy Sept Ocon!"

"Stipoburg and Ferroburg will stand with us."

"You can't be certain of that."

"They always have. Their fortunes are intertwined with ours. They have the same goals and grievances. Do you think I created this fleet without their help?"

"You're gambling with all of our lives."

"It's too late to turn back. Besides, I'm willing to bet that I can make an attack on the southern realm before the navy realizes what's happening. By then it will be too late. When Queen Silvanus retaliates, it will be open warfare and the Luminary Navy will be duty-bound to defend the archipelago alongside us."

Nixon shook his head. "Eventually, the war will conclude and we'll be held accountable."

Zayd's voice rose with a hint of madness to Nixon's ear.

"Our fleet will make offensive forays only, ensuring that we claim the

Tellusan land we need. Our efforts will be focussed, whittling away at the Tellusans' defences while they split their resources to mount a response. The Luminary Navy, on the other hand, will play a defensive role. Their mandate will prioritize protection of the entire archipelago. The navy will suffer losses while our fleet remains strong. When all is said and done, three of the original four septs will represent the dominant power within the archipelago just as it once was and always should have been."

Nixon remained speechless as he considered the audacity of the plan. He couldn't decide if it was genius or insanity. Clearly, his uncle wasn't as weak as he'd thought. He'd wrongly pegged the man as brainless. In truth, he was a megalomaniac. Could it really work? Nixon doubted it would be so easy. Still, it was true that the Luminaries had become complacent. He'd counted on that complacency for his own plans.

Nixon's lip twitched in amusement. Considering he wanted the same result as his uncle, some might well accuse him of megalomania as well. The difference was that his uncle wanted power for power's sake while Nixon deemed his pursuit of power as being for the good of the archipelago. He would lead them all into a new golden age. His was a righteous motivation.

Nixon admired the scope of his uncle's plan, but it had too many loose ends. He preferred a methodical approach where every aspect was accounted for. It was too late for that. Things were moving swiftly. For good or bad, he had no choice but to let events play out as they would. If by some stroke of luck his uncle's plan actually succeeded, Nixon would be ready to take advantage of the new political landscape. Until then, he had to assume it would fail. That meant distancing himself from his uncle when the time came. It was a hard decision that he'd already calculated as inevitable long before this revelation.

Despite his misgivings, Nixon found himself intoxicated with the idea of a secret base housing a hidden fleet. It had the potential to solve several shortcomings in his own evolving plan. If he played his cards right, he could claim the fleet without accepting responsibility for its creation. It was as though fate was handing him a gift as an endorsement of his purpose.

Zayd was smiling broadly and Nixon joined him with a smile of his own. Now that he knew everything, he could finally plan appropriately. The first step was an inventory of these new assets. In his mind, he'd already claimed them. The feigned solidarity came easily to his lips. "What do you need me to do, Uncle?"

Chapter 34

Transition from shroudside to solarside typically happens in one of two ways. The most common is through the many multi-axis turnstiles that ring a tropostate. Although policed with lax security, Valtteri felt the chance of someone confronting him was too great. He had to believe that Nixon would have people looking for him after he disappeared into the swath.

The other option was to traverse the service well, a hollow tube cored through the centre of a tropostate. The well housed conduits and pipes to carry power, water, and sewage. A Freefall or freerise to the plane of equilibrium at the mid-point of a well was quick enough, but the remainder of the journey involved a climb up a very long ladder centred within the tube. Generally, maintenance workers were the only ones who used it.

The well was a less public option, but Valtteri still wasn't comfortable with the risk. If he were spotted and challenged, he'd be exposed with nowhere to hide. Even if he remained unnoticed as he traversed the well, he would be clearly visible exiting the ladder. Somehow he would still have to walk the bridge from the centre of the well to its edge without being seen.

The central ladder didn't seem a viable option. Instead, he decided to scale the well using the massive array of plumbing attached to its wall. It was slow going, but afforded him nooks and crannies where he could take a break or hide. It would also allow him to slip over the lip of the well in a less conspicuous spot. At least that's what he hoped. He wouldn't know his options until he reached the surface. The climb had proven exhausting and he was resting more than he expected. *It doesn't matter how long it takes. I have to be careful,* he reminded himself. *I have to reach the admiral. He needs to know what Zayd Ocon is planning.*

The climb was tedious and Valtteri occupied his mind reflecting on events that led him here. In a very short amount of time, he had gone from a talented young officer with a future, to a man racing to expose the treasonous plans of his employer.

The journey to Opesburg had been a long one. Valtteri never left the tanker except for one time when they docked at Ferroburg, and then only briefly. Valtteri knew that Sebastian's family worked the forges there. It hadn't taken long to find the Arguso family and convince them to contact Sebastian with a message for the admiral. Fisher had already agreed to send a message, but the friaer couldn't deliver it directly until they ended their circuit on the water tanker. Even if he could get to it sooner, anything sent through an unofficial intermediary would get tied up in military bureaucracy and delay delivery. The admiral's staff would vet such messages and it was entirely possible he would never see it at all.

Besides that, Valtteri was convinced that all of his known acquaintances would be under Nixon's scrutiny. Fisher was well-known for his criticism of the Luminaries and Valtteri wasn't confident that he could get a message through, under the circumstances. Sebastian would also be monitored, but Valtteri didn't believe Nixon would think to watch his friend's relatives.

As far as Valtteri knew, Sebastian hadn't left Viburg Naval Base. He was still waiting for a new posting. That meant he had direct access to the admiral. Nixon's operatives had no authority on the base and Sebastian could approach the admiral directly without interference. Valtteri hesitated to involve his friend, but he didn't know who else to trust and it seemed like the route with the best chance of success.

The message contained one word. Aurora. The Aurora was a small single passenger decommissioned aeroguard class vessel that the admiral was refurbishing. Valtteri and Sebastian had spent many happy hours helping to strip it down. The admiral purchased a small garage on the fringes of solarside to house the craft. Valtteri didn't think many people knew about the admiral's hobby. He liked to keep his personal life separate from his naval duties. It would provide a good place for Valtteri to hide, and the admiral would know to look for him there.

Valtteri slowed as he neared the rim of the well. The pipes and cables turned ninety degrees and disappeared through the wall where they continued underground through a myriad of interconnected conduits. This would be the tricky part. The wall continued five feet higher than the pipes. He'd no longer have any handholds. His options were to try and balance on one of the larger pipes and reach for the top of the wall or use the grappling hook he'd brought along and risk making noise.

Valtteri knew that a well-manicured park surrounded the well. He'd visited it in the past on numerous occasions. He'd chosen this time of day thinking fewer people would be visiting. If he could get over the wall unseen, he'd look like any other pedestrian out for a stroll. He wasn't looking forward to crossing the empty space, but beyond that, he could quickly lose himself in the surrounding alleys. Valtteri made two heart-stopping attempts to balance on top of one of the larger pipes before dismissing it as an option.

Voices sounded nearby and he held his breath as they grew louder, then faded into the distance. Minutes passed, but he heard nothing more. The grappling hook rattled as it caught the top of the wall. The sound was deafening to his ears. He panicked for a moment realizing that if he stayed where he was, he would have no place to flee. It would be better to be spotted and run than stay where he was. Valtteri quickly scrambled over the wall and dropped to the other side, bringing the hook along. His head swivelled back and forth looking for threats, but no one was in sight.

Stashing the grappling hook under a bush, Valtteri sat for a moment. He willed his racing heart to settle. *I made it. Now I just need to get to the garage and wait.*

* * *

Two days passed, with no sign of the admiral. Valtteri occupied his time rewiring some of the gauges on the Aurora's instrument cluster. He found a few navy rations in the cupboard behind the small table in a corner of the garage. It supplemented the meagre provisions he'd brought along. The place had a toilet, sink, and shower. He wouldn't run out of water, but if the admiral failed to show up in the next few days, he'd need to go out and replenish his food supply. He worried that his message hadn't got through. *What will I do then?* Worst-case scenarios played through his mind. The wait was nerve-wracking and he was completely unprepared when he heard the rattling of keys in the door. Valtteri bumped his head trying to shift from his position under the console of the aerosiren. Rubbing his scalp, he ducked lower into the cockpit.

Quinto Soren's familiar voice echoed through the garage. "Valtteri?"

Relief washed over him. "Dad!" He climbed out of the cockpit and jumped to the floor. He strode quickly towards the admiral, but stopped short, suddenly uncertain. The admiral smiled and pulled him into a hug. "I'm so glad you're safe! I only got your message yesterday. How long have you been waiting?"

"Two days."

"I'm sorry it took so long, but I had to make sure no one would follow me. Things are a bit tense at the moment. What exactly did you do? I'm told you have a bounty on your head. Sept Ocon has charged you with treason!"

Valtteri had been expecting some sort of reprisal, but hearing it from the admiral forced the reality on him. It hit hard. "On what grounds? If anyone is guilty of that charge, it's Zayd Ocon. He's planning to attack Ludumburg and possibly other tropostates as well."

"Slow down. It doesn't surprise me that Zayd is plotting something, but I need details."

"I was sent to investigate the increased Tellusan military presence around Endelton."

Quinto nodded. "That makes sense. Zayd accused Queen Silvanus of sending troops across the limen."

"That's not what's happening. I've been travelling with a tinker who's filled me in on a few observations. The Guild has been building a case against the Luminaries for abuse of the tether tribes. I was introduced to a tribesman named Tallow. He said that the Luminaries were up to something at the base of the swath. A Vigil is sending tribes to work along one of the river routes leading to the interior. Nixon tried to kill me twice as I got closer to Endelton. I believe he was trying to prevent me from learning more."

"Hang on a second. Did you say Nixon Ocon tried to kill you?"

"Not directly, but he hired mercenaries and Swathcombers to do his dirty work." Valtteri shook his head. "That doesn't matter right now. With Tallow's help, I entered the swath to investigate. We discovered a minefield tethered to the base of the swath directly below Ludumburg. The mines will release en masse when triggered. We need to warn them. If those mines hit shroudside, thousands of innocent people will die."

"So that's what he's up to! Zayd is a warmonger, but I didn't think he'd go this far. Suspicions about Queen Silvanus's motivations are high. If Ludumburg is bombed, everyone will assume it was a Tellusan attack. Zayd will get his wish for war while taking out a political opponent at the same time. I wouldn't be surprised if he targeted Opesburg as well."

"You have to stop him."

"When I leave here, I'll warn Xandri and Dewai. They can train their telescopes on the surface and look for threats. For now, they'll have to move their tropostates out of the way, but the navy will deploy and permanently disable any minefields.”

Valtteri began to tremble as he felt the weight of a burden lifting from his shoulders. The stress had taxed him more than he realized. “I think I need to sit down.”

Quinto helped him to a chair. “You did well, son. Don’t worry, I’ll take care of it, but we have other things to discuss before I go.”

“Like why you never told me I was Iridogen?”

Quinto winced at the rebuke. “I’m so sorry, Val. You were always at a disadvantage within the swath. I didn’t want you to feel further removed than you already were.”

“After all I’ve recently learned, I think I understand your motivation. My biological family rejected me at birth, but my life could have been so much worse. You made a home for me — accepted me. It was far more than most would have done. From what I hear, it was a better life than most Iridogen enjoy. I want you to know how thankful I am for all you’ve done for me. If I’ve seemed ungrateful in the past, it was only because of my ignorance.”

Quinto stared at his feet. “I know I should have told you sooner. I thought I could protect you... not only from Sept Ocon, but from other agendas as well. I was foolish to think so and now you’re missing important information that could keep you alive.”

“Other agendas? Do you know why the friaers and the Tinkers Guild are so interested in me?”

“It’s complicated.”

“Empty answers. You’re as bad as Adis and Fisher.”

Quinto chuckled. “I don’t know this Adis fellow, but I’m quite familiar with Fisher’s ways. He can be maddening at times.”

“Fisher would only tell me a little. He said I needed to speak with you first. I assumed you knew Fisher professionally as a Hamo Sagitta instructor for the recruits, but he gave me the impression that your relationship involved more than that.”

Quinto nodded. “We’re very close friends. Actually, he’s my

mentor."

Valtteri looked up in surprise. "Your mentor? How can a Tellusan friaer be a mentor to an admiral of the Luminary Navy? And don't say it's complicated."

Quinto's mouth quirked in a lopsided grin. "Well, it is, but I'll try to explain. I need your word that you'll tell no one else. If you're willing to take an oath, I can explain more than I might say otherwise. I'll try to give you enough information to decide whether you want to take that oath. I'm sorry, but that's the best I can do. Understand that even the little I tell you now could cost my life and that of many others."

"You have my word."

Quinto nodded and cleared his throat. "The friaers and the tinkers will always have an interest in the Iridogen, if only out of intellectual curiosity. Both are collectors of information and both have a fascination with history. The Guild relies on precedent to function as effective arbiters, requiring a good understanding of the past. Having the most accurate documentation prevents governments from rewriting history to suit their ambitions. The friaers are also interested in history, but they focus their research on finding a cause for the inversion event. They sift through the confusion that remains, hoping to understand the will of God. Both groups have amassed a significant compilation of fragmented history. The Iridogen feature prominently in much of it."

"What could they hope to learn from someone like me? Surely they don't believe I have some magical knowledge of the past."

"Of course not. I would say they're more interested in learning about the curious qualities that Iridogen possess. I'm sure you've noticed some of those traits by now."

Valtteri shifted uncomfortably in his chair. He didn't want to dwell on his strange connection to iridomals and what that said about his humanity. The admiral seemed to sense his discomfort.

"Believe me when I tell you, Val. I love you and I will never think less of you for who you are. If anything, I see you as a light in these dark times."

Valtteri's memory sparked in recognition. "The phrase you told me to remember, 'a light to quell the darkness,' Fisher said it to me and so did Adis."

Quinto smiled. "Those who speak that phrase are people you can trust. It's a way for us to identify each other when circumstances dictate. Fisher told me that you were under the protection of a trusted tinker, but not the name. Be careful sharing the names of those who use that phrase. Their safety depends on their anonymity. If this tinker has taken you into his confidence, then he has placed his life in your hands."

It was a sobering thought, one that only raised more questions. "Why would he do that?"

"He belongs to an organization made up of like-minded individuals, a group who has access to information not available to most people. We're trying to fill in the gaps by bringing that information together. What we've discovered has the potential to change the world. The Iridogen are key to unlocking that mystery and precious few Iridogen remain. We protect them as best we can."

Valtteri felt his temper rise. "You need me for something."

Quinto held up his hands in surrender. "Ask Fisher if I haven't done everything I can to keep you out of this. It's part of the reason why I never told you. Our work is dangerous and I want you far from it."

"But you're telling me now."

Quinto sighed. "Fisher tells me that you've been recklessly pursuing answers. He said that you've learned enough to put yourself in danger, but not enough to protect yourself."

"I wouldn't say reckless."

Quinto laughed. "You're as stubborn as they come. I know you, Val. You'll never let this go and you'll risk your life to get the answers you seek. Fisher convinced me you're already in danger and that you'll be safer coming into the fold. Leadership has agreed to let me be your mentor if you agree to join our cause."

"So, Adis is more than a tinker, Fisher is more than a friaer, and you're more than an admiral. All of you are living double lives serving a secret organization that protects Iridogen for some mysterious purpose they have yet to glean. You'd like me to join your club so I can become even more of an outcast — living my life in the shadows to fulfill an unknown agenda at risk of life and limb. Is that about right?"

"When you put it that way, it sounds insane, I know. That's been my life and I really don't want that for you. It's okay to say no. I'll still do whatever I can to protect you. You don't need to join my world."

Valtteri stifled a cynical laugh. "Nothing sounds crazy to me anymore. The Luminaries raised me to further their plans and now they hunt me for that service. I'm already isolated, with precious few people I can trust. I know almost nothing about who I really am and where I belong, but I know this much, I will no longer serve the agenda of others."

"I understand. I'll let them know you're not interested."

"That's not what I said. You're also correct that I won't give up until I have answers. It sounds like your organization has more answers than anyone else. I'm in danger whether I join you or not, but you have resources that I may need for my survival. What I'm saying is that I'm moving forward on my terms. I'm tired of lies and half-truths. I need to know that I can walk away without reprisal if I don't like what I find."

Quinto held Valtteri's gaze and filled it with all of the sincerity he could muster. "We swear only to protect the identity of our contacts. Beyond that, anyone can leave at any time. We serve only because the truth we uncover compels each of us to use it to better the world through our own spheres of influence. Far too many wars have been fought over the origin of the swath. We share a common hope that when the final mystery is solved, it will be for the benefit of the entire world. Nothing we discover is withheld. It must be that way because we never know who will find an important connection. Some secrets rightfully belong to the world. The fact that organizations try to hide them drives us to uncover them."

Valtteri contemplated the admiral's words. "Then tell me truthfully, why do your superiors want me to join now? I was in danger from Zayd Ocon long before they made this decision. Surely his agenda has little to do with your search for truth."

Quinto closed his eyes and pinched the bridge of his nose. "I shouldn't share this with you before you take the oath, but the circumstances are extraordinary. Zayd Ocon inadvertently alerted us to a significant find. It turns out he was correct in his accusation that Queen Silvanus is hiding something. It seems that an ancient structure survived the inversion event. It was found deep in the southern realm. If this artefact is real, it could provide the answers we've all been searching for. More specifically, answers about the Iridogen."

"What reason do you have to believe that this is a genuine relic and not something that the queen is building for her military?"

"It's the nature of the report that intrigued us. The soldiers are ignorant of the significance, yet they thought it strange enough to mention."

A shiver crawled up Valtteri's spine as the pieces fell into place. "It's attracting iridomals, isn't it?"

Quinto nodded. "We need to investigate. Our sources say that Silvanus has been gathering the best scientific minds of her realm, but that they haven't elicited any kind of response from the structure. If it's drawing iridomals, the chances are high that the artefact will only respond to Iridogen."

"Of course," Valtteri snorted, "why would I expect otherwise?"

"I don't know what to say, Val. You're a navy trained operative who also happens to be Iridogen. Fisher assures me that you were taught Invicta Manus, giving you a coveted advantage. If you'd had any other kind of childhood, those opportunities would never have been afforded you. As much as I hate the idea of your involvement, you're uniquely qualified. It would take a long time to find and train another Iridogen who might be willing to investigate. Most would not wish to get involved, but I suspect you're already curious.

"Zayd, no doubt, had plans to send you south to uncover the queen's secret. You were already destined to head in that direction before things got messy. It's almost as though the universe was determined to send you there. I can't explain the timing of this discovery and your arrival at this moment, but the simple truth is that you might be able to learn something that has eluded us for centuries. We all want those answers, but beyond that hope, we have no expectations. We can't even hazard a guess at the benefits or potential consequences."

Valtteri smiled as the admiral related their lack of progress. "That sales pitch was as sorry as the navy's recruitment posters."

Quinto burst into laughter and Valtteri joined in. It felt good to lighten the mood. It reminded him of simpler times, something he hoped to reclaim one day. "I've lost faith in a lot of things lately, but you've never betrayed my trust and I believe you. I know you wouldn't be involved unless you thought it was important. I need answers as much as you do, so I'll take your oath. If it means stopping people like Zayd Ocon, so much the better."

Quinto held a finger to his lips and whispered. "What was that?"

The door smashed open and a squad of navy officers poured into the garage, training their weapons on Valtteri.

"Don't move!"

"What's the meaning of this?" The admiral shouted. "Stand down!"

The officers began to lower their weapons. "Admiral, what are you doing here?"

A dark form filled the doorway, blocking the sun. "He's conspiring with a traitor. Arrest them!"

"Nixon!" Valtteri leapt from his chair and moved towards the door. Several guns rose in response and Valtteri backed down.

"I said, stand down."

The officers looked from the admiral to Nixon, unsure what to do.

Nixon pointed at Valtteri. "That man is guilty of treason and archipelago law demands that he not be granted sanctuary. He's the property of Zayd Ocon and must return to Calcesburg for trial."

"I am no man's property!"

"You're pledged to Sept Ocon!" Nixon shot back.

"That pledge works both ways. I was under the protection of Sept Ocon. You invalidated that agreement when you tried to kill me without cause."

"Is that true?" The admiral asked.

"That traitor has no proof of such an accusation. He's coming with me."

"You have no jurisdiction here, Nixon."

"The law is clear. A Luminary has proclaimed Valtteri a traitor. He's an operative of Sept Ocon and my uncle is within his rights to make such a declaration."

"That is true enough, but I have yet to see the official documentation of this declaration and any orders to apprehend must pass through my office."

One of the officers spoke up. "We've seen the documented claim, Sir. It seems to be in order."

"Do you think it proper that I should take your word without seeing the document for myself?"

"No, Sir! That's not what I meant, Sir!"

"Whose orders do you follow when it comes to Luminary disputes?"

"The orders of the admiral, Sir!"

"Very well, I order you to return to your regular duties. I will consider Luminary Ocon's concerns and determine the proper course of action."

"Yes, Sir!"

"You can't do this!" Nixon raged as the officers filed out.

"You're in luck, Nixon. Opesburg is the judicial centre for the archipelago. If you'd like, we can head directly to the offices of Luminary Xandri. I'm sure he can clarify what I can and cannot do. I'll willingly defer to his judgment."

Nixon spat on the floor. "Everyone knows you're friends with Silas Xandri. His word means nothing to me."

Valtteri was done with the conversation. He took two quick steps and punched Nixon in the face, knocking him to the floor.

Nixon bounced back to his feet, fury on his face. Valtteri settled into a fighting stance and Nixon's eyes widened.

"It seems the two of you have something to settle. I won't allow you to command my officers, Nixon, but neither can I command you. I won't interfere if you make an attempt to bring Valtteri in on your own. That's well within your rights."

Nixon glared at the admiral. "Expect to hear from the Luminary Council. Both you and Luminary Xandri will be held accountable for this interference."

Nixon scowled and stormed out.

Valtteri rubbed his knuckles. "That felt good."

Quinto chuckled. "Did you see the expression on his face when you fell into a fighting stance? I'm guessing he's aware that you know Invicta Manus."

"He's been tailing me for some time. He must have seen me fight his mercenaries. That's going to raise questions if he brings it up in Council. Will that threaten your position?"

"Don't worry about me. Zayd has a lot to answer for. He may have allies on the Council, but his advantage is about to disappear. He'll lose majority backing once the truth about those minefields are exposed. Luminaries don't trust each other. I'm more worried about you. Treason is a serious charge. You'll need to go into hiding."

"I can take care of myself."

"I'd hoped to begin mentoring you, but now that we've been seen together, I'll be carefully monitored. I may not be able to talk to you for some time. Suspicion among the Luminaries is higher than I've ever seen it and I fear what's coming. You should leave the swath. Fisher and your tinker friend can answer many of your questions. We'll find some way to send messages back and forth through them, if you need to get in touch.”

Father and son embraced, both wondering if it would be the last time.

“You'd better go. Nixon might have his own operatives nearby. I hope you find what you're looking for, Son.”

Having nothing more to say, Valtteri simply nodded and jogged out into the street.

Chapter 35

Enzo Kiraz shook his head in confusion. "It had to be the Tellusans. Why would Luminaries target their own?"

Jayla Dewai of Ludumburg glared at him with contempt. "Don't be a fool, Enzo, you're as disposable as the rest of us."

Enzo slumped in the comfortable chair and finished the strong drink in his glass before refilling it from the crystal decanter in the centre of the ornate table. Ever the host, he had invited them to gather at his opulent estate. "It makes no sense. Voloburg has been nothing but welcoming to all septs. I have a good rapport with Zayd, Philo, and Tiago."

Silas laughed. "They enjoy the pleasures Voloburg has to offer, Enzo, but don't think for a moment that they regard you as an equal. The original three founders rely only on each other. The rest of us are just a means to an end. They control all of the essential services for life in the swath. We're tolerated only because they don't want to bother with the minutiae of maintaining systems for finance, education, research and frivolity. They benefit from what we offer, paying only for those things that enhance their own interests. We need them, but they only use us. Haven't you ever noticed their united front? They decide how to vote in advance at private meetings like the one we're having now."

"We have an equal vote in the Council." Enzo insisted.

"Do we?" Jayla spat. "Stipoburg, Calcesburg and Ferroburg agree on every issue ensuring they win fifty percent of the vote. When was the last time we had a stalemate? The answer is never. Silas and I have challenged them repeatedly, but you, dear Enzo, are so concerned for your bottom line that you vote with the majority every single time!"

"That's not fair! Voloburg relies on tourism. We can't afford to alienate our customers."

Jayla crossed her arms and glared at him.

"Haven't you made compromises as well?" Enzo responded in a weak voice.

"I believe that's the point Jayla is making." Silas interjected. "We're the ones who always compromise. They don't have to. Therein lies the inequity. If we become so weak that we can't afford to vote against the others, our influence will continue to diminish. Eventually, we will become part of the Lamina caste. What better way for them to accomplish that goal than with this threat of attack? Think for a moment, Enzo. Where would you be if the attack had succeeded? You would lose customers from two devastated tropostates. A collapse of the Opesburg banking system would mean that no one could afford to pay for your services. You would be entirely beholden to the unfair trading practices of the original three founders. I'm sure that's something you've already experienced to a degree. How can you possibly defend them?"

"The Tellusans..."

"Enough, Enzo! The Tellusans didn't plan this attack. It would've made more sense for them to target our naval bases. Why direct ordnance at three of the least threatening tropostates? Such a strategy offers no military advantage to the Tellusans. The only parties who stand to benefit are the original three founders. It's time for you to wake up or you may not see the next attack coming."

Quinto chose that moment to speak. "It's my duty to remain neutral, but it's also my responsibility to ensure the safety of the archipelago. That includes policing the septs. I appreciate the transparency you've shown by inviting me, but bear in mind that my presence here isn't acceptance of your position.

"If you agree to vote together and force a stalemate at the next Council session, that is your prerogative. I have authority to serve as a tiebreaker, but only to recommend a course of action that results in an equitable solution for all parties. I remind you all that the Luminaries established the navy to ensure a balance of power among the septs. I can't work to provide an advantage to one sept, or a coalition of septs, unless it's to counter a direct threat to the archipelago as a whole."

Frustration was clear in Jayla's voice. "Then why bother coming at all? I'm grateful for your warning about the minefields and I thank you for clearing them, but I know you don't believe that the Tellusans are responsible."

"What I believe is irrelevant. I can't mount a response without irrefutable evidence."

"So you're here to tell us that the navy will do nothing to address a threat from within?"

"Rest assured, the navy will respond when the threat is clear. However, we don't yet understand the extent of that threat. What I came to share may influence your discussion."

The room fell silent. Silas pulled out an unlit cigar and began to play with it, a nervous habit. Clearly, he wanted to light it. The others leaned forward ready to object. He put it back in his pocket and spoke for them all. "Your choice of words suggests that the minefields should be the least of our worries. I'm suitably alarmed. Please explain."

"I've discovered a fleet of warships hiding in the swath. From what I could tell of their numbers, it matches the strength of the Luminary Navy."

"Tellusan ships?" Enzo asked. Silas and Jayla both rolled their eyes.

"I'm afraid not. They were non-commissioned Aerish vessels. The same classes and types used in our navy."

"What more proof do you need?" Jayla exclaimed. "We all know who provides the raw resources, forges, and engines necessary to build a Luminary Navy vessel."

Quinto nodded. "We can guess the most likely source for parts, but not who is assembling them or for what purpose. If I recall, you are considering both local and external sources for your own construction project.

"What is he talking about?" Enzo asked.

"Never mind." Silas snapped. "We know who's responsible, and the navy can't ignore a threat of this magnitude. You need to destroy that fleet!"

"Unfortunately, it's no longer at the location where it was first discovered. I have search teams combing the swath. However, if we find and engage a rogue fleet, it won't be without significant losses. I'm not sure we can afford that right now."

"What do you mean?"

"Silas, you recently told me that you felt a war was on the horizon. Zayd Ocon has been accusing the Tellusans of provoking one and tensions are high. The creation of this fleet could be explained as a preparatory response for that possibility. The appearance of these minefields feed into Zayd's paranoid narrative. He will argue for retaliation. I suspect it will be discussed in the upcoming Council meeting. A decision to attack would ensure war with the Tellusans. In that case, we can't afford to diminish the strength of the Luminary Navy by battling this hidden fleet. At the same time, we can't allow a rogue fleet to operate within the swath, especially during a war. It must come under the authority of the Luminary Navy."

Jayla shook her head. "I have no doubt that Zayd is orchestrating this whole affair and you're playing right into his hands."

"I'm not ignoring the mounting evidence," Quinto insisted, "but we must be certain. I won't divert defensive resources for a hunt while there exists a possibility of war with the Tellusans. I suggest a different approach. It's entirely within my purview to request that the Council commission the emergency construction of new vessels. Let's see how the shipbuilding septs receive that request. If they've created a hidden fleet with altruistic intentions, then we should see those non-commissioned vessels start to filter into the navy fleet. The miraculously rapid appearance of these vessels will be impossible to explain, but no one will ask or complain because it will allow everyone to save face."

"And if the hidden fleet isn't offered?"

"Then I'll know that an ulterior motive exists and tensions will escalate."

"You've suggested a war with the Tellusans may be inevitable by that point. It will be difficult for you to fight a battle on two fronts. You should hunt them down now while you have the chance."

"I won't attack Luminaries without proof. You would demand the same consideration if the accusations were levelled at you. We have a little time. If we prepare for war, hidden motivations will come to light. A war fleet is built with the expectation of battle. The actions of the hidden fleet will determine its intent whether for civil aggression or to precipitate a war with the Tellusans. If it's the former, I will need to meet strength with strength. If it's the latter, I will need to ensure that the navy suffers less attrition than the hidden fleet. If I don't maintain that balance, I risk entering a civil battle at a later date with reduced strength. The best I can do is to prepare for both."

"How do you propose to do that?"

Quinto smiled as he glanced at Enzo. "That's where you come in."

Enzo squirmed in his seat. "I don't like the sound of that."

Quinto turned to Silas and Jayla. "I think a certain project will need to broaden in scope. Are you open to a third partner?"

The two Luminaries looked at each other and nodded.

"Silas and Jayla have been working on an 'agricultural project', Enzo. I suggest you contribute generously to their efforts if you want a stable future. I'll let them fill you in on the details."

Quinto turned back to Silas and Jayla. "Your project will need to expand dramatically. You'll have to rely heavily on your external source for construction materials. If civil war breaks out, I'll need to counter not only the hidden fleet, but also the smaller fleets of its allies. In other words, I need a secret fleet of my own. To ensure the future of the archipelago, I need more ships. Lots of them."

Silas ran fingers through his hair as he considered the logistics. "I don't see how we can justify a request for more engines. We were pushing things with our original design proposal."

Jayla raised her hand. "I have a thought. What if Enzo submitted the request? He could say that he saw our plans and wants to use the same concept for something like a sports arena. Better yet, go big and make it a betting track for small racing vessels. That way we could justify engines for both the facility and the racecraft."

Enzo warmed to the idea. "Could I really use it for that purpose?"

"Absolutely. I'll explain later, but the admiral will only be interested in parts of the superstructure. The rest would remain for you to use in whatever manner you wish."

"A second structure would help." Quinto nodded. "As for the propulsion systems... I can requisition spare engines and parts for the war effort. I'll cover any shortfalls in supplies that you may encounter. The safety of the archipelago takes priority."

Quinto turned to Luminary Dewai. "You mentioned that the university was experimenting with engine enhancements and new technology adapted for weapon systems. Normally, you wouldn't be permitted to move beyond the research phase without Council approval. However, due to the impending threat of war, I'm officially ordering production of those advancements to upgrade the Luminary fleet. Your outside sources can forge and provide parts as necessary, but all assembly must happen within the swath. I have a very large budget and would be happy to award the contracts to you three. Can you provide workers and build the assembly lines required to start production immediately?"

Jayla nodded at the other two Luminaries. "I believe we can make that happen, Admiral."

"All of this is conditional on your willingness to sign agreements stating that the work you're doing is for the war effort and all material you produce is property of the Luminary Navy. Will that be a problem?"

"Always the cautious one." Silas grumbled. "That won't be a problem, Admiral, no problem at all."

"I expect you all to support and emphasize the importance of war preparations at the upcoming Council meeting."

"Way ahead of you, Admiral. Leave the politics to us."

"Then I suggest we all get to work. We have a lot to do and very little time to prepare."

Chapter 36

How did they find me? Valtteri wondered as he ran. He felt confident that the admiral had covered his tracks. The only other person who knew about the garage was Sebastian. Valtteri's emotions bounced from disbelief to anger and landed on disappointment. Of all the people he'd known in the swath, Sebastian was the only person his age whom he'd call a friend. Sebastian had been his confidant, the one he talked to when he was depressed. Sebastian was the one who stood at his side against bullies. *He's like a brother to me.*

Some of the best memories in Valtteri's life included Sebastian. He didn't want to think what it might mean if those moments had been a lie. Valtteri had lost so much of who he was or might have been. The thought of someone manipulating his life to such a degree was too much to bear. *It can't have been Sebastian.*

Valtteri stopped at the edge of an alley opening into a clearing with a turnstile on the far side. The admiral's garage was in an industrial area of solarside. The only people likely to cross into shroudside from this location would be Lagan workers returning home after a shift. That was good and bad. He wouldn't have to fight a crowd to get there, but the turnstiles were always guarded, making it impossible to approach unseen.

One bored looking officer wandered back and forth in front of the gate, probably wondering what he'd done to deserve the assignment.

Movement from an adjacent alley caught his eye. *They're closing in on me. I have to move.* Valtteri abandoned caution and sprinted towards the gate.

"There he is!"

Valtteri recognized one of his pursuers as Joseph Admot, a Sept Ocon operative and the man tasked with his training. Valtteri recalled Zayd's warning regarding betrayal of the sept and Joseph looked eager to dispense a sadistic form of punishment. These were Zayd's elite operatives. They wouldn't be easy to elude.

The navy officer guarding the gate looked up in surprise as Valtteri barrelled towards him. The guard fumbled with his baton, unable to free it before Valtteri crumpled him with a kick to the stomach. Valtteri shouted a reflexive apology and raced past.

The turnstile was an older type without automation. Users negotiated hand and toe holds that spiralled them through a tube to the proper orientation on the other side. He didn't have time for that and dived through the gate as shots struck the ground where he'd been only a moment ago. The lone guard scrambled to safety as operatives swarmed out of the alleys.

Valtteri grunted in pain when his shoulder caught a handhold, spinning him in another direction. Disoriented, he grabbed at a rung to stop his uncontrolled momentum. Pushing off with his feet, he tucked into a roll as he entered shroudside. His reckless transition gained him a few precious seconds and he used them to reach an alley unseen.

Zayd's operatives emerged from the gate without slowing. They split into teams to search each alleyway. Valtteri ran as fast as he could, turning left then right, hoping to throw off his pursuers. With each step, he prayed that he wouldn't blunder into a literal dead end. He didn't know the shroudside of Opesburg very well, and this area, not at all.

The chase continued for over an hour. Valtteri was exhausted and completely lost. *I can't keep this up. I need to find a place to hide.*

The noon meal siren sounded and workers began to stream into the streets. Valtteri tried to blend into the crowd, but it was difficult to hide his heavier frame. He stumbled along, letting the flow of people carry him. Eventually, the crowd began to thin. The hungry workers were splitting up as they selected various eating establishments. Soon Valtteri would be alone in the street, exposed to his hunters.

His eyes cast about searching for options and froze on something unexpected. It was an eatery with a brightly coloured sign, a sign painted in familiar colours — Swathcomber colours. Valtteri frantically patted his trouser pockets searching for the bijou given to him by Bronto Knox. His fingers found what they sought and clutched it like a lifeline. He pulled it out and hooked it through his ear as he raced for the eatery.

Bursting through the entrance, he ran straight for the bar where a grizzled man in his forties was polishing a mug. Every eye in the room locked onto Valtteri. A few rose as he grabbed the owner's shirt.

"I need your help! They're after me."

"What's that to me, lad? If you're in trouble with the law, perhaps you shouldn't have done whatever it was ya done."

"My name is Knox," he hissed, "Valtteri Knox." Valtteri turned his head to display his bijou. The owner's eyes widened in recognition. His response was instant and commanding.

"He's one of ours, boys, you know the drill."

Everyone leapt from their seats and moved to the entrance, crowding around two men. They struck up a pseudo argument, ready to throw fists at each other or anyone unfortunate enough to happen upon the establishment.

"The name's Janus. My boys will run interference. Follow me."

Valtteri trailed Janus to a back room. Janus moved aside some carpet and pried at one of the floorboards with his knife. He lifted a two-foot square section of flooring, exposing the floor joists and a tunnel below.

"Drop down and follow the tunnel to the end. You'll find food, water, weapons, and a cot. Stay there and rest. I'll come for ya when it's safe."

Valtteri slipped between the joists and dropped to the tunnel floor. Janus passed a lantern down.

"Thank you, Janus. I owe you."

"No need for that, lad. Swathcombers take care of their own."

Valtteri lit the lantern, and Janus replaced the floorboards. The smell of the surrounding soil induced a moment of claustrophobia. He shook it off and started down the long dark tunnel. This wasn't his grave... not today.

* * *

Valtteri had no way to determine the passage of time, but he estimated at least a day had passed. His lantern ran out of fuel hours ago and he was anxious to escape the darkness. Not that shroudside was a brightly lit place, but right now he'd settle for shadows and room to move.

A knock sounded, followed by a blast of fresh air as an opening formed above him. He grabbed a knife from the cache and prepared to defend himself.

"Valtteri?"

The voice sounded familiar. "Valtteri? It's me, Sato."

"Sato? What are *you* doing here?"

"Janus contacted our family. I was making a delivery from Swiftwater and came as soon as I heard." Sato reached down through the opening. "Give me your hand."

Sato grunted as he pulled. "That lazy Tellusan lifestyle is making you soft and heavy."

"I'm going to let that slide since I'm so happy to see you."

Sato grinned. "It seems like I'm always getting you out of trouble, cousin."

"Are things that bad?"

"At least thirty operatives are searching shroudside and harassing the locals. I think you've worn out any welcome you may have had from the citizens. As for those who are searching for you, let's just say they're in a foul mood. You must have really upset some powerful people."

"Zayd Ocon considers me a traitor. I'm guessing that the only welcome mats I can expect belong to bounty hunters."

"So you're a tick on the hide of the Luminaries? Then you're truly a Swathcomber in both name and deed. Draw a little blood at a time until the day we drain them dry."

"Slugs and ticks against leviathan." Valtteri muttered.

"What was that?"

"Ignore me. I'm functioning on two hours of sleep. What's the plan?"

"I've seen no indication that the search will be ending any time soon. You can't stay here. We need to leave Opesburg."

"How are we going to do that? Zayd's men will be watching the ports and searching every vessel."

"Swathcombers are considered parasites by the Luminaries. We're happy to live up to their expectations by thriving within the framework of their tropostates. We use their infrastructure while eschewing traditional modes of travel. We'll be travelling on foot through several tunnels until we reach the world chain. After that, we'll let a chain walker carry us to our final destination."

"Chain walker?"

"It will be easier to show you than to explain. Let's go."

* * *

They spent the better part of a day travelling through tunnels or along abandoned maintenance corridors. Occasionally, it was necessary to travel short distances aboveground to reach a hidden passage. Eventually, they found their way to the world chain. Every time he saw the massive links that connected the tropostates, Valtteri was filled with awe. The chain anchored the archipelago's floating land masses to the mountain ranges, keeping them from floating across the limen.

They found their way to a hidden room beneath the foundation of a chain reel. Sato was pulling out an assortment of equipment and laying it out on the floor. "We'll wait until the siren sounds at evening meal. During the shift change, we'll have a ten-minute window of opportunity. The chain reel monitoring station is vacant at that time, so we're least likely to be spotted leaving. Once we're about a quarter of a mile out, we should be safe from discovery."

Sato handed him a bulky looking piece of equipment and a backpack. "The pack is for personal gear. It contains a few rations, some water, and a hammock. The hammock can be hung from a chain link if you need to take a break. Stashes of food and water are available every one hundred nautical miles. A chain walker can travel that distance in about six hours."

Sato released a catch on the side of the device and flipped down a padded surface. "This is where you sit. Keep your limbs on the seat side of the drive unless you want to arrive at your destination missing an appendage."

He turned the device around to expose a disk approximately two feet in diameter. "The drive contains a coiled spring which powers a clockwork mechanism that allows us to travel along the world chain. It's a good habit to wind the spring whenever you stop for a break. You'll find a crank clipped to the bottom of the seat for that purpose."

Valtteri watched in fascination as Sato pulled out three telescoping tubes and attached them to the disk. It looked like a clock face with hands at twelve, four, and eight. Sato partially extended the tubes and attached large articulated hooks to the ends.

"As soon as we leave this room, fully extend one of the arms. Hook it over the farthest chain link you can reach." Sato pointed at the links above their heads. "When you've secured the pole, hop onto the seat and swing away from the city. Don't forget to attach your safety harness to the drive."

Valterri nodded. "Got it. Then what?"

"Extend the two remaining arms and initiate the drive. The safety lock is right here." Sato pointed to a latch securing a larger lever at the front of the device. "Throw the big lever when you're ready. The drive will swing you forward. Keep an eye on the leading hook. Under normal conditions, the gyroscope will detect when you're at the top of your swing and turn the forward arm ninety degrees. It will hook the chain link on descent. The arm behind you will swing away from the previous link at the same time. You'll experience a moment of freefall. Don't panic, that's normal. You'll get used to it."

"You said, 'under normal conditions'. What would be considered abnormal?"

"If the wind is high, a gust could throw your leading arm out of alignment causing you to miss a link. The hooks are large and forgiving, but if it looks like you might miss your target, you can use this lever to compensate. The arms can be torqued inward or outward."

"What if I miss?"

"If you miss, the walker will derail. It's nothing to worry about. You'll just settle on the plain of equilibrium. Usually, you're close enough to the chain that you can just hook it with one of the arms and start back up again. On the remote chance you get blown further from the world chain, you'll find a thrust canister and grappling hook attached to your harness. Regardless, I'll be keeping an eye on you. If you run into trouble I'll be there to help."

"How far are we travelling?"

"The navy runs patrols within a twenty-five-mile circumference of a tropostate. We try to stay well clear of them. We'll aim for the hundred-mile marker and then we'll stop to rest. I've arranged for a Swathcomber platform to meet us there."

Sato finished rigging the second walker. "I'll go first so you can see how it's done. Once I'm out of the way, you'll have to move quickly. Do you think you can manage?"

Valtteri uttered a nervous laugh. "I think so?"

The shift siren began to wail, drowning out his voice. Sato was already running out the door. Valtteri grabbed his gear and chased after him.

Chapter 37

Nixon cursed his bad luck. Valtteri was in his grasp until the Admiral interfered. The man deliberately ignored Luminary law in order to protect an outsider. The Admiral could have taken Valtteri into custody, to hold pending proof of official documentation. It was, in fact, what should have happened, a normal procedure with the officers he'd brought along for the arrest. They were following policy until the Admiral demanded otherwise. The man didn't seem to know his place.

Sept Ocon's operatives had picked up the scent and chased Valtteri through shroudside, but Knox managed to elude them. That failure was maddening in itself, but worse was the silence that followed. Despite the combined assets of the Ocon intelligence operatives and his own personal network of informants, no one had seen the traitor. Nixon had the navy scouring the tropostate to no avail. All shipping ports were monitored, but no one had made a sighting or gathered any actionable intelligence about Valtteri's whereabouts.

The bounty for Valtteri was high and Nixon knew there would be no shortage of greedy Lagans hoping to cash in. The only explanation for the lack of sightings was that Valterri was no longer on Opesburg. He didn't know how that was possible, but he had to face the fact it was most likely true.

With Valtteri in the wind, it was only a matter of time before Zayd's activities came to light. Nixon needed to find a way to distance himself from the fallout. He considered the pieces in play. It was obvious to Nixon that Quinto Soren stood in direct opposition to the Ocon family. It was unthinkable that someone from the Lamina caste would have the temerity to stand against his betters, but matters seemed to be moving in that direction.

Nixon had a better appreciation of his uncle's concerns about Quinto Soren's loyalties. He shuddered as he considered what the Luminary Navy could do to the archipelago if a rogue element commanded the fleet. The navy had been formed to protect the septs, but now Nixon wondered if he could trust it to do so. His uncle's creation of a hidden fleet had seemed a dangerous risk, but now it felt necessary.

Somehow he had to protect that fleet and either remove Quinto Soren from power or gain his trust. He also needed to find a way to placate Opesburg, Ludemburg,and Voloburg. His uncle's habit of antagonizing them was making them suspicious. Rebuilding those relationships wouldn't be easy if they learned about his uncle's involvement in the minefields. Valtteri's escape made that seem inevitable.

Nixon didn't require a perfect fix, he just needed to make sure he had time to implement his own plans if, or more likely when, his uncle was exposed. If he didn't find a way to preemptively de-escalate the coming scandal, Sept Ocon would be removed from power. That was unacceptable.

Nixon worked late into the night preparing a list.

Chapter 38

Tensions were high as the Luminaries took seats around the small theatre aboard the aeronaught class warship.

"Couldn't you have found more comfortable seats for this assembly?"

"Oh, I'm sorry, Enzo." Zayd snapped. "How thoughtless of me. When you and your colleagues insisted that we convene on neutral ground, I should have made an effort to accommodate your profligate sensibilities. It's certainly more worthy of our time than any other reason for gathering here today."

"No need to be adversarial."

"Council has been convened to question my actions for a second time. What could be more antagonistic than that? My nephew arranged this venue. If you have complaints, bring them up with him. I have little patience for your questions and no time for your nonsense."

"Why do you assume this Council was convened to question you? Do you have a reason to feel guilty? Perhaps you're just so full of yourself that you imagine everything must be about you."

"Don't patronize me, Silas. I've heard the spurious rumours you're spreading."

"I, for one, find the venue completely appropriate. What better place to discuss the actions of a warmonger than on a warship?"

Zayd glared at Jayla. "If you have some indictment to make, Luminary Dewai, you'd better have proof."

Quinto spoke before Jayla could respond. "Let's proceed with some decorum, please. We're here to discuss our response to the recent discovery of minefields placed below Ludumburg, Opesburg, and Voloburg."

"I've repeatedly warned this Council about the Tellusans." Zayd asserted. "The navy must respond in kind."

"That would start a war!"

"The Tellusans targeted your tropostate, Silas. I would say the war has already begun. Where is your outrage?"

"I'll direct my outrage at the responsible party, not a Tellusan scapegoat."

Zayd sneered. "Yes, I've heard the ridiculous accusations you make behind my back but have yet to declare to my face."

"I've also heard these rumours," Philo Stol interjected, "but they seem untenable on the surface. Why would Sept Ocon weaken his allies while the threat of war looms?"

"Perhaps Luminary Stol should look *below* the surface if he wants to discover the truth. I imagine he'd be diving deep if Stipoburg had been a target. Interesting that none of the original three founders feels threatened."

Philo spoke with indignation. "An attack on any sept is an attack on us all. I'm not diminishing the threat. I agree with Zayd, we must retaliate!"

"Only a fool attacks before determining if the one he faces is friend or foe." Silas retorted.

"We know who our enemy is." Tiago Damira responded. "Queen Silvanus maintains a military presence along our border. Some suggest her troops have crossed the limen. Isn't that enough evidence that the Tellusans are responsible for these minefields?"

"I see that we entertain rumours when they suit us. Do I need to remind you, Tiago, that the Tellusans gather at our border because Zayd sent bombs across the limen? If that wasn't a provocation, I don't know what is. Even if the Tellusans were responsible for the minefields, we know who started this."

"That was an accident." Zayd countered. "I've already given a public explanation and made reparations. Queen Silvanus accepted both. This latest act of the Tellusans proves how duplicitous they truly are. We can't trust them. We certainly can't ignore the threat they pose to the archipelago."

"We all know that you orchestrated this, Ocon! You've been itching for a war with the Tellusans ever since your father died."

"This is tiresome. We stand on the brink of war and Luminary Dewei insists on wasting valuable time. If anyone here has proof to support these accusations against me, then share it with the rest of us." Zayd gazed pointedly at each of the assembled Luminaries.

Jayla glanced at the admiral with pleading eyes. Quinto shook his head. They couldn't mention the hidden fleet. He moved the conversation to more practical matters. "My duty is to protect the archipelago. Regardless of how we choose to respond to the current threat, I must prepare the fleet. By a show of hands, are we all in agreement that the Luminary Navy should make provision for war?"

Hands rose in unison.

"Let the record show that we have unanimous agreement to prepare the fleet. According to agreements made at the founding of the archipelago, you'll each supply the navy with material necessary for the war effort. Some of you will be providing ongoing supplies such as food and medical services. Others will be called upon to immediately bolster the fleet with spare parts and ammunition. My staff will be visiting your manufacturing facilities to conduct an inventory of any production capabilities that may be useful to the fleet. All identified inventory will be housed at naval facilities for the foreseeable future."

"That seems rather extreme." Tiago objected. "How will we maintain our existing contracts if we have no control over the items we produce?"

"Are you suggesting that your personal profit should take precedence over the safety of your fellow Luminaries?"

"Of course not, but some of us will carry a heavier burden and we need to maintain a regular income stream to support additional production."

"You can make a request from navy warehouses at any time. It should only cause a minor delay. I doubt your customers will notice. Over time, we'll all learn where to focus production for optimum results. War means sacrifice."

Tiago clearly wasn't satisfied with the answer.

"If it helps, you'll be happy to learn that I'm requisitioning the immediate production of new warships. The other Luminaries will be helping to fund construction so you won't suffer a significant loss in profit. You can expect that the majority of your contracts will be military ones."

"This is unacceptable!" Philo Stol exclaimed. "Luminaries maintain independent sovereignty. You can't just take over our industries."

"Yes, Luminary Stol, I can. We're on a war footing now. I'm fully sanctioned to take any precautions I deem necessary to protect the archipelago."

"You should be very careful, Admiral." Zayd threatened. "The Council can vote to replace you."

"That's true in a time of peace, but you've just voted to prepare for war. Do you wish to vote again? That is your prerogative. To be clear, any vote regarding the navy must be unanimous."

Zayd stared daggers at the admiral.

"What is your wish, Luminary Ocon? Do we prepare for war or not? It's all or nothing. War isn't a convenient matter."

Zayd opened his mouth to respond, but the theatre doors opened and redirected the focus of his ire.

Tiago spoke first. "You're interrupting a Council of the Luminaries!"

Nixon entered, pushing a cart into the centre of the theatre. It carried a chest displaying a Tinkers Guild seal. "Apologies, Luminary Damira, but I have information that will better inform your current deliberations."

Zayd seized on the unexpected interruption. "Let my nephew speak. Perhaps we can finally put to rest these rumours about me."

All eyes turned to Nixon.

"As many of you know, I've been taking on greater responsibilities for Sept Ocon, particularly in the area of intelligence gathering. The Tinkers Guild recently approached me with allegations regarding crimes against the tether tribes. I wasn't aware that any tribes still existed at the base of the swath, but I have since learned that they continue under Luminary subjugation. I'm sure many of you are as surprised as I was.

"The Guild provided evidence that Sept Ocon, among others, is complicit in these crimes. I agreed to support their investigation to uncover the truth about these allegations. The Guild has been quite thorough. One of the suspects on their list was a Vigil by the name of Eli Strom. I've learned that he's an operative for Sept Ocon. He has steadfastly refused to speak to the Guild, but was quite forthcoming to me as a commanding officer. Not only did he confirm the Guild's accusations, but the Vigil told me that he was tasked with the installation of three minefields at my uncle's command."

Zayd quickly rose from his seat. "This is outrageous slander. Who is this Vigil? I demand to question him myself."

"Sit down, Ocon!" Silas roared. "I will hear the evidence. You can defend yourself later."

Zayd held his tongue. His eyes turned to Nixon, smouldering with warning.

Nixon ignored his uncle, unconcerned. "I don't like surprises, so I undertook an audit of our operatives' recent activities. I found a number of cleverly concealed projects, but one in particular was too large to hide. In fact, it's the reason I chose this vessel for your meeting."

The Luminaries glanced at each other in confusion. Philo Stol and Tiago Damira squirmed uncomfortably in their seats. Nixon used the momentary confusion to send them a signal, stroking his left eyebrow three times with his fingertips. It was a gesture of solidarity known only to the original three founding families. He paused until they returned the signal, acknowledging that he wasn't about to betray them.

"We're aboard a non-commissioned vessel. This ship is not under the admiral's command. It's operating with a civilian crew posing as navy officers. This same crew is responsible for knowingly sending live ordnance across the limen, a clearly provocative act ordered by my uncle. The crew confirmed this during my interrogation."

Nixon turned to face Quinto. "Admiral, I've taken the liberty of contacting your men on the ship that brought you here. They have taken over this vessel and await your command. I'll leave you to deal with the ship and its crew as you see fit."

Quinto noted that Nixon only mentioned one of the ships from the hidden fleet. He didn't have time to ponder the reason as two officers quietly entered the theatre and stood by his side. One of them whispered in the admiral's ear. He nodded and motioned for them to remain.

Nixon continued, "Witnesses have given their statements. All evidence has been carefully documented and handed to the Guild for verification. This chest contains authenticated copies of all material in the Guild's possession. Everything within has been thoroughly investigated and substantiated by experts. You have before you the irrefutable proof of my uncle's transgressions."

Silas asked the question on everyone's mind. "If the Guild was only bringing charges regarding the tether tribes, why did you disclose these additional details? Why are you sharing this information with us now?"

"I might have kept silent but for one other crime noted within that chest, something from my childhood. I finally find myself in a position to do something about it."

"No!" Zayd yelled. "He's lying, don't listen to him!"

"Restrain Luminary Ocon." Quinto ordered. "If he interrupts again, gag him." The two officers bound Zayd's hands and stood to either side of him.

"Uncle Zayd didn't approve of my grandfather's reforms. One day, he decided to act on his exasperation. Unfortunately for him, his actions weren't as covert as he'd planned. I observed as he sedated his victim before threading a tube down his throat to fill the chest cavity with superheated steam. I watched in horror as he scalded his own father, inflicting invisible but fatal wounds. Grandfather perished shortly after. His legacy died with him, and now we find ourselves closer to war than the peace he envisioned."

"You claim to have evidence for this as well?"

Nixon nodded. "I have the weapon my uncle used. The Guild has verified that his fingerprints are all over it. The only other fingerprints on the device belong to the person who was hired to build it. He has given his sworn testimony, as have I. I also have testimony from the woman who sold the sedative used by my uncle to commit his crime."

The Luminaries looked at each other in shock. "What do you hope to gain by implicating your sept?" Jayla asked.

"My uncle has irreparably harmed the reputation of Sept Ocon. I want the opportunity to restore honour to our family name. I have already agreed to address the wrongs done to the tether tribes. I'm in discussions with the Tinkers Guild to consider appropriate reparations. As far as this Council is concerned, I give my humble apologies. I know that my uncle has treated some of you dismissively. I hope that by coming forward I can begin to restore those damaged relationships. I would also like to avenge my grandfather. He was a good man and didn't deserve his fate."

Zayd looked at his nephew with pleading eyes. "Why are you doing this, Nixon?"

Nixon allowed Zayd to glimpse a subtle smirk of satisfaction. "Because you've created costly and unnecessary chaos, Uncle. While this pains me, I have to make a hard decision."

Zayd blinked rapidly as he grasped the extent of his nephew's betrayal. "It's not what you think! I'm not alone in this!"

"Gag him!" Philo and Tiago insisted in unison. Quinto nodded, and the two navy officers guarding Zayd quickly silenced him.

Quinto took charge. "With the evidence presented, we need a vote. All who believe Zayd Ocon is guilty, raise your hand."

Silas, Jayla, and Enzo immediately lifted their arms. Tiago and Philo looked at each other before reluctantly raising their own. "A majority vote has determined Zayd Ocon's guilt. He is deprived of his status as a Luminary of this Council." Quinto turned to address Nixon. "It won't change the outcome, but as Zayd's heir apparent, you have the right to add your vote."

Nixon lifted his hand to declare his vote and cleared his throat. "With your permission, I'd like to request the right of the avenger to decide my uncle's sentence."

"By claiming that right, you can make a recommendation, but the Council must approve it."

"I chose this vessel as a venue for this meeting, but I also picked the location. Our current position is the spot where my uncle bombarded the forest of Queen Silvanus. I ask that we cast Zayd Ocon across the limen to plunge to his death. Any of the craters formed by his hand would make a suitable grave. I'd like to request that the sentence be enacted immediately. I suggest that we alert Queen Silvanus of this newly uncovered evidence and our corrective actions so she can verify the results of my uncle's sentence. With that accomplished, I recommend we stand down and return to a peace status before things escalate."

Quinto nodded and turned the recommendation over to the

Council. "Those in favour of the sentence, acknowledge your vote by a show of hands."

Everyone raised their hands.

"Those in favour of returning to a peace status?"

All hands remained in the air.

"Zayd Ocon, this council has determined your fate."

Quinto nodded to the two officers. "You've heard the sentence. Carry it out immediately and let us know when it's done."

The two officers dragged a kicking and screaming Zayd Ocon out of the theatre. They carried him over the side of the ship, attached a thrust canister to his back, and watched as it carried him over the edge.

Chapter 39

Valtteri stood at the edge of the Swathcomber platform staring off into the distance. He took a deep breath and exhaled slowly, relishing the slower pace. Someone was plucking a tune on a stringed instrument while others prepared the evening meal. If Valtteri closed his eyes, he could pick out the sounds of community. Men rolled dice on a table and laughed. Elderly women held hands and mumbled their prayers. Children squealed in delight as their siblings chased them. A young couple whispered tenderly to each other. It made him smile. These were all things worth living for, a life he'd never experienced for himself. He reserved a deep longing for it. Valtteri still felt like an outsider even though the Swathcombers openly accepted him.

Sato leaned against the railing next to him. "Are you okay?"

"Yes, I'm fine. My thoughts are just wandering again."

He and Sato had grown close. They were like-minded in many ways. Sato was fiercely loyal to family, but he had an equally strong desire to set off and explore the world. For Valtteri's part, he was slowly coming to adore his adopted family, but his new life here felt very constraining, and the Swathcomber way of life meant living in close quarters with limited options for travel.

Sato seemed to sense his restlessness. "It won't be much longer, Cousin. The bounty hunters will soon realize you're no longer in any of the tropostates. They'll assume you've left the swath and give up the hunt. Then you can start moving about freely again."

Information was slow to filter through the Swathcomber network, spread out as they were. The sporadic news they received was all good. Admiral Soren successfully destroyed the minefields before they could do harm. Valtteri had played a role in that success. That personal victory overshadowed his struggles, making it all seem worthwhile.

He still couldn't believe that Zayd Ocon was dead. The plot to attack his fellow Luminaries was brought to an abrupt end before it could provoke a war. In a surprising twist, the plight of the tether tribes had also come to light. Nixon himself had brought forward the evidence that Valtteri and Tallow had been hoping to reveal. Despite the apparent common ground, Nixon refused to repeal the treason charges. He insisted that Valtteri had acted in a manner that betrayed Sept Ocon. The bounty remained in place, and would for the remainder of his life. It hardly mattered to Valtteri. Even if Nixon invited him back into the fold, he wouldn't return. Nixon had tried to kill him several times. He didn't trust the man as far as he could throw him.

Nixon may have exposed his uncle for the tyrant that he was, but Valtteri didn't believe for a moment that it was for reasons other than to claim power. The unsanctioned fleet remained hidden somewhere. That was too much power to ignore. Nixon would show his true colours soon enough. When that time came, Valtteri vowed that he'd stop him.

So many unanswered questions remained. Valtteri wanted to learn more about the Iridogen and a possible link to the artefact in the southern realm. He didn't know when he'd see the admiral again, but he intended to follow through on his commitment to help Enigma.

It was strange. One way or another, he'd always felt like he was on the fringes of society, but now that he was officially an outcast, he had more friends than ever before. He recalled something Adis told him once. 'A family is made up of those who stick with you through good times and bad.' He'd found that, hadn't he?

One thing he knew for certain. No longer would he serve blindly. He'd do what he knew to be right, not out of obligation to a political agenda, but because he wanted to. Valtteri understood the cost. He'd be looking over his shoulder for the rest of his life. A smile spread across his face as this new reality settled upon him. He'd never felt so free.

"What are you grinning about?" Sato asked.

"I was thinking about that swill you've been brewing."

"You're joking, right? That's a quality ale you're disparaging."

Valtteri placed a hand on Sato's shoulder. "Perhaps you're right. I think my stomach has settled enough to give it another try."

"That's the spirit, Cousin! I'll make a Swathcomber out of you yet."

"I'm counting on it."

The story continues, in book 2 of the States of Inversion series.

I hope you enjoyed reading *In the Shadow of the Luminaries*. Please take a moment to post a review and tell a friend. You can find my author pages on Amazon, Goodreads and Bookbub.

In future novels, I plan to spend some time in the Southern Kingdom looking into the motivations of Queen Silvanus, and then there's the Unified Northern Collective where we'll learn more about the northern Iridogen. Let's not forget the tinkers, friaers and swathcomers. There's so much to explore in this world and I hope you'll come along for the ride.

If you sign up for my newsletter, you can download a free ebook *States of Inversion* novella that tells the story of Tallow and Sicily. It's titled *Grasping at Gravity* and provides the Tether Tribe backstory. Visit **www.kallensamuels.com** for details.

All the best,
Kallen Samuels